House of the Black Moon

William Xavier Chandler

First Paperback Edition, May 2025
Second Paperback Edition, January 2026

ISBN 979-8-9945846-1-3

Visit thewilliamxavier.com
Instagram: @williamxavierchandler
Facebook: William Xavier Chandler: Author & Musician

Cover concept & Design: William Xavier Chandler
& Jason Croft
Final Digital Editing: Nikola Simic

FURIOUS STYLES

ENTERTAINMENT, LLC

Publishing Division

Contents

PART II

PART III

House of the Black Moon

Prologue

"When one claims to know everything, they've only succeeded in proving what a true waste of existence they are. To taste of these particular souls is both satisfying, to expunge the whole of creation of their banality, and sorrowfully morose in how close to nothing they provide in nourishment."

--- Aylash Revall

Part I:
What Was

Chapter One: Some Back Story

There's a saying that Fort Worth is where the west begins. . . whatever the fuck that means. Try this one on for size: "Abilene-Sweetwater is where the west bleeds." Dust Storms of red and orange filth that stretch ominously like translucent, inescapable taffy all the way to Lubbock, infiltrating the smallest openings of homes and vehicles. Each grain feels like a rusty hypodermic needle being stabbed hastily into the skin. Tumbleweeds rumbling like a gang of Mad Max-inspired bikers covered head-to-steel-toe in barbed wire, ripping through the air with ferocity until they congregate, up to fifty at a time, along the corners, fences, and antennae of your property. Tornadoes and storms, or tornadoes *and drought*, depending on the universe's mood, ripping through your soul and home with impressive, almost boring ease, either flooding your defeated dreams or heating them to a broiling crisp. The sour, slimy stench of crude oil being raped from beneath the earth's surface; its scent bonding permanently in your hair follicles, clothing fibers, and back of your parched, dehydrated throat. Every ten miles along any and every highway, an abandoned ranch house or barn, or an exit down a dirt road that instantly recalls the Texas

Chainsaw Massacre and allocates a sense of inebriated dread and wonder into your bones.

A small-town network of associated wasteland, where owning an ever-addictive television (36" or bigger, if you're so lucky) deceives the youngest of locals into longing for some Hollywood (or Las Colinas) manufactured pipe dream, them not realizing how good they have it. Simplicity or lack of options, what-have-you; they keep Texas' pulse on the American Dream, while stomping down forcefully on such queer modern notions as creativity and individuality. A place where the summer and the winter both kill indiscriminately, this their only acknowledgment of inclusion. A place where we can agree that football, barbecue, chicken fried steak, and biscuits and gravy should be commemorated on a coin, or some new southern Mount Rushmore. A place where most have no hope but grasp tightly onto a symbol of faith.

A place where some escape, but most don't.

This is the miraculous nothing into which I was born.

But nevertheless, born I was. That event occurred in Merkel, TX November 2nd, 1998, but I languished most my life in Abilene. I grew up ok, always had one or two relatively close friends, but was never a really popular kid. In my town, popular's kind of hard to be if you're not rich or you're not good at football. Of course, I was neither. I suppose I never had *any* really special qualities. On the other hand, I wasn't sad, and I wasn't stupid; I was just. . . quiet. In retrospect, that quietness might have come off as just a tad creepy. I'm sure that my blank, half-asleep disposition aided that atmosphere. I won't lie; I did always have something *just a little bit* off about me, and looking back, I believe that was due to a combination of self-esteem and status issues and an unhealthy level of shyness. Additionally, good decisions and I just didn't seem to get on well. Case in point, I dropped out of Abilene High two months before graduation, working the typical jobs right after: Allsups, Texaco, family-owned video store, etc., most of these for just a couple of months before losing interest or being asked not to return. I spent almost three weeks in the oil fields in Post, reworking obsolete wells, before I realized that wasn't for me. Truth be told, that work was just physically too hard for me, and I know real quick when something's going to work out or not. So, I ended up back in Abilene, and figured that's probably where I'd just stay until I withered and ceased to breathe, drained dry from life and boredom.

In a sharpened, blood-tasting bit of irony, at the time that I was the most confused and uncertain about my next immediate chapter, my mom felt it would be a good time to tell me that she was really my grandmother, and that I'd never really known either of my parents. The words were almost a validation, confirming something I somehow knew without knowing. At the same time, that validation hurt and cut and twisted my insides like some violent invading parasite, and a well of questions sprang forth in my brain. Since that sweltering mid-September revelation almost three years ago, I've felt both a vast, hollow tunnel of betrayal, and an animalistic yearning for the world to provide answers for my existence.

931 N. Danville Drive, Abilene. It's the first home I remember. The first anything. I have no recollection of Merkel, or of my birth parents. They were virtually still children who had no apparent aptitude or internal fortitude to raise a baby. My "momma," Mona McCarty, raised me, and while I now recognize what a decrepit, rundown, outright desolate hovel 931 N. Danville is, my first few years' worth of memories there are gloriously joyful ones. Three-foot tall, rusty chain link fence covering only three quarters of the yard. Mildewy, exposed wooden doorframe wearing away from rain, moisture, lack of paint, and lack of love. Broken sidewalk; broken porch steps. Technically three bedrooms, but more like two and a huge in-house storage shed, which held the secrets of the McCarty universe and every non-perishable knick-knack and souvenir available. Momma Mona didn't gaze her eyes upon anything she didn't want to keep, or "might use later." Multiple towers of newspapers, documenting everything from Abilene's back-to-back-to-back state football championships in the 50's to President Kennedy's assassination, to who won homecoming queen in 1987. Clothes Mona hadn't worn since the 70's. Clothes she never wore. My birth mother's things, sitting in boxes never opened until I opened them to try and piece together something about her life. Porcelain dolls, porcelain plates, porcelain elephants, porcelain for the sake of porcelain. Children's books, their aroma so unique with nostrils pressed precociously into their crevices, which I pretended to read before I knew how, and never picked up once I did know how. Gravy bowls, olive green coffee cups, maroon hand-woven blankets that smelled like old folks' home, Time Magazine from

twenty-five years ago, Home and Garden from forty. A dream catcher that caught no dreams or anything remotely resembling a dream. Ever. You could have hidden bodies in that room.

No one would have found them.

Momma Mona and I were a team, albeit one with sizable cracks in its foundation, due to what I can narrow down as a (two) generation gap. A widow who birthed my mother very late in life for a housewife in West Texas, and then raised her alone for twelve years, she was loving in almost every way that only a grandmother could be, but didn't want to see much of me either before or after dinner. She was used to kids going outside after school, and playing until dinnertime, or until the sun went down, whichever came first. I, however, grew up on video games and cable television, allergies, and after school cartoons right before they died off into inevitable sucky-ness oblivion. The only chance to play with other kids was kickball or baseball in the sun-charred vacant parking lot turned overgrown field across the street, which ended for me when everyone else realized I wasn't any good. The kids in the lot preferred to make light of or ridicule my shortcomings rather than allow me the chance to improve or live my life without wanting to cry myself numb in my backyard. Mona would ask me "why don't you play football, or join the student council? Something worthwhile like that?" She just didn't get me, and I didn't make it easy for her to. I was just as shy expressing my inner monologues to her as I was my classmates. One major obstacle was that I didn't really *have* an inner monologue. All my thoughts very functional and direct: *She wore that same shirt three days ago. My head hurts. Two minutes until the bell rings.* Nothing about the turmoil in the world, or existential struggles with mankind or religion. I watched television and film like consuming fast food, never dwelling upon it once chewed up. And, without an older sibling to turn me onto anything different, I only listened to the music on our radio stations and watched what music still emerged at odd hours on MTV. I didn't fall in love with any of it, and didn't seek out music from obscure bands in the indie section of the cool CD shop in town.

Not yet at least. Not until one caught my eye and ear like a fishhook piercing through gills.

Chapter Two: Some Forth Story

Now, I'm about to share some things that will give you pause, make you question my sanity, as well as conjure some automatic visuals long implanted by books and television. But just as I did, you'll find many misconceptions about people bound to my condition shattered. I should go ahead and get a few out of the way, which will make the following accounts go down smoother.

First, I don't have some fancy French or Victorian name. I'm not an androgynous, bisexual type who wears makeup and has to tie up his clothes like in a weird, velvety male corset. I can't shape-shift, run or move faster than the speed of light, and I can't read your thoughts.

My name is Davis McCarty, the last in a long line of Texans.

And I. I am. I am a vampire.

Chapter Three: And Some More Back Story

Dead. Cold. Empty. Then fuming.

Not fancy or unique as descriptive words go, but that's exactly what I felt for months after I found out the truth about my parents. Since she was Mona's daughter, I focused more of my energy and, honestly, my disgust, on my mother. How could a woman with the same blood as my Mona end up so unbelievably opposite? I had many a schoolmate grow up with absentee fathers; one-night stands, rape, failed relationships, or basic cowardice pointed to this outcome. But in no instance could I think of one that had been abandoned by their mother. For almost two weeks, I didn't really speak to anyone, not even Mona. I felt a rare form of betrayal from her, understanding both the opposing joy and obligation she grappled with by raising her grandson, but resenting her passionately for over two decades of falsehood. Not being in her shoes, I couldn't fathom why she couldn't have just told me, at least when I was old enough to understand. I wasn't so fragile that it would have broken me. I spent most of those two weeks in my room, in darkness. The rest of the time, I would go on long, aimless walks around Abilene, invariably ending up on the I-20 access road heading west before my heels and hips would ache, and I'd realize I'd been on my feet far too long. Cowboy boots or cheaply made, nameless $10 tennis shoes from Walmart do *not* a good walking shoe make.

In time, my emptiness and anger turned into curiosity, and I sat down with Mona one Sunday morning and unloaded a linguistic tsunami of questions during one eight-hour period of grizzled, painful conversation. The vital points of this talk were:

1. My mother's name – Valerie
2. My father's name – Jackson Wilhoitte
3. Their ages when I was born – she 16, and he 17
4. What happened to them – they moved to Sweetwater together after a midnight jailbreak from the safety of their parents' fortresses, and broke up almost immediately thereafter. She moved in with a co-worker at Dairy Queen, had the baby, dropped it off on Mona's doorstep, and has never contacted her again. Jackson was killed by a drunk driver in a car accident at age 20.
5. Mona saw Valerie at a department store one afternoon when I would have been about three years old, made an initial motion to go and speak to her, but stopped herself. Mona instead waited for Valerie to turn down an aisle before making her exit, tears streaming, heart heaving, and hands convulsing.
6. The Box – there were several, actually; but this particular one, made of shiny, smelly cherry wood, held Mona's most cherished, and therefore most

tormenting, memories of her only child.

The Box was in the spare bedroom/storage room/vault/tomb, placed delicately underneath a deceptively stacked layer of old sweaters, t-shirts, and dresses belonging to the past. Out of sight and out of mind. The first time I attempted to open the Box, I couldn't bring myself to do it. I was able to frighten myself out of the room, thinking that it would crush me to see her face and come to the realization, whatever her excuse, that she abandoned me on a porch and went on existing like I didn't. I was afraid I'd see my face in hers, and that I would feel remorse, or longing, for her. Eventually – no, inevitably – I lugged it off a coffin of a loveseat, plunged it to the depths of the room's wood floor, and with both of my hands trembling as if afflicted with something like Parkinson's, I gripped it more with my knuckles than my fingers, and pried it open while forcing the anticipated lump in my throat down to my esophagus.

There she was.

She was beautiful. Barely above white trash, a spoiled, bad habit kind of smirk etched on her face in almost every image, but beautiful, nonetheless. Her eyes. That's how you could tell I was hers. Our eyes were the same. Forever a baby to a teenager in this Box, and not a day older. No record of anyone past sixteen years of age. She hadn't even learned to live yet. Her hair was much darker than mine, a true brunette, like Momma Mona before she started graying. My hair was a dirty brownish caramel and blond, no doubt taking after Jackson, or from some recessive gene attached to someone long dead. One thing that jumped out like a murderous clown in a horror movie was Valerie's complexion. She was a pale, milky white, in every picture, never having a tan even though the sun and its tantalizingly tricky dry heat hung up in the sky hard and intimidating eight months out of the year. It would coat roughnecks and farmers in a bronze protective layer and could sneak up on the unsuspecting with a fiery red sunburn before one could blink an eye.

I looked through the Box and buried my hands all the way to the bottom of it, pulling every card, picture, memento, newspaper clipping, and trinket out hungrily, putting it back, and then repeating, studying each item over again and again. I would stop on specific pictures and ask them questions, as if Valerie could magically blurt out an answer. Not until I'd gone through the Box several times had I realized I overlooked the fact that there was no picture of her and me. Not one, not in this house. I didn't know if one had ever even been taken. Upon this revelation, I cried. And I mean I *CRIED*. Forcefully. Violently. Melodramatically. I had never unleashed my eye ducts anything close to how I did that one solitary day in the spare bedroom/storage room/vault/tomb. And I never did so as violently again. Every stereotypical, self-analyzing, self-blaming, *wounded* feeling a child without his parents could feel, I felt it. Every possible question, I asked it. I asked it to the dark silence of the wood floor and the mirror covered in scarves and newspaper clippings. I went through all the other torturous relics in the room, looking to connect dots to a past, someone else's past, so that I might meet my present in the middle. Stopping short of demanding to hire a private investigator to find her, I most assuredly wanted to know more. I wanted to know *her.*

Her choice of attire at least gave me a place to start.

In almost every photograph of my newly discovered mother, she was wearing a black T-shirt celebrating a musical artist. A band shirt. I know that Mona didn't have the money or the trust to let Valerie go to concerts, even back in the 90's when they might have slightly more economically priced. I had no way of knowing for sure; I'd never attended a concert. But, yet, in an estimated four of every five pictures, she proudly or obliviously displayed a band across her bosom. Pantera, Korn, Nine Inch Nails, among others. She was apparently into the heavier musical tastes, the Beastie Boys notwithstanding (their look seemed to be out of place, so I had to Google them). But where did she get these shirts, where were they now, and what led her to be into hard rock, heavy metal, and alternative? There was a music store in town called Record Guys, and it turns out that this, Walmart, and Goodwill is where she got the shirts, and any CDs she bought. Mona must have been as generous as she could be with the funds, but I was very hard pressed to believe she'd be so approving of the artists themselves. I couldn't see my grandmother throwing up devil horns, rocking out to Metallica with her daughter.

I went to Record Guys with a picture of my mother and asked if anyone there knew her. Unfortunately, no one there was even as old as me, but the cashier said he'd ask around. A few days later, he bumped into me by chance at Grumps Burgers and told me that the original owner had befriended Valerie and a small group of her classmates, and that Valerie would get free swag by agreeing to make out with his employee Travis. Even though I didn't ask and didn't want to know, the kid assured me that "it never went past making out." It was as if he saw the terrified but quizzical thought pinballing around behind my eyelids. Travis Rutherford had only worked at Record Guys five months, but still lived close by, and, if there was a chocolate shake in it for him, agreed to come up there and answer any questions I had about Valerie. I tried to strictly refer to her by name when talking to someone about her. I couldn't bring myself to call her my mom, because she wasn't my mom.

She was a ghost.

Travis and I had an initially awkward, but ultimately really cool conversation about Valerie, and I found out that her first concert was something called Blockbuster Rock Fest in Dallas-Fort Worth in 1997, her first time getting drunk was when she was fourteen, and that it was a bad influence named Rusty who got her into rock music. He was also the one that got her that first drunk. She met Jackson in school, and their relationship was doomed from the start. He was a popular, good-looking kid, whose rich parents didn't approve of Valerie in the least. Travis also told me that Valerie was part of a friend group called the Skunk Punks, from a particular green leafy aroma that came from her friend Deena's Ford Taurus when they hung out. The Skunk Punks came up to the store almost daily while Travis worked there and seemed to really care about music. He said that this was rare for people their age at the time. I believe it's even more rare today. I asked him to show me what she listened to, and what she bought. He said she almost never bought anything, but listened to a "shitload of music" inside Record Guys.

While looking through the very same sections of CDs and vinyl records she had over twenty years before, I came across something. It was a piece of vinyl by an artist I automatically assumed was much more recent than any of Valerie's favorites, and it bellowed to me internally, drawing me in as if it had some movement spell over my legs and feet. The name of the band was Unholy Saint, and their album cover was an overhead shot of little kids playing spin the bottle, but with a crucifix instead of a bottle. The album title was *Tastes Like Death*, and I couldn't stop gazing at it. I picked it up out of the bin, inspected it front and back, and kept it under my arm the whole time I kept looking at the other records.

Upon leaving, I bought the album, still unsure why, and rushed home to listen to it. To be historically accurate, I first rushed to Walmart to buy a turntable.

Turning my head in the direction of that album at precisely the moment I did, while it was coincidentally at the front of its row, completely fucked up my life forever.

Chapter Four: Sainted

I can't explain what it was about the *Tastes Like Death* album, but I really liked it. Enough so that I started learning all about Unholy Saint and bought their other two releases; one self-titled EP released independently in their hometown of Santa Ana, CA, and their newest full-length album, *Salvation*. It was a markedly improved collection of songs from their major label debut. The band itself sounded, and I'm quoting Rolling Stone Online, "like a hot mug of Bauhaus, mid-80's White Zombie, Fugazi, and Ministry topped with the soaring, syrupy hooks of Big Country, Erasure, and STP to help drink them down." I had to go back and research almost all those bands, and after at first thinking the journalist didn't know what they were talking about, I ended up confirming that very description. It only took me thirty or so listens to the album to agree.

I guess the mashup of influences shouldn't be too much of a surprise, as its members appeared to be vastly different people. The singer, Daniel Sepulveda, was half Argentinian, one quarter Mexican, and one quarter white American. He was 6'4," had jet black, shaggy hair and piercing, burning brown eyes that could melt you or frighten you. The guitarist, Alister Amaranth, who hailed from Connecticut in one article, Pennsylvania in another, and Massachusetts in yet another, was rather diminutive by contrast. Standing at 5'7," with thin arms standing on thin legs, Alister appeared even shorter and more fragile than that. It's a wonder he didn't fall over playing his Gibson Les Paul; it seemed to weigh just as much as he did. In onstage pictures, he's always looking down at his guitar. I've never seen one of him facing a camera. The drummer, Robert M. What could you really say about him? He travelled south to Santa Ana from Fresno, had a mustache and a dad bod, but visibly strong arms, and didn't speak in interviews – at all. The bass player, a young lady named Devin Sikorsky. She was blond, mysterious, and beautiful. She'd lived her entire life in Orange County, but articles would never nail down specific cities. I noticed a pattern that whenever a journalist would ask her a deeply personal question, she would laugh like they had told a great joke, and then gently say "Next, please."

No article ever mentioned the ages of the band members, and the band members would never say. I thought that was an odd secret to keep. None of them were pushing old age, or even close to 30 in my estimation. I don't know how they figured this amalgam of disparate personalities was going to work, but I was damn glad it did. Their music was dark and dangerous, while also seemingly playful and light. A perfect blend of substance *and* style. I couldn't believe it; I was a bona fide hard rock music fan.

Ironically, the song that sunk its hooks deepest in me, with no intention of letting go, didn't sound like the typical Unholy Saint song. It closed the *Salvation* album and was just Devin and a piano, on a beautiful but sad, aching slow ballad called *Collide*. Those lyrics and her voice. You could feel the whisper bubbling through her teeth and tickling the edge of her lips. You could empathize with whatever pain caused that song. It wasn't born out of thin air; it was a result of suffering.

The giddy intoxication of falling in love with music, and specifically with a certain band, was so foreign and so *wonderful* to me. I felt a warm excitement in my abdomen when I'd see an online article on them or when one of their songs came on my Spotify, which I got soon after falling in said love. I would go look for magazines at Books-a-Million that might have something written on the band. If I found one that did, I bought it. They actually got the cover of *Underground Rock* when *Salvation* came out, and it was the best interview with them I'd read yet. Highly informative to a degree, but still just toying with fans eager to learn more. The band kept many details in the dark and refused to divulge whole sections of their past. It only made their following hunger for more. It made me start to open myself to an outside world I thought was done with me. It made me think about. . .

Seeing them play live.

Just out of curiosity, I looked at their calendar on UnholySaint.com and saw that they were *PLAYING ABILENE*!!! The show was four months away and would be held at the Paramount Theater on Cypress. That was big time in my mind, and I wondered if they'd be able to sell out the venue. I would never find out. A large contingent of the community's "moral" leadership got together to protest the band playing the Paramount, and the city gave in to their objections. Unholy Saint would instead perform at Guitars and Cadillacs, plenty big enough but not as prestigious and conservative. The main reason for the protest? The band's imagery and lyrical content. That was the only part of the band I was having trouble fully embracing. They were less than thrilled with organized religion and had a huge problem with Christianity. I wasn't really religious at all and had stopped going to church with Mona around high school, but I also didn't like to disrespect the beliefs I'd been taught or the people who believed them. "Live and Let Live" was my stance on all religions, as I didn't practice a one, but had no issue with any. Unholy Saint, on the other hand, were very outspoken about their adversarial stance on organized religion as a whole and Christianity in particular, and that bothered some people. Unholy Saint was just fine with bothering people. All the cities on their tour itinerary were ones that had prominent Christian colleges or universities in them, Abilene Christian University of course being ours. If they could, Unholy Saint booked their shows on campus or as close as possible to the college. Now, here in Abilene, nothing was *really* far from anything, so a twelve-minute drive from school to venue for a young person was nothing, although it might have seemed too long for someone Mona's age to waste their evening on. As the months shrunk down to weeks, I felt some hesitance in biting the bullet and purchasing a ticket to the show. I'd never been to a concert, small or large, before and felt that: 1) doing so would take me across a threshold I wasn't ready to accept – fully acknowledging that I was a helpless, dedicated Unholy Saint fan boy, or Disciple, as they're collectively known, and 2), being out and about as such might exclude me from certain potential employers in Abilene who want nothing to do with a "sick, heavy metal, satanist homo" as our former neighbor Milton Mader once described them.

On the other hand, this might have been my only chance to ever see them play live. I had no plans of leaving Abilene, temporarily or otherwise, and after their performance Abilene might not have plans for them to ever return. In fact, Abilene might have direct, iron clad plans to *prevent* them from returning. Procrastination is something I wish they gave out jobs for, because not only would I do my job well, but I could see myself in a big fancy corner office as Vice President of procrastination. I'm *that good* at it. So, I waited until eight days before the show to buy a ticket. General Admission, which I had to ask the girl at Guitars and Cadillacs what that meant. I went straight to the venue to buy a ticket. I wasn't confident in my online ticket buying skills, as I had none. But I got my ticket, for a steep $24.57 after taxes and fees. Hearing the cost had me do a double take and made me ask if I was getting a VIP ticket, because I just wanted a regular one. What the hell were they charging $24 a ticket for? I wondered if bigger acts charged more.

Those eight days couldn't have gone by slower if God or Superman grabbed the earth by the ass and held it down, only allowing it to spin at half its normal speed. With no job and no booked social schedule, I had a lot of time for contemplation on my hands. For some time, I didn't even understand *why* I was so tense and wound up. Mona, far wiser than I ever gave her credit for, could see it from a country mile, and finally decided to shed some light on my dilemma two days prior to the show. She explained how natural it was for me to be both nervous *and* excited about going to a concert for the first time, perceiving the environment without having ever experienced it before. Hearing her keen deduction finally got me to settle, but the night before the show only produced a grand total of two, maybe three hours of sleep.

What I wouldn't give to go back to my bed on that night, and never wake up again.

Chapter Five: The Night I Died. . . And Then Wished for Death

Finally, the day of the concert arrived, and all the agonizing and anticipation would soon be worth it. I showered beforehand, knowing the futility of that gesture, and that I would probably end up drenched in sweat. It was more to wake up my senses and keep me alert rather than clean. Less than four days removed from almost a foot of snow from Cisco to Snyder, my bones were still achingly frigid, but my blood more than compensated by boiling my insides to a revved engine, enough to generate a bit of perspiration on my temples and collar. I couldn't stop pacing as I debated internally about what time to hop in the truck and head toward the venue. Too early and I would stick out as some obsessed freak or a dork who didn't comprehend the etiquette of concert going, which I didn't. However, I was more concerned with showing up too late. I wanted to get as close to the stage as possible and knew that might take some doing. I'd seen on Facebook that Unholy Saint disciples were coming from all over the state, as this and their Lubbock show were the only two in Texas on this leg of the tour (that I knew to refer to it as a "leg" made me feel so astute). And judging from YouTube videos of past shows, the first 20 or so feet in front of the stage is not for the un-indoctrinated meek, but for the aggressive. The time on my ticket said 9:00pm, but that would be for the opening act. Unholy Saint didn't take any bands on tour with them, but instead let the venues work with local bands to open each show. This evening would have two bands going on ahead of my new favorite. I didn't know anything about either and can't remember their names, except that one had the word Rattlesnake in it. That band must have been really good because they'd also been allowed to open up for Basil Rathbone and the Dead MacBeth, who'd come through Abilene two weeks earlier. According to fan sites, Unholy Saint wouldn't come on stage until close to 11:00, and they would play for approximately two hours. Depending on the mood of the band, they might treat the crowd to *Collide* and/or something off their E.P., but the night would have to be stellar for that to happen. They ended every other show on this tour with a cover by one classic heavy metal artist or another, followed by their astonishingly epic song *Immortality Fades*. I couldn't fucking wait.

I decided to leave my house at 8:00, and when I pulled up outside of Guitars and Cadillacs, I was met with an already long line of anxious people about to be let in, but also a decent if underwhelming number of moms, grandmas, and other Christians protesting the concert. I'd heard of protests like this outside of Kiss concerts in the 70's, and just couldn't believe that such spectacles were still being staged in the 21st century. I managed to accidentally make eye contact with one of them, an elderly woman named Mabel Nadine who used to sit next to Mona at church. They'd always smile and hug each other, and sit in the sixth row, on the aisle, left of center. Every single Sunday. When she saw me, I could tell she was thrown back a bit by the fact that I was attending "such heathenistic filth," but she didn't pursue any direct confrontation with me, thank goodness. Eventually, I got to the front of the line, got my ticket scanned, and catapulted my ass in the building as fast as I could. The front of the stage, and anything near it, was completely filled in by rabid fans, at least half of them younger than me.

Standing through the first two bands was a welcome initiation into concert life, as everything moved along pretty chill and uneventful. I rarely drink, but did down two beers quickly to settle myself in, and their liquidity sloshed along nauseatingly in my belly far too long. They were the most expensive beers I've ever purchased. The music was OK and both bands did their best to expend their energy and connect with the audience. Since they're both local, they had a commendable amount of their own fans cheering them on. The closer it got to Unholy Saint's entrance, though, the more palpable the tension and unrest grew. People had waited long enough. As soon as the "Rattlesnake" band said their farewell, what was once a huge chasm in the center of the floor evaporated and transformed into a pond of rustling, jostling humanity. Close to 600 Disciples were ready and willing to open up their lives to these four mysterious, California gothic monoliths, eager for a catharsis. I just wanted to see them play their songs.

I looked nervously at my watch to see that it was already 10:05 when all of a sudden, the lights went out almost an hour before the internet's prediction and the crowd went nuts. A large subset of them lunged forward to get to the front of the stage, discarding anyone too small or weak to hold their position. The collective roar everyone erupted with was quite impressive, and a little jolting. At first, I was too shy to participate, but then decided to join the masses. I started by producing an adolescent creaking yell, but soon found my throat and delivered some manly, Texas-sized war calls, which I would throw out less and less awkwardly after each song. A video screen behind the drum riser flashed a lightning quick image of a crucifix, which then stayed on screen and began to spin clockwise like the spin the bottle icon on the *Tastes Like Death* album. As it came to a slow crawl, recorded moaning sounds, like sex, grew louder and multiplied, causing the younger concert goers (and I) to squirm and blush. As the cross stopped in an upside-down position, the swarming bee guitar of *Blood Harvest* filled the room, and the rest of the band exploded into the first verse of the song. They wouldn't let up, or even pause to acknowledge the crowd, for the next 30 minutes or so.

To put it mildly, Unholy Saint was everything I'd hoped they'd be and then some. At some points droning and pulsing, and at others destructive and menacing, they seemed to be seasoned veterans well advanced for their relatively short existence, keeping the show going at an amazingly brisk pace. Daniel was brash, upfront, and almost antagonistic, while Alister was a calming, controlling, commanding influence. I don't know if others in the crowd could tell, but he would give direction, changing the order of the songs, deleting or adding as they went. He would call on their drummer to speed up or slow down, depending on the reaction his fingertips and ears got from the volume, or what energy he was drawing from the crowd. Devin was the living, breathing definition of the word cool. Although, as the show went on, that coolness seemed more akin to aloofness or detachment. She seemed to be looking through the crowd or above it, to the next show, the next town. Robert M. played the drums. Sometimes pulverizing hard, sometimes feather soft. Through it all, his facial expression never changed, nor did his line of sight. His cranium was connected as if by chains to his hi-hat. His head never turned elsewhere. Subconsciously or otherwise, I ended up gravitating from the center of the floor towards the left, to be somewhat in line with where Devin stood, and during their song *Solemn*, I think she locked eyes with mine for more than a few seconds. In that brief time, I stood mesmerized, embarrassed, *and* turned on, growing slightly swollen, if you know what I mean.

The band had played for approximately an hour and a half, when the stage went completely dark, and a few moments later, a spotlight lit up Daniel Sepulveda's grinning, perspiration-soaked face. He stood silent, glaring at the crowd, and then spoke these words in an obviously mocking accent:

"Howdy, y'all. Thank you for coming tonight. We hope you've enjoyed yourselves as much as we have. Since we're here in Texas, we have a little something special for you."

Please let it be Collide, I thought to myself. *It's going to be Collide.* Jesus, I felt like a schoolgirl watching the Beatles in those old black and white clips.

"This is for all you boot scooters and shit kickers."

With that, the rest of the band reemerged, seemingly from thin air, and they kicked into a faster, edgier, almost punk rock version of Brooks and Dunn's *Neon Moon*, slowing down to sing the end of the song as it was written, Daniel countryfying his voice. The audience was stunned and applauded voraciously in approval at its completion. They then played a more expected *Communication Breakdown* by Led Zeppelin, before closing the night with the inevitable *Immortality Fades*. Although they had included a song off their first E.P., and gave us two cover songs instead of one, there was no *Collide*. I felt a swell of disappointment or longing in my stomach, which then flowed upward into my heart. Although I was blown away by what I'd just witnessed and had no frame of reference to compare this show to, the exclusion of my favorite song left a slight sting of "what could have been." As the masses filed out of Guitars and Cadillacs, I overheard at least two other people also displeased by *Collide*'s absence. I guess it wasn't just *my* favorite Unholy Saint song. Before exiting the building, I stopped by the merchandise booth and contemplated getting a shirt. This sense of my mother, who I couldn't even remember, heaved itself onto my shoulders, and I felt that this is exactly what she would have been doing at this moment, were she here. I then thought to myself "*she actually might be*" and scanned the room to check. No sign of the target, but I did see a slew of vaguely familiar faces from high school's past, some I didn't expect to be at any type of rock show, let alone a sacrilegious one.

The potential for seeing my mother extinguished, I reset my mind to the shirts but couldn't convince myself to pull the trigger on something that cost $25. *All musicians must be millionaires*, I laughed to myself, mind blown at the audacity. Resigned to the fact that my first Unholy Saint experience was now in the books, I shuffled slowly out of the venue and into the cold Texas night. A surprising number of people were still just milling about outside, and a sizable group congregated near the band's tour bus, which was parked well behind the venue, on 39th Street. I sort of bumped into a young couple who'd made the trip all the way from Weatherford, who told me that everyone near the tour bus was hoping to meet the band. I shook my head in amusement, not thinking meeting the band was even a remote possibility, and made my way to my vehicle on the opposite side of the building. I was almost at my truck, away from all the commotion, when I heard a female voice cut its way through the darkness.

"Hey. Do you have a cigarette?"

It was Devin Sikorsky.

It was Devin Sikorsky.

Devin Fucking Sikorsky.

"Uh. Uh, no. I'm sorry. I don't."

"Did you see the show?"

"Uh. Uh, yes. Yes, I did."

"How did you like it?" Her voice seemed exhausted

by asking this question, as if it was the millionth time she'd asked it of someone.

"I... I liked it a lot. It was really, really... great. That was my first show."

"Your first Unholy Saint show? Sainted and soiled."

"My first show ever. By anybody... You looked at me at one point. I mean, I think you did.

Didn't you?"

Her eyes rolled like I was feeding her some line she'd heard too many times before, or if I was clearly more enthralled by a moment she didn't even register.

"No. I didn't. I've never seen you before."

"Can I tell you something?"

"Please don't be weird."

"No, no! Of course not."

"Okay, then."

"Your song, *Colli*---"

"Come closer."

My back stiffened, and I grew nervous. "Your song, *Collide*. It's my favorite Unholy Saint song. It might be my favorite song, period."

"Oh, really? And what do you like about it?" She seemed uninterested in the answer.

"Your voice. How simple and tender it sounds. The song, not your voice. Your voice isn't simple. It's---."

"Come *closer.*"

I couldn't breathe. Much closer and I would be invading her private space. She put her hands on my unbuttoned black jean jacket, and pulled me gently closer to her, close enough that her forearms were pressing slightly against her chest. My body shivered violently, instantly ten degrees colder than before, but also simmering with an emerging heat that started at my toes, and encompassed the shrinking space between us. I could see how blue her eyes were, and made out a few lines in her face and forehead that told me she might be older than I previously guessed. She was at least four inches shorter than I was. Dark roots peaked gingerly from beneath her blond crown. She smelled like lavender and rose petals, and you couldn't tell that she just spent almost two hours playing a bass in a virtual oven under hot, exploitive light. I was a little scared.

'Are you scared?" she asked with a hint of a laugh. 'Lean down a little. Let me whisper in your ear."

I felt movement in my groin. I dipped my head down. I was able to make out a bit of saliva on her lips as she put them to my right ear, and her voice felt like wind tickling an abandoned tunnel.

'Your neck smells of sadness and uncertainty. I fear that this may be the highpoint of your young life."

It was.

'You never told me your name."

"It's Dav---"

Before I could finish dribbling it out, she'd gripped

my hair vice grip tight with her left hand, pulling my head downward, and thrust my jaw to the left with her right, popping the bones in my neck. Her fingers felt like they were sinking into my skin, absorbing the flesh underneath. I could barely notice a fiery red and yellow-white maniacal gleam in her eye as her mouth opened wide, exposing jagged, yellowing molars, and fiercely pointed, porcelain-like canines. She bit down firmly on the side of my throat and cupped my mouth with her right hand to keep my screams from alerting anyone. I couldn't believe how freakishly strong she was, or what was even happening. My eyes rolled up into my head, and my body from scrotum to Adam's apple wanted to vomit. I could feel blood – my blood – soaking the collar of my jacket and running the length of my shirt. Through throbbing ears, I could hear her mouth make a hard sucking sound, as if she was searching thirstily for the last drops of soda through a straw. Something ruptured and exploded inside my neck, filling everything from my sinuses to my esophagus with blood. My trachea refused to relax or allow me to breathe, my legs went limp and were close to giving out, and my arms, which I thought were trying as hard as they could to break myself from Devin's vice, were about as effective as an infant's. My brain snapped out of reality, and then back into it, and I made amends with the thought that this woman was killing me. That I was about to die.

Fortunately, or unfortunately, as hindsight would instill in me, two members of the night's event staff walked around the corner to see something, not sure of what, happening.

"Hey, no drug deals or sexual favors here. This is a

family friendly environment."

Devin's eyes enlarged, surprised by her interruption. She un-suckled her mouth from my throat, grabbed me again by the jacket, and flung me in the gentlemen's direction. I managed to soar backwards at an alarmingly easy rate, traveling approximately twenty feet. Now realizing that this was not a consensual transaction, the two enacted their "professional event staff" training.

"Carl, get help! You, two - stop where you are!"

I remember thinking, *Stop? I can barely move*, before trying to make it to my knees and then passing out completely, flat and facedown, for at least several seconds. As I was told after, Devin ran towards the back of the building, turned the corner, and was a glimmer before the guy could even get a glimpse of what she looked like or who she was.

Event staff superintendent Dave Spencer, whose little brother went to school with me, and his co-worker Carl, tried to help me to my feet as more members of their crew started to gather around, but my body turned into dead weight comparable to a block of unchiseled stone, and they settled for turning me over on my back and adjusting me into a sitting position. It was then that they noticed the blood covering my torso and the wound spitting out more, like a tapped oil well.

"Somebody call 911! This guy's hurt bad!," a muffled voice in a distant land called out.

Dave's eyes contained the reaction of someone who was experiencing a horror film, but in real life. His voice sounded frail and frightened.

"Shit. He's... lost a lot of blood, and he's turning gray and green."

I had indeed lost a lot of blood. I didn't know how much the human body held, or how quickly it generated it, but I knew that I would never find out. I didn't have time for anything. I was at the end. And I *still* couldn't piece together *WHAT THE HELL HAD JUST HAPPENED*! Just then, as I could hear sirens in the distance, my body seized from head to toe, moving like pennies on a nightstand during an earthquake, and a painful, invisible, barbed wire electricity shot through my arteries and out every pore of my body. The event staff all jumped back about three steps, gasping, mouths to the floor, as I convulsed uncontrollably. I could hear a voice shout out "You can see his veins!," but had noticed that all the voices, going back several minutes, seemed far away and distant like my ears had been stuffed with gauze or sponge. My head ached like President Kennedy's must have when the second bullet exploded through it, and my screams of agony had to have been heard – no, felt – by cattle tens of miles away. I gazed helplessly at my outstretched hands and just like Dave Spencer said, my skin was graying, with strong streaks of green mixed in. My veins were visible and protruding, and what blood left in them was dark and violent. My blood vessels mushroomed in splotches on my skin, and my eyes turned a neon, bloodshot, translucent purple.

The ambulance and police cars arrived, their inhabitants fumbling out of vehicles with equipment and protocols in hand. But I... refused. I didn't want them to come near me. I didn't want them to... discover me.

Discover what I was. I didn't even *know* what I was, but subconsciously, my body already did. It knew the outcome of this chance meeting with one of my new heroes, and knew that I couldn't divulge, verbally or otherwise, the unfair truth of my resulting condition. Nor did I want any consequence to befall Devin, even though she clearly deserved some for the brazen attempted murder I was beginning to come to grips with. Even so, I felt this deep-down need to… *protect her*? So, I painstakingly hobbled onto my hands and knees, analyzed the scene in front of me, and when I saw an imaginary breach in the pattern of various humans coming to my aid, I dizzyingly stood on one foot, then the other, and ran. As if my limbs were trying to go in different directions, I ran forward, following the pattern my brain had sketched out for me, and when the event staff tried to stop me, I stiff armed, and elbowed, and hip tossed my way to freedom, running atop one of the police vehicles, and hightailed it away from all of them. As I ran, my bodily marionette show stabilized, and my balance righted itself. I ran, and ran, and ran all the way to Mona's. I burst through the door, hurried to my bathroom, and stared at myself in the mirror. I couldn't believe what was looking back at me. "What the fuck?!" was the only phrase that came to mind, and I repeated it over and over again.

I heard footsteps and then a knock on the door.

"Davis, honey? Is that you? Are you alright?"

Fuck.

Chapter Six: Revelation

I stood there, staring at my left eye in the mirror, watching it morph from hazel to black to charcoal. My fingernails split into a thousand streaks, and my cheeks sank in deep, grasping hard onto my jawbones for comfort. I couldn't let Mona see me like this. I had to think quickly, and I had to resolve this dilemma without her finding out anything about tonight's activity.

"Hi, momma. I'm sorry I woke you. I'm just a little sick from too much alcohol. It doesn't rest easy on my tummy. I think... I think I'm too much of a light weight when it comes to drinking."

"Can I help you with anything? I knew you shouldn't have gone to one of those... concerts. They're just a playground for bad behavior and bad influences."

"Oh yeah? Mabel Nadine was there," I joked, tears streaming down my gray face.

"Davis McCarty! Do not use your tongue to spread lies about another person, least of all one of God's most precious and perfect creatures!"

"Understood. Momma Mona, can we please talk

about this later? I'm *really* not feeling well, but I'll be alright in the morning, and you need to get back to bed. I don't appreciate being the cause of your disturbance."

".. Are you sure?"

"Yes, ma'am. I'll talk to you in the morning."

I had no intention of talking to Mona in the morning. I had to leave the house as soon as possible and leave it forever. A peculiar thing occurred as she was standing outside the bathroom door, debating with me. I could smell her through the door. Through the walls. I could smell her blood; tasted its sugar content on my lips. And I wanted it. No, I *required* it. I needed to consume my grandmother's blood, just to remain alive. Instincts that didn't even exist in me an hour before shined bright like freshly installed software with a brand-new car smell. They were automatic and they were damn real. And they scared the living shit out of me. I was thinking of drinking my grandmother's blood. That's vampire shit.

And that's when it finally dawned on me, destroying my gut like I'd jumped on a grenade in Vietnam, and shredding my quickly deteriorating brain like some toxic amoeba: Devin Sikorsky was a vampire, and she turned me into one as well. Then, almost as quickly, another painful truth clawed its way up my back and through my perceptions: she hadn't meant to turn me into a vampire. She had meant to feed on and kill me. Only the unexpected interruption of the venue's staff stopped her. But where was she? *Did she make it on the band's tour bus? Did she get stopped by a police officer needing an explanation for crazy chick covered in blood? Did the rest of the band completely freak out on her upon seeing her appearance? Did they know her secret?* A whirlwind of thoughts and questions pounded my skull from the inside out, and I didn't have one fucking answer.

I knew that I had to get out of that house, though. I couldn't live with myself, whether *I* was actually alive or not, if I caused my Mona any harm. *Any* harm. I don't think anyone outside Guitars and Cadillacs knew who I was, and I didn't see anyone I recognized as I tore ass back home. I doubted it would be on the news. I stuffed some clothes into a duffle bag, crammed the last thirty-five dollars I had into my jeans pocket, wrote Mona as gentle and honest a goodbye letter as possible, and slipped out my bedroom window, knowing there was an abandoned grain mill along the highway I could lay low in for the duration of the day. I assumed that since I was now apparently a vampire, I must not be able to go out in the sun. I would use that time to figure out what to do next. Where to go.

Mona was the only parent I'd ever known, and as bad as I felt for her when she found the letter I'd written her, and what devastation it would undoubtedly cause, one person stuck in my memories and weakened my heart even more than she did.

Annie Moore.

Chapter Seven: Annie

Dropping out of school felt like I'd broken my momma's heart, but something somewhere triggered that decision (I can't even recall what anymore), and once it was made, there was no thought of an alternative. I made no clear concession for the repercussions of my action, and clearly had no concept of the ache it would plunge into Momma Mona. Like any responsible, tough love spewing parent, she gave me the tear-filled walk to the front porch, an anguished squeal coming from the rusted screen door as it fought to open, and told me that her home was no longer mine, not until I went back to school or could return with a job that paid half of the mortgage payment (I didn't know that she'd already paid the house off years prior). I was able to sleep on the flower-patterned, stain-drenched, forgotten-by-time couch in my friend Nathan's garage. Detached from the house, deteriorating rapidly, and serving no noble purpose, his parents had allowed him to convert the garage into a hangout of sorts for his many friends (two friends), and its Capri-Sun and sweaty clay smelling couch served me adequately in my time of need.

Almost exactly a month later, Momma Mona called

the residence and asked me to come back. She felt guilty something awful, and said we could work out some form of agreement. Truth be told, I think she simply became lonely, lonely enough to abandon her previous position. I was overjoyed, but played it cool, agreeing to come back the following afternoon. It was a sunny, but uncharacteristically chilly April evening. We hugged, we cried, we had salmon and fried okra, and we got on with life. She was never quite the same again, though, and for several years I couldn't explain why. Not until she told me about my parents, and how much my knack for screwing up reminded her of Valerie, would that puzzle piece mysteriously materialize and fall into place.

One big hurdle I had to overcome to follow through with my decision to leave school prematurely, and, in hindsight, one factor that led heavily to that decision, was a girl. Annie Moore. We weren't friends, but she was kind to me on several occasions, when all her popular friends ignored me or worse. She didn't wear the most expensive clothes or drive the most expensive car; she was really down to earth, didn't take her privilege for granted, and didn't put stock in material things. She was beautiful on a level I couldn't explain, sophisticated and attractive, but also quite plain in her beauty. She somehow had brown *and* blond hair, as if she had dyed streaks in it. Alas, they were real. Inviting light brown eyes, the cutest dimples and button nose, a fit but not overly athletic figure, and an amazing ass. She was the total package, and I don't even know if she knew it. She could have owned every heterosexual male in Abilene High, or the whole of Abilene for that matter. I would have been eager to be her subject or her slave.

Annie first swerved into my orbit in seventh grade, which is to say I can't remember her at all before that. Her father, Robert "Bob" Moore, was the owner of the biggest tractor and farm equipment franchise in the region, and they were more than well off. When we were sat at the same table in seventh grade English, she immediately greeted me with a "Hi. You're Davis, right?" I couldn't believe she knew my name. That six weeks we sat at the same table, she always included me in group discussions and asked my opinion on essay assignments, etc. We only had one more class together from junior high all the way to senior year, when we shared two electives. Other than those, she was in much more advanced classes than me, our grades separating us like any other indicator of a modern class system.

One of those electives was journalism. I really didn't even know what possessed me to take it, other than the fact that I was done with physical education. Both were assigned during first period, I didn't want to be sweaty and uncomfortable for the rest of the day, and I wouldn't have showered at school even if the P.E. kids were allowed to. That she was also in journalism assured me that I had made the right choice. There I found out that she was really into writing (I should have known in seventh grade English), and that she planned on being an author and "investigative journalist," whatever that was. She alluded to the fact that her father was not a fan of that plan, and wanted her to take over the tractor franchises, of which Bob now owned three, with one in Shallowater and one just outside Slaton. I was just happy we had a couple of classes together, and that she didn't make me feel unworthy of her presence. She was very different from her friends, apart from maybe one or two, who all seemed very vapid, vain, and unintelligent.

The day I realized that I had a *HUGE* crush on Annie was November 1st, 2016, one day after Halloween and one day before my 18th birthday. Annie had invited me to her and Wendy Taylor's joint Halloween party. I did not attend, and the next day Annie asked me where I was. I couldn't believe she noticed my absence. I couldn't believe I was on her mind at all. She told me that she wouldn't be in class on the 2nd because she had a doctor's appointment in the morning and would then be travelling with the basketball team to cover the first away game of the season for the school paper. Therefore, the only time to give me my birthday present was today. *Birthday present*?! Momma Mona was the only person who'd ever given me anything for my birthday or Christmas. Yet, here was Annie with an incredible gesture of thoughtfulness and fellowship. I was speechless, evidenced by my thunderstruck, silent stare at her gift, which I had to unwrap in the hallway of our school. I could have done without the attention, to be sure, but I was over the moon that she cared enough to actually get me something. It was bigger than I would have expected for something coming from a relative acquaintance. I set my books on the floor and tore into the package methodically. It was a gift basket that contained two gift certificates to my favorite movie theater, which I'd only attended three times in my life, two gift passes to the Abilene Zoo (I'd been only once before), a blank journal, a blank artist's sketch book, a John Deere hat, a Coke, and a big bag of Peanut M&M's. I didn't know what to say, except thank you repeatedly.

She must have thought I was a record skipping for all the times I said it. Annie was a nice person. A good person. That was the kind of gift I'd expect a high schooler to give one of their best friends, or someone they had romantic feelings for, but she did it for a mere classmate. I told her as much the next class period I had with her on November 3rd, to which she responded, "You *are* one of my friends, silly."

I was in love.

At least I *think* I was. I really hadn't felt feelings like that before, didn't know what to make of them, and had no grasp of "next steps." I definitely didn't expect those feelings to be reciprocated. I mean, no matter how much she thought we were friends, we were on completely different ends of the social pecking order spectrum, and people just didn't cross those boundaries. I never saw it once. In fact, on more than a few occasions I saw such foolishness stamped out like a small fire starting in a wastebasket. I watched Becky Halford tearfully have to break things off with my classmate Jose at her parents' insistence. They wouldn't have her "ruining her father's reputation and messing up her life dating a Mexican." I saw much of the same when one person from one side of the tracks started, or tried to start, mingling with someone from the other. The two main obstacles were race and income. If I hadn't made myself clear up to this point, Momma Mona did the best she could for us on temporary work, side hustles, and odd jobs for straight cash, but she and we did not have much money. Nothing close to it. When I did concede to a social request and went to Annie's house for a party Spring Break of senior year, her father and the family's staff kept a stern eye on me at all times. While her other friends were free to move about and use one of the upstairs bathrooms, I was told which exact downstairs one to use, ordered not to deviate from it or wander around the property. When Annie grabbed me by the hand to coerce me into swimming with everyone, her father's brow raised a few inches, and his grimace was undeniable. He didn't want her touching my poor, filthy hands, and he most assuredly didn't want me touching any part of her.

The more we spoke in class, the closer we got, and the harder I fell. Knowing the futility of such emotion, I had to find a way to mitigate and eventually extinguish it. I started by altering my route to and from classes to reduce our exposure. I figured if I saw her less, my feelings would dissipate. When she noticed that route change, I had to begin taking longer restroom breaks and would on occasion be intentionally tardy to our two classes. I would strike a quick conversation with our teachers after the bell rang, pretending to need some details on a random assignment. I knew that she hated to be late to class and couldn't stick around to say a few words or walk with me.

Aside from the issues with caring for Annie, my grades had started to drop significantly, and I felt a large cloud of unrest and hopelessness about my future, both in the world and at Abilene High. I knew college wasn't in the cards and felt that a diploma wouldn't help me attain the kind of job and wages I was destined for anyway. So, one early April 2017 morning, with a heavy heart but a made-up mind, I just stopped coming. I would hang out at the diner near school, and when that raised questions and ran its course, I would hang out in the wooded areas of the park. I didn't want to be a coward, and didn't want to continue deceiving Mona, so I eventually came clean, hence my dreaded month-long expulsion from the house. *But two days before that admission*, I got a knock on the door in the afternoon. Puzzled and suspicious, I opened the creaky screen door to find Annie Moore on my broken porch. I wanted to die. I didn't know she was aware of my address, and now that she was, I was sure my home's visual first impression would be its last and repel her in perpetuity. She looked concerned for me, and then annoyed to find me otherwise well.

"Uh, hi," I slipped through a mostly closed mouth sheepishly.

"Hi? Where have you been? You haven't been to school in almost a month."

"Yeah, about that. I kind of dropped out. What... what are you doing here?"

"I'm checking on *you*!"

"How did you... How did you know where I live?"

"It's not hard, Davis. I just... Wait; dropped out? Why would you do something so---"

"Pleeease. Please don't. I don't have a good answer, but I know it's for the best."

"For the best? Dropping out of school two months before graduation, and not getting a diploma is for the best? Okay. Whatever you say."

"I'm sorry, but I'm just a little confused. Why are

you here?"

"Are you serious? I was *worried about you*!"

"You were?"

"YES!"

"Oh. I'm sorry. I didn't mean to worry you. But why would you...."

"God, never mind, Davis. Never mind. Good luck."

She turned and walked to her car. She closed the door behind her, gripped the wheel tight with both hands, and sat there staring straight ahead for several seconds. She turned her head to find me gawking at her and gave what looked like a long sigh before starting the engine and peeling away slowly like a delicate band aid. It felt like there was something Annie wasn't saying, but I was painfully oblivious as to what. In all honesty, I was completely shocked by her visit. It seemed like such a drastic breach of teenage etiquette, even for someone who had an adequate level of self-esteem. The wrong pair of eyes as a witness and one mouth could spread the virus of rumor until it was pandemic level damaging. Did she really see me as that close a friend? We didn't hang out outside of school, and we didn't talk on the phone. I wasn't completely crazy in my confusion, *was I*? I was touched, though. Nathan was the only other person to contact me about my absence, carefully intercepted phone calls from the school notwithstanding. Almost instantly, I wished I could go back in time and replay that whole scene again. I would say a lot more than the mute imbecile that answered the door. What was done was done, though. Now possibly I could go on with my life without feeling the tug of my feelings for Annie Moore.

I wouldn't see her beautiful image again for over two years.

One blazing summer day, I was in her father's store searching for some soil and some gardening tools for Momma Mona. I was heading to the cash register when I heard that voice call out to me.

"McCarty!"

Oh no.

"Davis! Davis McCarty."

I turned on a slow-motion swivel, knuckles tightening, muscles clinching.

"Annie? Hey! How are you?" My voice sounded feeble.

She was more stunning that ever. Her teeth were whiter, her skin smoother, and her smell was of an expensive, sweet perfume.

"I'm good. How are you?"

"I'm… the same, I guess. Just getting on with it."

"That's great. It's so funny that we bumped into each other. I just got back in town a couple of days ago. I'm home from KU for the summer. I didn't see you last summer at all. Do you still live in Abilene?"

"Yes. Yes, I do. I'm still at home with mom. I was in Post for a while, but---"

"OK. OK, great. We should get together for lunch or something."

It was as if she had never left my front yard angry and let down that day. It was as if we were even better friends than we were. I was just as confused by this as the day she knocked on my front door.

"Yeah, sure. I mean, of course. Whenever you have free time."

How could I get her to pay for mine without appearing like a complete loser, is the thought that ran through my head. I expected her to forget about our run-in and go on with her wonderful life in Kansas before going on to bigger and better things like a career, marriage to a hot millionaire, and vacations with their kids in places like Vail and Cabo San Lucas. Two days later, though, she called Mona's and asked if I was available for Mexican the next day, her treat (Yes!). I checked with my imaginary schedule planner and told her that I could "just squeeze her in amongst all my mergers and acquisitions." That's literally what I said, and it caused her to spit out her drink, she laughed so hard.

We went on that lunch date, and had a great time. About twenty minutes in, she did give me *the talk*: why did I drop out, why didn't I call her after I did, etc., to which I provided an unconvincing but ultimately accepted slew of lies. But, aside from that awkward but necessary interlude, we enjoyed ourselves immensely, and time flew by before she had to be back at the house for a family function. We agreed to do it again, though, and did once more before she went back to KU for her third year.

Over the next year, her final year of undergrad study, we got together once at Christmas break and started talking on the phone about once every two weeks. We were finally actual friends, and I'd even forgotten my insecurity about our respective social standings. However, one thing she never brought up in our conversations ate at me and kept me up at night: boyfriends. I figured there was no way that she didn't have one, or at least date casually. It was a big campus, and she was an absolute catch. She never brought it up, though. I was afraid to, thinking that if I willingly opened pandora's box, she'd unleash a life's worth of relationships and conquests, allowing me to be her springboard and shoulder to cry on. I didn't contain that resolve. After all, I was in love with her again.

May 20, 2020. A day that could have been the restart to my life, instead became one more example of my inability to let a bad decision dissolve unfulfilled. Annie had been back home for a week, having obtained her bachelor's degree in journalism a year ahead of schedule. She called and asked me to come over at my earliest convenience so we could hang out. She then made a point of saying she had something to discuss with me. I was intrigued. I was frightened. What I wasn't was going to wait long to find out what the something was. The next day, late morning, I headed over to her parents' house and was greeted almost lifelessly by Annie's father Bob. His look of disapproval and maybe even disgust was hardly hidden from his smoldering eyes and sunken jowls. Slowly, he opened the door and stepped back for me to enter.

"Annie's coming down, shortly. Feel free to wait at

the breakfast table."

Before I could finish my "Thank you," he was out of sight, with his study door closing loudly behind him. I could only shake my head, wondering how such a sweet, kind soul came from his stereotypically prejudiced loins. I could hear Annie's socked heels prancing down the stairs swiftly, and turned to see her eyeing me with a huge smile. At the bottom of the stairs, she almost leapt into my arms with a big bear hug.

"I am soooo glad to see you, and soooo glad to have that degree!"

"Congratulations, again. You deserve it, and everything else that's coming with it."

"That's what I wanted to talk to you about. Let's go sit by the pool house and talk. Ilona will bring us some fruit and waters."

Once seated under a still-friendly sun and seen to by Ilona, the Moores' beautiful new Lithuanian housekeeper, Annie hit me with a sucker punch of a scenario, one that I was in no way prepared for. She said that she had already registered for her master's degree at KU, but that she would transfer somewhere closer to home if I wanted her to, even as close as Abilene Christian. Wait, *what*? Instantly dehydrated. Throat gasping for air and linguistics. I couldn't formulate concrete thoughts, much less get out the words to combat this assault on my senses.

"What do… what do… what… do you… what do you mean, if I want you to?"

Real smooth.

"I mean, if you wanted me to go to school closer, I can."

"Why?"

Her look was a mixture of slightly shocked and slightly perturbed.

"Because I thought you'd like that."

"What, what, what... Why?"

If there was an annual award for inserting your foot in your mouth, I was definitely getting a nomination. It's nice just to be nominated.

Without missing a beat, Annie transitioned to Plan B while I was still trying to wrap my mind around Plan A.

"No, never mind. Disregard this whole confusing, embarrassing exchange. I'll go back to KU in the fall." Her jaw tensed, and her posture straightened, facing forward, removing her leg from brushing against mine.

"No, wait. Let's continue this conversation. I'm just confused is all. Why would I have a say or an opinion in where you finish college? That's a big deal, and it sounds like that should be a decision between you and your parents. They're paying for it, anyway, right?"

"I just thought we might want to be closer to each other, so we could see each other more often."

As she said these words, she lengthened certain ones while leaning her head to the right, as if she was using her entire skull and shoulder structure to bite through an overcooked bite of steak, trying to lead me to the same finish line she crossed sometime before I even knew we were running. My expression must have looked entirely ignorant, which caused her next words to burst out more drastically.

"Don't you want to date?"

Oh Shit.

"Date? Ohhh. Like date. Date, date. Date *me*. You would want to date me?"

"Well, wouldn't you want to date me?"

I wanted to say yes. I *wanted* to say, "That's all I've wanted for the past eight years." I *WANTED* to say, "Let's move in together and get married and have your dad fund our lifestyle for the foreseeable future." What came out of my mouth was:

"I think so."

I was clever.

"I think so?" she repeated, in complete exasperation. 'I *think so*?"

Uh oh.

"I just don't want to be the cause of anything that derails your life. I'm not someone who has the future you do, and... how long have you been thinking about this?"

She pushed her hands up either side of her face and ran them angrily through her tantalizing shoulder-length hair, still surprised how completely dense I was.

"It doesn't matter, does it? You obviously don't feel the same, right? Let's just..."

A quick opening of the back door, followed by a quick gust of wind, and the silhouette of Bob Moore's head could be seen before unveiling his stern, determined visage in the sunlight.

"Annie. I need to talk to you. Davis, you'll have to resume your visit at another time."

I can swear that I remember possible tears welling up in Annie's eyes, as they peered through mine and out the back of my itchy, swarming head. Now that she was being forced to end it, she wanted to continue our talk and tried to voice her words with her eyes, but I just didn't speak the same ocular language. I raised both of my eyebrows, hoping she would understand their meaning, trying to convey that I cared more than she knew. More than she could ever know. We both rose from the pool house breakfast table, defeated and hollow, and she led me to the front door. We peered through each other one more time, and she gave me an almost silent "bye," and I walked down the driveway to my truck, a sad, lonely idiot. I thought, once again, I had seen Annie Moore for the last time.

Once again, of course, I would be incorrect.

Chapter Eight: Without Purpose, Yet I Persist

Alone. The sounds of cars roaring past on I-20 cascade against the cawing sounds of birds that apparently do not fly further south than Texas for the winter. I pulled a mildewing, stuck-together handful of burlap sacks from the temporary shelter I'd encased myself in and lay them over me, thinking that if my skin met sunlight, it would burn instantly, and I might possibly perish in flames. Shivering. Shivering from the cold, and from this unknown metamorphosis, which is freezing my veins from the inside and frostbiting my skin from the outside. I can almost peer through my epidermal layers, to the arteries, capillaries, and veins that used to sustain me. Now their existence is a reminder, an alarm clock informing me that soon my transition will be complete. Soon I will act as the beast I've become, or I will die from an agonizing, self-imposed starvation. This isn't the peaceful, sleep all day/party all night vampire's routine I've been led to believe in. I can't sleep a wink. Hell, I can barely close my eyes or function at all. I fear my teeth chipping and breaking off from the clinched chattering they're doing. I don't feel any fangs, which surprises me. I don't bother to take my phone's cracked, glassy, mirror-like screen and get an update on my complexion; I figure I don't have a reflection anymore.

Well, maybe I'll check just *one more time*, just in case. I open up my phone hesitantly. No electricity in this long-forgotten hovel means that it is almost dead itself. I turn the screen toward me and bear witness. Not to an invisible man, but a highly visible, decaying one. My eyes are resembling those of a White Walker from Game of Thrones. My skin, already graying and greening, is now blistering and opening. *What the fuck is happening to me*?!! My stomach feels as if it's been starving for weeks, and my lips are cracked wide open. *God, this HAS to be a dream*! *A horrible dream, but one nonetheless, where I wake up, and still haven't gone to the concert. It's still a few days away, and everything's great, and I make an acquaintance there, and they offer me a well-paying secure job, and Annie shows up, and professes her undying, long-lasting love for me. We kiss, and then I get called up onstage by Unholy Saint, and I get to sit next to Devin as she sings Collide, and she hands me the mic so I can propose marriage to Annie, who of course says yes, and then…*

Then I vomit. I'm writhing in acidic, otherworldly pain, and black bile is spewing from my mouth. I try to keep it shut, but the bile is seeping through my teeth and down my chin and throat. I know it must wreak, but my nostrils can't detect it. The sense of smell is suddenly missing. My skull feels like it's being turned to jelly by some paint shaking machine at Home Depot, and my limbs start to spasm. Just outside, I hear barking. A dog is barking, and I can tell just from the sound that it's a medium to large size dog, most likely a Labrador. He uses his nose and front legs to push through an opening in the warped, decaying doors, and sure enough, I'm correct. A chocolate and auburn, malnourished lab. It's barking at me. I don't know the exact reason, and I don't really care; the dog has blood. Warm, flowing, living blood. This of all things is what returns my sense of smell, and incidentally taste, to me. After three seconds of debating the carnage I'm about to engage in, my necessity takes control of my conscience, and I lunge, trampolining through the air, crushing down hard on the dog's head. With my right arm, I hold the dog's muzzle shut and with my left I push down triumphantly on its ribs. I bite through its coat, through its flesh, and through its defenses. I feed, and now feel the equivalent of heroin or dilaudid flowing elegantly through my body's interconnected rivers. While the dog whimpers and then comes to a stillness, my pain is subsiding, replaced with a rush of relief. My skin is improving slightly. My spasms regulating. Blood. It's my savior.

With my body in relief and my conscience in denial, I peek out the mill's doors, checking to see if anyone is looking for the dog. It had no collar or tags, so I think I'm in the clear. I drag its body to a corner and place some of the burlap sacks atop it. At night, I'll move him out back. I decide now would be a good time to sleep, so I make sure I'm out of the sun's harm, and doze off for what seems like five minutes when I start to feel the acid rush take hold again, and my body, from pinky toe to longest hair follicle, stings and tremors like a miniature quarterback on the electric football game I'd seen packed up in Mona's spare bedroom/storage room/vault/tomb, never knowing who it belonged to. I check my phone, which, along with showing seven missed calls and five voicemails from Momma Mona, says I've been asleep for basically two hours. Two hours? That's the only respite I get for taking a poor animal's life, and ingesting I don't know how much of its blood? I can't take this. I wasn't strong enough to survive the oil fields for more than three weeks; I won't be able to take another day of suffering or killing, much less an eternity of it. *How was Devin Sikorsky able to appear so normal, so composed, and so attractive?* I zone out and shut down, not knowing what to do. My mind kicks back after a bit, and I can almost visualize my thoughts as they speed back and forth on an Autobahn-speed mental highway. *Can I kill myself? Can I even die? If I choose to starve, how long will it take to consume me, and will the result be worth the pain to get there? Should I walk out into the day? Since it's overcast, is there enough sunlight to kill me? How will it happen? Will I burst into flames, or will I just blister and burn to a charred crisp? Should I make a stake out of some wood, and throw myself on it like some disgraced samurai? Who will find me, and how long will it take? Will they find a perfectly intact body, or a puddle of black ooze similar to the bile that forced its way out of my gut?*

The thoughts are all too much, and I begin to weep. Thoughts of Mona and how scared and frustrated she must be. Thoughts of her identifying me at a morgue. Thoughts of Annie. Knowing that we had not only just repaired our relationship, but began to shift into a more important and intimate headspace. Everything just abruptly ended, forever. I weep, and I weep, and I pray. I never prayed before. I don't even think I really believed in God. But I'm praying now. I'm looking for any type of solace in this infliction. Any assistance would be greatly appreciated. My stomach is churning and eating itself. My muscles are contracting continually, and it's exhausting me. I still can't muster a normal sense of smell, aside from blood. My nose is now a hound dog's against the smell of blood. I'm able to deduce that the dog still has a little left. But now it's cold and coagulating, bloated with the heightened aroma of aluminum. I dare not feed on a dead dog. What a glorious existence. I've been "infected" for a little more than twelve hours, and it's been without a doubt the worst twelve hours of my life. What would Bela Lugosi and Christopher Lee think of me?

Just as I'm about to make the decision to end it, or try to end it, I hear tires grinding to a stop, and an old door shut crankily. Uneven footsteps are coming closer, making their way to the abandoned vessel's entrance.

"Spaniard," an elderly gentlemen's voice calls out, hopeful but uncertain.

"Spaniard. Are you in there, you mischievous bastard?"

I see a shadow, and then a curious, old face.

"Is anyone in here? I'm looking for my dog. I noticed a truck parked out back, and I know there hasn't been a truck parked out back of this place in a while."

The sound of his voice told his whole story. He was once a good-looking, arrogant, man's man, but his destiny didn't match his predictions for it. He could be kind, but he was mostly smart ass and provocative to the point of antagonism. I could hear estrangement and loneliness in his voice, perhaps from his offspring. The only companion he had left was his dog. I felt sad that I had taken this last sole companion, but before I could feel *too* hard about it, I justified myself and hardened my heart by thinking that if he loved his dog so much, he wouldn't have let it get away and wander into such a den of horror.

I couldn't understand how hearing someone's voice could unlock their pasts and personalities, but knew that this was a benefit of the vampiric affliction I'd been cursed with. Everything I'd formulated by hearing this old timer speak, I knew I could virtually count it as gospel. Unfortunately for him, the greatest sense I'd gained was the smell of blood. Even though I was relatively new to this game, I could detect that his was particularly unappealing. It was corrupted by nicotine and cholesterol, his arteries constricted by both. Alcohol was an omnipresent co-conspirator in his bloodstream, and the thought of drinking this blood caused me to dry heave. I didn't know when I might have another opportunity to feed, though; especially without leaving the confines of this hideout, and the old timer was already without his best friend. I don't think he had anything left to lose, but his life.

"Hello," I cautiously cast into the air as I slipped out of hiding.

"What are you doing in here? This place is out of commission. Could be dangerous to go messin' about. Have you seen my dog? He's a lab. Answers to Spaniard."

I don't know exactly why, but in a very short amount of time, I'd developed a resentment toward this man and sought to feed on him as some sort of vindication for his failure as a human citizen. It may have been some built-in justification defense mechanism for being a vicious, animalistic murderer. In any case, I was starving and dying, and knew that even in my compromised state, I was this man's superior. His ender.

"I hate to tell you this, sir, but your Spaniard is dead. He's laying over there in the corner." At first, he couldn't tell if I was serious, joking, friend, or foe. The changing expressions on his face revealed he'd eventually made his decision as to which.

"What? Wha, wha… What happened to him? Did you kill him?"

I could see the slight turn of his eyes and torso toward the doors he walked in through, knowing he was thinking of the pistol in his glove compartment.

"Sir, I really didn't want to hurt your dog, and don't want to hurt you, but if you're thinking of running to your car to get your gun, I need to tell you that you won't make it."

"Is that so?" He stuck out his chest, arrogantly dismissing my statement as an ill-advised challenge.

"Yes, sir."

The dead-panned assuredness in my voice gave him pause and made him uncomfortable in a way he hadn't been in a long, long time. He parted his lips in a faint gasp and leaned back on his heels, and I could tell he was going to turn and hightail it toward his vehicle. He hadn't noticed that I'd been inching closer and closer during our brief introduction, and was now about fifteen feet away, more than close enough to cut off an old man's route. Before he could make another move, I leapt, remembering exactly how my body propelled itself at Spaniard and, looking like Superman, was almost horizontal in the air as I grabbed the old man by the throat with my right hand and punched him in the mouth with my left to disorient him further as we flew downward to the abandoned building's cold, solid floor, its dust pillowing up like a mini atomic cloud around us.

I could hear him gurgling out "please" as I was about to sink my teeth in his throat. Seeing the fear in his eyes sent an adrenaline through my pores and into my soul, but it also... made me stop. I was still human. I was still a good person, I thought. I sympathized with him. I *empathized*. This man didn't do anything to deserve this. I was acting on instincts to survive, but also being manipulated by my own brain. Manipulated into malicious thoughts, turning me against my former self. Deep inside, I knew that I was still going to eventually feed on this man, but I tried every mind game I could think of to plead with myself to delay the process, and maybe even convince me that I was still indeed dreaming, and the only way to wake up was biting an imaginary human.

"What's your name?" I asked aggressively, making sure to project an image of dominance.

"Ah. Ahh. It's... It's Lester. Lester Hansen... Please don't hurt me."

Why did I ask his name? That makes him a person, not a victim. It also makes me search my memory banks.

"Hansen? You own the Hansen's Auto Shop?"

"No, but that's my son's shop. He's had it since---"

"So Malcolm Hansen is your… grandson, then?"

"Yeah, yeah. That's right. You know him?"

I had gone to school with Malcolm my whole life. For some reason, I always remembered his birthday was two months after mine. It was the first birthday our teachers would recognize after we came back from Christmas Break. I couldn't believe the situation I was now in, about to kill Malcolm's grandfather by draining him of his life's blood. I also realized that the estrangement I'd sensed in Lester's voice was on point. Malcolm had mentioned several times through the years how his dad and his grandpa barely talked or saw one another, even though they lived less than fifteen minutes away. How Lester would make rude, hurtful comments at family dinners and other gatherings, making his daughter-in-law, Malcolm's mother, cry. How Lester and his son would actually take swings at each other when the temperature and volatility got too hot to turn back, each man too stubborn and unrelenting to stop the damage it was causing everyone around them. Even with the family situation as it was, I know Malcolm, wherever he was, would feel sadness when hearing of his grandfather's "freak accident." I couldn't let it look so brazenly like cold-blooded murder. In fact, if I could, I would hide the body, and hopefully no one would locate it. A disappearance would have its own heartbreak, but at least no one would have to try and explain why

Lester's blood was all but missing.

"What the hell's wrong with your face?" Lester asked, when able to focus his eyes and get a closeup look at me.

"Nothing. Nothing. I just don't get enough calcium."

"No shit." This made Lester laugh. Even in such a compromised state, he was able to let out some condescending banter.

"Look, I'm real sorry it's come to this, and I'm sure somebody's going to be sad you're gone, but I got no choice, sir. I've got to survive, and to do that, I gotta feed."

"Feed? What the fu---."

And with that, I forced my weight down on Lester's chest to keep him from squirming or breathing, and forcefully turned his head aside to get a free rein of his throat. Even with my normal sense of smell failing me, I was close enough to catch some sort of alcohol pouring out of his skin, and the distinct combination of chlorine and shit on his breath. I closed my eyes and said a quick, silent prayer to myself, then reared my head backward before swinging it down like an executioner's ax on Lester. My teeth sank in the side of his neck and my cheeks started their vacuum of sucking. At first, my mouth was uncomfortable; it had to find the right position and strength to do this correctly. His blood burst in my mouth like a flash flood, but then slowed considerably, making me work hard for the last bit. I knew that I had to consider drinking enough to: 1) be full, 2) kill him and not turn him into what I'd been turned into, and 3) delay my hunger pains as long as possible. As he got close to death, his legs started to shake violently, and his fingers gripped to my arms with a vice-like intensity. And then he just stopped moving all at once. I'd fed on my first human. I'd killed a fellow Texan for the first time. And I felt… I felt horrible.

I pushed away from Lester's body, fearful like I'd just discovered him, and crab walked backward until my head and shoulders smashed against the nearest wall. I brought my knees up to my chest, and pulled them tight, rocking back and forth. There was no way to measure the guilt and astonishment I felt for the act I'd just committed.

"I'm so sorry. I'm so sorry. I'm so sorry. I'm sorry. I'm sorry. So sorry. Sosorrysosorryl'msorryl'msorrysorrysorrysorrysorry."

In a bit of wishful thinking, I felt that if I said it enough, he might come back to life somehow and forgive me. I also thought if I said it enough, it might make me stop feeling it. I just sat there for about ten minutes, staring at Lester's eyes staring back at mine. He was at peace, but not peaceful looking. He looked frozen in time, in a startled, horrified gaze. I had to figure out what the hell I was going to do with him, and with myself. I couldn't just stay here in this grain mill waiting for random people to come looking for their pets. And what if the police came to do a vagrancy or loitering check, or what if the place just gave out due to neglect and toppled on me? I couldn't remain here much longer, and I knew it. But first I had to erase any trace of Lester Hansen at this location. I dug into his pants pockets and found the key to his vehicle, an ancient Chrysler something-or-other. I'd never heard of that brand of automobile, and certainly didn't recall seeing one on the road. It was dark blue at one point, now with a healthy dose of rusty discoloration on its façade. I got in it, facing the resistance of stale cigarette smoke and fried eggs, cranked the engine on, and slowly guided it behind the building, next to my truck. If you drove by, you wouldn't be able to see either vehicle; you'd have to pull into the overgrown grass and weed infested parking lot and pull around closer to the rear to notice any new activity in this locale. It hadn't been in operation for over twenty years. For the next five hours or so, I waited for the sun to set and the dark to relieve me of my hiding place. In that time, I was able to sleep some, albeit lightly, and only started to go through mild withdrawals, now knowing how much blood I needed to consume in one feeding to satiate my insides.

At around 7:30, I couldn't take being couped up any longer, and thought I would escape into the night to do some reconnaissance, but would play it extra safe, so as to not be detected by the police or anyone else Mona might have enlisted to form a search party. I also knew that I would have to feed again before the sun came up. It would be the only way I could sleep through the night. I drove all over Abilene and the surrounding towns, scouting out possible hiding spots, possible prey, and all the while it felt as if I was saying my farewell to this city. I have no earthly idea why, as I'd never lived farther than Post, and never for more than a few weeks. This was my *home*. This *is* my home. I'd never asked for anything more, anything exotic or surreal. I never aspired to anything unrealistic. I suppose Mona never let me. She didn't sugar coat my life, and she didn't hinder me; she just told me how things were. It bruised me deeply to think that I must somehow leave this place, as if there was a vampire friendly community somewhere outside the laid-back country-life confines of West Central Texas. I settled in briefly at the Starbucks on Buffalo Gap Road as it was the furthest from any of my stomping grounds, and used the opportunity to recharge my phone. I didn't order anything, and didn't make eye contact or verbal communication with anyone. I couldn't risk being questioned or ID'd. My phone was only at 80%, but they were about to close, so I tore out of there and headed just south to the McDonalds to complete the phone charging process. In hindsight, I don't even know what having a phone would accomplish. I was no longer going to be concerned with current events or trivial news stories from the local or national government, or the entertainment world. I didn't plan on calling Mona or Nathan or Annie to chit chat about our day. I was for all intents and purposes a member of a new world, a world without the living to accompany me. At the moment, though, it was second nature to make sure it charged enough to get through the night. Unfortunately, a guy who works at the convenience store nearest to our house recognized me and made himself known.

"McCarty. Hey, it's Willie from the corner store. Your mom is looking for you, and she's all kinds of---."

"Yeah, thanks, Willie" I blurted out as I got up and took off within four seconds of him engaging me.

I could hear his words trailing faintly behind me as I speed-walked to my truck.

"Hey, are you alright? Do you want me to let your

mom know…"

Shit. Shit. Shit. What am I going to do? I need to get out of here, but I don't want to get out of here. Where am I gonna go? I don't even have more than $35, and I need to fill up my tank. At least I won't have to spend any money on food for the next 1,000 years. HAHAHA! I needed that laugh. I won't ever laugh again. Shit. Shit. Shit. What am I gonna do?

I was really starting to lose it. The streetlights and headlights, and noises of the city were beginning to get under my skin and make me wince with irritation. Sensory overload like I'd never felt before, but had previously experienced by way of my shyness and inadequacies. I needed to just worry about finding some blood to drink before getting safely back to the grain mill undetected. Oh shit, the grain mill! I didn't get rid of Lester or his dog. They're still in the building, and by tomorrow they'll start to stink. I needed to bury them and make his Chrysler disappear. I also needed to remove any evidence that I was involved in the disappearance. I headed back to the mill to face the repercussions of my actions; housekeeping, in other words. About five minutes from the building, though, I got a nauseous sense of dread crawl up the crack of my ass, along my spine, and into my temples. I think I was being followed. Unsure but pretty damn sure at the same time, I varied my speed to gauge the reaction of the vehicle behind me. I then sped up on the highway, doing about 95 mph, went waaaaay past my exit, and doubled back, making an oblong circle before cutting my lights, pulling behind the grain mill, and cutting my engine next to Lester's beat up something-or-other. I hunched low, my torso almost perpendicular to the ground, and shuffled quickly into the building through the back opening, threw the burlap sacks over me, and lay flat and still. A few minutes later, I could hear a car pull into the parking lot, stop in front of the building, and turn off its lights and engine. While my heart pounded and my breathing spiked, my ears were hearing a foreign car, most likely a coupe or sedan, and then they heard the careful, scared footsteps of someone light on their feet as they slowly made their way to the side doors of the hollow, pitch-black building. One might ask why a vampire, even a newly created one, was hiding from a mere mortal instead of waiting nonchalantly with a wink and a smirk. Afterall, what weak human is a match for a supernatural being, no? In all honestly, I still didn't feel superior to humanity and had no idea who the person following me was, or if the person who parked outside the grain mill was the same person who appeared to follow me for almost half my drive back to the building. Also, although I needed to feed at least once more before the night was through, I was still trying to be as selective as possible. What if this was Willie from the corner store, or my grandmother, or some elderly woman desperately searching for Mr. Hansen. I didn't want to murder and feed on an old lady. Some big bad wolf that would make me, my victims a dog, and old man, and an old woman. I didn't want that kind of reputation to hang forever around my neck as I started my career in vampire-dom.

I listened intently as the footsteps came ever closer, and I could hear rustling as the person negotiated internally on what doors to pry open and enter through. Their decision made, I heard them attempt to jimmy open the front double doors, which had been troublesome for some time, probably even prior to the mill shutting down its operations. Successful, they entered the cold, silent building and I could feel their eyes moving left to right as they searched for something, or someone, in the darkness.

"Hello? Are you in here?"

A male voice, late 20's or early 30's at most. Frightened, rigid, almost shivering. They must be rail thin, their presence in the building is frail and lacking in authority. They hold up the flashlight on their cell phone to assist the moon in illuminating the room.

"Who are you looking for?" I asked in a solemn, monotone register, still lying flat on my back, with the burlap sacks covering me.

"I'm pretty sure you were at the Unholy Saint concert last night."

Intrigued, I tossed the sacks aside and rose confidently to greet this individual face to face. Like earlier today, I tried to project an image of dominance. It was still just that, a projection.

I was not surprised to find a rail thin, frightened male in his late 20's.

"How did you know that, and who are you?"

"My name's Aiden. Aiden Morales. I was there. I was at the concert, too. I..." He cocked his head to the side as he finished his sentence, and the whiff of healthy – at least healthier than Lester's – blood wafted up into my nostrils. I could sense something different about it, almost chemical, but I was still rather new to this. It seemed fresh. Satisfying. I couldn't help myself. But instead of flying through the air like a madman, I adopted a new approach. Sensing that Aiden Morales was no more a threat to me than an ant to a hippo, I just started walking toward him methodically, shoulders broad, my eyes never leaving his. I grabbed two handfuls of his hoodie's material and, in an attempt to simply pull him to me, I lifted him off the floor. It couldn't have been more than a couple of inches, but it was fairly easy. Shocked, I paused for a second, regrouped, and intentionally tried to lift him. Imagine my surprise when he levitated over a foot into the air. *Was I getting superstrength?* Aiden's eyes were opened so wide I thought they were going to pop out of their sockets like a squeezable yogurt being commanded out of its tube. His fear was incomparable. I quickly made note of his three-day stubble, cheap cologne, and light caramel and olive complexion, and could tell that his insubstantial disposition was caused by something medical. In any case, I was about finished analyzing, and turned my attention to drinking him. I put my hands on either side of his skull, applied enough pressure for it to be highly discomforting for him, and pulled him to my mouth, when he threw me for a complete loop.

"I know what you are! I know what you are.

"And I know who did this to you."

Chapter Nine: Slightly Less Blurry

"What?"

"I know who did this to you. It was them, right? Unholy Saint, or someone associated with them?"

"What would make you think that?" I softened my grip on his skull before reapplying my grip down to his hoodie.

"Because even though it may not be exactly the same, they did something with my brother."

This got my attention. I let go of Aiden, placing him delicately as I tried to ignore my body and its frustrated reaction to thinking it was going to feed only to stop abruptly. An instinct was being stifled, and I didn't know how long my intellectual parts were going to be able to battle my instinctual ones. I took two steps back, as if this would somehow be a safe distance.

"Your brother?"

"Yes. Miguel. Miguel Morales. He and I---."

"Wait. Stop. Morales? You don't look Mexican. Are you from Spain or something?" In my head I thought about Hansen's dog Spaniard, and laughed to myself at how crazy it would be if I'd come across a dog named Spaniard and an actual Spaniard in the same day, in Abilene of all places.

"I'm half Mexican American and half Anglo American. Brown dad, white mom. No big deal. We're everywhere nowadays."

"No offense. I was just confused. So, your brother."

"Miguel. Last year. Last year was a hard year. I'd been fighting leukemia for over two years, and had fought my way to remission. Miguel wanted to do something for me, to celebrate, and even though it was kind of more for him, he talked me into seeing this band Unholy Saint. They were on the road supporting their debut album and were playing Fort Worth. We live in North Richland Hills, so basically the same city. I could tell from the name that they weren't going to be my thing, but whatever. My little brother wanted to take me out, and he'd been very supportive of me during my battle, so I thought 'what the hell,' right?"

I was starting to feel bad for Aiden, while also feeling the urge to open his veins and gorge upon him.

"So, we go out to this place Lola's, and lo and behold, Unholy Saint was pretty damn good. Not earth shattering, but very entertaining, especially for a brand-new group. After their show, Miguel wanted to meet them, but I didn't need to do all that, so I just hung at the bar and waited for him to shake a few hands, maybe get an autograph, etc..”

I can feel Aiden starting to shake as his memory recalls and replays the details of his story, and I can hear his heart beating faster.

“I can see him talking to the guitar player at the foot of the stage, and then he starts bouncing up and down on his heels and gets this big goofy smile on his face, and then he starts looking around the room, and spots me. He comes running over to me and says he’s going to get to go on their tour bus, and asks if I want to join him. I decline, and he looks disappointed, like if this band was Led Zeppelin or something. He takes a step back, looks me up and down, and says “Seriously?” to which I reply in no uncertain terms “Seriously.” Miguel couldn’t believe it, but then pivoted and asked if I’d be alright if *he* went on the bus. I had no problem with that, and let him do his thing. However, after about 45 minutes, I was pretty anxious to leave and went outside to go get him. That’s when I saw that the bus wasn’t there anymore. I asked this chick who was still hanging around outside where it went, and she said they’d pulled out more than fifteen minutes ago. Except Miguel was nowhere to be found. I went back inside, and it was almost empty now. I went into the men’s room and called out for him, but he wasn’t there, so I called his cell. It rang and rang, with no answer, so I hung up and called again. And again. And again. Eventually, after about six or seven calls, it just went straight to voice mail. I started texting him, but no reply. I walked around the block, looking everywhere, but no Miguel. I checked the parking lot, and his car was still sitting right where we parked. It seemed crazy to me that he would have left on the bus with them, but he's always been a pretty impulsive kid, even way back when we were little. I checked the band's website, to see if there was a phone number for a manager or someone I could call to see if he was still on the bus. Nothing. I then saw that they were set to play San Antonio next, so I decided to follow that route, knowing they would most likely be taking 35 most of the way. At this point, the tour bus has been gone over 30 minutes, but would be on 35 for over three hours, and I can drive fast. I had a key to Miguel's Corolla, and I hopped in and started booking it in that direction. It took a little over an hour, but I caught up to them at a large truck stop/tourist trap just north of Waco. I remembered their logo on the tour bus from when we got to the show, so there was no mistaking it for somebody else's. I screeched my tires to a halt right next to the bus, got out and started banging on the door. I was met by a very large, very angry-looking bodyguard named Zander. "What the fuck do *you* want?" he asked calmly but intimidatingly. I told him I was looking for my brother who got on their bus after the show. He laughed to himself, amused that I'd driven almost an hour and a half to look for him, and told me that Miguel was not on the bus. I asked if he could double check, and just as he was about to tell me to fuck off, I heard a voice tell him to chill, and that it was alright. That voice belonged to their guitar player, Alister. He tapped Zander on the shoulder, and Zander fled back into the bus and Alister met me at the door. "Your brother was here, but he got all weird and handsy, so I had to remove him. He probably went home sulking." I told him that A) that didn't sound like my brother at all, B) he couldn't have gone home in his car because I was driving it, and C) he wouldn't have left me there by myself. I told him I wanted to know exactly what the hell happened on that bus, and where my little brother was, and I didn't care how big his bodyguard was. Alister just stood there staring at me. His head dipped lower and lower until he was raising his eyes to see me. I remember him running his hand through his styled, stringy hair, and his eyes turning like a glowing silver, and him telling me "Go home. Go, now. While it's safe. You don't want to know what happened, and you don't want any part of this, little boy." He had to be the nerdiest, tiniest looking dude, but his voice and his eyes scared the living shit out of me. It was then, as the light above the door's entry came on, that I saw Alister had a teeny bit of blood on the side of his mouth. Then I realized it was on both sides of his mouth. He noticed me notice it, wiped one side of it off with the back of his hand, and said "I hope you enjoyed the show. I know I did," before pushing me back from the door with one hand, closing it, and sauntering in silhouette as the bus came alive and pulled out of the parking lot. It headed onto the highway and out of sight. All I could do was just stand there and watch it fade away. I was paralyzed with fear. I knew something horrible happened to my brother, and I knew it was because of them. And after driving like a NASCAR driver to catch up to them, I just let them float away. There was nothing I could do about it."

I had listened to Aiden relay the story of his brother's last known whereabouts and the subsequent deep dive into Unholy Saint and their mysterious, possibly sordid pasts, unburdening himself fully. Tears now welling his eyes, he recounted the multiple avenues and angles he took to try and find Miguel or justice for him, all to no avail. While I truly sympathized with him, and was appreciative beyond belief that his story sparked a flame of inspiration in what my next steps would be, the more pressing matter, for me, at least, was the fact that I was starving and scraping by a thread to hold it in. Knowing that there was a 99.9% chance that Aiden would be the quickest possibility of sustenance for the rest of the evening, I had to make a decision, make it quickly, and be prepared to live (or die) with the consequences.

"Aiden. Aiden. Please. That's good. That's enough. I've got it, and I'm sorry. Really. But nowhere in that story does it tell me that you know what I am, or why. What I am, whether you can fathom it or not, is a bloodsucker, a creature of the night, a vampire. And it's well past my dinner time. So, out of respect for your already screwed up last few years on earth, and for the ungodly sized pair of balls on you for coming here, I'm going to give you approximately two minutes to wrap things up, and approximately a ten-second head start to get to your car. After that head start, I can't be held accountable for the things out of my control."

"OK. Wow. Two minutes. Two minutes. Got it. I started following Unholy Saint whenever they would come as far south as Oklahoma, as far west as New Mexico and as far east as Louisiana. I hoped to find anyone who could and would corroborate the rumors I'd read online, or my own personal hunches. I stopped getting any access to the band after they recognized me. They would see me coming from a mile away, and I was also a little afraid of Zander and the rest of the band's security death squad."

"One minute left."

"Then they were playing this show in Abilene, and I came to check it out, and what do I find but Devin Sikorsky running off into the night faster than Uṣain Bolt, and some dude bleeding out in a parking lot, who then manages to push his way through a whole gang of dudes heavier and tougher than he is, that were trying to help him. I don't think you realize how crazy that scene looked, how much ground you covered between jumps, and how fast you ended up running. So I asked around, did some investigating, and got your name and address. I went to your house, told your mom some bullshit story about you accidentally getting my wallet at the show, and just looked for you. It didn't take too long."

"Ten seconds starts now." I couldn't stop the burning pain in my gut from causing my legs to shake and my veins to bulge. I was visibly under distress, and Aiden was the only one who could ease my suffering. As he started to backpedal and then burst through the doors of the mill toward his car, he was fumbling with his keys and yelling "If you can kill her, I think you'll go back to normal. You'll go back to normal. If you can---."

It was the same car as in Aiden's story. It was Miguel's Toyota. A white Corolla with a smashed driver's side bumper and a missing hubcap. I spent the entirety of the moon's regulatory shift dropping Lester's and Aiden's vehicles in random remote places in Abilene where no one would notice them for at least a few days. I had to run back to the mill each time, and it helped me to understand that I was now exponentially faster and more agile than I ever had been. Additionally, I had stamina I'd never even dreamed of. I did fear that such physical exertion would facilitate my hunger pains that much quicker than if I didn't expend any energy, but what had to be done had to be done. After I'd dispatched both vehicles, I dug, with my bare hands, a single burial place for both Lester and Aiden, as well as Spaniard, back behind the abandoned grain mill.

Once done with the required tactical activities, I was able to rest and reflect. In some ways, I felt much more guilt over Aiden than I did Lester, but in others, I felt less. I was more numb. One way I justified it is that Aiden kind of knew what he was getting into, even if he didn't comprehend the full extent or the full conclusion. He'd sought me out, after all. He could have gone back home to Fort Worth or wherever, and not spent the time looking for the thing that would be his ending. I was just making excuses, though, for the part of me that still pretended to be a normal human. And by the way, *What the hell was I?* Clearly, I needed to drink blood, human or otherwise, to remain somewhat functional. Also clearly, my body was adapting, attaining qualities it did not have previously. However, the stereotypical vampire from pop-culture's past, I clearly was not. What did Aiden mean, *if I could kill her, I might go back to normal?* How would he know? He didn't even know I was a vampire. Was he just saying anything he could to stall or prevent the inevitable? Could he actually be correct? I had to find out, and set my mind to do some research, but first I needed sleep. I would have a lot to do in the morning. I checked my phone to make sure it still had enough charge, and saw a text message from Mona.

"If you have to take this journey, so be it. I will pray for you," it began.

"... but you have to do it on your own. I won't be paying for your phone any longer."

Oh shit. She *had* been paying for my phone.

Chapter Ten: Now with Purpose and *Direction*

Vampire or not, I needed access to a smart phone. It would be my only link to the regular world. To the past. To the everything. Unfortunately, I didn't have any money left. Fortunately, I didn't give a shit anymore. I figured the rules applied to people bound to live within them. I for one, didn't even know if I was alive anymore. I basically sweated out the cold, sunny day in the mill like a druggy going through withdrawals, praying for dusk to come. Once it did, I shot out of that sarcophagus like a bat out of the bridge in Austin, fed on the first cat I could catch off guard, and sought out the nearest ATM. It was now time to put my increasing strength to the test. As I struggled not to starve to death, I noticed an unexpected benefit to every muscle in my body contracting as if it was ingesting anabolic steroids – bigger, stronger muscles. This must be what causes the stereotypical superstrength in vampire lore, and now I know it's partly true. After breaking into the local Salvation Army Store and relieving them of some less than conspicuous wardrobe, I donned a disguise, found an ATM and, covering my face, smashed through what I deduced to be the weakest spot on it with a clinched missile of a fist. Its plastic and metal shredded the skin on my knuckles and hand, but I was successful in ripping the panels apart and grabbing the cash that lay helpless inside. Hopeful that neither the store nor ATM crime scenes identified me, I changed clothing yet again and purchased a prepaid smart phone and three months advance service at a pharmacy. Now I could begin to hunt down the same intel that Aiden had, my search focused more on my condition than his brother's assailants.

I researched vampires for hours back at the mill, mostly uncovering nothing, until I could just catch a glimpse of change in the skyline outside. One thing that was paramount to every myth and description of vampire existence was the unflinching and untimely fate that sunlight produced to all stricken with this disease, regardless of the authenticity of the source material. I decided to test out the theory, and waited until about 7:00am, before covering myself almost head to toe in sweatpants and a hoodie. I exited the mill on the side not facing the sun, and stuck out my hand to get a taste of its kiss. Nothing. No change at all… at first. Then, it started to itch, and a slight rash formed on the back of my hand and wrist. Uncomfortable, but not unbearable. Nothing near life-ending. *Could all the stories be false,* I thought to myself, giddily. *Could I exist in the day?* I removed the hoodie, and let the sunlight hit my face and head. Again, nothing at first, followed by an itch, a rash, and… searing pain! A constricting but bursting pain branding its will upon my flesh. I screamed out in agony, covered my own mouth to keep from alerting anyone who might be driving by, and hurried back into the confines of the mill's seclusion. I took a bottled water and doused my head with it, praying that it would alleviate the effects. I had found out over the course of the last two evenings that water was still a much-needed resource, and that a vampire can dehydrate as easily as any other human, so I bought a case of water along with my new phone. Turns out the sun is without a doubt no friend to the vampire. By this point, I could confidently say that vampire is what I was. I drank blood to live and found the sun to be a very strict deterrent to the outside world, even in small doses on my skin. What was positive, though, was that the sun did not cause me to burst into flames, nor did it make me start to decompose nastily like the vampire in Fright Night. I remember being scared to death by that movie in elementary school, when a friend's older brother was watching it. It may be the only vampire movie I've ever seen.

After making sure that I was safely in a spot inside that no position of the sun could penetrate my defenses, I resumed my search of all things vampire, but also started to look closer at Unholy Saint. I wasn't looking as a fan any longer, but as a detective. They, both individually and as a collective, were an enigma. No embarrassing high school or college pictures of them. No former girlfriends with gossip for TMZ. Anything and everything about them came directly from the band. They didn't have outside management or representation. Unholy Saint was a self-contained unit. In that case, I returned my attention to vampires in general. I couldn't get out of my head what Aiden was trying to say about returning to normal. I read dozens of stories on various websites and didn't see anything related to such a solution until I came across CarpathianChalice.com. It was almost by accident that I stumbled upon it, but once I did, I believe that I'd found the site I was looking for. Carpathian Chalice gave as extensive and compelling a history of the vampire as I'd ever read, and one that included details I'd never heard of. For one, it gave a brief account of the "first vampire," a man named Aylash Revall, from some 2,500 B.C. It also explained that vampirism, starting with this Revall, is an infection that corrupts and kills the blood cells, requiring basically daily transfusions to keep ahead of the grim reaper. It stated, with no real evidence other than a list of supposed vampires, that the average infected person only lives less than fifty more years with their situation. Hardly the window to immortality that popular opinion paints it. More relevant to me was the small detail of "freeing oneself from the infection of sanguine corruption." In addition to a slow, painful immunity process to the sun that made it possible for vampires to walk the earth in the day, the site stated that in a few instances, one's infection was reduced or deleted when the afflicted managed to drink the blood of and then kill the vampire that infected them.

This of course would mean locating and killing Devin Sikorsky. A week prior, I would have been almost willing to do her bidding, following her utmost desires to the letter. Now, killing her didn't seem so bad. After all, she was more than happy to end *my* life. Unholy Saint still had seven dates left on their current tour, as they made a path back home to California. Now that money would not be an object, and my instinct for survival far outweighed the moral dilemma of theft, I would be able to fund such a mission without trouble. I went back to the list of "known" vampires on the Carpathian Chalice list, and didn't see Devin Sikorsky on it. Just in case, I also checked the rest of the band, and didn't see them either. No need for confirmation, though; her teeth in my neck and the subsequent result were all I needed to know that she had in fact infected me. Unholy Saint had just played Lubbock last night, and were no doubt on their way to Hobbs, NM. I wouldn't make it there in time, I thought, but could make it to their next show in New Mexico, or perhaps at their show in Glendale, AZ. Yes, that's where I'd set my sites on Devin, and ending my horrible nightmare. I racked my brain with all the possible scenarios, and how I could even bypass Zander to get to her. *Was Zander a vampire? How long had Devin been a vampire? Could I even defeat her, let alone kill her?*

I started to plot out a driving schedule, as I would most likely have to park while the sun was out, unless I could block out the sun with my vehicle. I looked up how that exact thing had been done in a vampire movie called Near Dark, but to disastrous results. No, I had to play this more safe than sorry. I would only drive at night. Ha! Now I would have thought Hobbs, NM was a world away, but in figuring out the driving distance to Glendale, I realized I could make it to Hobbs in less than four hours. That meant I could drive tonight and be there with more than enough time before tomorrow's show. I didn't have to wait for Arizona! I focused my energy on finding out everything I could about their upcoming show just outside the campus of The University of the Southwest. Stage set-up, overhead views, possible exit routes, etc. I needed to get this right if I was going to have revenge, or redemption, or both. It helped that the band put at least an entire day of rest between their shows. But *why* would they? Did their concerts take it out of them? Did they need an extra day for Devin to feed enough to get her through to the next town? I researched the previous stops on their tour and checked the news sites for any murders or missing persons' reports the nights of or before those shows, and sure enough, there was at least one every city. Now that didn't mean Devin was responsible for all of them, but it was too coincidental to be a "coincidence." Even though Unholy Saint was the first band I ever really cared about, and their music touched something deep down inside me, I knew that I had no choice but to kill Devin Sikorsky.

But how, exactly? I read up on stakes through the heart, burning, decapitation, plunging into icy waters, but were these all just old wives' tales; myths and legends dreamt up by the Bram Stokers of the world? Would all it take is just me abducting her and starving her? Not feeding seemed to cause me enough pain and discomfort to want to die, if not be dangerously close to it. If given the chance, could I even really do it? I'd been raised to be a gentleman. Could I kill a woman? Yes! I had to keep telling myself, she's not a woman. She's not human. She's a demon, a creature absent from God, bent on destruction. If I didn't kill her, how many more star-struck young men would she lure into her web after a show, devouring them the same way she tried to do me? How many had she done that to, before me? In a vain attempt to somehow turn back time and/or reveal all the last two days' events to be nothing but an illusion, I went back to the internet for some more info on Devin. Something that would present an alternative to execution. Something that would endear her to me. Instead, I found maybe what Aiden was referring to when he mentioned rumors about the band. It was a Reddit page titled Unholy Truth, and contained several juicy but unverified stories about orgies, cults, illicit drug use, and other things the members of the band might be indulging in back home in California. The stories all referenced a place on the dividing line between Huntington Beach and Newport Beach. An "ultra exclusive social club" called the House of the Black Moon. Three different accounts on Unholy Truth were from people who claimed their siblings or friends gained entrance into the club, only to vanish without a trace the same day. None of these disappearances seemed to be solved, and no real help was provided by local law enforcement. I vowed to myself that if I couldn't accomplish my task on the road, I would venture all the way to Cali and this House of the Black Moon. I would get justice not only for myself, but for these other helpless, tortured souls. I waited until sundown and then headed out west to Hobbs. It would be my first time crossing state lines. My first time leaving the solace of Texas. I'm man enough to admit that I was more than a little scared. Conversely, I was also becoming self-aware enough to know that I had basically no time left in Abilene before I or my victims were discovered. I wasn't just leaving on a mission. I was possibly leaving for good.

I thought it might be a good idea to call Annie and let her know.

Chapter Eleven: Her Voice

I had just got to Seminole, TX when I couldn't take the pains anymore. On this third day of vampire's existence, the pains came with more of an urge, a hunger hanging just on the lips and salivary glands. I didn't want to, but I was going to have to kill something. I'd read on Carpathian Chalice that previous, morally conflicted blood drinkers had tried to feed solely from blood donation bags but found that any blood not inside a living body when consumed was off limits. In each case, the vampire suffered a horribly excruciating result, comparable to extreme food poisoning. I guess it was sort of cheating the system, and whoever was responsible for this cursed existence, intentional or otherwise, made that an impossibility. So, on top of being hungry to the point of agonizing, near-death misery, the patient also cannot drink the very drink that can end that misery. What a mindfuck.

I thought that Abilene was "small town," but compared to Seminole, it must have been like Dallas. There wasn't much going on in the middle of the night, which made finding someone out and about a little difficult. I didn't like the idea of breaking and entering, and didn't know if I even could. *Would I have to be invited in, like in the legends?* That entire premise sounded completely stupid to me, but I hoped I wouldn't have to find out. I drove around a little bit while my body still had some control over itself, and saw that the employees of Taqueria Jalisco were just about done for the night, and filing out. Things close up early here, so in hindsight, oversleeping and getting a late start on the road proved beneficial, as it lined up nicely with this closing time. I parked a little way down from the restaurant. One by one, wait staff and bus boys got into vehicles close by and sauntered off into the night, save for one unlucky individual. A middle-aged man, a little overweight, was walking with a slight limp, away from the building, but to no close-by awaiting car. He would have to do. I felt bad about it, to be sure, but had no choice. It was me or him, and it *wasn't* going to be me. At first, I thought he was heading toward the Seminole Inn, and there wasn't much in terms of coverage to take him in hiding. But he started veering from that direction into the darkness. If I had a chance, this was it. I slipped out of my truck quietly and started a slow walk tenderly on my heels, which quickly became a fast jog. Ultimately at a pace faster than any sprinter, I startled him from behind, tackling him to the ground. I could feel the air being knocked from his insides, and the pain of such a hit cause an anguished groan in his mouth. I turned him over so that we were facing each other, and saw a curly, black haired Mexican American. I could smell a large amount of beer on his stale, putrid breath, so I don't know if he was actually an employee, or if he was simply a patron who it took a long time to escort from the establishment. His eyes grew large with fear, then anger.

"Que? Who are you, pinche guero?"

"I'm sorry," was my only reply.

I slammed my head against his neck and jaw, and sunk my teeth down on his flesh. His neck was sweaty, and his blood alcohol content made me a little nauseous as I drank him down. His instincts forced him to grab and push at me, but then he just froze there, terrified, until he went still with death. I made sure to drink all my stomach could handle. I didn't know if I would get another chance before the next sunlight came and went. There were no streetlights on to the immediate east of the Taqueria and the Inn. Nor did there appear to be any threat of anyone driving up soon. Still, I couldn't leave this man dead in this spot, or he would be discovered come morning. I didn't exactly bring a crime scene cleanup kit with me. Hindsight is a learning experience that never stops educating. I ran to the truck, hopped in, and pulled up to my victim. I heaved him in the bed with surprising ease, and drove around looking for a place to dump him that would allow me to keep on safely to Hobbs before he was found. I took I-62 to 214 until I was basically in the middle of the universe with no human around for light years. There was a small network of valleys in the vast untarnished landscape, and I hefted the man up on my shoulders and carried him into the night, settling him down in a basin that no one could see from any street or angle. Only the coyotes or a low flying single engine plane would locate him before I wanted anyone to. I don't know why, but even though I knew it was a mistake that would mess with my heart and head, I reached into the man's pockets and found his wallet. Oscar Jimenez, aged 52. A few bucks and a single picture of him and what might be his granddaughter. That was it. And now it was over. I had to move on but somehow knew that I would end up pulling the wallet of every victim hereafter. I must be a glutton for punishment. Who would have guessed?

I drove on to Hobbs with tears in my eyes and a lump in my Adam's apple. I was now a predator. A murderer. A flood of thoughts came pouring from me. *If I was technically still human, would I be considered a serial killer, or mass murderer? Would being caught and exposed instantly give Mona a heart attack and kill her, too? How come no vampire has been caught yet? How many vampires actually exist out there? How many of them are American and how many are international?* I felt aimless. Hopeless. The need to call Annie was now a task that couldn't be put off. I felt that it was the wrong move to make, but one I couldn't avoid; not without keeping a three-ton boulder tied to my shoulders. I couldn't breathe. And I needed to hear her voice. Her soothing, lovable, sexy voice. A friend's voice.

After losing my cell service, I didn't have enough patience to transfer all my saved phone numbers to my temporary phone manually, so I did so with only two numbers, Mona's and Annie's. I wrote down the other recognizable ones in a small notebook I had in the glove box of my truck for God knows how long. However, as I mulled over a potential conversation with Annie in my head, a pulverizing thought, like a large Hawaiian wave, came down upon my sense of paranoia, and I felt strongly that I shouldn't make the call from my cell phone. I didn't know if it could be tapped, or traced, or in any other way used to track me down and bring me to justice. I knew Annie wouldn't recognize the number, so I wondered if she'd even pick up. If she didn't, I didn't know if I would leave her a voicemail. Maybe I would just call over and over to hear her voice on the message. Oh crap! I *was* still in love with her! I found a 7-11 where I could wash my hands and face, and then searched all over for a still-working, old school pay phone. Once I found one, I repeated picking it up and putting it back down on the base at least a dozen times before I could bring myself to pop in the required amount of change needed to call a long-distance area code. It was after midnight, and I didn't know if she'd be awake to answer, or be completely pissed that someone was inconsiderate enough to call so late.

"Hello?"

"Hi... It's... It's me."

"Really?"

"Am I calling too late? Were you asleep?"

"No. I'm up. What number is this?"

"It's a payphone."

"*Payphone?* What the hell? Do they still have those?" I could tell by her voice that she was holding in a fair amount of rage, and not saying what she really wanted to.

"Are you... are you upset?"

"Upset? Why would I possibly be upset?"

"Come on, Annie."

"No, really. Why would I possibly be upset, right now?"

I paused, trying to choose my words. Trying not to cry, actually. What came out was a long, frustrated sigh.

"Is there any particular reason that I should be upset, right now? Angry? A little mad? Maybe a little FUCKING PISSED OFF?!"

"Annie, I'm sorr---"

"Is it okay? Okay, if I'm a little fucking confused and heartbroken?"

Whoa. I didn't expect the word heartbroken to come out of her mouth. But I should have. I searched my memory banks for the files to our most recent conversations, and I could see things from her end.

"First off, yes. Yes, it is okay."

"Oh, thank you so much for giving me permission."

"Annie, PLEASE!"

She could hear the anger, and the creaking emotion in my voice. She was surprised. A hurt, tired voice responded.

"What do you want, Davis?"

"I want to explain."

"Go ahead."

"I apologize for not calling, and just sort of dropping off the face of the earth. It was not my intent, at all. Something happened." I didn't know exactly how to approach the next sentence. I stuttered and paused.

"Oh, something *happened*? Oh, I'm glad we got that out of the way."

"Annie."

“What happened, Davis? And did it happen at that concert by those devil worshippers?”

“Actually---”

“What’s her name?”

“No, it’s not like that… Believe it or not, it’s actually much worse.”

“What? How?”

“That night. I was attacked.”

Her voice softened, and I could hear the concern immediately entering her throat.

“Attacked? Are you ok? By whom?”

“A member of the band.”

She went through a scenario in her head and described an over-excited me jumping onstage during a song, and being thrown off the stage by a bouncer, etc. etc.

“I wish that was the case, Annie. I was… bitten. Bitten on the neck by the bass player.”

“Wait; the *girl* bass player?”

Oh shit. “Yes, by the girl bass player.”

“Look, we only kissed one time, and yes, it was just a peck, but I have feelings for you, and I don’t need to hear about some kinky rock star shit phrased as an---"

“This wasn’t anything like that. She was trying to kill me.”

“Yeah, right. How the hell is she going to kill you by *biting you*? What is she, a werewolf? Or a vampire?”

I gulped hard, and then proceeded. “The latter, not

the former."

I truly believe she was caught off guard by my witty sense of wording. I could actually hear her shaking her head, trying to make sense of it.

"What do you mean, the latter?"

"Vampire. I mean she's a vampire."

"Fuck you."

"I'm not joking. I'm completely serious, right now."

"FUH. KHA. YOU."

"Annie. Please." My voice withered like long-dead vines, and almost silent, I began to weep. She could hear me plain as day.

"Why would you lie to me like that?" I could hear her eyes' faucets now turn on.

"Annie, I'm not. I'm not lying. I'm not lying to you."

No words from her, just a stifled, muffled crying. She must be holding her sweatered sleeve to her mouth. I could imagine which sweater, and she looked beautiful in it.

"Annie. Annie? Please believe me. I want nothing more than for it not to be true. For the last three days to not have existed. There's nothing I can do now."

"Where are you?" I could hear her spine stiffen as she went from slumped over to sitting straight up.

"I'm... I'm in New Mexico."

"New Mexico? Why?"

I could feel a suspicious bend to her voice.

"This is where Unholy Saint is playing tomorrow

night. Hobbs, New Mexico."

"What the fuck is in Hobbs, New Mexico, and why are *you* there if that's where they're playing?" I could hear her emphasize and lengthen the syllables in Hobbs, New Mexico, and it made me laugh – on the inside.

"I need to kill the bass player. Hopefully, that way I can become normal again."

"Normal? Normal, again? What do you mean, normal again?"

"It's really a complicated story, you see."

"Oh, really? Try me."

"Ok. Ok. So… when she bit me, she was trying to kill me." I could hear the eyes rolling in Annie's head, and hear her struggling not to call complete bullshit. At least she was trying to keep it in.

"But she was interrupted, just by chance, by some guys who worked the venue."

"So, she was in the middle of killing you, when they showed up? So, great. Great news. Davis lives to fight another day."

"No. Not exactly."

"Spell it out!"

"By not killing me, she turned me."

"*Turned* you? Into w h a t?" Her mouth spread out that last word like it was hot caramel being pulled from a machine and given to a small, eager child. I'm certain her brain knew what I was getting at, but I don't think she was ready to say it herself. I had to come out and get it over with.

"Into a vampire." I'd done it. I'd said it. I'd said it to

the person I cared about most in the whole world. That revelation was itself an astonishment; I never thought I would love someone more than I loved Mona. But had I just screwed up any chance of Annie Moore ever speaking to me again?

"Into a vampire? McCarty, I'm trying really hard not to hang up. Not to smash my phone on the floor, and break my hand punching the wall. Not to absolutely lose my shit on you right now. But… do you know how fucking idiotic and insane what you just said to me sounds?"

"Yes. If I hadn't experienced what I had the last three days, I would completely agree with you. But, unfortunately, as much as I've tried to wake up and have this all be a bad, bad dream, it's the truth. I am now a vampire, and the only hope I have right now of not still being one is to kill the person who did this to me."

"Davis? What have you experienced the last three days?"

Oh shit. I realized in about .03 seconds that I wasn't ready for the rest of this conversation. I had to abort, regardless of the long-term finality of its conclusion.

"I can't. I can't get into that. Not right now, at least. I need to try and get a little more reconnaissance done before the sun comes up, and then I need to try and get some solitude and darkness before tomorrow night." I didn't mention also needing to get some blood.

"No. Please. Don't go yet. Tell me what the last three days have been like."

"I'm sorry. I can't. I've got to go."

"Please, Davis, don't. Don't do this! I lov---."

I hung up the phone. And then I took it off the hook,

in case you can call back a pay phone.

"---e you."

I knew she said it. I couldn't believe she said it. I was SO HAPPY she said it. And so pissed. She could have told me years before. Or months before, or weeks. I couldn't bear to hear it now. Now it couldn't mean anything. It could never mean anything. Not unless: 1) I was actually successful in killing Devin Sikorsky, 2) the curse of vampirism actually left my body, and 3) I could come back to Abilene completely scot-free of the two innocent victims I ended. No. Now those words would be hollow, tormenting words. A glimpse of a future we could have had, but never would have.

I loved her, too. I always had. But now it was time to bid her farewell.

Forever.

Chapter Twelve: Are You *Hunting* Me?

I had to get out of my own head. I had to just for a few minutes pretend I was somewhere else. Someone else. I could start to feel pressure from within turn to stones being heaped upon me. I thought back to a book I was forced to read in high school about the Salem Witch trials, and how one of the people in the book died by having stones piled atop him. In this moment, in a run-down parking lot in a run-down neighborhood, I could completely relate to that poor, unfortunate soul. I could hear nothing but hollow silence, and it was louder than a freight train. I believe I was finally and fully starting to go insane. I went back to the 7-11 where I washed up, and realized that I had done so not to get rid of any blood or other evidence of Oscar, but because I felt this need to be "clean" when I called Annie. As if washing away the proof would absolve me of the guilt and keep her from hearing it through the phone. Like I said, I was going insane. Going back to the store was two-fold, I think. Part of me didn't want to admit it, but I needed to interact with another human. Twenty seconds talking to a convenience store clerk would have to suffice. It would help me feel normal to fill up my gas tank, walk in, grab something from a shelf and pay for it, even though I ceased needing anything the store had to offer. The other reason, which I also didn't want to admit, was that I was scouting out a potential feeding. A clerk would be too "high-profile," but what other patrons were hanging out at this time of night? Would one of them be of service, in case my veins burned through Oscar's blood too quickly? Possibly. There was an aimless teenage couple. They looked like they were breaking some sort of curfew by being there. The boy appeared to be at least two years older than the girl. The only other target was a haggard woman who looked twenty years older than she was, and who my nostrils told me was an alcoholic prostitute. She was speaking loud, random gibberish. I got the eerie feeling that both of these options were more trouble than they were worth.

As I carried out my transaction with the clerk, I noticed myself in the fish-eye security mirror behind the register, and a myth's origins pierced my heart like a heavy steel sword from the Middle Ages. The world's been led to believe that vampires have no reflection. That always sounded so stupid to me. And it is completely false, to be sure. The truth, though, is that vampires can't stand to look at themselves, especially when being reflected next to a perfectly healthy human being. The process of dying a slow, infected death causes the eyes to jaundice, lose the ability to see most colors, and eventually lose their eyesight altogether. This process mixed with a declining appearance makes a vampire's reflection difficult to endure. I looked like a shell of a human and I knew it, but the clerk could only see a seemingly burnt-out, drugged out loser. I saw a gray-green fading away of a person. I saw the skewed perception of a vampire form, from within the eyes of a vampire. No wonder mirrors are the enemy.

Melancholy as I was, I had to switch my attention to tomorrow night's, now this night's, show, and getting my revenge and hopefully rebirth. I looked up all the details I could find, and saw that they were setting up an outdoor stage in between the activity center and the baseball field. A local news story explained that while Unholy Saint couldn't get a permit to perform on any campus facility, a loophole gave them the right to set up on this one piece of land still owned by a Native American family whose ancestors were robbed of most of it by the Mexican government in the mid-1800's. The lot was vacant and insignificant, but the family refused to sell it to the university. It was unknown why or if they granted Unholy Saint permission to use the land, but here we were. I drove around the campus for a bit before finding the stage being set up. I was more concerned with where I'd be able to get to the band before or after the show. Amazingly, I was met by their tour bus staring straight at me. There they were. Were they wide awake, as it was close to 3:00am? Was Devin out on the prowl, eating some poor bastard tasked with erecting the stage, or some unsuspecting student just returning from Christmas Break? I parked safely away from the activity, but not safely enough from campus security, and a guard pulled up behind me, tapped on my window, and asked me to state my business. Unable to provide school ID or a proper reason for my loitering, I was asked to move along.

As I was driving slowly away through the campus, I noticed a shiny blur streaking behind the buildings. I could feel the security guard's vehicle still behind me from a distance; he hadn't noticed anything. I couldn't do anything to draw his attention, but a queasy, uncomfortable feeling crept up my spine and raised the hair on my neck. There had to be some connection between that streak and the band's presence. Just then, another streak flew by my peripheral, followed by a loud, crashing sound and lights going dark behind me. In my rearview, I could see the security guard cut right abruptly, driving his car directly onto the property. He got out of his vehicle and ran to the sound. I stopped the truck, and just sat, waiting to see what happened next. I looked back through my mirror, and saw Devin standing behind the truck. I thought about gunning it in reverse, but she might get away, and that might bring back the security guard. Instead, still eyeing her in the mirror, I unlocked the door and started to open it. As I stepped my foot out, she was at the door.

"Hi."

"Oh, shit!" There was no point in denying it. She startled me. I felt like an idiot.

"I'm sorry." She was hiding a giggle in her mouth, and took a couple of steps backward to show me she was letting me out without incident. "Don't be afraid. You can step out."

I had gone through several different daydream scenarios about this very moment, and now that it was here, I was scared shitless. It didn't matter that I was a vampire, too; or that this was a fight between an able-bodied man, and a petite, artsy girl. She was my superior. She was an experienced monster, while I was still figuring out how to become one.

"I created a little diversion, so you and I could talk uninterrupted. Well, mostly uninterrupted." On the curb next to my truck, seemingly out of nowhere, were Zander, Unholy Saint's head of security, and another guy. I hadn't seen him at the Abilene show. He was even bigger and more intimidating than Zander. My new skills detected something about the two. Zander was a normal human. The other was not.

"We won't have too much time to talk before the security guy comes back to his car, and I really don't think we should make him disappear the night *before* our show, so we better make this quick. How can I help you?"

"Uh. Ummm."

"Wow. You have a lot to say. I think I'm a little disappointed. I had a feeling you might show up eventually, after I couldn't finish my feeding. You obviously had a few days to prepare for this meeting, and you're tongue-tied?"

I stood there, dumbfounded, and her face morphed from playful and amused to deadly serious.

"Look. I'm sorry I transformed you. I didn't mean to prolong your suffering, but only to end your meaningless existence. I got careless, and defied protocol. Alister was *not* happy. But the facts are facts. You are what you are, and now you can use that. It's gonna suck for a while. No sugarcoating that. But we can help you. We can make it easier, at least. We just have to finish the tour, and then we---"

"Meaningless? Meaningless? Are you kidding me? You don't know me. You have no idea what I might have done with my life. I might ha---"

"Come on, David." She didn't even remember my name. "Get real for a second. You weren't going to become President, or CEO, or even assistant manager at In-n-Out. There's a reason why we can feed at every single tour stop along the way, and no one gets wise. It's because our victims are insignificant bit players who don't have wonderful futures ahead of them, or concerned families looking for answers for too long before they move on with their own unimportant lives. Our paths crossed, and that's where it was supposed to end. That's where your story was supposed to end. Now that it hasn't, make the most of it. That's why you're here, right?"

"I, uh---"

"Damn, what is it with you? Are you still scared of me?" She was clearly annoyed now.

"No, it's just that I was actually coming here to... to kill you."

You could see her jaw drop, and her face go cold with surprise, confusion, and maybe respect?

"*Kill* me? Were you *that* pissed off about what happened? Wait. Did you have a guurrlll friend?"

"No, not exactly. But I had to try anything. Anything

I could to return to normal."

"*Normal*?" Her eyes squinted really tightly, full of spite. "I don't know what you may have seen on the internet, but... Wait a second. Are you *hunting* me?" That playful look returned to her face momentarily, like she was happily obliged to accept a challenge.

"Maybe. I don't know. Whatever you want to call it." I could tell that Devin had seen the blurry silhouette of the university's security guard making his way back into view. A split second later I could hear the thud of his steps on the cold ground. Her face went back to serious.

"Zander, Cyrus. Deal with him. Don't kill him. David---"

"It's Davis, Goddamnit."

"Whatever. You didn't finish getting it out before. Get in your truck and drive away. Out of obligation to the fact that I fucked things up for you, I'll give you some time to think things through and come to a solid conclusion. You can either go your own way, or you can make your way to California and seek guidance and shelter. Choice number three is that you can end your own life. No doubt you'll be saving lives if you do. But whatever you decide, don't show up tomorrow. Don't pursue the path you're on. It won't end well."

If I was going to continue my mission, I took into account that I had to deal with not only Devin, but Zander and the other guy, in addition to the campus security guard. If I could even kill her by myself, what good would it do me to possibly be human again only to get killed seconds later by her attack dogs, or arrested? I started to get into my truck while overhearing Zander tell the security guard that they had no idea about the vandalism down the road, but that I was an overzealous fan that was staking out the band, hoping to get an autograph or a picture, and that they run into this all the time. The guard bought it and said he'd let them get me to go on my way having met "my favorite member of the band." I started my engine and pulled off slowly, defeated and sunken. I had to regroup and plan my next move. I found an abandoned office building, pitifully fed on two dogs in the alley behind it, and then holed up inside, laid flat out in a supply closet plotting out my future.

As my interaction with Devin played out over and over in my brain, several things she said stuck with me. One, that other security guard, the one she called Cyrus. He was a vampire. You could smell the mixture of others' blood in his system, as well as his own unique scent of decay. At first, I just thought he was a white guy, but as he moved in the light, I could tell he was mixed, probably half-black. His existence meant that there was positively more than just one vampire in the Unholy Saint camp. Devin said that she had broken protocol, and that Alister was not happy. The only logical reaction to that statement is that Alister either knows what Devin is, or that he is also one himself. There must be some rules and/or patterns to their feeding, like time of night, location, etc. Devin had probably sought out her prey too soon after the show and much too close to the venue. She created a crime scene with a cast of witnesses, and that *had* to be bad for business as well as uncharacteristically sloppy. She didn't mention anyone else in the band, so maybe it was just the two of them and Cyrus. There was no way to tell, but I figured that the more I pursued her, if I did indeed continue, that the more layers to the onion there would be. She had also said that they could help me. *Help me what? Learn how to live with being a vampire? Live with them? Did they have a nice, peaceful vampire commune in Cali? Was the House of the Black Moon their compound?*

Finally, she told me not to show up tomorrow. Not to continue on this path. If she didn't feel at least a little threatened, she wouldn't have had Zander and Cyrus with her tonight. Did part of her think I could have a malicious intent to my visit? I didn't have any idea how old she was or how long she'd been a vampire, but she'd had to have seen a bunch in her time to confidently tour the world as a musician. I couldn't have been the first vampire she created, or the first one that confronted her afterwards. *What was her track record in terms of new recruits? Had she had to put down one of her own dogs before? If I did show up, regardless of my intent, would she heed that as a challenge to her direction and eliminate me no matter what?* I put my hands over my face and racked my brain for some answer, hoping it would magically materialize and guide me. According to her, it sounded like becoming human through killing her was an ill-advised assumption, but could that have just been a ploy to prevent me from trying? We didn't have the chance to finish that part of the conversation. I could feel the coldness of the hard closet floor on my back, and I sat still listening to the quiet. I could make out the six-legged rustling of roaches in the walls and the scampering of rats in the ceiling. I wondered to myself, is this all I am now? A cowering, dying person, forgotten by the world, destined to hide in darkness among rats and insects. Christ, I had eaten dogs for a late-night snack. This didn't seem like any acceptable way of life. For anyone. I couldn't let this be my final act. Even if I failed, or found out I was wrong, I had to try. I *would* show up tomorrow, and I *would* make my move. The result would be death; of that, I was sure. Either mine or hers, or more.

The time on my phone was now 6:15am, the day of the show. I knew Mona would be up, having a biscuit and a cup of coffee. In a time of weakness, and a lapse of judgement, I sat up on my butt, pulled my knees to my chest, and dialed her number. I sat there looking at those digits on my phone for a small eternity. I wanted so badly to hear her voice, and to tell her things would be alright. But I knew they wouldn't be, so I clicked the cancel button and set the phone on the floor... so I thought. I laid back down flat and stared up at the decaying ceiling tiles, dried and brown from leaks in the roof, and tried to drift to sleep when I heard a faint voice. I paused and then heard it again.

"Hello? Hello? Hellooohh?"

Oh no. I couldn't have. I looked at the phone, and could see its display lit up. I had hit Send somehow. I picked up the phone and ended the call as fast as I could. I held the phone in my hand, and sure enough, a few seconds later, it vibrated in my palm. It was Mona. I didn't answer. I couldn't do this to her. To us. The break wasn't exactly clean, but it was necessary. It was final. I let the vibration fill my hand until it went out, and waited to see if she called again or left a voicemail. None came. I didn't know it would be the last opportunity I ever had to speak to her.

Chapter Thirteen: Hobbs

9:45am. I'd only got three hours of sleep when the assorted sounds of traffic outside aroused me and opened my eyes. The closet was pitch black, except for a slight crack of daytime let in below the door. Even outside of this closet there was no threat of daylight burning me. All the windows were opaque and stained with filth from lack of care, and half of them blacked out by graffiti. Still, I had to be wary. I didn't know what surprises befell this building during the day, or what other visitors, lawful or otherwise, it might entertain. As much as I wanted to go back to sleep, I knew that it would be a futile effort. My insides were tied up in knots thinking about what lay ahead tonight, and my head was a tornado of opposing thoughts and philosophies. I talked my way through so many different scenarios, but none of them ended without bloodshed. Since I was interrupted last night during my recon mission, I had to revert to other tactics to get a good schematic of the playing field. To that end, I'd stumbled upon a very advanced satellite imaging site called Your Earth Now, which could provide an up-to-date overhead view of almost any spot in the western world, and some of the most far-reaching places on earth, within seconds from real-time. I typed in University of the Southwest, Hobbs, New Mexico, and it gave me the whole map. From there, I could zoom in or zoom out, and navigate my way around however I pleased. I came across the roof of the stage, and noticed a lot of other structures around it. Thrown off, I went to the band's website, and saw that, to entice people hesitant to come out because of the cold temperature, a carnival-like atmosphere had been created, along with hot chocolate and cider to drink, games to play, and a few rides to ride. Also, because of apparently low-ticket sales, an offer of two-for-one tickets was available until an hour before showtime. I guess Hobbs, NM wasn't as keen to name Unholy Saint the future of alternative rock music that Texas was, but how nice of them to give their fans a deal before they dine on their blood and discard them in nameless graves or random dumpsters and ditches along the highway.

I could see that the tour bus was still in the same spot it was parked in last night, and from there, I plotted out my attack points and escape route, etc. However, one fact remained that I couldn't dismiss: Devin knew it was me last night; before I could spot her, and even before I parked. She or they could smell me from a proverbial mile away, and that meant that any element of surprise I thought I might have would be for not. Tonight had to be perceived as a do-or-die, almost kamikaze-style mission, lest I succeed. I tried to do some research on the undead Mr. Cyrus, but there was nothing to be found. The road crew for the band is listed on their website, and he's there underneath Zander, but only since two days ago. Before him, someone named Isaac was in that spot. The website only lists first names, for reasons unknown. Cyrus' body resembled Arnold

Schwarzenegger's circa 1980, if Arnold was also six inches taller than he was. Not someone I wanted to get into one-on-one combat with, assuming that Devin didn't rip out my throat and stomp on it herself. I knew I was "punching above my weight," but I also felt amplified by the fact that I had nothing to lose. I'd said goodbye to Mona internally, and I'd said goodbye to Annie literally, so… wait. My phone rang.

The name read Annie.

How did she get my number? I called her from a payphone.

Should I answer it? What the hell? Why now?

I accepted the call and put the phone to my ear shakily, almost as if I was afraid Freddy Kreuger was going to come through the phone and stick me with his knife hand. I didn't say anything right away. I just took in a deep breath, and waited.

"Are you there? Davis?"

"I'm here… How did you get this number?"

"Your mom."

My mom, I thought to myself. *How? Ohhhhhh.* It finally settled after rolling around in my head like a pinball.

"My mom. My grandmother."

"Your *mom,* Davis. She's still your mom. Anyway, she called me and told me she got a weird phone call early in the morning, from a number she didn't know. She said whoever called didn't say anything, and then the call dropped. She told me that she had a feeling it was you and not some accident or prank call, so she called back, but you didn't answer."

"I couldn't."

"Why not?"

"What would I say?" I really countrified my accent. 'I'm sorry, momma, but I'm a vampire now, and I gotta go kill another vampire'. Hold up. She *called* you? How did she get *your* number?"

"I came over the day after the concert. If you don't recall, I called and texted you that night, and the next day, with no response. I thought maybe, just *maybe*, you had such a great time that you lost your phone, or had a bad hangover, so I dropped by. I dropped by to find Mona a crying, terrified wreck. She told me about the letter you had written her. She didn't let me read it or anything, so I didn't know the full extent of your absence until you called me."

"Wait... why didn't you tell me any of this when I *did* call you?"

"Honestly? She asked me not to. Just in case I got a hold of you, she didn't want you to know that she had gone to pieces so emotionally. But since you're probably never coming back anyway, who cares if I tell you?"

"I do, if that means anything."

"Doesn't mean much at the moment. Look, I'm about to pull into an auto shop, but can you let me know if you're alright, and that you're not going to that show tonight?"

“I’m not alright, and no, I can’t tell you that; cuz I am.”

“Alright. We’ll see. Gotta go. Bye.”

“Wait. What do you me---?” *What did she mean, “we’ll see?”* Even though I wanted desperately to call her back and get into it, I didn’t have the time or energy to focus on her just then. I was instead plotting my possible suicide… by homicide.

It was now 5:38pm, and sunset was less than 15 minutes away. It couldn’t get here soon enough, as the noises from outside this building kept getting closer and louder. At one point, I was awoken from a brief nodding off by what might have been young punks looking to get high or further mess up the place, but they were on a different floor and on the opposite end of the building, so I remained still and calm. No one discovered me, nor was I looking to be. Although, in hindsight, I maybe should have looked for at least *one* person; I was going through blood withdrawals and needed sustenance badly. At the show, I would need to look as normal as possible, so as not to draw attention from authorities and concert goers alike. Walking in convulsing and pale gray would contradict that approach, so a solution was needed. I stepped outside of the supply closet and looked for a clear line of sight to the street below, and the one visible working business on the block, an antique and knickknack shop across the street. *How was this place still in business?* Almost everything else was boarded up and/or empty. It closed at 6:00, so if I was going to feed before the concert, maybe Helen’s Gifts and Resale Shop was going to be my best bet.

Right before closing time, I slipped out of the business building and ran across the street fast, avoiding any detection. I went to the back of the shop, and found that the back door was unlocked. I was getting exponentially better at being silent, and was able to enter without so much as a peep. I then walked through the back room of the shop, drew back a barrier-like curtain, and peeked out into the store carefully, seeing if anyone was inside. Hearing and seeing nothing, I waited until whoever, Helen I presume, went to lock the front door. I prayed silently to God to forgive me for what I was about to do, waited for the employee to cut the lights, turn and walk back toward the backroom, and then jumped to take her by surprise. Surprised she was, but not without heart. She punched and clawed and spit at me through the entire ordeal, calling me a "fucking cowardly bastard" before I accidentally snapped her neck plunging myself into her throat. As I drank, I almost had to stop prematurely due to the strong scent of her perfume. I couldn't make out what it was, but it was entirely too much, and all over her neck and chest. As I had predicted I would, I searched her body for her ID and found her to be Helen Reid, 54 years of age. I looked around the store, puzzled by how many people's formerly cherished possessions could be on sale for pennies of their former worth. I studied the pictures on the wall of Helen and previous customers or local celebrities, none of whom I recognized, and tried to deduce if she had any children or grandchildren. A portrait somewhat larger than the others gave me some insight. It was Helen, seated center of the picture, surrounded by three adults, and six children of various ages. I pulled it off the wall, and turned over to see these words on the back: "To memaw. Love, Jack, Tracy, and Deedee." I couldn't tell if those were the three adults, or three of the children, but I got a stone-like lump my throat, and tears, sour with guilt, welled up in my eyes. I couldn't believe what was happening, as if I was watching a horrible crime unfold on television instead of carrying it out myself. Doing these deeds was so much easier and instinctual in the moment, but the aftermath wasn't becoming easier to deal with; it was becoming, as least for me, much worse. I vowed that successful or not, after I killed Devin, I would take my own life. I prayed to God again not to let me go back on that vow. There was no taking Helen out to a desolate valley; I didn't have time or secrecy to do that. I dragged her to her backroom, stuffed her in a cabinet, and hoped that it would be someone other than the people in the picture that found her.

I was satiated, and looked somewhat passable as human. I turned my attention on getting to the show, and was on campus within fifteen minutes. I parked my truck relatively far from the event, hoping to not be discovered so soon. As I got to the entry way where event staff was scanning tickets, I could see that the carnival vibe had worked a little, but not nearly enough to conceal me amongst a large crowd. It was a little sparser than Unholy Saint would have hoped for, no doubt. Anonymity would be difficult, and I decided to delay my entry until they went on. I could hear the opening band from a distance, and they weren't that bad, and they weren't that good. Surveying the spot I had predetermined as my attack point, I noticed that it had more than doubled its muscle-bound event security. I meandered over to the other side of the stage, and it was the same there. Devin had made sure I wouldn't be interrupting anything. As the opening band concluded their set and the crews changed out the gear, a large influx of people made their way from the rides and fairway games to the concert's entry way, and the crowd size ended up being much more respectable than previously thought. Still, I didn't think I could blend in, and hung back, outside the official concert area. At 9:05, the lights went dark, and Unholy Saint's entrance music filled the PA system. Then they were onstage, and the now-familiar opening notes of *Blood Harvest* filled the air. I stood just outside the concert area and watched, and started to revert back to being a fan, mesmerized by the performance of these disparate personalities on display. I can't explain what attracts a person to a particular band's music in a way that grips them so uncontrollably whole. There's just a connection between an image, a sound, a melody perhaps, and a person becomes a follower; a "disciple." In these first three songs from Unholy Saint, I had to be reminded that, no matter what, I loved their fucking music. A lot.

And then she saw me. Devin was in her standard stage left spot, looking straight ahead, when I think she got my scent, and cranked her head directly in my direction, lightning quick as if in a horror film. Her head started bobbing slightly, and she got a small half-grin on her lips. She stared straight through me, and mimed the words "bad idea" before turning away and switching spots with Alister, now engaging the crowd at stage right. Already caught, I thought I'd get a slightly closer look, scanned my ticket, and integrated into the general admission crowd. At first, I tried to stay as far back as possible, but I couldn't stop my legs from inching closer and closer, until I was about 25 feet from the stage, just left of center stage. This is basically the same spot I was in for the show in Abilene, and I have to admit, I loved it. I loved the songs, the energy. Everything. Now time for the encore, Daniel did another country boy voice greeting and talked to the audience for a bit, announcing again that they had something special for the crowd. The lights went out and then slowly absorbed the stage in a dark blue and purple hue, with a small spotlight on Devin, who was now front and center. She sang a beautiful and sad version of the Cowboy Junkies' cover of *Sweet Jane*. After the song ended, Devin stood in the center of the stage frozen still in a silhouette, while one of the road crew walked out and hung her bass back across her body. As she took her pick and scratched it against the strings, the band kicked into *Immortality Fades*, and the energy of this final song was recognized and reciprocated by the crowd both inside the concert area and the one outside it, resulting in those in the thoroughfare rushing the cordoned off area, blitzing through the event security team, and barreling to the front of the stage to join the obsessed disciples. Not only did the once harmless mosh pit grow in size and intensity, but a large number of individuals took turns climbing over the barrier between floor and stage, hopping onto the stage and diving off. Some would get flung back or shoved forcefully to the floor below, while experienced others were adept enough to dodge the staff and fly back into the crowd head or feet first.

Eventually, too many people jumped the stage at once, and just stayed there, trying to get the affection of the band or simply gain attention from the crowd. I could tell things were getting slightly out of control though when Devin looked at the security guys with a confused, angry look, and Alister actually looked up from his guitar, took it and smashed it on the floor before running offstage. Daniel and Devin followed his lead, and exited swiftly while the crowd grew more raucous. I don't think anyone expected this turn of events, especially with how much effort was made just to get more people to attend, but I took it as a sign and an opportunity to achieve what I'd set out on my road trip to accomplish. I ran up onto the stage, pushing anyone in my way out of it, and made a bee line to the side I'd seen Devin escape to. As I approached the side of the stage, two security personnel advanced on me, and I punched one directly in the nose. I did so intentionally light, as to not kill him, but it did knock him out cold. I grabbed the other by the right arm and hit him with an arm drag that any wrestling fan would have approved of. Once I was clear of them, I scanned the backstage area for any sign of Devin, but she was out of sight. The entire band was nowhere to be found. I turned around to view the crowd and caught the band's head of security Zander escorting someone in a black, hooded robe through the carnival section. I took two large strides and then leapt off the stage, accidentally too vampire-like, in hindsight, and landed some thirty feet from the barriers. I crashed into an audience member's back with my right thigh, sending them spiraling painfully to the ground. Not affected in the least, once my feet hit, I was sprinting to the figure in the black robe.

Nothing was going to stop me from getting to them, so I thought. But, as I sped through the crowd, I got a scent in my nostrils, my heart stopped, and my legs slowed considerably. I stopped altogether and tried to narrow the scent's source, my eyes coming to a stop on a ring toss game. The grotesquely large, pink, stuffed bear prizes caught my attention for a split second, and then I saw her. It was Annie. She was there. Almost simultaneously, she saw me. *What is she doing here? Is she going to try and talk me out of my mission?* I couldn't let that happen, but now I also couldn't let her get hurt. As I tried to shift my gaze slightly back to the hooded figure, it was gone, replaced by something much more clear – Devin. She was leaning coolly against a brick wall, staring at me with a look that said, "You wanted me; come get me." I looked back at Annie with a concerned wince, and she turned toward Devin, who then looked toward Annie before cocking her head in confusion and staring me down again with a look that now said, "What the hell is this?" I had to make the abrupt decision to forget about Annie's presence and pursue Devin, but before I could, a hand was firmly on my back, ushering me in a mandatory stroll. It was Daniel Sepulveda. He had on a standard pair of black shades, and a black jean jacket. As he pushed me along, he put his arm around me like we were friends having a conversation.

"Look, bro. I know you had a big revenge thing planned out, and you think this is somehow going to bring you closure, but it's not. We have to finish our tour, so we can get out of these god forsaken shit holes and get back to home to start working on our new album. This next one, man. I have a feeling it's going to break us wide open. I mean, when we rehearse, we're coming up with new shit every DAY! We're on fire right now."

As we walked, I noticed people in the crowd realize it was Daniel. Some had thought to run up to him and ask for an autograph or a picture, but stopped, too timid to do so. Others that did have the nerve were discouraged by the outstretched arms of two large security members following closely behind us. I also noticed that the grip around me was one that I didn't have the strength to break free of, even if I'd tried my hardest. What startled me more than that fact, though, was the smell coming off of him. It wasn't just the sweat and beer from a hard-earned musical performance; it was the stench of a lonely body trying not to decay. It was the smell of cursed death. It was my smell. Daniel Sepulveda was a vampire.

"So, being that as it may, I can't have you fucking up our plans with your little death wish, right? I'm going to have to ask you to leave peacefully. You go your way; we'll go ours. No longer shall our paths intersect."

Daniel then stopped our walk, spun me around to face him dead on, and ripped off his glasses in a very 80's soap opera villain type way. I had to crane my neck up at a sharp angle to look him in the eyes, which were almost completely white, like a comic book character's, except for a little shade of blue interspersed. He leaned down so close we were basically nose to nose, and then warned "Don't follow us again, and I won't have to fuck you up permanently. Understood?"

There wasn't one trace of humor or irony in this warning. He was completely serious. And before I could acknowledge his warning one way or the other, he grabbed the back of my jacket with one hand and threw me through a window. I didn't just land inside the building, though. I sailed through the building, shoulder tackled a brick pillar in the center of it, and exploded out a window on the opposite exterior wall. My legs banged against the wall, and I collapsed thuddingly harsh onto the cold, stiff, gravelly earth. Apparently, even though his physique didn't appear anything close to muscular or active, Daniel Sepulveda was not a vampire one should fuck with. I was not impervious to pain, and I laid there flat on my back looking up at the stars, the air knocked out of me, bruises and abrasions forming rapidly. Then, from atop the building I'd just been flung through, Devin peeped over its old, cement ledge, and peered down at me, disappointed. I think disappointed in herself more than anything.

"I don't know what it is about you, Davis. You're like an adorable helpless puppy I can't seem to suffocate or stomp to death with my Docs. There's a soft spot there for you, and I don't know why. Maybe because you've got guts. You called my bluff. I thought I could just kill you myself and be done with it, but the concert got all out of hand, and even before that the boys could tell something was off inside me. I don't like to let them down, but Daniel was determined to interject himself and save the day. Lead singers, am I right?"

As I stared up at her, this overwhelming feeling of failure found itself to the center of my chest and in my face, which had grown heavy and warmed a few degrees. I could hear faint voices becoming louder and footsteps trampling across the ground, and figured she would have to jump down and end me before being spotted. At the same time, I also sensed that she may be letting me go without eternal death. Now *I* was disappointed in her.

Even *I* knew that allowing me to breathe was a sign of slippage in her world, and I didn't even know her world.

"I made Daniel promise not to kill you, and in return I promised never to let you puppy dog me into weakness again. So, little man, be thankful for this second chance. You're exactly the first person I've ever given it to. Be smart. Don't cross my path again. You'll be impaled by a stake from crotch to brain, decapitated, and pissed on before being thrown into a dumpster and set on fire. I caught a scent in the crowd tonight. Another loser from your precious Abilene. It would be a shame if anything were to happen to her. Do I make myself fucking clear?"

Annie! My pulse and my breathing both accelerated, and a montage of horrible atrocities befalling her at the hands of my favorite band shuffled through my brain just behind my eyelids at four hundred miles per second. Before I could even answer, a young man's voice was asking me if I was ok, and Devin was gone in a flash. I was left alive. I had failed.

"Yo, K.U. I think I found the dude you're looking for."

The voice I'd heard belonged to a fellow concert goer, and his drawl and dialect had me convinced that he was firmly lacking in brain cells from years of mind-destroying narcotics and copious amounts of weed. My ribs and back were stiff and instantly sore from the high-flying act I'd involuntarily taken, while my thighs were in considerably worse shape. Even in my ever-growing "superhuman" state, getting thrown through a building still hurt like a sonofabitch. All I could do was lay there and listen to the sound of footsteps that I never really isolated before, but now could pick out from a lineup of a thousand.

Annie Moore's footsteps.

Chapter Fourteen: Were You Hunting *Me*?

"Davis!," Annie shrieked, panicked. "What the hell happened? You were there, and then you weren't there. Did you just ignore me?"

"I didn't ignore… I'm sorry. I saw you, but I had to complete my… I had to finish the job. I couldn't let you stop me from that."

"Fair enough; we can get to that statement in a second. But how did you just disappear, going from that side of the festivities to this one, and why are you all cut up, and unable to move?"

The stoner guy that was obviously drafted as part of my search party was still hovering around us. I wasn't sure why. "It's a long story, and I really need to tell it in a more private setting, if you get my drift." Our eyes both settled on stoner guy, patient but annoyed that he wasn't taking the hint. He just stared at me blankly, still under the influence of whatever it was that was supposed to make his night "really epic." Several seconds passed before it finally clicked in his head that I wanted to be alone with Annie.

“Oh, I got you, dude. You go get it,” he said with a mischievous grin. I could feel her roll her eyes as he slouched off into the New Mexico night forever.

“Fine. Come on. Let’s go be private, Prince of Darkness.”

“Can you show me a little empathy? I’m the victim here.”

“Have you killed anyone since being turned into a vampire?”

I couldn’t answer. My mouth opened, but nothing would come out.

‘Have you?”

Silence.

‘Davis?” My name on her lips hinted of “You can’t be serious… can you?” I could sense her mood transfix from pissed off to frightened. She still didn’t believe me, all the way from Abilene to Hobbs, and even up to now. I got the feeling that she was starting to, though.

“Do you really want the answer to that question?” I was hoping she didn’t, but already knew what her response would be.

“Please?”

“I had to feed, and in feeding, that meant I had to drink blood. Warm, fresh blood… Do you want to hear more?”

She just looked at me with a long, quizzical stare, asking herself questions in her head before she asked them of me.

"I'm going to ask this just one time, or one *more* time, depending on how I may have worded this question recently. Are you telling me truthfully that you believe yourself to be a vampire?"

Words at this point were meaningless. I knew that I would just have to prove it to her. Completely alone, away from all of the temporary chaos that was the concert/carnival, was a car parked by its lonesome. "Come with me," I beckoned in a short, commanding tone. Noticing that the band's tour bus was no longer anywhere in sight, we walked over to the vehicle, a black Hyundai Sonata. I ripped open the trunk with my right hand, cupped the back of the car, and lifted it one-handed in the air, similar to photos of proud fisherman holding a marlin or large catfish. Annie jumped back, amazed… but still skeptical.

"Ok. So you're really strong. What if that's just steroids or adrenaline, like when a mom lifts a car to save her baby? Why didn't you just show me your fangs?"

"I don't have fangs, Moore. And steroids? I'm still about a buck thirty. Wouldn't I, you know, look the part?"

"Then how did you do it?"

"Cuz I'm a fuckin' vampire, Annie!"

I clinched my fists and dug my heels into the ground, and it caused her to step back again. Her reaction was slight, but it hurt me. I could feel her fear, and I never thought she would exhibit it toward me. Because of me.

"Are you afraid of me?" I asked wounded.

"No! No... I don't know." Her eyes were an emphatic "Yes!"

"I would never hu---"

She pulled out a necklace with a cross on it, and held it tight.

"Would this hurt you if you gazed upon it or if it was placed it on your skin?"

Inside I laughed a little, but didn't want to diminish or ridicule her momentum.

"I don't know, Annie. Why don't we try it and see what happens."

"Seriously. What if it hurts, or what if it kills you?"

"I don't think it will. But wait. Why would you bring that? If you didn't even believe me, why would you take that precaution?"

"Because it's just that, Davis – a precaution. I didn't believe you, but I heard honesty in your voice, like *you* believed you. So, just in case---"

"You were going to humor me?"

"It wasn't my intention to placate you; I just---"

"I don't know what placate means, Annie."

"I didn't know what I was going to find when, or

even if I caught up with you. I was just covering all my bases."

"Well, let's get it out of the way. Scientific experiment number one. Hold it up to me, so I can get a good glimpse with my darkening, evil eyes."

She could read the sarcasm in me. "Don't make this difficult."

"Oh, trust me. You don't fucking *know* difficult."

"Please don't talk to me like that." She was firm and disappointed.

I immediately stiffened my face and flattened my lips. "Come on, then. Do it."

She unhid the cross from her grip, and held it boldly in front of me. No effect resulted.

"Put it on my forehead." A memory from that damn *Fright Night* came flooding into my brain, and I cringed from the possibility that I might react the same way. She edged closer and closer until she was near enough to set it gently on my skin, and then I moved closer still to really impress its shape to me. Again, no result, but I let out a little scream just to mess with her, before collapsing in a fit of laughter.

"Aaargg! You asshole! So you're obviously not a vampire."

"Are you kidding me? Why would looking at or touching a cross kill me?"

"I don't know. Aren't they supposed to?"

"Yeah, in movies. This isn't a movie, Annie. This is real life. I'm really fucked. And I just blew my chance to..."

"Your chance to return to normal?"

"Yep."

"And why would that work?"

"I don't know. I just heard that it might."

"Is there any other proof of vampirism you can provide, just for my sanity's sake?"

I breathed deep and exhaled hard. I knew that she would always have some doubts if I didn't drive my point excruciatingly home. So that's what I did.

"I'll tell you what. Why don't you drive out to the abandoned grain mill on 20, back home, go to the back of it with a shovel or a large excavator, and start digging up the ground about forty feet from the back door. That's where you'll find the bodies of an Aiden Morales and Lester Hansen, my first human victims. Buried with them is Lester's dog, Spaniard, who I got lucky enough to eat just before I would have suffered an unbelievably painful death of my own. I had to suck the blood of a goddamned animal to keep from deteriorating and decomposing from something that looks like cancer and feels like fire." I could feel Annie stiffen from both my words and from the cold. The temperature had decreased some fifteen degrees from the beginning of the concert to the current time, and it would continue to do so. My words, though, are what really started to chill her. "Then, go ahead and head back through Seminole, and search the barren, cracked valleys along 214, and you'll maybe come upon the body of Oscar Jimenez, if he hasn't been devoured by coyotes and domestic animals yet." Annie's face had turned a pale white, all the blood drained from it and running down to her legs. "But before all that, just head on over to Helen's Gifts and Resale shop here in the beautiful paradise that is Hobbs, Neeewww Mmexxxiccco (I made sure to mimic how she pronounced it on the phone), and you can have just a dandy time cleaning up the crime scene of Helen Reid's untimely murder. Or is it a buffet? I can't tell anymore, Annie. I really c---"

Annie turned around and started running. Fast. *Oh shit, I need to catch her.* Luckily, that wouldn't be hard... except that I was still banged up from being hurled through a building by Daniel Sepulveda. I rose to my feet quickly, and then wobbled around woozily until I gained my balance and my direction. Then I was off to the races. Even a hobbled vampire was faster than a normal human. And while Annie was faster than I ever gave her credit for, she wasn't track star fast, much less vampire fast. I caught her from behind as she got to her Lincoln Navigator, and I smashed the door closed with the edge of my palm, clutching her from behind. A few of the handful of leftover fans from the concert raised their heads like deer and watched for a bit, but they checked it off as a couple arguing after a cool but tense night. I held her arms to her sides, and squeezed tighter than I'd ever squeezed anyone, but made sure not to harm her. I still was far from knowing my own strength's limits.

Instead of screaming for her life, she laid her head back against my chin and chest, and just sobbed quietly, pleading with me to let her go. "Please, Davis. Please. I won't tell anybody. Just please, please let me go." I was mortified. I couldn't believe she thought I could ever hurt her. But then I asked myself, *"Was it possible for me not to*?" I spun her around and put my hands on each side of her face, ensuring that she was at full attention for my proclamation.

"Hey. Hey. Everything's OK. I'm not going to hurt you. I lo… I. You're my best friend. Hell, you've been my *only* friend for a while now. I would never. Could never… Do anything to hurt you."

"Are you so sure? I bet you never thought you could kill someone either."

"I never thought I'd be a vampire." She didn't know whether or not to laugh, but I know I saw a little gleam of a smile, ever so briefly.

"You killed those people?" she asked frailly.

"I didn't want to… But I did what I had to do. It's no different than a wolf hunting deer. If the wolf don't eat, the wolf don't live. I'm not ready to die."

"But you're not an animal. Davis, you had a choice. You *have* a choice."

"I am an animal, Annie! I'm becoming one, at least. This isn't humanity, what I am. This is a sick joke played on humanity."

Annie curled her bottom lip up into her mouth and nodded her head rhythmically.

"So now what? What happens now?"

"Well, I just was told in so many words that if I keep following Unholy Saint, they'll kill me in a fantastically gruesome way. They also told me they know about you."

"Me? How the hell do they know about me?"

Dropping my head and burying my chin in my chest, I didn't know if I should, but –

"Devin could smell you."

"Smell me?!"

"Yes… It's one of the things that leaves completely, but then grows stronger as almost everything else about a vampire withers away. They're not dumb, Annie."

"OK. So once again, now what?"

"I'm going after her."

"WHAATT?!" Again, the leftovers from tonight's audience raised their heads briefly, and then returned to their own lives.

"They wouldn't think I'd still have it in me to persist, not after what just happened, so I have the element of surprise. Two, I st---"

"What *did* just happen?"

Scratching my head, I couldn't believe it myself, what I was about to divulge. "I found out the lead singer of the band is also a vampire, which makes three confirmed vampires in their camp so far. I found this out by smelling him, and the fact that he threw me through a damn brick building, from one side of it clear through the other. That's why you saw me and then didn't see me."

"Why go after them? It's obvious you're outnumbered, out experienced, basically in over your head. And they know about me?"

"I didn't even get the chance before I was caught off guard. I won't let that happen again."

"You won't get another chance, Davis. They're going to smell you the moment you enter the same city limit they're in, then they're going to ambush you again with even more vampires than before, and you'll disappear and never be heard from again... If you're lucky."

"I have to try. Not just for me, either. But for the other people they're going to kill without a second thought, and to make it up somehow to the people I've killed. I have to redeem them."

"Redeem them? Look... Sweetheart... They aren't coming back, and no matter what, their deaths were unfortunate and unfair, and there's nothing you can do to absolve that. You don't have to join the dead, though. Not by getting slaughtered like them."

If Devin's last threat was more solid than her first, my death sounded a hundred times worse than anything I put anyone through. I wasn't going to share the descriptive details of that threat with Annie. I could tell that the more we talked, the more Annie would try to dissuade me from my chosen path, and even though I didn't think she'd be successful, my gasping, hyper-pumping heart was feeling those feelings for her as I looked in her eyes. Unrelated, my hunger was starting to rear its head in my veins. It was actually less safe for her the longer she was within my reach. I started to back up in the direction of my truck, when I caught a glimpse of the cargo area of her Navigator. My eyes opened wide, and my jaw dropped.

"Are these for me?" I questioned. It was just a joke.

"What? Oh." She took a step, and then froze and dropped her arms to her side.

"What *is* this?" At first, I saw what I thought were For Sale sign stakes, and then I noticed that they were thicker and rougher, hand carved. I opened her lift gate to find a total of four of these rudimentary but sturdy wooden stakes and a Walmart bag filled with more crucifixes, alcohol, lighter fluid, raw garlic, vials of water, and matches.

Still looking inside the Navigator, I posed a simple statement. "I thought you didn't believe me."

"I didn't know what to believe, but like I said earlier, just in case."

"Just in case. Yeah." I looked up at the stars again, tears peeking out of my eyes, and a feeling of betrayal and hurt enveloped me. "So, if I *did* turn out to be a vampire, you were going to use this stuff on me? Were you hunting *me*?"

"Of course not."

"Then what? Were you bringing these things to help me hunt down and kill my enemies? You wanted to make sure I was armed enough? Is that it?"

"I don't know why I brought them. I didn't know what I'd find, or what you'd look like, or act like. I didn't know you would---"

"You didn't know I would what?" I was starting to simmer with anger, and that simmer would soon start to boil with rage if I didn't remove myself from the situation. Annie started to tip toe closer to me, baby step after baby step.

"You would still be---"

"Still be what, Goddamnit?"

"Still be you." And she rushed up to my body, threw her arms around me, and kissed me. Passionately and deeply. I was completely stunned, and then...

"Oh, God! Your breath smells like a trash can!" She jerked her head back, whiplash quick, and then released her arm from my waist. "What the hell is that? Don't you still brush your teeth?"

My body shrunk down in itself, broken from embarrassment. "What's the point, Annie? I'm dying. Even with new blood in my system, I'm constantly dying. Feeding is like getting a temporary reprieve from a death sentence. It acts as a blood transfusion or dialysis, like what Scotty Turner's grandma used to get every week. It just delays; it doesn't stop. My body is altering and improving certain aspects of itself as a sort of defense mechanism, but the insides of me. The basic building blocks of life, those things are deteriorating and replenishing, and deteriorating, and replenishing. I eat when I'm hungry. After I do, I'm good again. Depending on how much I drink, that time period could be nine hours, but might only be two. This shit is not all it's cracked up to be, and it's definitely *not* like it is in the movies." She just stared at me, now hanging on my every word, as if she was back in journalism class. "My veins and arteries are stretching and boiling. My skin and my breath and my sweat and my hair smell like they're going sour, because they are. I'm a dead man that just isn't dead yet. I have an infection. A blood infection, and it's killing me. And I love you, but I have to go now."

"You what?"

"I have to go now. You're not safe here. Not with---"

"No. Before that. What did you say?"

"Oh. I said I... I said I love you."

"Wow. That's what I thought you said."

"I'm sorry."

"No, it's OK. It's fine. It's just *really bad* fucking timing."

I didn't know what else to say. She was right. It was bad timing. I didn't mean to say it, and I don't think I even meant it romantically, but once it was out there, why deny it. I did love her like that, and had, for a long, long time. And, since I did, I needed her to get as far away from me as fucking possible.

"I need you to go back to Abilene."

"What?"

"Yep. I need you to get in your car, fill up your gas tank, and shoot right back home, and when you're supposed to, I need you to get your ass back up to

Kansas and finish your Masters, and then go be some rich newspaper person or tv reporter. Hell, go write a book and become a famous author. You can even write about this, someday, if you want."

"Davis, I can't go back. I can't leave you. I can't let you do this alone."

"I am alone. I have to do this myself, and I have to succeed, or I have to die trying. Either way, I c---"

"I can't just go back to college, now. What the hell am I going to talk about? 'Oh yeah, I think me and my best friend might be more than friends. It just sucks, though, cuz he's a vampire and all'." She was able to instantly put on a wonderfully stereotypical but accurate West Texas hick's voice.

"You're not safe with me, and more than that, you're not safe around me."

"I thought you would never hurt me."

"I'm not worried about me." That wasn't completely true. I didn't know what my urges were capable of. I was already secretly and automatically inhaling the sweet aroma of her blood, and it was the healthiest and most tantalizing I'd ever had the pleasure of inhaling. "I'm worried about them."

"I can't let them kill you." A tear streamed from each of her eyes, running down the curve of her cheeks before resting against the sides of her mouth.

"You don't have a choice. There's nothing you would be able to do to stop them."

"Can't we call the police?"

"Whuuut? Do you think blowing the lid on an alternative rock band that also happen to secretly be a gang of vampires is the most sane thing to do? Don't you think others have probably done so in the past? How do you think that worked out for them? How many do you think got more than ten seconds on the phone before being hung up on or thrown out of a police station?"

"I don't *know* what to do, Davis, but you hunting them down when they really don't seem to be bothered by your efforts doesn't sound too smart either."

"One thing I do know is that they increased their security significantly when they thought I would still be stupid enough to come after them. That tells me that they're at least a little worried about me, and what I might be able to do. And the plan to use Devin as a decoy so Daniel could sneak up on me and send a message? That had to be worked out and discussed in advance."

"Yeah, so they discussed it, and had a plan, and that plan got you thrown through a building. They aren't the underdog, here. You are. And don't think for a minute that three of them is all there are. One thing I do know from vampire movies is that they have a whole "army of the night" waiting to be unveiled in Act III."

"Wow. That sounds a little dramatic. Did you take theater as well?"

"I did, but that's beside the point. You know everything I just said is true. Don't do it, and if you're stubborn enough to *still* do it, let me *help* you."

"Look… I appreciate you, and your offer to help. But I just told you I love you. I'm not going to be responsible for destroying the only girl I've ever loved. And regardless of the outcome of my struggle, I can't let you see me suffer with this, or see me feed. I *will* have to feed. And I mean tonight. Soon. I'm not worthy of you. I never was. I'm not ashamed to admit that. But I'm really not worthy of you now. I need you to go back home, and forget about this night, and forget that I was your friend. At least until you write that book."

Her head hung low, like on an executioner's chopping block, and she clinched her fingers onto my hoodie. "Davis." Her voice was weak with loss and failed hope. "Please don't do this."

"I have to." I slowly pried her fingers from me, and in a flash, I dashed off to my vehicle, quicker than she would have ever been able to follow, threw myself in my truck, and drove off into the night. I didn't care about Unholy Saint's next stop; I just cared about finding a victim to drink from. Tears just trickled from my face as I thought of Annie's expression in those last moments. I wondered what would become of her. She was the kindest, most complete person I'd ever known, and I would hope to never come across her again.

As I drove west, Annie stood in the same spot I'd left her for about five minutes. She thought about the victims I'd enlightened her about, and about the band of vampires I just had to go and fall in love with. She thought about how I told her I loved her. Then she came upon a decision.

"I love you, too, Davis. But whether you like it or

not, I'm going to follow you. And I'm going to help you. And, even if it kills my soul to do it, I might end up having to kill you."

Part II:
What Is

Chapter Fifteen: But No Cigar

Stillness. Cold, but tolerable. A swirling mixture of black, purple, and navy blue paints the sky before it wakes with vengeance. Approximately an hour before dawn, this city rustles up a whistling breeze and a sprinkling of bright, beaming headlights, but the world at large still appears to be drenched in the comforted sweat of slumber. This place known as Glendale, AZ is a desert, but a hospitable one. At least in winter. The bells on the door of Shirley's Diner clang around my head in an echo long after I walk through its scuffed and flyer-covered glass threshold. It smells of wood, mildew, and cigarettes, a scent long forgotten by my hometown eateries; even in Abilene, safety now comes first. But not at Shirley's. This could be the prime filming location of a diner for any film or television series looking to revert back to the 70's without falsifying one square inch of the façade. Not currently hungry, I stop in and attempt to blend in among the truckers, retired regulars, and uniformed military men able to walk about in the sun. My hope isn't just to fool them; it's to fool myself. It's only been about three hours since I drank of a homeless man in Tucson, and ten since I drank of two deer in El

Paso. Also a desert, El Paso carried a much heavier weight upon it and a much colder bite to its nights. It's by far the largest city I've ever set foot in, and was a bit overwhelming, even for a vampire. If I was still an ordinary human, a naïve, inexperienced young adult like me could get into trouble there. *Would I even be able to stand under the behemoth that is Southern California?* I can't provide a review one way or another of Tucson. I only sought out its grimiest, dingiest parts of town, and boy, did I find them. Delirious from much driving, no rest, and still-fresh wounds, I located a target who wouldn't be missed, one who would lessen the load on my heart for ending them. I sacrificed the health of the blood I was drinking for the ambiguity of not caring about my aftermath. This man had no ID, no name, and no home or family to mourn him. He did have some peculiar aromas to his blood. No doubt, I'll one day find that those aromas are the result of disease flowing through him.

Here in Glendale, though, I'm going to try and bury the memory of the homeless man, and stay as far from its seedy nightlife underbelly as possible, while I hunt Devin, Daniel, and the rest of Unholy Saint for that matter. *Anyone who gets in my way* is the mantra I will utter as I carry out my new life's work. But as I find out that they're playing a place called the Wet Beaver tonight, seedy and underbelly are two words I think I'll be placed smack dab in the middle of. After my complete failure in Hobbs to do anything remotely resembling what I hoped to, the band played their next show two days later, but then added five more to the itinerary, including a second, private Glendale show in addition to their scheduled Christian college tour date. I sat in wait as the show at Arizona Christian University came and went, hoping to throw off their perception of when and if I would reemerge. The band's Instagram page showed them standing proudly and sadly in front of the former Alice Cooper'stown Restaurant, which looked to have been closed down permanently for a while now. It also displayed highlights of the band's gig two nights ago at the University's King Auditorium, and explained that it was actually Alice Cooper, himself a fan of the group, who'd made it possible for Unholy Saint to get the approval to play there by calling in a favor of the university's president and board of directors. Reviews of the show online all seem to be almost nauseatingly positive, making me resentful for both missing it and being unable to prevent it. A bit of salt in the wound, their encore on this evening did indeed include *Collide*, but also two Alice Cooper covers, *Desperado* and *Black Juju*. I didn't really know any of his music, aside from *School's Out*, so I went back and listened to those two songs, eventually loving them both. The band must have really been feeling it that night, as they went over their agreed upon, and contractually required, ending time of 11:00 by 40 minutes, incurring a fee of $40 grand for doing so. They essentially lost money on this show. I was so jealous of Glendale.

If I stick to my plan, tonight's show won't happen at all. I intend to catch Devin by surprise right before they go on. They'll have to stay in the tour bus until nightfall, and then they'll be whisked into the club quickly. It will be then that I strike, from the rooftop of the English-style pub next door. The plan, how I envision it, will unfold like this: I sail down like a heatseeking missile, head and hands first, vice-grip her head with both hands, and rip it from her body before anyone can aid her. Then, whatever happens, happens. Maybe I get swarmed by the security team and Daniel, and maybe they do to me what I did to her. Maybe, just maybe, I end up getting away, everyone too surprised and distraught to take action. Then what? *Will I return to human? If so, will it be instantaneous? Will it be painful?* The more I think about a proposed reverse metamorphosis, the more I realize how stupid that bit of wishful thinking sounds. Then again, if someone had told me that the bass player in my favorite band would bite me on the neck and turn me into a vampire, I would have also thought *that* was pretty stupid. So maybe my hope isn't so far-fetched.

The sun is setting on Glendale, and I'm watching the clock in my truck intently, about to get out and to make my way up the ladder in the back of the pub. I need to time this right, so I've basically covered every inch of my skin so that I can be on the roof before the night is completely upon us. My legs are shaking violently. I'm gripped by a nervousness that far exceeds what I felt in Hobbs, or the first time I had to kill a human. I don't know exactly why. I figured I would feel the opposite. In both of those previous scenarios, I didn't know what to expect. With Lester, I let instinct guide the bulk of my actions. With the Hobbs carnival concert, I had a vision in my head, but didn't take into account any uncontrollable events that would alter or defeat my vision. This time, I knew the players, the terrain, the time, and the strategy. Nothing would stop me. Comically, I almost had to smile as I began my ascent and heard:

"Hey buddy. What do ya think yer doin'?"

I hopped down from the second rung of the pub's ladder, inhaled a deep breath, and turned coolly around to face my inquisitor.

"I'm just checking the power up top. The pub and the club are tied to the same generator, and tonight's band is going to be using a lot of juice." I was pretty proud of myself for coming up with something so believable, so abruptly.

"Is that right?" the gentleman asked, unconvinced. He was short and round, but looked like he was hiding more muscle than fat underneath his white undershirt and red, lumberjack flannel. He had lines caused by a hard life etched across his face and forehead, leading me to believe that he was actually younger than his living mug shot relayed. His eyes seemed almost black and non-expressive.

"Yes, sir."

Three other men walked up behind him, with virtually identical sneers and arms crossed in a "he doesn't look too impressive" stance.

"Uh, your name wouldn't be Davis, would it?"

What was that about uncontrollable events? I looked down at the ground, exhaled the earlier breath, and immediately lunged at the red flannel guy, knocking him off his feet and straight into the air with a right uppercut. While he was still up there, one of his buddies was already making his way toward me, and I managed to catch him in the testicles with a swift straight legged kick. I performed it so well, though, that his crotch basically formed to my shin, and as I tried to shake him off, one guy engulfed me, tying up my right side while the fourth sent a brass knuckled hook to my jaw and eye socket. Getting hit in the face with brass knuckles hurts a vampire just like it does any human, and I was sent sprawling backwards, trying to keep my balance with one watering eye closed and my legs a little weak. I knew that focusing my attention on brass knuckle guy would be priority number one, and as he advanced toward me confidently, I met him with a left to the gut and swept his leg with a spinning trip that I had no idea would work; I'd never been in a real life or death fight before. He fell legs over head to the cracked asphalt and sparse grass floor, which allowed me to come down with all my power in a hammer fist to his nose. I could feel it crumble into pieces underneath my clinched palm and pinky, giving me the feeling he might be dead. All three others were now back to their feet and lumbering toward me, spreading out to surround and box me in. I made a quick gesture to the left, as if I was going to flee in that direction, and all three shifted their stance that way. I used that quick fake to run straight into the guy I hadn't yet engaged. I shoulder tackled him to the ground, sprang to my feet, and stomped on his chest and head three times in quick succession. His sternum, breast plate, and ribs turned to soft soil underneath my boots while a giant red-purple hematoma formed along his forehead and down the side of his face. I could hear him whimper a frantic but stifled gasp for oxygen. In a matter of moments, his lungs would fill with blood, and he would drown in himself. With my foot still on the poor gentleman on the ground, I stared directly into red flannel guys' eyes, and could sense that the easy conflict he thought he was entering was now out of hand. He smacked his friend across the chest, and they both backed up, turned and ran. I started to dust myself off while four other men picked up my two vanquished foes and drug them back into the Wet Beaver, when a familiar scent flitted its way daintily into my nasal cavity.

Zander was basically within an arm's grasp of me before I caught whiff of him, and he set his hand on my shoulder like a loving father would before delivering some bad news. The bad news in this case was a clubbing forearm to the back of my head. It propelled me forward, but I don't know why he was so aloof in his attack. He was after all, still a human, while I was… *more* than human. As he stepped forward to inflict more punishment, I jolted around, ducked under a massive swing from his impressive arms, and caught him with a left to the chest that stopped him immediately. Surprised, but not deterred, he proved to me why he was chosen to lead the security team of an undead, blood drinking rock band. Face to face, he was faster than me, and much more skilled in combat. I noticed a USMC tattoo on his right arm and realized that he's had professional military training. Blocking and punching, dodging and advancing, he was backing me down and connecting with his strikes. He couldn't have been physically stronger than me, though, and at the right moment, I caught his left fist in mid punch, dug my nails in the back of his hand, and clutched tight, breaking his bones in my palm. He screamed out to the sky in agony, but then struck me flush in the face with a well-timed, well-placed head butt. My nose exploded with whatever actual blood was left in my sinuses, and a drowsy, nauseous, icepick-to-my-temples feeling evolved from nose to brain stem. Pain or broken hands weren't going to end a fight with Zander.

As I gathered my eyes to refocus, I sought to kill him and end this once and for all. I'd failed to notice the gray sky above me growing darker, its clouds dropping petite morsels of rain, and the automatically awakened streetlights. Just as I confirmed those transitions in my head, I swiped away Zander's ax handle swing coming down for my bloodied face, grabbed him by the throat and crotch, and lifted him over my head. His face turned magenta from the cutoff blood to his arteries. My plan was to snap his neck, liquify his testicles, bring him down on my knee, and break him in half. However, a faint piercing whistle, like a fighter jet's missile falling from high above the atmosphere, caught my ear, and I was speared in the gut and chest by some very fast object. I flew back in its grip, unable to breathe, and barely glimpsed Zander thumping to the ground, reaching for his sore jugular. My missile was Devin. She crawled across my torso as we sailed, and we locked eyes just inches away from each other's faces, close enough to kiss. She then proceeded to hit me with repeated palm strikes to the nose and jaw. My nose was already broken, and was now being obliterated by this woman, who I believe was *FLYING*! We'd been horizontal and not touching the ground for several seconds and several dozen feet. We finally came to rest against an alley dumpster with the force of a car wreck. The back of my head collided hard enough to cause a dent in it. Devin put both hands on my throat and started squeezing. If she was wringing out a towel, there would be no moisture left. I fought her off the best I could, but I couldn't free myself from her grip. I tried punching her, but she held me down by my throat with one hand, and dismissed my attempts with the other. My eyes started to bulge forward, the whites turning egg yolk gray and stretching well past my lenses. As I struggled, I let my body go numb and cleared my head to think of one last solution. I then took both hands and pressed them as forcefully as I could muster into her thighs, fingertips infiltrating her flesh. She growled in my face with a contemptuous "Ooohh, you shit!," and loosened up ever so slightly. This momentary lapse allowed me to startle her with a spit in her left eye, and a stealthy knee to her vagina. I was *not* proud of myself.

Not finished in the least, Devin started peppering my forehead with elbows, but I intercepted one, lifted her arm and guided it to the side to give me a straight shot, and then nailed her in the throat with the side of my hand. I could hear her insides make a sound like a balloon leaking air, and her eyes welled up with water. I took a page out of Zander's book, locked my fingers around Devin's neck and thrust her face down on my forehead. She wilted and crumbled, arms and legs limp as they enveloped me from either side. For a second, neither of us moved. I felt what little heart beat a vampire has weakly pulsing between our bodies. I gently pushed her off of me, and she made a soft moan as she lay on her side. I had enough strength to get one shoulder on top of her, and I grabbed a brick that lay in the alley, it unaware that it would be used to smash the skull and brains of a young woman to death. I stared at her face for a few moments, noticing the soft beauty of her eyelashes, and the stark, dark river of veins contrasting just below her milk white skin. She had started to apply her night's makeup, but it looked jagged and unfinished. She most likely had to exit her tour bus abruptly to prevent *her* bodyguard from being slaughtered. *Ironic*, I thought.

"What the fuck *IS IT* with you, man?"

Whose voice was that? I tried to crank my head and neck behind me to see, when a diminutive but strong hand clasped my hair and yanked me off of Devin and the ground, and into the air. Alister Amaranth held my beaten, exhausted body in the air with his one arm. His teeth clinched and his veins throbbed with anger.

"Why wouldn't you get the hint? Are you literally brain damaged, or do you just have a death wish? Not one other singular person on this earth, human or otherwise, has been the total pain in the ass that you've been. It's been a *real* drag, to say the least. Is this the Texan in you?"

He now grabbed me with the other hand and brought me closer to him, my feet still unable to touch the ground. "I want you to see me. I want you to know that I am frustrated to no end that I have to lower myself, my standards, to deal with you. I've got too much to do. Who do think manages a band that doesn't have a manager? I do! But, if you want something done right, I suppose you have to…"

The next two seconds moved in slow motion. Alister opened his mouth wide, and I peered into his gaping, dark, bleeding gummed opening. His teeth, all of them, were sharpened. I'd never noticed before. I can only assume he was going to pull my throat apart with his mouth when sirens and blue and red lights intruded on us. “Freeze!,” I heard a police officer yell from the beginning of the alley as at least three more began running toward Alister and I. Things were going south quickly. Would this be the day that a rock star guitarist went on the lamb as a cop killer? From my peripheral, I could see Devin stagger to her feet, hunched over and groggy. She was facing the opposite direction as the police, ass up, so they wouldn’t be able to recognize her, even if they knew who she was. She put her hands on her knees, took a moment to catch herself, and then sprinted off into the night faster than I’d ever seen anyone on two legs run before. The whole time, Alister held me in the air, his eyes never leaving mine. A grin spread across his face wider and wider. His expression grew more amused and mischievous by the second.

“Stop, now!,” the policeman called out to Devin, but she was long gone before his sentence stopped on his lips. As the group of officers approached closer, Alister had to make a decision, and I could only hang suspended and wait on what that decision would be.

“Davis!,” I heard screamed in my direction, and that’s when I discovered that Annie had followed me to Glendale, and that she had undoubtedly been the one to alert the police. Why she had chosen this strategy, I couldn’t figure out; the ramifications were ungodly in the negative. There was a slim chance, though, that she had just saved my life.

Alister cocked his head to one side, rolled his eyes disapprovingly, nudged me closer to his face, and whispered through gritted teeth, just loud enough for me to hear. “Are you into the band Anthrax?” he inquired. I was deeply confused by this question, as our freedom and secrets were seconds away from shattered.

“Uh, no. I don’t think I’ve ever liste---"

“I hear your momma calling you. I hear your momma calling you.” He sort of *sang* these words. I had no idea how that had anything to do with his question, or why he even asked me that at a time like this, but knew for damn sure that he was referring to Annie as my “momma.”

The cops were upon us, and a little startled by the fact that this little skinny guy was holding someone at least twenty pounds heavier and two inches taller in the air like he was no heavier than a coat. The main mouthpiece for this unfortunate authority parted his lips again, raising his volume so we could know he was serious.

“You, put him down and walk toward me with your hands behind your head.”

“Yes, sir. I *certainly* don’t want to do anything to alarm you.” He gently and methodically slid me down his body, pressing our torsos together, and smiled at me as he paused to think of his next words. “On second thought, though.” The officers all reached for their firearms. “I’m fairly bored by this interaction. I think I’m done.” Alister put his forehead against mine, ran his fingers through my hair, and whispered “Close, Davis. Close. But no cigar.” He then hoisted me onto his shoulder, lightning-fast, like positioning a large duffle bag, and catapulted me to the ground with what wrestling announcers call a spine buster, causing the officers to jump back three feet or so. My shoulder blades and back of my head hit first, and I lost consciousness for a bit, barely able to hear Annie scream out in horror.

"No! Davis!," she screeched as she ran toward us.

The cops descended upon Alister with guns and Billy Clubs drawn, but he trampolined fifteen or so feet in the air between them, landed on the window ledge of a closed real estate office, and kicked in its glass, disappearing inside. Three of the four officers gave chase to the back door of that building, while one stayed with me and Annie.

"I begged you not to follow them! I begged you, Davis!" She was admonishing me rather sternly, and, with drool puddling out of each side of my mouth, I began to worry about what she had told the police about Unholy Saint and me. I wasn't prepared to have the curtain pulled back on this subculture of monsters, and I sure as hell wasn't prepared to be the face or scapegoat of that subculture. I was just trying to coexist with myself one minute while trying not to commit suicide the next.

"Annie, I told you to go home. Why did you follow me?"

"Sir, I don't mean to break up your domestic disagreement, but I need to take a statement and ask if you want to press charges. Do you know your assailant?" I couldn't believe we were going through this.

"No. No sir. It wasn't an assault. It was just a disagreement, and I had it coming to me. I don't want to go into it any further, and I won't be pressing charges." I also wasn't going to divulge that I was starving and about to absolutely lose my shit. Neither he, his partners, nor Annie were safe. The officer eased up in his stance a bit, relaxing his shoulders and adopting an annoyed look on his face. All of a sudden, he transitioned from officer of the law to pissed off football coach type.

"Can you at least tell us who that was, and what the fuck just happened?" Annie must have sensed my body language and deduced that any longer an interaction might lead to worse things. She chose to interject herself in the conversation.

"What *happened*? What do you mean, officer? I had called you because I was afraid my boyfriend was going to get beat up for defending my honor." The cop's face grew considerably more annoyed at the complete failure to play dumb that Annie had just attempted. Meanwhile, I was surprised that she had used the term "boyfriend" to describe me.

"I mean how the hell was a little nerdy guy holding a grown ass man in the air like he was a newborn? And how the hell did the same guy jump up almost twenty feet in the air and land balanced on top of a three-inch window ledge before smashing through it?"

"Sir, I don't know how, and have never seen that gentleman before. I think that—"

"But you knew that this fella was following them. *Them*. You said *them*, so there must be more than one. You must know who some of these people are. And I'm sure they're associated in one way or another with the Wet Beaver. This place has been nothing but... eventful, since it opened."

"Is that fucking right?" a coarse, grizzled voice's question fell upon the chilly night air. The three of us turned to face the voice, as the other officers emerged, empty-handed and perplexed, from the real estate building.

"Yes, actually, that's right, Sinjin. The number of DUI's, car wrecks, petty theft, drug possession, public intox, and prostitution busts within a mile to the front door of your establishment since it opened are numerous enough to fund the whole of the Glendale Police Department."

"Oh, is *that* fucking right?"

"Yes, sir. That's fucking *right*."

"Well, you heard the kid. He's not pressing charges, and whatever the shit just happened back here spooked a band from out of town that was supposed to take the stage in a couple of hours, and they split. So, now I've got no headliner, police in my backyard disturbing the "ambiance," and I'm pissed. So, pretty please, how about you and your fellow homos get the fuck out of here, so I can try to recoup some of my business and get some music up on the damn stage tonight?"

Forgetting for a moment that the band he was referring to was Unholy Saint, I expected the policemen to gang up and beat the shit out of this old man, whose skin and disposition looked like he'd seen a lot and lived a long and wild life. I thought he was completely bald, but then noticed as he turned to his profile that he had a long, braided ponytail jutting out the back of his age spotted and dry-scalped head. Instead of the impending but assured police brutality, though, the officers looked at each other warily, bit their lips, and slowly started to retreat back to their vehicles. The head officer at the scene holstered his firearm and tapped two fingers to his forehead and then to Sinjin, in a farewell/salute type gesture.

"Just keep the place quiet, tonight, and keep the calls to a minimum."

Dismissively and sarcastically, Sinjin replied. "Yeah, I'll be really fucking quiet, tonight. Take a hike." A younger, rather muscular member of the police force took offense to this last comment and made a move back toward the old man, but was stopped with a hand to the chest by his superior. All four then slumped away, less powerful than they thought they were when they woke up this morning and put on their uniforms.

"I'm sorry we ruined your show, tonight," I apologized to Sinjin. I have no idea why I cared or felt some deference to him. I think I just viewed him as some frustrated business owner caught up in something that wasn't his business and shouldn't have been his concern.

Annie wasn't as obedient, or as oblivious. "Yeah, really sorry your murder-cunt band of blood bitches can't play tonight."

"You!" The old man aggravatingly pointed his finger right at me. "You get your ass in here." Annie took a step back and put her hand on her hip. I'd never seen as much attitude from her the entire time I've known her as I saw in the last five minutes.

"I'm sorry; what the fuc—"

"Davis McCarty. Annie Moore. You get your asses in here right now."

How did he know our names? Annie and I stared at each other, stunned, and both suddenly felt very unsure of ourselves.

"What are you waiting for, a nice invitation and balloons from Party City? You need to feed, right? Get your ass inside before you kill some helpless bastard out on the streets, or worse, get your pretty little girlfriend here damaged beyond repair."

Who the fuck is this guy? I took Annie's hand in mine, noticed her pull back slightly and shiver when she felt how cold it was, and draped a protective arm around her shoulder. We slowly shuffled our feet toward the old man, who peered oddly seductively at us over his bifocals. He extended his hand graciously and smiled an arrogant, dangerous smile.

"The name is Sinjin Pierce. We've got a lot to talk about. If I feel good about you, you'll walk out of here before the sun comes up. If I don't, and right now I don't, neither of you will ever walk, or breathe, or live, again. Welcome to the Wet Beaver. This is my home away from home. Get the fuck inside." Annie's eyes grew bulging big, and she locked in with mine and swallowed a gulp deep down her throat. We stepped into the darkness that beckoned through the venue's backdoor.

What the fuck have I done?

Chapter Sixteen: A Glimpse Behind the Curtain

Dim lights hung the atmosphere that lined the back of house of the Wet Beaver. I could hear dishwashers clanging plates and beer mugs in sinks, cooks grilling meat and chopping vegetables, and waitresses yelling out orders to the kitchen and bar from some unseen spot in the establishment. I felt the absorption of the PA system's bass through the walls and under my heels, while the muffled wail of Led Zeppelin and AC/DC filled the air. Black-painted brick made up the walls as Sinjin Pierce led us through the bowels of his home away from home, and he said nothing until we got to a door protected by a tough, but dumb, looking guard with dark curly hair and a nasty, greasy stubble. He stood there, hands crossed behind his back and deadly serious like he was a member of the Secret Service.

As we entered this exclusive sanctum of the club, dim LED bulbs gave way to black and red lit lamps and more contemporary electronic music served as the soundtrack. I could smell an interesting conglomeration of vampires and normal humans in this place, and I could detect newly consecrated death. I clutched Annie's hand firmly, and she scrunched up her face and bit her lip; I'd gripped it too firmly. A large, smoke-filled room with the words Beaver Den painted on the ceiling in neon entertained both types of inhabitants concurrently, and each seemed to know of the other, all lounging and drinking on furry, black sofas. Behind more closed doors, I could hear the sounds of sex in some and the sounds of confrontation in others. No screams, though. No one being tortured or raped or devoured violently. I was thoroughly confused.

"I opened this place 28 years ago, taking over a saloon run by some green businessmen," Sinjin offered up without my asking. "They had no clue what they were doing, and were losing money hand over fist, so my stepping in was a blessing."

"What is this place? Not… Not the club itself, but this. This place within the place?"

"You mean the place *within the walls*?" He made his voice sound cheesily eerie, like a late-night TV horror movie host.

"Sure."

"It's where the night drinkers come to get away from things and relax in this part of the country. I own two more similar to this one; The Naked Huntress in Laughlin, NV and the Ham Steak in Bakersfield, CA."

"The *Ham Steak*? Are these like the House of the Black Moon?"

"How the hell do you know about the House of the Black Moon?"

Annie butted in. "How the hell do you know our names?"

"Oooh, fierce. I, and we, know a lot. It wasn't hard to find out about you, especially after Davis made it clear to Devin that he wanted her to remember his name." Annie snapped her head around to stare in my eyes, asking without words what the hell *that* meant. "So, anyway, no, this is nothing like the House of the Black Moon. This is a rest stop along the way. The House of the Black Moon is more like..." Sinjin stopped to scratch his head, debating whether or not he should even be telling us this, and then... "More like a headquarters. The American Embassy if you will, for vampires. I can only assume that your intention if you get out of here alive is to keep after the band. And, if that's indeed the case, that's where you'll eventually find yourself. If you were smart, it's where someone with your condition would seek shelter. Guidance. Acceptance. You don't look like someone who's smart, though; you would probably go there looking for a fight. A fight wouldn't last long for you. It wouldn't end in your favor."

"I'll take my chances."

"You'll take whatever the hell I decide to give you. Anyway, there used to be eight places like the House of the Black Moon. Now, there are only four, and one of them is on its last legs."

"How do you know all this, and why are you "in alignment" with them?"

Sinjin took off his glasses and beat them against his hip while silently staring through my eyes. He drew up his nose a few times like a rat sniffing for crumbs on the floor and then floored me and Annie with a haymaker of a revelation.

"My two older siblings were cursed with this same affliction. One became this way much like you did, and the other chose it. They neither killed me nor allowed any harm to come to me, so when I was able to return that favor, I did. I opened up this place first, then the other two followed. There's a network of likeminded half-way house kind of hangs all over the country for the night drinkers. I just wish that my brother and sister could have seen it."

"That's the second time you've referred to vampires as "night drinkers." Is that their preferred name, like African American or---"

"That's what I call them! You can call 'em whatever the hell you want." A rustling and some thuds came from inside one of the closed doors, and our eyes all shot towards it, intrigued. Sinjun laughed to himself, cocked his head to one side like Robert DeNiro in the movie Goodfellas, and once again stared right through me. "Oh. *You* want to see inside. Do you think you can handle it?"

All of a sudden, I didn't know if I could. I was equal parts terrified and enticed.

"Little lady, I'm sure you can't, so I will strongly suggest that you wait outside. Davis, you probably don't have a choice. You need to drink. You can do that, here."

Annie was little more than offended. "You don't know shit about what I can or can't handle. What I want to know is why did those cops just up and leave because you told them to, and what gives you the pull to talk to them like they're your employees?"

"Haha! Damn. I like you. It's going to be a SHAME if I end up killing you. A damn shame. Really." They then stared at each other, neither one flinching or making any movement at all, before Sinjin relented and answered her question. "I've got friends in high places, just like I've got friends in low places. I own many reputable businesses here in Glendale, and I contribute a lot to local efforts and charities. Pierce Automotive Group. Healing Hearts Foundation. The Glendale Fine Arts Academy and half a dozen other things. All mine or partly mine. Also, the chief of police has a daughter who's "run afoul" of the law more than a few times. She of course made her way here. Instead of helping to string her out or string her up, I made sure she's steered clear of this lifestyle. I've got more than a few favors in my back pocket."

"You sound like a real philanthropist. A regular good will ambassador."

"Easy. Easy there. Don't assume that you can speak to me however you want in *my* place of business. One word, one snap of my fingers, and the clientele here will rip you apart and piss on your souls. You don't want to go in there, because you *shouldn't* want to go in there. It's something that no mortal should ever be privy to. Davis *has* to go in there, because if he doesn't, he's going to feed on you tonight. He'll either do it here, or he'll do it out there somewhere, and then he'll be dumping you in an unmarked grave or in a dumpster, or in Lake Havasu or some shit. Neither one of you want that, am I right?"

I had to reassure her that nothing of the sort would be happening. “If it’s all the same to you, I feel safer with her next to me, or within arm’s reach, just like your siblings probably felt about you.”

“My siblings. Are dead. And don’t mistake one second of this grand tour as being safe. The dance floor at the Wet Beaver is not safe. The men’s room at the Wet Beaver is not safe. Once you walked through this door, safety was one of the last things you should ever expect to find. Together, separate, makes no difference. I was trying to be a gentleman, and spare you, Annie, the extreme displeasure of watching your beloved Davis drink the blood of another human.”

“You don’t let vampires kill people in there! Do you?”

“Of course not! What the hell do I look like? A monster? A sociopath?” Annie and I were both perplexed.

“Davis, I’m sure you’ve noticed that there are both night drinkers and humans hanging out here together, in symbiotic bliss. Everyone on this side of the door is able to control themselves with minimal to no drama between the two classes. The players on the other side of the door, however; they still have a little problem with control. Their urges, their lusts, are still fresh. Harder to get reins on. Like me, there are humans who are sympathetic to their plight, and willing to lend a helping hand, or vein, that is.”

“Are you saying that they let vampires turn them?” Annie asked sheepishly. She was playing out an entire scene of carnage in her mind.

"God, no! No one dies in the Beaver unless I give the OK, and NO HUMANS are turned or slaughtered here! And, just to let you know, that's what I call it when a vampire kills a human and drinks of them. Slaughter. It's not pretty, and it's not subtle. It's an abomination." Sinjin's hands started to tremble, and I could tell he was holding back both rage and pain. I was unsure of just how much I could ask, and how far I could push him. I *had* to find out a few things, though.

"Sinjin. How did your siblings become vampires, and how did they die?"

"You slimy, snotnosed, punk son of a bitch." He approached me rapidly, and a handful of minions followed right behind him, surrounding Annie and me. "Maybe it's my fault for divulging so much. Maybe I gave you the false impression that you could ask and receive anything you wanted here. That is not the case, my steers and queers Texas friend." He got directly in front of me, his eyebrow tickling my eyelash. I could feel his breath on my chin and throat. It was warm and tainted. I felt afraid. My stomach was hollow and nauseous, and my temperature spiked. It didn't help that I was less than ten minutes away from a full-on hunger meltdown. My adrenaline and the need to protect Annie were temporarily repressing the urge, but that would only last so long. I felt now that I'd really screwed up by asking the question, and *really* needed to get on the other side of that door. Sinjin grabbed my chin gingerly, and then ran a long finger-nailed index finger down my left cheek.

"Just fuckin' with ya! HAHAHAHAHAHA!" He and all his acolytes erupted with laughter. He had tears in his eyes, and couldn't stand upright from how hard he was laughing. "Oh! Oh, man. Let me catch my breath. That was good. That was really good. Oh, man, Davis. Your expression. Priceless. Truly. Thank you for giving me the best laugh I've had in ages." I was starting to get pissed off, and I could tell that Annie was getting more and more concerned with this roller coaster of emotions that Sinjin had strapped us into. "If you're going to learn anything about what you are, and how your piece fits into the puzzle that is this "sub-culture," I'm going to have to give you some rope. You're either going to use that rope to pull yourself to safety, or you're going to use it to hang yourself, snapping your neck like a frail switch from a pine tree. It's up to you. I honestly would prefer the former, because I know you didn't choose this, and you shouldn't have to just live with feeding on homeless guys and prostitutes, etc. But if you choose the latter, I really have no problem putting you and the girl next door here in a meat grinder and serving you on a grilled bun. That's how absolute the repercussions of your decision are. That's how absolute they *have* to be. So, do you want to hear how my siblings became vampires and how they died?" I didn't know if this was a trick question that would result in more laughter, or a trick question that would result in him exploding and killing Annie and me, both. This seemed like a game to him one minute and a history lesson the next. And I *REALLY* had to feed soon.

"Yeessss, I guess."

"Ha! You frightened little bastard. This is what

happened." Annie and I both leaned in closer to him, and then she made herself right at home, sliding down onto one of the furry black sofas, braced her hands on her knees, and asked for a whiskey and soda.

"My family and I were travelling the south for the summer, from Florida to California. It was 1958. My father was a preacher and a salesman, and could work on the road. He had just purchased one of the first Winnebagos ever to touch the road, and was eager to test it out. My mom was a quiet, amazing housewife who took care of my brother Jack, my sister Milena, and me. I was the baby of the family. About half-way through the road trip, one night we stopped the Winnebago in Flagstaff to camp out and sleep, when in the middle of the night we woke to scratching sounds on the top of the Winnie, and then all the windows got smashed in. My memory is of our door getting yanked off the hinges and a tall, thin man with glowing red and yellow eyes and long, wolf-like fingernails stepping aboard. He grabbed my father by the throat as he struggled to put some shorts on, lifted him in the air, and broke his neck. My father's head was turned far inward, his ear resting on his chest. After dropping him to the ground, he grabbed my mother by the back of the neck, pulled her head backward by her long, beautiful brown hair, and sank his teeth in her neck. The moment probably took ten seconds, but it seemed like a lifetime in my head." I could sense Annie tensing up, and looked to see tears streaming down her face. "My brother Jack was 15 years old, and he jumped up and started punching on the tall man, but his punches had no effect. The tall man cast my mother's lifeless body aside, grabbed Jack and bit down on his neck. I remember blood flowing down

Jack's collarbone like a clogged river. He only drank of him for a few seconds, though. During this time, Milena grabbed me and stuffed me in the storage compartment under our breakfast bench. The tall man pushed Jack down onto the passenger seat of the Winnie, and slowly walked toward her. 'I smell a little boy. Did you think you could hide him from me?' Through the muffled barrier of the breakfast seat, I could hear new voices inside the vehicle. They were discussing something. Then I heard the tall man's voice again. 'Your brother is one of us now. My name is Warren. Warren Winston. The only humane thing to do with the rest of you is end your suffering before it continues'. I hadn't talked with Milena about this until a few years later, and what I found out then was that she knew what the tall man was and what he had done to Jack. In a very short window of time, she had made a few key decisions, and as Warren grabbed her by the buttons of her cotton nightgown, which I can still feel and smell, she started bartering."

'Make me one, too. Turn me like Jack, and take me with you. I won't fight, and I'll do whatever you need, but let Sinjin live. Let him go live with our aunt and uncle in New Mexico. Please. He's only a little boy. He deserves a chance'.

"I could feel the Winnebago explode with the laughter of our attackers, and heard the tall man reply. 'Deserves? That's a good one. No one is entitled to anything on this earth. No one deserves anything, and bad things happen to good people. Tonight is just a page in our story. Your story was predetermined to end tonight'.

'Why Jack and not me? Why take him?'.

‘I need a soldier. I’m building an army’.

‘I can be as good a soldier as he can. I can do anything you need. Just please let my baby brother live’. With that, she grabbed a coffee mug that had been left on the breakfast table and threw it at one of the vampires standing at the door. He caught it in his hand and gently set it on the dashboard.

‘How old are you?’.

‘12. I’m about to be 13 in two months’.

‘Well, 13, you’ve got guts. And you apparently have smarts. But I have to think about this’.

“The stillness and quiet of Warren and his group mulling over Milena’s proposal was killing me. I still didn’t really even know what was going on, but I knew that it could possibly end with me being separated from my siblings. And that was a terrifying thought. I thought about busting out of the storage compartment and making my own case, as enthralling as that could be from a seven-year-old. But, before I could, a large commotion interrupted everything, and I had to struggle hard to figure out what was going on. The sound was chilling, and it was something I’ll never forget; not as long as I live. It was my brother.”

‘Hey, 13. Are you sure you want to join this? I want you to watch what the transformation looks like. I want you to see what living death is, and to know that anytime you don’t have fresh blood pumping in your veins, delaying your decomposition, this scene, this feeling, this sound is exactly what you’ll experience’.

Sinjin went on to describe Warren holding Jack by the hair as his cardiovascular system burned from the inside out and how his skin and flesh changed color and went into convulsions while Milena was forced to watch. I knew the transformation well, and Sinjin's tale forced me to dive back inside my own. It was a very traumatic experience that I hadn't realized that I'd avoided revisiting. I don't even think that was intentional; I was just too busy and focused on my hunt that I'd stopped thinking about it. *Was I becoming comfortable in my new life?* He continued his account, and described Milena's screams and pleas for Warren to help Jack. Right before he allowed Jack to die from his illness, he saved him, but it was the most savage and sadistic form of salvation I could have ever imagined.

"You see," Sinjin choked out as strong as he could, "my mother was still just *barely* alive; so blood-drained that she would have died eventually, but so infected by whatever sickness is contained inside a vampire's saliva that it kept her breathing and in just as much pain as Jack was in. He told Jack that if he didn't want to feel the pain anymore, he would have to drain the last pint from his own mother, to ease both of their suffering. Jack didn't want to, but he also couldn't resist his own selfish need for survival. Part of me was hopeful that he was also thinking of saving me and my sister in one way or another. He looked at Milena shamefully, and asked Jesus for forgiveness before latching onto our mother's neck. Since she only had a little blood left, Jack had to suck harder and harder to get it. His patience wore thin, and he basically bit a large chunk out of my mother's throat while she cried quietly, too weak to fight or move."

Annie's tears were now accompanied by audible sobs. My legs were shaking with hunger pains, and I could tell Sinjin knew it. He shifted his weight from one leg to the other, and glanced toward the door holding my apparent dinner on the other side of it.

"You don't need to bore yourself anymore with the rest of my trip down memory lane. It's time we got Davis fed, yeah?"

"But what about your sister?" Annie cried out. "How did she come about her choice, and did they get you to your uncle, or did you live with them like a little pathetic mascot? You got me way too far in this story to leave all that out."

"Your boyfriend doesn't have too much longer before he has to make a decision about you, so are you sure you want to keep him waiting?"

"What?"

"Well, I mean, you're going to be the one he feeds on."

I jumped backward and grabbed Annie, placing her protectively behind me. "Not a chance in Hell," I growled at Sinjin.

"Hahaha! I'm just fucking with you! You are too easy a mark. Long story short, even though Milena hated Warren for what he'd done to her family, killing her parents and turning her and her brother into cold blooded predatory animals, she did what she did to save my life. What good would four dead Pierces be when she could reduce that number by two? She brought me out of the storage compartment, and I got to see Jack's new, disgusting transformation before apparently passing out, sound asleep. The next thing I remember was being walked to my uncle's front porch in Albuquerque, by Milena. She hadn't been turned yet. She gave me a kiss on the cheek, told me she was sorry, then rang the doorbell and ran off into an awaiting blue station wagon. Maybe I'll tell you the rest of the story some other time." Sinjin walked toward the door, typed in a four-digit code, and opened it. "But now, paradise awaits."

As the door opened wider, a blinding white light played havoc with my eyes, and I had to shield them and look away. Annie did the same. My pupils eventually adjusted, and I stepped through the door into a completely white room with multiple bright white lights. Its brightness reminded me of what descriptions of heaven look like when someone has a near-death experience. Half-walls adorned with eight-inch subway tiles held about a dozen people in place with medieval looking chains and shackles. These weren't humans, though. These were vampires, and normal humans were walking freely amongst them.

"What the hell is this room?" I questioned Sinjin.

"Why, it's the feeding room of course. All the humans in here want to help the night drinkers drink, but they also want to stay human and keep their normal day jobs and watch reality TV, etc. etc. blah blah blah. So, in here, they can cut themselves open enough to let that sweet nectar run, and it can drip down into a drinker's mouth. The brightness is so night drinkers can have a minor reminiscence of what the sun is like, without the ultraviolet rays cooking their compromised vitamin D. It's a win-win."

"Then why the shackles?"

"Great question. Like I mentioned, some of these drinkers are new to the game. Also, sometimes, maybe a vampire waits too long to knock on the door, or sometimes the blood he or she is tasting is too enjoyable, or coming out too slowly. Patience is not the most observed virtue in the night drinker's toolbox. So, because of that, and an "incident" about 15 years ago, the structure and protocols of the Beaver Den required some process improvement." I stood watching for a moment, trying to take it all in. "Go ahead, sit down at any vacant shackle, and we'll get you locked up and hooked up. A willing server will walk up eventually. They love new guys."

"No," Annie spoke up.

"What do you mean 'no?'," I asked. "Annie, I don't have a choice. I have to feed now."

"No, you won't drink some random person's blood. I'll give you mine."

I stared in stunned silence, and then Sinjin and I locked eyes.

"Damn, Davis. I think this one's a keeper! Although, I only know of maybe one or two vampire-human relationships to really make it work. All the other ones just ended in blood and tears, sometimes in that order."

"Annie. I can't let you do this. I won't let you do this."

"I'm not going to let some random ass vamp-hag drip their blood into your mouth. If you need to feed, let me help you." She was beginning to sound territorial, almost like a jealous girlfriend, which technically she was not.

Sinjin interjected. "If you're going to do this, you need to get in here, and do it quick. I know when a night drinker is about to run out of time, and he actually should have chained up about fifteen minutes ago."

I started to talk her out of it. "Annie, ple---"

"Don't try to stop me." She slowly stepped foot in the bright, bright heaven room and surveyed the scene. She closed her eyes, breathed in deep, and upon stepping on some blood drops, vomited all over the bright room's otherwise pristine floor.

"Really?" Sinjin asked, disappointed. "I thought you were tougher than that. You talk a good game, but---"

"I can do this!" She looked at me longingly. "Davis. Trust me. I can do this."

I walked over to Sinjin and pulled him aside, whispering a few things I didn't want Annie to hear, before turning back to the shackles.

"OK, Annie. You win. You can do it." I walked over to the last set of chains on the wall nearest the door, sat down and held my arms up. Two employees of the Wet Beaver then slid the shackles around both wrists and secured them in place. I motioned for Annie to come stand in front of me.

"OK, so how do I do this?" she asked Sinjin. With a

nod, he commanded a platter be brought over. On that platter were several instruments for the occasion. "These daggers are sharp and sterile. You can poke one into your forearm and apply enough pressure, and you'll get what you need for Davis. After you poke, you discard it to the floor, and someone will pick it up. You hold your arm over Davis' mouth and let the blood fall. He'll drink it up, and voila, he continues to breathe."

"Is he alive?"

"In a way. He's not *undead,* and he's not eternal by any means. He's only preventing the death wrought by being infected. Every drop of fresh blood adds more time to the clock. Every night drinker who keeps on going gains a little more experience, a little more perspective. More tools in their supernatural toolbox. Some get to the point where they thrive, and where less blood is needed to satisfy them daily. These are the exception, not the rule."

Annie looked over the selection of fine metallic daggers placed in front of her, and chose a smaller, pointier option. She held it to her forearm, hesitated while keeping her thoughts to herself, and then stuck it in at an angle, not quite parallel with her arm. She winced, paused, and then stuck further, watching the blood start to pool around the opening. As it dribbled out, she dry-heaved and closed her mouth tight to avoid another embarrassing secretion. She dropped the dagger as instructed and held her forearm over my face. I tilted my head back and opened my mouth wide, as to not waste any time or precious plasma. At first, Annie looked incredibly disgusted and a little horrified as I drank her blood from a safe, non-life altering distance, but then she eased up, and her look was more of sympathy and sadness.

"What is it, Annie?"

"I was thinking about how I'm so sad for you. How you were just trying to go to a concert, and be a part of life, instead of sitting alone in your grandma's house. I'm thinking of how you won't ever get to have a normal life. How we...." I could see her eyes start to water. "How we... won't ever get to have a normal life. It makes me sad for you." And with that, she stooped down to my face, and she planted a soft, sorrowful, loving kiss on my lips. It was a perfect distraction for Sinjin to come up behind her and inject her neck with sodium pentothal. Annie spun around and tried to slap Sinjin out of existence.

"What the fuck are you doing?!"

"Annie, stop. I asked him to do it."

"You what?" She looked confused, then betrayed.

"I had to. I couldn't have you participating in this any longer. I need you to go live your life. I need you to fulfill all the potential you have." She started to weep, and to wobble. The anesthetic worked its way through her system quickly.

"No. Why would you do this? Whyyy... wooouuulddd... youuuuu... dooooo"

"I love you, Annie. I love you so much. That's why you have to go, and never come back."

Her eyes were half shut and rolling up into their

sockets. She turned her head lazily in Sinjin's direction. "Not finished... withhhh yourrrr storrrry."

"Another time," he replied calmly. Before she fell to the ground, two of Sinjin's minions held her up, and began to carry her out. A sweaty, youngish-looking, shy redhead with short cutoffs and ample, bared cleavage wandered over to me, and let me drink some more. It must have been obvious that I didn't get enough from Annie before she was stabbed in the neck. Addressing Sinjin, commanding but still chained, I confirmed our whispered agreement. "Remember, she gets dropped off at 7001 Encinata Lane, Abilene, TX, with no accidental drug-induced rapes, finger-fucking, or abuse of any kind. I need her to live the life she was meant to, and to get as far from this horror show as possible."

"Of course," Sinjin replied. His voice didn't sound convincing, and I immediately second guessed my proposal, but I had no choice. He had me at his mercy. Additionally, we'd made a deal that I wouldn't kill anyone in the Beaver. "But do you really think she'll stay away? She's got a little thing for you, like a sad puppy at the animal shelter. God, man. They're either trying to change us or save us. I've got two divorces that will attest to that. In any case, she won't be harmed on her trip back to Abilene. You have my word. You just make sure that you live up to your end of the bargain, both inside these walls and outside of them."

Not killing anyone inside of the Wet Beaver wasn't the only stipulation of my release. I had also promised Sinjin I wouldn't attempt to kill Devin any longer. I didn't necessarily lie to him, because my goal wasn't to kill Devin anymore.

It was to kill Unholy Saint. Every last one of them.

Chapter Seventeen: The Huntress

Drowsy. Droning. The monotony of the road has me sleepy and uncomfortable. I've been driving on I-93, getting off at random exits, taking treks down random dirt roads. What should have taken three and a half hours to get to Laughlin, NV will have taken over two and a half days when all is said and done. I made a detour to Lake Havasu, and was amazed by the still, tranquil beauty of the lake in February. I tried to visualize what this same spot would look and sound like just a month later when the Spring Break crowd would try its best to demolish it and themselves. It was early enough in the morning that the sun hadn't honed its burning control over me, and I observed a group of college age kids not much younger than myself camping out in a tent. Their lack of stress and responsibility made me envious but grateful that there were still people enjoying the world. The juxtaposition between them, grilling hot dogs on a small portable unit while laughing and shooting the shit, and me, feeding on and disposing of an early morning jogger who picked the wrong place at the wrong time, couldn't have been more stark.

Before that, I'd gone the opposite direction and eventually made my way up to Prescott National Forest, spending the night among the juniper trees. I fed by the light of the moon on a mule deer, the carcass of which I donated to a mountain lion. I believe the mountain lion had first sought to dine on *me*, but changed its mind, and wouldn't come near me. My hypothesis is that my scent scared it. It was probably unsure of what to do with a dead person who refused to die. I was amazed by how beautiful nature was. I don't think I'd ever really stopped and looked at it before. I definitely didn't have something so beautiful in West Texas to compare it to, and never went to any national parks in Texas. Hell, I didn't even know if we *had* any national parks in Texas. I think I saw a family of black bears, but didn't get close enough to confirm. *Shouldn't they be hibernating?,* I thought to myself. Being so awestruck made me angry at how much of nothing I'd done and seen in my short life as an ordinary human. How much I'd taken for granted.

On the way to Lake Havasu, I stopped at Alamo Lake. I just thought it would be cool to visit somewhere that shared the same name with a Texas landmark. Subconsciously, I must have been missing home. Not too long after I bid farewell to Glendale and the Wet Beaver, I stopped in Surprise, AZ to steal some money from another ATM. I only really needed money for clothes, gas, and water. I didn't want to look or smell like a homeless person, and I didn't want to continue stealing clothes, so I figured ATM theft was the lesser morally of two evils. The reason I chose Surprise as my scene of the crime is that I recalled hearing that name back home for some reason. After searching my memory hard and long,

I realized that the baseball players at school would talk about Surprise, Arizona being where the Texas Rangers baseball team had Spring Training, and that two of our ballplayers were there, trying to make the major league team. Neither ended up making it past Double A.

Eventually, I stopped my road tripping and crossed the threshold into Laughlin, NV. Almost as if drawn by some spiritual lasso, and even though I never said it out loud, I knew that I was travelling to the Naked Huntress, one of Sinjin Pierce's other rest stops for "night drinkers" as he called them. Since I was one of this group, I felt that it should welcome me with open arms. I'm pretty sure that Sinjin also assumed I would be heading this direction, or to Bakersfield, CA and the Ham Steak. Every time I thought of that name since he first said it, I giggled a little at how random and ridiculous it sounded. I didn't get a chance to ask the origin of the name. I chose the Naked Huntress because it was much closer, and I knew I would have to feed soon after arriving in town. *Wouldn't it be better to not have to kill for my dinner?* The sun had been down for about three hours when I entered its parking lot, which apparently was still a tad too early; the parking lot was only half full. The outside of the place looked a little more classy, but also like it was hiding something. I got out of my vehicle and headed to the entrance, when I saw it: Cabaret and Private Club. For all intents and purposes, this was a strip club. I opened the double doors and walked in to find a decent looking if not too beautiful a hostess, dressed more modestly than I had expected.

"Good evening. Welcome to the Naked Huntress. Is this your first time with us?" She smiled sincerely, and seemed very jovial, *like a good hostess should be*, I thought.

"Umm. Yes, actually. This *is* my first time here."

"Perfect. We have a full bar and a full kitchen, five dancer platforms, plenty of seating in our main area, and an upstairs VIP area for an extra $50. If you just want to sit downstairs, that will be $20."

"Ok. Do you... Do you have a... Beaver Den, here? By Chance?"

"I'm sorry. A what?"

"Like in Glendale, AZ." I leaned in close to her and quieted my voice, as if we were spies in an action film. "Like a *secret* VIP?" Her face dropped, her eyes sunk back, and her mouth sat half-parted for five seconds. I think she literally went into some other zone in her brain for a bit.

"Oh... Your... People... Usually... They go in... through the... other... door."

"My god, I'm so sorry. I didn't know. I don't know the protocol here. I'm so sorry."

"No. No. It's ok." I could feel her start to tremble with these subtle little quakes, and the part of her bare skin I could see was instantly covered in goose bumps. Either she hadn't actually interacted with vampires before, or she *had* and was traumatized by it. "It's really ok. I couldn't tell. I didn't know, because you didn't... you don't act... like.... Like them."

"Like what?" I played coy, intentionally.

"Like *them*. You know. *Night drinkers*." Bingo. I made sure to give her as sincere and welcoming a smile as she gave me just moments earlier.

"And what do they act like?" I inquired.

"Well, I don't mean to... They don't *all* act the same. But for the most part, they're either really arrogant, or really mean. Like cold and dark mean. You're not from around here, are you?" I could feel her ease up around me, and it made me want to cry, knowing that before me stood a human who not only knew what I was, but was not looking at me like I was a monster.

"Well I hope I never act like them, then." This caused her to blush and give a shy little smile. "Look. If there's only one way into that *secret* area, then I'm eventually going to need to know the directions to that other door. But, right now, I just want to pretend to enjoy a life I'll never get to have. So I'll pay the $20 and sit down here."

"I'm going to give you the VIP access – for free." She carefully took my right hand and stamped it.

"Thank you. Thank you, very much..."

"Crystal. My name's Crystal."

"Well, thank you, Crystal."

"You're welcome..."

"Davis. My name's Davis."

"Well, you're welcome, Davis. And if you go up to VIP, ask for Braxton. There's a way into... the place you want to be, through VIP."

"Thanks again." I couldn't believe the only positive, heartwarming conversation I'd had since being turned was with the hostess at a strip club/vampire hangout.

I'd been inside a strip club exactly two other times in my life, and while there were similarities, this one seemed to be head and shoulders better than those two places. The design, the architecture, and the *women.* Even though it was still early, these women on the platforms and main stage were Hollywood starlets compared to what I'd seen back home. If this is what Laughlin had to offer, I wondered how amazing the dancers must look in Las Vegas. It also made me wonder if the Ham Steak was also a strip club. I'd only walked through the main floor of the Wet Beaver after closing hours, when Sinjin wanted to give me a brief tour as we parted ways. But, ironically, given its name, it was only a bar and music venue. Pictures of a few of the servers showed them to be pretty scantily dressed, but nowhere near naked.

I walked the floor a little before settling on a seat far enough from the stages that I didn't feel like a pervert or stalker, but I almost immediately felt uncomfortable and decidedly not in my element. Almost as immediately, one of the dancers jiggled over to me in her high, high heels, and placed a leg in between the two of mine. "Do you want a dance?"

"No, thank you," I replied softly, looking mostly downward.

"Oh, you're shy. No worries, handsome. I'll loosen

you up before the night's over." She smiled and winked, then quickly made her way to the next mark.

Before I had to go through any more of those awkward interactions, where I felt bad about not accepting a young lady's offer, I decided to head upstairs and find this Braxton. My time pretending to be a normal dude had lasted four minutes. I found a winding, semi-spiral staircase and took it to the second floor, where I was met by a bouncer who had to verify my stamp. Upon said verification, I walked over to the bar, and ordered a water.

"A water?" the bartender asked, puzzled.

"Just to start," I assured him. He didn't look impressed. "Do you know where I could find Braxton?"

"He's not here yet. He doesn't come in until 10:00, which is almost 30 minutes from now. He won't get on the floor until 10:30. So, get ready to fill up on water. What do you want with Braxton?"

"The hostess downstairs said I could find him up here. I just need to ask him a question. A personal question."

"Do you have a crush on him or something?" The bartender seemed humored by himself.

"No. Nothing like that."

"What's your name, friend?"

"Davis."

"Davis from Texas?" *What?*

"Uhhh. Yesss. How do you know?"

"Ah, well. It appears that I have not one, but two messages here for a 'Davis from Texas'. You're the only Davis from Texas here right now, and something tells me that you're going to be the only 'Davis from Texas' here tonight."

"Yes, it would be a relatively safe assumption, I guess."

"Well, then here you go. One message from Sinjin Pierce and one message from…." He paused for dramatic effect, and to keep me on my toes, uneasy. "Alister Amaranth." *Alister Amaranth? Was I so predictable?* "Thanks. Thank you."

I started to read them there at the bar, when a dancer came up from behind me and started rubbing on my crotch. She ran her fingers through my hair and gave a playful nibble on my ear, whispering "Do you want a dance?" Damn, I wasn't going to be able to get away from them, at least not in *this* part of the club. "No, thank you," I replied politely but firmly. "Maybe later." "Yeah, sure," she snapped back sarcastically and walked off, automatically uninterested. I decided to switch to a less inviting seat in the corner of the VIP section, and sat down to read these messages that had been waiting for my arrival. I chose a good news first/bad news second approach, and opened Sinjin's first. I'd no sooner read the first line than glanced up to find another gentleman sitting across the room staring directly at me in an almost blind, dumb trance.

"Pay him no mind," a waitress called out to me. "That's only Felix. He'll sit there like that for hours if we let him. We sometimes forget he's there, and start to lock up until he says something."

"Great." I zoned him out and attempted to lock in on my correspondence.

‘No doubt you paid my Huntress a visit. I would hope that you’re doing so strictly based on my description of the place and your new, growing interest in vampire culture and desire to be a more productive member of its community. Unfortunately, I fear that you’re only stopping there on your way to break your promise to me and try to kill various, specific members of Unholy Saint. It truly will break my heart if you spit on my trust. Especially since you don’t know if I kept my promise and returned sweet cheeks to Abilene in one piece. I guess we’ll never know. While you’re there, get a dance from Electra. She’s a true pro. And try the desert stargazer. It’ll get you halfway there. So powerful, you’ll almost forget you’re not human anymore. Until we meet again’.

I held the note in my hand and re-read the part about Annie several times, as if doing so would gain me some insight into how and if she made it home. I had called her more than once since they carried her off, but got no answer either time. Checking my phone every few minutes didn’t produce any magical callbacks from her either. After reading the note one last time, I looked up to see that same guy staring at me like I was a suspenseful, thrilling program on an invisible television. Neither his expression nor his body moved an inch. As intrigued as I was by receiving a message from Alister, I almost didn’t want to read it. I knew his hand couldn’t reach out of the paper and grab me by the throat, but I didn’t *really* know it. I couldn’t delay any longer, however, and I unfolded the paper and peaked slowly at the first sentence.

‘What’s up, Texas? I was hoping that slam I gave you crushed your head like an over-ripe pineapple, but we can’t win ‘em all, can we? I spoke with Sinjin, today. He’s got a soft spot for our kind, so I knew he wasn’t going to end you. It really would have been better for everyone if he did, but… we can’t win ‘em all, can we? I wasn't lying or blowing smoke up your ass when I told you that no one has ever given us this much trouble before. That's an accurate statement if ever there was one. Don't fuck with our remaining shows. I repeat, don't fuck with our remaining shows. If you somehow get all the way to the Black Moon, be prepared to come in peace, and I'll do the same. I can walk you through the rules, the history, the future. You can decide if you want to join us. That sounded so gay. We're not like a social club. Anyway, if you come prepared for war, it won't be much of one. It'll be a small skirmish ending in your visceral, eternal, senseless demise. I'll personally deliver your remains to 7001 Encinata Lane in Abilene. Or better yet, maybe I'll personally deliver them to 3419 Park Oak in Lawrence, KS. The choice is yours, Texas. Choose wisely, because... we can't win 'em all, can we? Yours, truly. Alister'.

He had both of Annie's addresses. Even hers in Kansas. That told me that she got home safe. At least got home alive. It also told me that their patience was up, and that they'd done a good amount of due diligence in researching us both. If she had just listened when I told her to forget about me, not to follow me. If she wasn't so damned stubborn and determined to do the right thing. I was so engrossed with Alister's note that I hadn't noticed the VIP section fill up around me, completely naked dancers grinding and writhing on customers, and the volume in the building increase exponentially. I also hadn't noticed a handsome, muscular man with a square jaw in a black suit staring a hole through me. When I finally did, he beckoned to me with a come-hither wave.

"Braxton, I presume?"

"You presume correctly," he replied in a deadpan, monotone voice.

"Can I get behind the curtain?"

"Is that some sort of reference to the Wizard of Oz?" That unintentionally broke the clear tension between us, and I laughed out loud.

"No. No. I just don't know what this place's secret spot is called. In Glendale, it's the Beaver Den, so this is…?"

"Oh, I follow. This doesn't have a name, but if you need to call it something, call it the Lair."

"Got it. Can I get into the Lair?"

"You already know you can. The shimmering, metal door to the left of the bar. When the red light above the door turns green, all you have to do is open it. Be warned. This shit is a little more depraved than the Beaver Den, if you can believe that." I actually hadn't seen anything too crazy in the Beaver Den to be honest, aside from chained up vampires drinking from open wounds in humans.

"Alright then. Warning heeded. I assume there are volunteers for someone like me, who needs to feed sooner rather than later?"

"There are."

"Great. Thank you."

"Don't mention it." Then Braxton's face stiffened into a serious, soldier-like scowl, and he smoothly grabbed me by the arm and stepped into my personal space. "I'll have you know that we've been instructed to watch you, closely. No one seems to know what to make of you yet. So, on one hand, they're – we're – going to try and indoctrinate you, and on the other, we're wary. To that end, if you do something crazy, and we have to step in and have you erased, so be it."

"Also noted. Wouldn't it have been smarter to not

mention that to me, so my guard was down?"

"Would your guard have truly been "down"?"

"No. I guess not. Good point."

"Enjoy yourself. Eventually, Electra will visit you." *What is it with this Electra? She must be God's gift to stripping.*

I moved swiftly over to the shimmering metal door to the left of the bar and stood there patiently, watching and waiting for the red light above to turn green. A few seconds later, it did, and I opened the door, not knowing exactly what depravity lay in wait for me. *Holy Shit.* I think I repeated those two words in my head several times. I walked into a large room with red and burgundy sofas arranged in a square, and on each of them were vampire clientele sitting down while naked strippers straddled or stood over them, *COVERED IN BLOOD!* The vampires were licking blood off of bellies and sucking it off stiff-nippled breasts, or having it drip from the dancers' open wounds into their gaping, lusting mouths. These dancers were at least as beautiful as the ones downstairs, some more so, but they also looked a little more lethal. Some were done up in a very goth style, dyed black locks, black eyeliner and lipstick. Two girls stood out because of their ethnicity; an Indian or Pakistani girl, a little older than the others, and a very voluptuous Latina. Their striking beauty and different skin tones casted a significant but welcome contrast against the salt and pepper sea of buxom, tanned skinned white and African American workers. *None* of these vampires were chained up. *How dangerous*, I thought. This could be an explosive mistake. But everyone seemed to be on their best behavior, and having a great time.

Off to one side was a long, sleek, cherry wood bar manned by one bartender. Just like in Glendale, vampires and humans were drinking together, socializing, no one different than or superior to the other. Behind the center of the room, was a raised floor with small rooms. Inside those rooms, through opaque translucent doors, I could see people having loud, passionate sex in various positions. I had never seen anything like this in my life, so it was a bit much to take in. With all this going on, I noticed that I didn't get physically aroused. I couldn't explain it. It didn't take so much as a beautiful girl in a bikini to have me "standing at attention" when I was a teenager, or even as a young adult, which seemed like only a short few months ago. Could this be what happened to men when they became adults?

"You can't get hard when you're a vampire," Braxton startled me from over my shoulder with this bit of information. "What ultimately causes an erection is the flow of blood directed toward the penis. You don't have any blood to flow. The only way to get it to happen is to feed. You've got maybe 10 to 30 minutes tops after you feed to get any activity going on down there. It's not like they make it seem in movies and TV; vampires aren't super horny or romantic. They're lonely, melancholy, and uninterested. I feel for you guys."

I had never thought about it, but I hadn't had any sexual thoughts since Devin turned me. Not even for Annie. All I could think about is how much I loved her, and felt for her safety. Nothing carnal ever entered my mind. "So, are all those men behind the doors vampires?" I asked.

"Most of 'em. Some of those vampires might even be women."

"Really? What happens to *their* libidos and biological functions after they're turned?"

"Pretty much the female version of what happens to

the men. I don't really feel like elaborating. So, you see anything that you'd like to lick on?"

I didn't realize *how* much I was in love with Annie until I heard that question. I automatically associated it with something sexual, and the thought of sex with anyone but her didn't interest me at all. In fact, it kind of disgusted me. Since I never really had a girlfriend, I guess I never knew how monogamous I was. It was settled; I was a one-woman man. A woman that I told never to contact me again, and had drugged and smuggled across state lines.

"I think I would rather just have someone hold an open cut over me."

"Suit yourself. Are you needing yet, or can you hold off a bit and take in the atmosphere? Would you like some alcohol?"

"Would a desert stargazer be an alcoholic beverage?"

"Why yes it would. Want one of those?"

"Sure."

Braxton held his hand up to the Lair's bartender, positioning his fingers in some kind of code. He didn't speak or even mouth anything. Ten seconds later, "One desert stargazer. Sip it. Don't down it."

Unsure of where to sit, I just ended up taking a seat at the end of the bar, facing the wall of bottles. I needed a moment to compose myself, to try and relax. This place was an assault on the senses, and I was and still am an introvert. I took the first sip of this highly recommended solution, and it instantly threw my head backwards. I couldn't tell if I liked it, or I hated it. There were so many flavors, including some that were quite foreign to my uneducated tongue. That searching, ambiguous reaction was exactly the same for the next two chugs. Somewhere along the way, however, I ended up really enjoying it. I finished probably a little too quickly, in opposition to Braxton's advice. Just when I was about to order a second, I got a hand placed gently on my shoulder.

"Hi. I'm---"

"Electra," I finished her sentence for her. "How couldn't you be?"

She couldn't have been more than 25, but her eyes belied more life experience than most people twice her age. She had a semi-dark tint to her skin, but I couldn't decipher if it was tanned, faked tanned, or if she was Hispanic or some other ethnicity. Her face looked and her voice sounded white, and right out of L.A. or some other California town. At least, my perception of what they sounded like. Unlike virtually every other dancer there, she wasn't completely nude. She had a sheer, white, see-through negligee covering black, barely-there lingerie. She had styled dark brown hair with some highlights, comforting big green eyes, a tiny mole on her left cheek, and another between her left nostril and her upper lip. I can't explain why, but those moles were extremely sexy. She wasn't tall or short, and was fit but curvy. I thought her breasts might be fake, but...

"They're real," she stated, matter of fact, as if being able to read my mind.

"I can't read your mind, just your eyes." Wow. Sinjin was right. Electra was a true pro.

"You're Davis, right?"

"I must stick out like a sore thumb."

"A sore Texas thumb. But no, to be completely straight with you, Braxton pointed you out to me. I'm not a psychic or a witch."

"What are you?"

"I'm the most talented dancer this town's ever seen, the most talented stripper in maybe the whole country, and probably the best piece of ass anyone who's had me will ever have." Somehow, when she said this, it didn't sound like boasting. More accurately, it didn't sound like she was wrong.

"That's definitely quite a headline for a resume."

"I'm going to speed-round this introduction for you. People I've been with, man or woman, fall in love with me, promise me big things, and buy me big things. They come in here and spend thousands on me nightly. The clientele behind the closed door who've had me wish they were humans again. If you want to fuck me, it's normally $5,000 an hour, and people don't regret a damn penny of that five grand. If you want to drink from my body, it's normally $8,000. But, for some reason, some rail-thin, wet behind the ears, young country boy from tumbleweed and dust storm Texas gets to come in here and I'm told by management that it's "on the house." You must be the second coming or some shit."

"I'm not special at all, I don't think. I'm the most inexperienced vampire in this or any other place, and I wasn't much better before I was one. I'm a simple guy with no real interests and no real skills. The only time I ever really started to fall in love with something, it turned on me. Made me this. The only woman I've ever loved... at the very least is destined to live a normal life without me, and at the very worst, is in grave danger directly because of me. So, I think the only reason I'm getting this special treatment is they want to butter me up."

"Why would they? What do they care?"

"So I won't make trouble."

"For whom?"

"For vampires in general and Unholy Saint, in particular."

"How did I know?"

"How *did* you know?"

"Look, I try to stay out of such matters and mind my business, but when you have such a unique and normally hidden creature so out in the open trying to actually *gain* popularity and notoriety, things are eventually going to get screwed up. Let me guess, it was the girl, right?"

"If by 'the girl', you mean the bass player, Devin Sikorsky, then yes. It was 'the girl'."

"Of course it was. It doesn't sound like them to make another a vampire, though."

"That wasn't her intent. It was more---"

"An accident? Shit. No wonder you're making trouble. This turned your whole life all kind of upside down."

"You could say that."

"I just did, silly. Well, what do you say we make good use of your in-house credit? Whatever you want, it's free." Electra then removed the white, see-through negligee, and stood there displaying her body for me, like I was appreciating a car in a showroom.

"I don't know what I want; I just know what I need."

"To feed. Well, you can do that. Come wth me." We walked over to the very occupied sofas, and as we got to one, a blonde, petite dancer and her customer just up and removed themselves, swiftly relocating somewhere else. She was straddling his lap, not even facing us, and Electra didn't have to say anything to her. She is definitely the alpha among the ladies. It was very impressive. "Sit here," she commanded. I sat down on the sofa and Electra took a step back and then removed her black lace bra, exposing larger than average, perfect breasts. She untied one side of her customized, braided thong, took a razor blade from the end table next to the sofa, and created a small incision on the front of her hip where the string was. Blood started to bubble up and pour out. "Don't suck on the wound itself. I don't want you infecting me with your vampire shit. I enjoy my sunning in Mexico and Vegas. As soon as the blood runs down toward my pelvis, lick it off of anywhere. *Any*where."

I waited until it was in this weird sort of Bermuda Triangle between her thigh and her crevice, and lapped at the blood like a dog before it could get to her pubic region. I felt invasive, embarrassed, and stupid all at the same time. This might be sexy for some, but not for me. As I fed on her blood, she took my right hand and stroked it gently, but then placed it on her left breast. She squeezed my hand so it would squeeze her breast, and I pulled away abruptly.

"Don't. Please don't do that. I don't want to do anything but rehydrate and rejuvenate."

"Oh. OK." She was startled by how strongly I asked. I don't think she's ever been rejected before, especially not here. She didn't try to talk me into anything more, at least not right away. "That's a good way to put it: 'rehydrate and rejuvenate'. I'm going to start making people call it that." I fed for approximately three minutes, which doesn't seem like long for eating a regular meal, but is rather long when you're drinking blood, and the cut that it springs forth from is less than an inch long. I could tell she was getting a little done with the process, and maybe a little weaker, from her increased fidgeting. “Are you close to full?” she inquired, hopeful at my answer.

“Yes. I’m sorry. I’m almost done. You can tell by the lack of visible veins on my arms, and the return of some color resembling normal on my skin. Not completely normal, but passable as human in a crowded space. I’m a little flushed, actually. I could use---”

“Another desert stargazer?”

“Yes! I was just about to say that. How do you know what I’m going to say?”

“I’ve been around long enough, Davis. Longer than someone my age should be, but long, nonetheless. You move on over to that loveseat in the corner of the room, and I’ll get us a couple stargazers.”

I watched her as she slipped her see-through negligee back on sans bra, sauntered leisurely but confidently to the bar, and spoke with the bartender while he prepared our drinks. For a small moment, I wondered internally, *could I do something sexual with her? Could I actually have sex with her? Why am I feeling so warm, and why am I entertaining this?* It definitely felt out of character for me, but the atmosphere is what it is, she was an exquisitely beautiful woman, so sexual thoughts *should* be commonplace here. That’s what I told myself. Still, something felt off about my thought process. She returned with our drinks, and after she wiped and bandaged her cut, we sat side by side on the oversized one-cushion loveseat in the corner. A few seconds of uncomfortable silence followed, until she opened the conservation with some philosophizing.

“Did you ever think you’d be here, in this time and

place? Could you have even fathomed that vampires existed or that you'd one day walk among them?"

"I never even thought I'd set foot outside of Texas, much less set out cross country as a vampire. The biggest struggles I faced the day I became a vampire were *what do I wear to the show, and should I apply at Home Depot or Hooters?*"

"We take the little things for granted."

"How about you? Did you think you'd ever be a stripper, or prostitute, letting people drink blood off your body?"

"I mean, the answer can't possibly be 'yes', but I've been different, and my life's been different, for so long that I can honestly say I'm not *too* surprised how things turned out."

"Are you happy?"

"I don't think anyone's happy, Davis. I'm content, though. With my life, with my freedom. I can come and go as I please, and I can travel the world at a moment's notice. There's some happiness in that. Are my life choices, or my career choices, limiting in some respects? Of course they are. Do I wish I had a relationship with my family? Sure. Do I cry about it? Not for a long, long time."

At the same time, as if subconsciously able to sense staring eyes, we both swiveled our heads toward the bar to see a gentlemen dressed in a sloppily put together suit talking to the bartender while looking and pointing at us. I couldn't tell if the look on his face was anger or sadness, but he definitely seemed uneasy and pushy.

"That's Roosevelt," Electra informed me. "He's become one of my semi-regular, human customers, and he has the mistaken perception that if he's here, then I should be attentive to his presence. He'd be wrong of course. I'll keep him waiting for another hour or two if I please. Your blood flow is still in working order. Are you sure you don't want to fuck me?" The bluntness of her question shocked and embarrassed me. It also put a dumb smile on my face, while my body got warmer and "dreamier."

"Umm, no ma'am. I think you're stunning, and I kind of like you as a person, but---"

"Are you a virgin, Davis?" Again, the bluntness of this question really caught me off guard, and I squirmed in my seat.

"I… I don't think I… no comment." My inability to communicate properly, and my body language gave her all the answer she needed.

"It's OK. You don't have to say it." She popped up from the loveseat and threw her hands on her hips while staring over in Roosevelt's direction. "It's time our paths intersected, since they will not intertwine. But can you do me a favor, and I promise this isn't trying to lead you somewhere?"

"What?" I asked nervously.

"Can you feel my ass, and tell me what you think?"

"Why?"

"I just want an objective opinion."

I thought about it for a few seconds, with a dumb look on my face. It was getting harder to concentrate on words or concrete thoughts, and I couldn't figure out why.

"OK, I guess. Just for a few seconds, and just to help you out."

While now staring directly into Roosevelt's eyes, she grabbed both of my hands and placed them with a slap on each buttock. She then slowly guided my hands up and down on the curve of each. I think she knew that I wouldn't have a clue how to analyze or caress them myself. And secretly, I think she *was* trying to get this to lead to something. Someone as confident and sexual as she was probably didn't appreciate me resisting her charms. She took one hand and cupped it under my chin, lifting my head upward so she could gaze down upon me.

"Well. What do you think?"

"I've never touched someone's ass like this, so I don't have a basis for true comparison, but it's probably the best bottom I've ever seen. That's including magazines or movies, or in person. It's a very nice… bottom. Or ass. Or bottom." I sounded like a child. I noticed my loins starting to move like a normal human male. I was one part relieved, and one part ashamed. I didn't want to betray my feelings for Annie.

"It's not cheating if you're not with her, Davis." *How does she do that?* "And it's natural for you to get turned on by rubbing the best ass – bottom – you've ever seen." She was grinning, trying not to bust out laughing altogether at my inexperience and shyness.

"Why do I feel this way? This isn't what drunk feels like." I was very aware that my brain and body were undergoing some sort of chemical change that was extremely foreign from how Bud Light made me feel.

"That's probably the ecstasy and ketamine you're feeling. Have you never tried those before?"

"What? No. I've never had ecstasy or ketamine before. What the hell is ketamine?" Those desert stargazers are something else.

"Everything's fine. The drink is put together to put you at ease, get you in a party mood, and heighten your enjoyment of certain pleasures. Vampires tend to handle the effects better than normal folk, but this is your first time, and you had two. My goodness." She smiled at the visible haziness in my stare, and the innocent stupidity in my smile. "Are you sure you don't want to check out one of the private rooms? Could be the best time of your life."

"I don't think I have a life, Electra. I do have a direction, though. And I need to be heading on down the road."

"Not in your condition, you won't. At least not for a while." She stood and stared at me for a bit, searching for the words, while Roosevelt grew audibly more impatient at the bar. "Wow. I can honestly say that you're the first person ever to turn me down. First time for everything, right?"

"I suppose so. Can you answer me something, though, if it's not too personal?"

"Ooooh, that sounds interesting. Sure."

"What *are* you? Nationality, I mean."

"I thought that was spinning around in that noodle of yours. You really want to know?"

"Yes, ma'am." Hearing herself referred to as ma'am now a second time seemed to upset her.

"You just made me want to throw up in my mouth a little bit, calling me ma'am. What the fuck? I'm an American born half Israeli and half Lebanese."

"You're really beautiful."

"Yes, Davis. Yes, I fucking am." She dropped her head down, a little bashful-like, which surprised the hell out of me. “Davis, please take this bit of advice. Get laid. Find yourself a community of like creatures, if you’re going to remain alive. Don’t try to fuck with Unholy Saint. You’ve managed to not be torn in pieces. Quit while you’re ahead. They’re only the head of the snake, if you get my drift. There’s much worse you’ll have to answer to if you continue to pursue them.”

Electra gave me a hug, pulled my head down and gave me a tender kiss on the cheek, and walked me to the shimmering, metal door, so I could make my exit and resume my journey. “Later,” was her farewell to me. As I entered the cool, Laughlin night, thoroughly discombobulated and woozy from the drinks, I was heading to my truck when I heard a voice behind me.

“Hey, man. You want some company?”

It was the creepy, almost catatonic guy from inside the VIP.

“My name’s Felix. You’re a vampire, right?”

Chapter Eighteen: Kindred Spirit

Let me paint the scene for you. The guy from inside VIP with a staring problem was sitting in a wheelchair outside of the Naked Huntress, next to the curb. There's no telling how long he'd been waiting for me, or even *if* he was waiting for me. His name was apparently Felix, and he knew I was a vampire. He had greasy, stringy, neck length hair with a bald spot on the back of his head, and his clothes looked and smelled like he hadn't changed or washed them in four days. He wasn't in a wheelchair inside the club, so I was confused by the magical addition of one. He was wearing lightly tinted, hippyish eyeglasses, a long sleeve plaid shirt under a dirty orange puffy vest, with tan cargo pants and cream, falling apart Converse Chucks hanging for dear life to his feet. He looked like he was in his sixties. I'd find out later that he was a few months from only his 49th birthday.

"I figure since you ain't got nobody with you in the club, then you ain't got nobody, period. And since I know you're heading out to California to find all those other vampires, I figure you need a road trip buddy."

"You figured wrong, friend. And how do you know I'm a vampire? And how do you know I'm going to California to 'find all those other vampires'?"

"I can read lips."

"Read lips?"

"Yes, sir. I can read lips, and I can speak and read five other languages. That was my specialty in the military. I helped clean up all the dead bodies in Kuwait when I was a teenager, and found out that kind of work wasn't for me. So, I decided to learn a whole bunch of languages, learned to lip read, and became a linguistics specialist. I went to Afghanistan and Iraq, and eventually got blown the fuck up in a firefight. I got to go home, and I ain't been worth a shit since."

"I don't think all that info about vampires and California was exchanged in VIP. You weren't allowed behind the secret door, were you?"

"Maybe I was, maybe I wasn't. I guess we'll never know. The important thing is, I'm right. I *am* right, aren't I?"

"It appears so."

"So here's the thing. I know all kinds of motels and vacant, abandoned buildings we can stay in to keep you out of sight, or out of the sun. I can get you materials and gas, or handle reconnaissance, during the day. I can even suggest places where you might be able to find a safe victim to feed on. I just ask that you take me with you, and that you don't feed on me."

"Why? Can you just leave Laughlin with no advance

notice?"

"*Leave* Laughlin?" Felix laughed, doubling over and almost falling out of his wheelchair. "Buddy, I ain't got nowhere else to be."

"I don't have time to push you around in a wheelchair all night, and can't do it at all during the day. It sounds like---"

"Hell. I don't need this thing. I just sit around in it when I'm tired." Felix got out of the chair, stretched his back far, causing several loud pops across his vertebrae, and walked towards me on wobbly, bowlegged knees with his hand out. "Felix. Felix Hendry. Nice to officially meet you."

"Felix Henry?"

"No. Hendry. Like Henry, but with a D in the middle. If I had a dime for every time someone's gotten that wrong… let's just say I'd have a lot of dimes." His arms and fingers moved about as if independent of his control. I thought he may be on methamphetamine, but felt for some reason that it was impolite to intrude, and didn't ask.

"Look. I need a little bit of time to think about this, OK?"

"Sure; take all the time you need. You probably need a few minutes to half an hour to try and shake off the effects of those stargazers, anyhow." How the hell did *he* know about the stargazers?

"Thank you." I walked gingerly to my truck, got in, and sat there. At first, I didn't think about Felix, or anything. I just tried to get the view to stop spinning. I don't know anything about ecstasy, but I'd be surprised if there wasn't something else in that drink making me feel this way. Given another opportunity, I don't think I'll be trying one ever again. Taking on a passenger wasn't really anything I'd given any thought to. I didn't talk much, and didn't have any real experience conversing with a stranger for long periods of time. The main activity I'd adopted while driving through Arizona and on to Nevada was listening to new music (new to me) or Unholy Saint, trying to unravel any mysteries in their songs that would have given their secret away. I should have known they wouldn't be so foolish, but there is a lot of innuendo and imagery in their lyrics. Additionally, Felix's first impression was definitely on the creepy end of the spectrum. The thought of travelling and committing to the whims of my detours with him along for the ride didn't give me any kind of positive feeling. Right when I was going to make up my mind and let him down easy, he tapped on my window.

"Look, man," he started. "I know you've got a mission to complete, and I know you were probably a loner to begin with, but you look like someone who needs to talk. Even if you don't know that yet. People can't go forever without human interaction. And you've got a *STORY* to tell! Wouldn't it be nice to tell it? Tell it to a person who already believes you?" He had a small point. "I'm not going to get in your way, or be in your hair. This is your automobile. You're the boss. You can dump me anywhere at any time and I know that. I'm just trying to help, and see the country at the same time. And don't forget about me being able to move about in the daylight for you. That's got to be a benefit. We might even be able to fashion some sort of darkness for you, so I can drive during the day."

"Let's not take it too far. I'm still thinking. Just a minute longer, I promise." I let his words swirl around in my head, before he dropped a small bomb on me.

"I know you're taking this road trip hoping to return to the living. I know someone who's done it. So it can be done. I'm sure you've got a lady and a momma you're dying to see again. Let's give you the chance to do that. Let me help you do that."

"Hop in, Felix."

We peeled away from the Naked Huntress and over the next two days, we took things slow and easy, feeling each other out, so to speak. Felix told me his stories of being a Navy brat who'd been all over the world by the time he was in high school. He spoke of following his father into the military, spending some time stationed in Texas, and the aforementioned body cleanup in Kuwait. I started by introducing my boring former life, before giving into his requests for the account of my cursed fateful first concert experience and the ensuing aftermath. We travelled southwest to Joshua Tree, before I found out that Unholy Saint was going to be in Lake Tahoe for a few days of rest between their show in Las Vegas and their hometown tour finale in Santa Ana. That detail caused me to cut back up north, basically going round in a big circle before we stopped at Mojave National Preserve, and then at Kingston Range Wilderness.

Of course, under the circumstances, it wasn't all site

seeing and male bonding. By the light of the moon, I had to feed on a cage full of rabbits on a quiet estate near Palm Springs. The owner's bedroom light came on during, but no further activity occurred, for which I was quite thankful. I fed on a hitchhiker I picked up at a desolate intersection in Barstow, CA, dropping Felix off at a local diner once identifying a victim. In neither of these situations did I ask Felix for his assistance in coordination or disposal. In both, he offered it, gaining my trust at a rapid pace. His mannerisms and unchecked spasms eventually went unnoticed, and he was not only knowledgeable about seemingly every square inch of road, milestone, and renowned oddity we passed, but was also equal parts hilarious and encouraging. He kept me from feeling sorry for myself or self-pity, and added a level of humility to counterbalance my increasing strength, speed, and ambivalence to killing.

I decided that we would spend a day or two at Death Valley National Park before trying to locate the band in Tahoe, so I filled up three large containers full of gas, purchased a tent, black sheets, and portable space heater, and stocked up on snacks for Felix. I'd grown up hearing of people who get stranded and die in Death Valley, and, whether that was just an old wives' tale or not, I didn't want me or my new companion to suffer the same fate. Most of the activities there were best accomplished in the daytime, but I was still excited about the place, if based on nothing but what I'd seen on the road thus far. I was especially anxious to see the night sky out in the middle of nowhere. I'd heard that it leaves people speechless, and since darkness was to be my new best friend, I figured we should get properly acquainted. The only thing that worried me was possibly ending up starving with no one to feed on. No one but Felix.

Chapter Nineteen: Death Valley

As the first peak of dawn clawed its way through the sparse gathering of clouds over Death Valley National Park, Felix and I switched spots, him now behind the wheel, and I in the passenger seat, covered in a hoodie with a pillow between me and the window. I pretended to be asleep as we pulled up to the welcome gate, and Felix paid the $30 each for us to gain entry. I never looked at the park employee, but could tell she was tired, uninterested, and anti-social from her curt responses. We were given a map and told to enjoy ourselves. There was a hint of sarcasm in that statement, and I felt that she thought we were lovers. I never expected the enormity of this place. It was clearly larger than anywhere else I'd seen, and even though it was mostly desolate looking, I found it beautiful. Until that day, I had no idea that they had filmed parts of Star Wars there. Trying to visualize certain memories of the film, knowing that I would be coming up on those same spots, filled my heart with heaviness and happiness at the same time. It took me back to when I was a child, and momma Mona had me watch the Star Wars saga in story order, so I could marvel at how good it got instead of how bad it got. She actually didn't really know. She was just going off of what Valerie had told her. The memory was bittersweet.

We spent the first hour locating a place within the back country roads that would shield the truck as much as possible from the sun, and I unfolded the new black sheets and tacked them up hastily to form a cloth isolation booth of sorts in the passenger seat. We wound through the vehicle trails, gazing up at the rock formations around us, when Felix looked forward just in time to avoid running over a backpacker, me unaware in my shroud. He screeched to a halt, I shot forward into the glove compartment, and she threw her fists down on my hood.

"What the fuck?! Watch where you're going!"

Technically, she was the one who was supposed to watch where *she* was going. This area was designated for motorists, not pedestrians. I wasn't going to give her any trouble, though, and Felix rolled down his window and apologized.

"Sorry, my ass!" was her forgiveness, and she went on about her way. I felt bad about it, but I made a mental note that she might be someone who could satisfy my hunger tonight. I observed which way she was heading, and captured her scent in my sensory databank. It was sometime shortly after Glendale that I realized my sense of smell had not only returned, but was significantly upgraded. Instead of only sniffing blood, I could catch a whiff of perfume from a hundred yards away and locate which wrist or side of the neck its client sprayed it on. In this particular case, the almost pancaked traveler smelled of new sweat and no foul odor, indicating that she had only been on her hike for a relatively short time. She faded from view as we made one turn around the trail, and she made an opposite one.

"Haha! I know what you're thinking," Felix exclaimed, giddy from his correct deduction.

"What? What am I thinking?"

"You're thinking that, if someone has to die tonight, it didn't do her any favors acting like a rude bitch." He smiled at me, from ear to ear.

"In her defense, you almost ran her over. I would be mad, too. But, yes, and not in those same words, I was thinking that she might make a good option tonight." His smile got even wider.

"I knew it."

"Shut up," I mumbled while repositioning my sheet.

There were several places where the rock along the path was high enough that sunlight didn't penetrate all the way to the ground, but we also had to factor in pulling over and parking in a spot wide enough for other vehicles to pass us. My sleep schedule would be during the park's busiest time window, and having to move along or interact too much with the general population could prove inconvenient. We settled on a spot that resembled a large, natural courtyard. It contained a little more exposure to the sun than I wanted, but allowed plenty of room for others to go around us. Besides, I had the sheets as coverage. After having a cinnamon roll and a water for breakfast, Felix got out of the truck, stretched his legs, and decided to walk around and investigate our surroundings on foot.

"Don't let anyone run you over," I called out, and lay my head back to get some actual sleep. About an hour into my slumber, I was awakened by two sets of footsteps, roaming slowly toward the truck. I could tell one was male and one female, both wearing hiking boots. There was a knock on the window. I reached my hand carefully out of the shroud and let down my window a crack, not setting my face outside it.

"Yes?"

"Hi. Do you have any weed on you?" She sounded cute and about twenty years old. She was apparently the spokesperson for the pair.

"No. I don't smoke. Sorry. I'm just trying to get some sleep."

"Are you sure?"

"What? Of course, I'm sure. I don't smoke weed, so I wouldn't have any on me. I haven't slept because of a very long drive, and I'm just trying to get some in before I can enjoy the park." I rolled up the window and withdrew back into the curtain. The male of the two then spoke up.

"You don't have to be a dick about it." I remained silent. I didn't want a simple request to get high to escalate into something further. The young man, a little older sounding, but not much, then punched the door of my truck. It's twelve years old, and hasn't been pretty since it rolled off the lot, but it's *my* truck, and an anger boiled into rage in my belly, up my esophagus, and out of my breath and nostrils. I wanted to step out and slit his throat, but yet again, I remained silent and didn't move. Just around that time, I heard Felix coming back around from his site seeing to ask what was going on. He startled the two, who were suspicious of his look and possible reaction. After calming them and hearing their perspective of what happened, which was more or less the truth minus their description of my tone, Felix pacified the situation.

"No worries, amigo. I got a joint right here, and it's all yours. Just leave my compadre alone so he can get some shuteye. A matter of fact, here, you can have two. That still leaves me one, which is more than enough to keep me high the whole trip."

I sensed that no one had left, and then I heard the man whispering something. One of my new heightened senses was hearing, but he must have been virtually mouthing his words. I couldn't make them out. Then Felix raised his voice a little.

"Take it easy, amigo. Don't make me regret handing over two joints."

The girl then intervened, and I could hear her pulling her partner away from the truck, and then from the area. Felix opened the driver's door and hopped in.

"Man, I'm too old to be hiking and climbing and walking around this fucking desert."

"What happened at the end there with that kid?"

"Kid? He's basically your age. He has a little bit of a

hard time accepting a gift. More importantly, he has a hard time letting things go when he thinks someone's wronged him."

"He thinks I *wronged* him? He called me a dick, but he thinks *I* wronged *him*?"

"I'd say that's pretty much his deal."

"Well, what *did* he say? He got awful quiet when talking tough about me."

"Oh, it ain't nuthin'. Just something about he doesn't like being disrespected, and hoping he never runs into you cuz he doesn't know if he'll be cool. Some bullshit like that. He's probably never been in a fight where it wasn't five guys against one."

"Oh, they have that guy in Nevada, too?" I jested.

"Davis, they have that guy everywhere." Felix was convinced that the threat "weed boy" posed was harmless, but scent and direction mental notes two and three – check. The ability to analyze a person from their voice and body language installed itself almost instantly in me back at the grain mill in Abilene, and I was using it to diffuse the bad feeling I got from the couple. She was originally a very structured, by-the-book good girl who'd gone hippie free spirit yoga girl after having her universe expanded in college. Somehow, she fell for an uptight, spoiled, rich kid who used his parents' wealth as an introduction to worlds he'd never be invited into if he was me. He uses that money like his expensive cologne, too loosely, to gain influence and attention. He thinks he's the smartest, most enlightened person in the room, any room. But behind his back, most people think he's just a bitch. I intended to prod Felix a little more about weed boy's aura, but his eyes were drooping lower than a cartoon character's, and his skin looked grayer than mine. He growled at me in a low, cranky murmur, "I'm going to get some sleep, too."

We both did just that, until Felix arose late in the afternoon and heated himself up a can of chili that he spread out over a bag of Fritos. He sat his aching bones down atop a hill and ate while he watched the sun get lower and lower on the horizon. Lunch never seems so unhealthy and gross as when you literally don't need to consume it anymore. At one point, before I'd crossed over from Texas into New Mexico, I thought I might still be able to eat regular food since I appeared to still be human, just a human with a really dire infection. I was also afraid that I wouldn't be able to get Mexican food nearly as good as what I'd been spoiled on my whole life, so I grabbed a couple of street tacos late one night, and tried to force them down my throat. It didn't go well. I couldn't taste them, as in they had no taste. I stuffed one in my mouth as fast as I could, let it dribble down my throat and into my belly like slow flowing crude oil, where it sat like a rock before exploding its way back up my digestive system and all over the parking lot of a shithole of a rest stop. Like an idiot, I tried to do the same with the second one. It ended much like the first, except with the added bonus of burning diarrhea. One thing I still haven't figured out or been told is why a vampire can no longer eat solid food, or why they *can* consume alcohol and other liquids. My body still required water to survive, and I seemed to put down those stargazers in Laughlin pretty easily. No food, though. And Frito Pie, once one of my top five favorite cuisines, now felt as atrocious as it would a toddler trying Brussels sprouts for the first time. The thought of taking one bite brought back the feeling of those tacos in my Adam's Apple, where it just sat and festered. You've got to take the bad of vampirism with the good, I guess.

Sundown fell over the park, and I finally managed to get out of the truck and stretch my legs. I felt exhausted even though I had just slept, which is where water is so important to a vampire's continued existence. The underlying cause of the vampiric condition is in the substance that infiltrates and corrupts the vascular system while the victim's blood is removed, a sort of viral backwash into the veins. That corruption never seems to leave, and begins to kill the victim if they don't find replacement blood constantly. It's like cutting out a malignant stage 4 tumor that reforms within hours of its removal. While the body attempts to keep on keeping on, the impact that water normally has on the rest of the body is magnified tenfold. Dehydration is a real problem, and part of the reason most vampires can't control or compose themselves. In addition to the consistent demand for blood the infection puts on its victim, the pain and frustration are too great a stress on the body. Fuck. So I immediately down two 16oz bottles of drinking water and begin to venture out into the park on foot. The temperature has already dropped considerably in less than an hour, and my already cold frame has plummeted into a walking icicle. I'm down to about two percent body fat, which removes any remaining insulation I once had. Not that it would have helped; I'm essentially in a constant dying process.

This place is amazing. For a moment, I think of just

staying here, playing out my final days feeding on various mammals until I'm bored and ready to end it. I used my physical advantage to bound halfway up the apropos Coffin Peak exponentially quicker than a human, before finally getting winded. I could swear that my heels weren't even touching the rock as I sprinted and clawed my way upward. The exertion came at a price, though; I forced myself into a starvation I hadn't experienced since early on in my brief history as a "night drinker." I lay my back against the cool, stiff mountain and scanned the terrain silently. Another new feature my ever-changing form had graced me with was a night/heat sensing vision. I was able to visualize the heat signatures of a living creature, much like wearing night vision goggles. I remember watching *Silence of the Lambs* with Mona, and thinking that the killer's NVG's were really cool. Now I had a built-in pair. This gift was ironic, since my eyes were concurrently deteriorating. I was almost color blind, surprised I could even make out the different colors of skin and fabric in the Naked Huntress.

I was very grateful for this gift, for it allowed me to locate my dinner that night, a large four-legged animal that resembled a ram. There were seven of them, actually, so I figured even if they scattered upon noticing me, I would get at least one. One was all I needed, but two would keep me engorged until the next evening. They were approximately three hundred yards away, and about as far above me. I had to regain my energy, so I slumped down quietly against the rock and sat down, breathing deeply in and out. I kept my eye on the small herd, and they remained as still as I did, some standing. A few began to lay down, and I figured this must be their collective bed for the night. Once my hunger gained peak capacity and my lungs peak tolerance, I stood and raced upward and diagonally, with the rams locked in my sight. I was within thirty yards when they caught wind or sound of me and began to separate in multiple directions, attempting to escape whatever predator was coming near. One in particular, though, stumbled in the surprise, skidding downward in a slant. As it struggled to right its balance, I moved in ever closer. It contorted its body to get a vision of the creature climbing full speed to meet it, and once it did, gave me a kick with a hind leg, and then a full steam head butt with its battering ram of a horned head. It was out of position, though, and I grabbed it by the horns and sunk my teeth into its powerful throat. The horns were surprisingly rough and jagged, and they opened small slices all over my clinched hands. It took all of our strength and agility to remain upward and on our feet as we careened down the mountain. The ram was more adept at survival than I anticipated, and it began striking at me with its front legs. The pain was intense, and my torso felt the effects instantly, but I would not relinquish my grip on his neck. We came to a thud on a wide plateau, and my suckling stranglehold on him grew more intense. His eyes were large and protruding with fear, but his energy eventually waned, his body going limp and still. My hunger satiated, and my body wrecked with large abrasions and bruises, and possible fractured bones, it was impossible that I would be able to find and defeat another of these creatures tonight. They are after all large, muscular, violent creatures. I lay with my head on the ram's chest for all of twenty minutes, before dragging it inward away from the edge of the mountain, and placing it behind a gathering of free-standing stones. Upon returning to my truck, I found Felix sitting on its tailgate, having a beer and a joint.

"Howdy. How'd it go?" he asked sincerely.

"It went. I fed off a ram on this mountain. I'm pretty sure, judging from the map, that is was Coffin Peak."

"Ram? I don't think so, amigo. You probably fed on a desert bighorn sheep. How the hell did you pull that off? Those things are huge, and one butt from those horns should be able to destroy a human like an automobile destroying a housecat."

"I'm a vampire, I guess is the best answer I can give."

"Hot damn. You guys must be something. You're not even at full monster, yet. Just imagine what you'll be like 100 years from now."

His second sentence didn't register in my ears. I was too busy being stuck on his description of me as a monster. It hurt and angered me at the same time. "Is that what I am to you? A monster?"

"No, I didn't mean like that. It's like if you call a bigger than normal football player a monster. A man among boys, if you will. It's not a fair playing field to pit humans against vampires, especially when even the novice vampires can take down an animal that would trample over the biggest, nastiest football player like he was a schoolgirl." His explanation helped slightly, but I didn't appreciate the connotation. I would never feel comfortable being characterized or categorized as a monster. If that's all I was, there was no hope, and no reason to go on to Orange County. The House of the Black Moon be damned. In my agitated state, I brought up a topic I'd previously avoided addressing. I didn't have any such reservations at the moment.

"Felix. I've got a question for you. Who was it you knew that was able to go back to being human?"

"What's that?"

"Back in Laughlin, you said that you knew what I was going to California for, and that you knew someone who had done it."

"Oh! Oh, yeah. That's correct."

"So who was it?" Felix got a nervous, panicked look on his face, and I was starting to second guess the nature of our friendship, as well as the duration of it.

"Who *was* it?"

"Yes, that was *my* question." I walked over and picked up a small boulder, no bigger around than twenty inches, but far too heavy for a normal man my size to even fantasize picking up, and walked back over to Felix, where I pulverized it in my hands. "Who was it?" Felix gulped.

"Whoa. You don't have to go all intimidating on me, Davis. I'm just trying to remember the name is all. I'll get there. I don't have all my marbles, on account of my injuries."

"You've been able to remember every detail of every rest stop, hole in the wall, plaque on the side of the road, and national monument for hundreds of miles, as well as tell me exactly what kind of animal it was that I ate tonight. So, pretty, pretty please, who the hell do you know that became a vampire and then went back to human?" My patience, already dwindling in general, was at an all-time low.

"Donovan. Ruben Donovan. That's who." He sighed a big sigh, as if a weight had been lifted.

"Ruben Donovan? Who's that?"

"He was a musician that came through every now and then. Not bad looking, with a decent voice, but more of an oddity than a serious talent. At least, everybody knew that but him. He sang and played guitar, but to say his original songs needed work was an understatement. Now what I'm about to tell you is a combination of what I heard second or third hand from the people who were there, and then Ruben's account years later, after we'd met, so don't go taking it for gospel or anything. He had just got finished with a set at Whiskey Dick's in Laughlin, where some people had left halfway through, laughing their asses off as they exited. They made sure he knew they were laughing at him. This kind of reaction to his music had happened too frequently, and he was pissed. He believed that 1996 was going to be his year, and now it seemed like his dream was over. Crushed. He needed to let off some steam, so he went to the brand-new strip club in town, the Naked Huntress. He thought he might get laid, or get a hand job, whatever. But when he sits down at his table, he takes a look upstairs and sees the very people who laughed their way out of his set, walking into the VIP section. He takes his angry ass and marches up there, trying to get in without paying the extra, which at that time was more than it is now, because of the newness and everything."

I thought he might be adding unnecessary details to stall. I even thought it possible that he was making the entire story up, so I made sure to keep my bullshit detector on high. "Skip anything superfluous." My face was dead serious.

"Oh yeah, OK. So Ruben starts making a scene at the VIP entrance, saying he wants to talk to the sons a bitches that just went in. The security guys ain't letting it happen, but the owner, Sinjin Pierce, pops his head out of this shiny metal door by the bar, and says, "Let him through." They do, and Ruben goes in. Only, Ruben doesn't come out. Not for the rest of the night, or the next night, or even the night after that. Fast forward twelve years, and I meet him for the first time at the Naked Huntress. He's there meeting some people, and we get to talking, and he tells me his whole story. Before I know it, we're being asked to leave by the manager, and the place has been closed for half an hour."

"How?"

"How, what?"

"How did he return to being human after being a vampire? How did he become a vampire, and who made him one?"

"OK. Let me think back. The guys he was looking for, they were vampires, and one of them bit him, but was stopped before he could finish the job. Sinjin then had his people look after him. Sinjin had already developed a method for human/vampire interaction that resulted in no murder or transformation, so the Huntress was a safe haven for Ruben, even though he was highly resentful of the vampires that caused his. That group was nomadic, and came and went regularly. One night, while they were in town, Ruben decided he was going to get revenge, and kill as many of that gang as possible, but definitely the one that bit him. He waited until he'd drunk enough courage to make a move and then he made it. He walked up behind the guy while he was at the bar, and he sliced his head off with a samurai sword. The whole bar jumped back, frightened and bewildered, and the place went nuts. As soon as the vampire was dead, a swirling tornado of light and wind enveloped Ruben right in the middle of the bar, lifting him up in the air. When it placed him back down like a baby on a pillow, he was human again."

"Who told you this story?"

"The part about him killing the vampire and turning human, that came from Ruben himself."

"And you believed him?"

"Well, yeah, sure. Why not believe it? He was back to being human."

"And you know he was a vampire?"

"Well, I never... I didn't know him until after he was human again. He was human before I came back from Iraq... Why wouldn't you believe him?"

"It's just that it sounds like complete and utter bullshit. Just hearing *you* tell the story makes me want to slice you into little pieces."

"Well, I don't have any reason not to believe that's how it went down. He ended up being a regular at the Huntress. If he was a liar, especially about something like that, I don't think the vampires would have taken too kind to him."

"And you don't think they would have felt a little negatively about him cutting another one's head off in front of a whole bar full of humans and vampires?"

"Uhhh."

"I would really love to talk to him. Where does he live?"

"Well. That would be a slight problem. He died about five or six years ago. Throat cancer."

"Cancer?"

"Yes, sir. It had spread all over by the time it got him."

"If he was your friend, I'm sorry to hear that."

"He was, I guess."

"Is there anyone, anywhere, at all, that can corroborate his story?"

"I reckon there might be, but I would need to think about it."

"Well, why don't you hand me one of those Miller Lites while you think about it?"

I tried to stomach down the beer in front of Felix, who was surprised that I asked him for one. After I had calmed down, I tried to look and act more like a regular guy, as to remove the “monster” image from Felix’s mind. I didn’t want him associating me with anything but a road buddy. I didn’t need a fan or a groupie; nor did I want him in constant fear of me. He certainly didn’t fit the bill of a biographer. But I shouldn’t have been so naïve to think that we were anything close to peers. He was human and I was vampire. There would be a line of demarcation forever between us, between me and anyone. After another half hour of drinking and listening to the sounds of the night, Felix climbed in the bed of the truck and tried to sleep there. I already knew that it was too cold for him to be comfortable, but to each his own. I walked off a ways and stood staring up at the night sky. The stars that lit up the night were magical. So many, even more than I was used to seeing back home. As I began to head back to the truck, I thought I caught something reflecting in the distance. I focused a little more, and detected the heat signatures of three people running. They scurried behind a hill and disappeared. I didn’t know what they were doing or running from, and I was too tired and full to think about feeding on one of them. I chose to give them peace instead of horror.

It's funny how that decision came back around on me.

Chapter Twenty: Death Valley... Literally

About two hours after dawn, I woke to find the assorted sounds of birds, nature, and scattered humans enjoying a vacation or a day trip proceeding with their day. My plan was to leave sometime today, but realized it would have to be after dark, and after I fed, before we could get back on the road. If only Felix could hunt something and bring it back to me, I could feed before nightfall. Unfortunately, that was not an option.

I struggled with the story of Ruben Donovan all night. I dreamt that I ran into him at Sinjin Pierce's Ham Steak in Bakersfield, interrogated him about his supposed vampire/human breakthrough, convinced him to confess his lie, and then set him on fire while people ran from the club in fear for their lives. The dream ended with me having a seat at the bar, watching him burn until he evaporated and starting floating upward. Once he got to the ceiling of the establishment, he was forced downward and his vaporized remains descended to Hell like he was being flushed down a toilet. I told myself that if I can, I'm going to talk to someone about Ruben Donovan and find out all I can. If he's even a real person, but his story was bullshit, then there's no use in wasting time and energy on trying to kill Devin. The only reason I would have is revenge, and revenge for revenge's sake seemed pretty petty at the moment. I mean, shit happens. At the same time, though, she tried to kill me, and by afflicting me like this, she basically still did. So why not get a measure of eye-for-an-eye vengeance for her wanton carelessness?

Felix was not around when I came to. I remember him hopping out of the truck bed and into the cab sometime after I'd closed my eyes. I could sense that things might be a little silent between us for a bit. True to my forecast, we didn't speak much when he returned from exploring. We just communicated with looks and grunts, him outside of the vehicle, and me safely in. An evening removed from a tense exchange, for which I was mostly responsible, I'd had a little time and perspective to dwell upon, and realized a few things. 1) The guy who looked like a creepy mute had become a welcome change of pace on this trip, and opened himself to reveal an intelligent, humorous road trip companion who didn't appear to judge me. Not even in the least. 2) Just by being around me, he was putting himself in potential danger, and he'd come along anyway. In hindsight, I felt like a dick for the display with the boulder. It was an unfair threat. I just hope to God he's not intentionally lying about Ruben Donovan. Internally, I can feel myself caring less and less about the humans around me and what I must do to them to stay alive. I would hate for my anger to make Felix an unfortunate casualty of that lack of regard.

As dusk settled upon the sky, I got out of the truck

earlier than one would wisely suggest, wanting to clear the air as soon as possible. Felix had spent the afternoon hunting squirrels and was cooking up one for his dinner. I must have made a disgusted face, because he laughed out loud when he saw me.

"No, it *doesn't* taste like chicken, if that's what you've heard. I can't say that I would choose blood over it, though."

"Neither would I, if actually given a choice."

"Touche." We both burst into laughter. The interlude provided exactly the ice breaker I needed to speak to Felix about more important matters. It would end up being a shorter conversation than I anticipated.

"Hey, man. I want to apologize for last night. I shouldn't have—"

"No need. Really. It was a misunderstanding because something I said came out wrong. And you're perfectly within your rights to ask about the Ruben thing. That's what got you to let me tag along, right?"

"Still. I don't want you to be constantly worrying about me doing something like that again. You've been a pleasant positive on this trip since Laughlin. The *only* positive. I appreciate it."

"Thank you."

I accompanied Felix as he ate his meal, and we sat around a fire trading stories from our respective pasts. His life as a war-time soldier was safer than most because of his specialty, but ultimately not safe enough to shield him from irrevocable damage. I believe the mental damage might have been more impactful, though, and it seemed he didn't realize it until he was faced with speaking to someone about it in confidence. When recounting the story from his injury in Iraq, he froze, hands shaking frenetically, and started to tear up. Afterward, though, it was as if a peaceful, warm exhalation of energy moved through and out of him, and he sat at ease, a grateful grin on his face. This night was the first I'd really opened up about Annie. I gave all; my first impression of her, the first time I knew I had real feelings for her, the confession of fantasizing about her when I masturbated. Everything. He tried to envision every possible scenario that could lead to us being together, in a normal, romantic relationship. He also asked what the hell she saw in me to begin with, provoking another bout of laughter from the two of us. As the night wore on, though, my hunger arrived, and I had to bid Felix farewell, so I could satisfy it.

With true darkness now covering me, I sprinted off into the night, bound for Desolation Canyon. The name reminded me of the Unholy Saint title, *Desolation Merry Go Round*, so I figured *Why not?* I arrived at its mouth fairly quickly, surprising myself. My speed had picked up significantly, and I felt as if my feet were coming off the ground as I ran. I decided I was going to try and have Felix time me soon. I could have just stood pat and assessed the available prey with my heat sensing, but I wanted to get some exercise and purge some pent-up energy from my system. Now that I was in my desired area for the night, I poked around quietly, looking for a vantage point by which to observe and strike. I found an ideal perch that would hide me from any human or animal below, but allow me to duck behind a hump and jet out for a peak at anything coming through the canyon. I sat in that spot for over an hour before hearing any sound at all. Unfortunately, that sound was emitting from a rodent or mammal far too small to waste my time on. I let it scurry past uninterrupted and continued to wait. Another hour would go by before the sound of human footsteps caught my attention. The person's scent filled my nostrils, and it was familiar; the girl who'd asked me for the weed the day before. I should have felt bad, but I didn't. However, I knew she wasn't alone, so I delayed in making any advance. Sure enough, I heard and smelled her partner, coming up behind her.

"Morgan, do you see anybody?"

"Not a soul."

"We saw something head this way, and I'm pretty sure it was on two legs." *How did they see me, and what were they looking for?*

"Yes, but there's nothing here now."

I waited until the young man had caught up to his partner, and then I flung myself over the hump in the rock I'd been hiding behind and sailed down to the ground below, landing on both feet, facing the startled couple.

"What the fuck?! How the fuck did you do that without breaking your heels or ankles?"

"That's not really what you should be worried about, right now."

The girl shifted her head to the side, detecting something familiar. "That's the guy from the truck."

"Oooh. That's too bad for you, bro. I was hoping I would run into you."

"Oh, really. Have you been keeping tabs on me and my buddy?"

"You mean your homosexual life partner?" His voice hinted of a less than intelligent person who thought he was intellectually superior to those around him.

"Very clever." I focused on the girl. "Morgan, right? That's what he called you? You might want to talk some sense into him. His fate is sealed, regardless, but the brutality of his destiny can be amended, if he keeps his mouth shut or his demeanor respectful."

"What are you talking about? And Fletcher, please don't do this. We're just supposed to be enjoying ourselves. You promised you guys wouldn't do anything stupid, and you've already broken that."

You guys? There were more of them somewhere. Coincidentally, as I had that thought, I heard four more sets of steps running into the scene behind Fletcher, as he was now known. Felix was right, five against one was his preferred method of combat.

"Morgan, he disrespected me, and you know how I can't take that."

"My God, Fletcher! Grow up! Learn to let things go. He didn't have any weed. So what?"

I took an inventory of his buddies. He was clearly the alpha in the brains department, and most likely the guy bankrolling their little trip into the desert, but he wasn't the most physically imposing. That distinction belonged to a tall, muscular guy around the same age whose body resembled a swimmer's. The other three guys looked comparably harmless. They were all about my age or older, so I'm thinking that they've been friends since before college, or became really close in college and graduated together. The girl, Morgan, she was younger than all of them, so I don't know where they met. I just know that she could have done better. The alternative to Fletcher is that she would have lived past her twentieth birthday. The reality is that she won't.

"This won't take long, and I promise we won't hurt him too bad." He was clearly confident in the outcome, given the odds.

Before he had even finished uttering his sentence, I was already speeding past him, right for the muscular swimmer guy. Out of the corner of my eye, I saw him flinch and put his hands up like a frightened child or someone having a gun pulled on them during a theft. I left my feet about eight feet from the big guy, and extended my arm in an open palm strike to the guy's face. I drove his nose back up into his head, and kept my hand gripped across his face, slamming it into the ground as if I was doing so to a basketball. There was no need; he was dead basically as soon as I'd struck his face. I then immediately grabbed the next nearest guy, lifting him upside down by an ankle. I held him there for a split second before kicking him in the face, turning it into a bloody dough. I dropped him onto his head as another one of the group bear hugged me from behind. I jerked back with the rear of my head, catching him in the trapezius area. It was enough to break his hold, but didn't kill or damage him. Now he and the fifth idiot were both squared up and facing me while Fletcher finally decided it was safe to start moving toward the fight. I lunged quickly and held both guys in a front head lock, dropping my weight on them while they tried to push me forward. I dug in tight on one of them, choking off his oxygen. I could feel his face warm and bloat with red before I crushed his windpipe and vertebrae in my forearm. I let him go, and eased up on my headlock to the other, allowing him to stand face to face with me. I then held him with one hand and elbowed him repeatedly in the head and face with the other. He dropped to one knee, and I stopped to look at him. His eyes rolled back in his lids, and then closed, him falling face first in a growing pool of blood. The entire time, Morgan hadn't moved more than a foot, and Fletcher had taken his time, never reaching arm's length. He watched his friends die instead of attempting to assist or save them. He was a coward, and he was going to suffer a cruel consequence for conducting himself like one.

I walked toward Fletcher with disrespect and no fear of threat in my mind. He started to backstep franticly, so I dropped my arms to my side to induce him to act. He threw a weak left jab, and then a wild, uncertain right hook. I shrugged off both easily. As he continued to move backward, Morgan inched closer to one of the guys, realizing for the first time that he was dead and not just unconscious. She shined her phone's flashlight on him, revealing the caved-in bruise that was once a face. I could hear her tremble and squeal as I kept blocking Fletcher's stupid punches. I finally had enough toying with him and grabbed him by the shirt, hip tossing him to the unforgiving earth below. His hip and knee touched first, and he yelled out in pain. Morgan turned to face the sound, and her fear had her weeping uncontrollably. Her tears now squeezing her eyes together almost shut, she thought on one hand to try and flee, and on the other to be there for the man she loved. So, she stood… And waited.

"Get up," I sneered to Fletcher, dismissively.

"Pppleeease, man. Please don't hurt me. Us. Don't hurt us… please."

"Oh, don't hurt you? What happened to you hurting me?"

"I didn't mean it. I was just messing around."

"Oh. I just misunderstood. Everything's good then."

"Really? Are you serious?" His expression momentarily broke in slight relief.

"You dipshit." Fletcher's head dropped to his chest, and his shoulders shrunk, while Morgan lifted her hands to get our attention, almost like she was in elementary school.

"I told you y'all shouldn't have messed with the old man." *What?*

"What old man?"

"The guy that was with you. The one that gave us the joints." I turned to Fletcher.

"What did you do to him?"

"We just roughed him up a little."

Morgan knew how negatively their situation had

been altered, and had done an about face on Fletcher. "They beat the shit out of him! They broke his leg, and probably his ribs."

My insides boiled over with blind madness, and my eyes must have looked straight white, like some illustrated demon. The time to end this had come, so I could get back to Felix and attend to him. I grabbed Fletcher by the back of his shirt, yanked him backward onto his back, and stood on the center of his chest. He looked up at me, terror in his eyes, my heel pressing and digging into him.

"Morgan, come here." I was firm, and all humor had exited my voice. I wanted to make sure she knew this was a command, not a request.

"Please don't hurt me. Did you kill… Did you kill all of them?"

"Yes. Yes, I did. Come here."

She shuffled her feet forward, with her head pointed downward, clutching her hands together, intertwining her fingers. "Please."

"Stop. Just… stop." I gently placed my hand out to take hers, and she limply complied with her left. I took it slowly, and then jerked her close, and gripped a handful of blond, light hair. She screamed, and folded, her legs giving way under her. I stared down at Fletcher, prepared to dispense my verdict. 'Young man, I don't know you, but I can *feel* what a shitty person you are. I can hear it in your voice. With nothing but a short interaction on a lazy, carefree morning, I was able to deduce that you're one of the most selfish, manipulative, unsatisfied pieces of shit I've ever met. You actually don't deserve Morgan, and she sure as shit didn't deserve this'. Hearing that last part made her cry out and shiver again. 'So what's going to happen here is I'm going to make you watch me kill Morgan, so you can know and experience what I'm going to do to you."

"Pleasepleasepleasepleaseplease. Don't. Don't. Please don't do this to me. Please don't kill me. Please don't kill me."

"Morgan. It's ok. It won't take long, and I'll be as gentle as I can."

"No, I'm not ready to---"

I jammed my head down on Morgan's neck, stopping before contact, and then slowly latched my open mouth on the base of her neck and shoulder. I bit down strong, and she gasped, then shrieked, caught completely unaware. Her blood was the sweetest, purest sample I'd ever tasted to that point, and I worked hard and methodically not to waste any. Fletcher was horrified, and he started slapping, punching, and pushing at my leg. I couldn't believe how miserable and hollow his strikes were. They didn't feel like a person fighting for his life with all his remaining strength. They felt like a schoolgirl slapping at a silverback gorilla. Morgan grabbed each of my arms and held onto them. Her simultaneous grip was at first rigid, but then relaxed, as she was encountering the solace of impending death. I could hear her breath start to studder and spit as the final ones attempted to escape. I bit down further and sucked hard to complete the process, then I placed her down delicately on the ground next to Fletcher. Her eyes remained open, and I instructed him to look at her.

"Look into her eyes, Fletcher. Look at what your actions did." He started to weep. 'Your turn. I don't have any sympathy for you, and I won't be as fragile with you as I was with her."

"No. No. Nononononono." I clutched his styled, pretentious hair and jerked him up on his ass. He sat, helpless and slumped over, gasping for breath. I then knelt down, wrapped my arms around him, and tore into his neck like a rabid lioness in Africa. He held his arms out wide. I couldn't tell if he was praying or trying not to get blood on his sleeves. He screamed and cried and groaned, which caused me to bite with even more ferocity. My hunger had been alleviated by Morgan, but my rage was being quelled by violence. I braced my left hand on Fletcher's shoulder and cranked his head to the side with my right as I bit and fed and drank. I got more of his blood on my face and his clothes than in my mouth. The sinewy tissue of his flesh started to stretch and flay, and before I knew it, I'd ripped his head from his body. Tossing it to the ground triumphantly *and* regretfully, I stood and raised my arms to my side like a posing body builder or a conquering gladiator from Roman times. Part of that vulnerable pose was maybe me asking God for forgiveness. I threw my head back and stared into the cloudy, wind-soaked night. I knew that a milestone in my transformation had been complete. Felix was correct; I *was* a monster.

Felix! I'd forgotten what predicament he might be in. *How could I have taken so long?* I had to wait just a second and take in some air before I could sprint back, but sprint is exactly what I did. As I plowed through the ground with focused legs and heavy feet, my speed picked up and picked up, and accompanied by the wind, the balls of my toes did come off the ground. Instinctually, I increased my speed to its limit, lifted my feet off the ground, and... flew. I flew. Well, actually, I was *carried*. The wind aided me along as I floated through the air. When I got too close to the ground or a flurry weakened, my feet hit again, and I ran. As the wind picked back up, so did I, soaring through the air like someone in a Las Vegas Cirque de Soleil show. It was glorious. I wanted the feeling to never end. *This must be where the flying vampire myth comes from*, I thought. I was back at the truck in no time. Felix laid there on the ground next to the bed of my Ford, his head resting against the rear passenger tire.

"Felix, are you alright? What happened?"

He looked up at me, confused. Not all there.

"Oh. Hey. I'm alive. Would you look at that?"

"What happened?"

"That kid from yesterday. Him and his friends ran into me while I was taking a piss. I thought we were getting along fine, but then he---" Felix reached for his ribs. I think Morgan was right about them breaking. "He started getting all smartass, and I don't really go for smartass. So maybe I mouthed off a little bit, and as I walked back up to the truck, one of those little fuckers hit me from behind. And then they all started stomping on me. The one kid, Fletcher; his girlfriend was screaming and shrieking at them to stop, but he picked me up and propped me against the hood of the truck, and swung an aluminum bat on my ribs. He then swung it on my knee a few times. I really wish we'd brought that damn wheelchair."

I tried to lift Felix as gradually and softly as I could, cupped him up in my arms like he was my blushing bride, and laid him onto the bed of the truck. Looking over the damage they'd caused to an outnumbered, basically disabled veteran refueled my extinguished rage yet again, and the guilt I felt for not being there to defend him gnawed at my belly something fierce. Felix must have sensed this.

"Don't feel guilty about this, amigo. You were on the hunt. You had no idea what was gonna happen. Hell, who knew that kid was going to still be sore, and have four friends with him?"

"You did! And so did I."

"Well, if you hadn't fed already, I would have a few suggestions about who you might go after. I can't see too well, but that does look like blood all over your shirt. Smells like it, too."

"It was them."

"*Them* them? *All* of them?"

"Yup."

"Even her? Even the girl?"

"Yup."

"I'll be. Welp, that's the game. That's the cost of doing business."

"Spoken like a true player of the game. Spoken like a soldier."

"I don't feel good about the girl dying, but tell me you made that fucker pay at least a little bit."

"I'm not going to go into details, but yes, I made him severely regret his actions, and gave him just a small moment to ponder those decisions."

"Very diplomatic, your choice of words. You saved him for last, didn't you?"

"I didn't have to. His punk ass stepped back and watched all his friends get butchered right in front of him. He didn't even try to protect Morgan."

"Shit. You know her name? That's a damn shame a girl as cute as her had to get mixed up with a jerkoff like him."

"Yup." I paused for a moment, staring down at the ground, zoned out completely, replaying my respective interactions with her. It *was* a damn shame. However, there was no choice. She couldn't be spared. Doing so would have just made her a witness. And to be perfectly honest with myself, if she had been someone else, or even alone in the canyon without Fletcher, she would have been my prey. Her death was inevitable, either as a means to my survival, or as the prop exhibit for my vengeance. If I had to shake myself free of virtually any remorse, Felix was already way ahead of me.

"I said, don't feel guilty. She had to go by way of association. Sometimes, you pick the wrong guy, he does you dirty, and then you hopefully learn your lesson and move on. In this case, picking the wrong guy provided a permanent lesson. And *we* move on."

"I know you're right, and that's not ultimately what I'm hung up about. I'm conflicted because I'm trying to *manufacture* a greater guilt and sympathy than I have. I don't care even half as much about her fate as I would have last week, and last week I cared less than half as much as the week before. There's a line between light and darkness in all of us, and less than a month ago, when I was just some loser kid in Abilene, I think mine used to be about ninety percent on the light side. Now, it's about seventy to eighty percent the other way. When you literally have to kill to live, I guess that's also the cost of doing business… But enough about that; we need to get you to a doctor, and fast."

"Oh, no. Don't think you're leaving me here in a desert medical office and heading to the coast, only for the locals to find six dead bodies they can question me about. I'm coming with you, and we can just hole me up in some $40 motel to lick my wounds while you do what you need to do with that band. Bones'll heal. I can heal. Don't leave me behind, brother."

I stretched my shirt out in front of me to get a long, hard look at the rusty, crimson result of a site seeing detour. *This* was to be the result of any and all site seeing detours in my future? It didn't seem worth it to cause so much death. So much anguish for the families that will be contacted about their babies' violent endings, most likely via a phone call. Until I was done with my collision course with Unholy Saint, one way or another, one location or another, there would be no more left turns or out of the way rest stops. What good were they to me anyway? I'd never be able to just drive somewhere, stop, and hop out to enjoy nature, or life, in the middle of the day. I had no life. The only things I had in this world were a goal and Felix. I guess taking him would be better than not taking him.

"Alright. I'll get you out of here, and we'll head on to the west coast. Forget Lake Tahoe. I don't want to stop for anything but sleep or food until we set up a home base near the House of the Black Moon. We should be able to get there before sunrise. Worst case scenario, if we do need to make a stop or two, you take the wheel for a little bit at dawn. Their place is actually in Newport Beach by a place aptly called Castaways Park. I found an abandoned retirement home not far from there online. It's currently being used as a homeless squatting spot when the cops aren't clearing everyone out. I think we set up shop there. I can assess my approach, and settle upon a course of action. Let's – Felix? *Felix!*"

I thought he was dead. But he opened his eyes, startled.

"What?! What the fuck?!"

He'd passed out, and hadn't heard hardly anything I'd just said. And then he went back to sleep. I gathered him up and safely eased him into the passenger seat of the truck. There was no way in hell he could take the wheel and drive, even a little bit. He was messed up. I started the engine, and slowly pulled away from Death Valley National Park, stopping on a hill to gaze upon the vast dark beauty of it all, one more time.

Orange County, here I come.

Part III:

What Can Never Be

Chapter Twenty-One: Loss

California is just like Texas. Except for all the differences. I imagine that the suburbs of Dallas have to look almost exactly like this. Crowded. Congested. Busy. Schools, fast food, and shiny glass office buildings built up all around like an impenetrable fortress of humanity. There are even lots of Mexican restaurants. The differences, I think, must be the design of the architecture, the feel of the weather, the types of trees, and the ethnic majority. Both locales are very diverse, for sure, but the overwhelming majority here appears to be Latino. Back home, they're commonly referred to as Mexican or Hispanic, but here there is a more complex, more diverse melting pot of associated backgrounds. I could tell that just from the hour I'd spent entering and driving around Orange County, California. I thought I would have time on my hands to coast along the highways, but the sun rises early here, even though I've been led to believe it's basically the last place on earth the sun rises. I have to get us to that abandoned retirement home as soon as possible, and get Felix and myself to a safe spot in it. I've fed enough that I'm content to shake off any hunger withdrawals and wait out the sun until nightfall. I'm more concerned with Felix not being able to defend either one of us while I sleep. In a flop house, he's an easy target if anyone senses that he has anything they want. Lucky for him, and me, he really doesn't have shit.

As observed online, the "Horizon Vista Retirement Community" consists of four buildings and a total of 320 residences. There are four different floorplans, depending on the resident's, or resident's family's, ability to pay. This place went belly up when concerned children of residents reported various types of abuse, abnormal mortality rates, and in four cases, missing elderly. The missing were never found, the abuse was proven to be true, and half of the dead displayed signs of foul play. In almost every mortality case, the victim had been drained almost completely of blood. It shuttered its doors, and the head of the facility escaped to Costa Rica with several hundred thousand dollars of the residents' money. He was found in a beautiful villa along the beach, crucified and drained almost completely of blood. A peculiar coincidence? I think not. In fact, my theory upon reading about this facility is that the dead and missing almost certainly had something to do with the retirement home's proximity to the House of the Black Moon, especially the victims' lack of blood. Of the three articles I'd found online, only one of seemed to uncover that the ownership of the business was a network of shell companies, and that the person ultimately responsible could not be identified, much less located. As such, they remain the owner of the property and land, and refuse to sell or demolish the buildings.

A little after 6:30 in the morning, after dropping Felix off at the entrance and parking the truck further down the road, near the park, I broke a padlocked chain locking the front door and entered the lobby as quietly as I can. I swiped a wheelchair from a 24-hour emergency clinic in the middle of the night, and I've got Felix securely in it, to move him with as little pain to his broken bones as possible. Going over the threshold of each door in the main building caused him some discomfort, but so far, he's been a real trooper. I can hear sounds, but see only one drugged out vagrant on the floor of a long hallway that houses many rooms. They obviously get in and out as they please, the padlock worthless. This main building was for single room tenants, the poor paying folk. It also appears to be where the sick and helpless were located. Felix needs to use the restroom, so I locate the men's room and use his chair to open the door. We're both immediately pummeled by the ham, sweat, and chocolate smell of ass, our nostrils obliterated like an upper cut from Mike Tyson circa 1986. Even worse is the rotting weeks', months', and years' old stench of urine, pissed in urinals and toilets whose maintenance has been long neglected. There's one man standing at a urinal, his forehead against the wall, pants still zipped up. He's not moving at all, then I realize he's simply pissing his pants. I can hear another in a toilet stall, mumbling to himself. I don't know why, but I investigate. I think I want to know the fellow clientele I'm dealing with. I take a peak between the door and the wall, and I see a short, plump, wild-haired gremlin of a man, using the toilet seat as a lounge chair, injecting something into his arm. That's all I need to see, and Felix and I wheel on out of the men's room.

I need to find somewhere safe for Felix to recover

and me to sleep, so we exit the main building, and I leave him in the courtyard, cover myself completely with an oversized, hooded parka I swiped outside a dollar store, and begin to search the other three buildings. Luckily, the sky is rather overcast, so the sun would be unable to touch my skin regardless, but the parka is added protection. I hear it never rains here, but the sky would tell you otherwise. It apparently enjoys teasing. I skip the two nearest buildings and make a line directly for the one in the back. This must be where the fancy, apartment style units are, as they're large, single standing structures. I get to the porch of one of them, and am met by a tall, skinny fellow smoking a cigarette.

"Nah, bruh. Members only," he laughed. I can hear other people inside the unit laughing at the hopeful comedian's joke. "You have to carve out a spot in building #2. This section's all filled up."

"Is that so?"

"That's what I said." He tossed his cigarette to the ground and stared me down, trying to impose his dominance. I flipped off my hood and matched his stare with serious, dead eyes, causing him to relent in the rigidness of his stance. Much more polite, he clarified his statement. "Really, there's no room here. Everyone covets the big units, and we're all packed in." His eyes now seemed to be a little worried. I know I don't look *that* tough.

"No problem. I'll check out building 2." I turned and headed back whence I came, and I could hear him speak into the window of the unit. He lowered his volume considerably, but my ears are very adept now.

"Yo, he's one of them. I could tell." *One of whom? Does he know about vampires? Could he tell just by looking at me that I am one?* Interesting.

I took Felix's reins and backed my way into Horizon Vista Building 2, dubbed on the entrance "Sunset Lagoon," whatever that means. This building looked very similar to the main one, but with larger units inside, instead of the prison looking, one-room paradise some endured. Many more people in here than in the main building, but almost none of them in sight. More like rats scurrying in walls and attics, you can hear their clothing and jerky movements scratching on surfaces. Muffled arguments behind closed doors, a few stifled grunts and moans of sex. I pushed Felix up and down the halls, peering first into open doors, finding years of past squatters' belongings piled and decaying. Old beer cans, old junkie paraphernalia, sweatshirts, socks, shit-stained underwear, etc. etc. Twin size mattresses with all sorts of undecipherable stains soaked through to the floor. Stripped sheetrock unveiling the pipes and studs beneath. These doors were open because no one, not even homeless drug addicts, found them livable. Debating whether or not to open closed doors, I first used that honed hearing to eliminate the rooms clearly containing a living person inside. I found one that was dead silent, and slowly opened the door. On the floor of the "living room" were three mattresses, and three people sound asleep. I quickly moved on to the next one, finding two people on a blue sofa, nodded off with their heads hanging at a ninety-degree angle. Eight more rooms, eight similar scenarios. As I got to the end of one hall, I came to the door nearest the back exit, and found it locked. I gave it a harder try, just to make sure it wasn't stuck, and then forced it open with a short blast from my forearm. In the corner of the room, aiming a pistol at me, was an elementary aged boy.

"What the fuck are you doing, fucking up my door? Are you trying to jack me?" the boy exclaimed, with some semblance of authority in his voice. 'I don't play that shit, homie. I'll put a hole right through you." He was far less grubby than anyone else here, and he had the softest cheeks and most beautiful eyes. He was a little kid, and he was threatening to shoot me in a drug den.

"Whoa, whoa. I'm not trying to jack you. I don't even know who you are. I'm just trying to find a room where me and my friend can chill for a while."

"Well this ain't the room. You don't even knock. If the door's closed, someone's in it. If it's locked, stay your ass outside. What the fuck is that accent? Are you from Texas or some shit?"

"Yes, actually. I *am* from Texas."

"Ain't that some shit. The stereotype is strong with you, homie."

"What are you doing here? Shouldn't you be in school?"

"School? Man, I haven't been enrolled in school since the second week of first grade. I'm a working man, now. What you need?"

"Need?"

"Yeah, man. I got anything and everything. If I don't

got it, I can get it by tonight." It finally clicked in my naïve head.

"Ohhh. No, I don't need anything. Like I said, I was just looking for a place to crash."

"Well you don't pay when you check out at this luxury resort. I need money upfront."

"Do you, now?" I couldn't believe I was negotiating rent at a drug house with a child.

"I do."

"Nah, I don't think so." As the little guy furrowed his brow and started to debate me, I grabbed a steel rod that had been sitting randomly on the floor, and bent it like it was as soft as a spaghetti noodle, causing the boy to jump backward and cower in the corner.

"Yo, man! What the fuck?! Daniel said he wasn't going to mess with me. He said you guys were going to leave me alone." It was obvious he was frightened, and that he knew what I was from my display of power.

"Daniel *Sepulveda*?" I asked.

"Yeah, man. The singer. He said y'all were going to leave me alone."

"Y'all. That's a southern term."

"Is this the north? Everybody uses 'y'all' now. It don't belong to your Texas ass."

"Fair enough. Why would Daniel Sepulveda be "messing" with you? You're just a kid."

"Not here, I'm not. I'm either helping or I leave, or I'm dead. I was helping by moving product and making money for the night people. But Daniel took over being the liaison between them and us, and things got sideways. That bitch is crazy, and he's sadistic. My partner Jose tried talking to Alister, to ask him to go back to the way things were. Jose got eaten by five people right in front of us. Then I took Jose's spot as the connection here in the retirement home. Daniel will send one of his followers here every now and then to fuck with me. They're always threatening to do me like Jose."

"Why would Daniel or the group even be involved with this place?"

"Dude, they took over this place. *Before* it became a drug house. It's just another source of income, or food. They're not rock stars yet, and real-world shit costs money. And they got a lot more mouths to feed than just the band. Their church is hundreds, maybe thousands, now."

"Their church?"

"That's what I call it. You could call it a gang, or a cult, or an army by now, shit."

"Are all these "night people" at the House of the Black Moon?"

"I'm not allowed to say that name. Don't you know this? Aren't you one of Daniel's bitc---, people?" He immediately stood at attention as if he'd overstepped his boundaries.

"No, I'm not. Just the opposite."

"Either way, you're one of them, so I'm going to ask you not to eat me. What are you even doing awake right now? And why aren't you at Building 3?"

"Should I be?"

"That's where your kind stay. The ones that ain't at the... you know. The place you said."

"I think I'll just stay here."

"Whatever. Just don't eat me. There's a gathering of night people in building 3 later tonight. You should probably go to that."

"We'll see... Hey, kid. What's your name?"

"Business. The customers call me Business."

"What's your real name?" The kid looked inward to himself. I think it's the first time in a long time someone's asked him that.

"Ben. My name's Ben."

"Nice to meet you, Ben. I'm not going to eat you. Ben what?"

"We don't have to get into all that. If you see me around people, just call me Business."

"Alright, Ben. I'm going to find a place to sleep."

"Remember, open doors are available. Closed doors are occupied."

I wheeled Felix back through all the open doors, and we tried to agree on which one was the least disease and filth ridden. I was fading fast, and needed at least a few hours of deep sleep. We found a room with two mattresses, and I turned them over, hoping to find a cleaner surface. We'd found that they'd already been turned over and we'd *been* on the cleanest surface. I could tell that Felix was less bothered by any of this, as he'd not only seen warfare in a foreign country, but was probably staying in similar accommodations in Laughlin. I was the one who had a harder time with it. The abandoned grain mill back home was a palace compared to this place. I laid down uncomfortably but drowsily, and closed my eyes. For a few minutes, I thought about my interaction with Ben and the gathering he spoke of happening tonight. I planned on attending, and started to think about my entrance. Then I passed out. When I opened my eyes again, it was dark outside, and Felix was still asleep. Alive, though, as his loud, rambunctious snores announced with pride. I walked back to the truck to find it still there, and untampered with. I drove until I found a Weinerschnitzel, and bought Felix his dinner for the night. Upon returning, I parked in a different spot in the same parking lot, so it didn't stand out as so suspicious. I got back to our wonderful resort room to find Felix just now grumbling awake. I plied him with Tylenol and chili cheese dogs, and left him to his thoughts, going into more detail about the kid and the gathering I was about to head off towards.

"Be careful, Davis. You have no idea what you're walking into."

"No worries. I'll be fine. If things look like a problem, I'll abort."

"Please do. I've now seen what a vampire can do to a man. And I can imagine what multiple vampires can do to one."

"Like I said, if there's a problem, I'll abort."

I closed our door behind me, saying a prayer to myself for Felix to be unbothered in my absence. I took a small stroll through Building 2 and noticed that the people were emerging from their closed doors. They gravitated into small groups, chit chatting in the main hall, or smoking cigarettes together in a circle. Most of the inhabitants, though, formed a line outside Ben's door. A bulky, tatted up Mexican bodyguard who resembled a biker from a movie ushered them in and out efficiently, keeping the peace and the line moving. I decided it was time to visit building 3, and chills ran up my legs, through my torso, and out my arms. I couldn't believe it, but that chill was fear. I was afraid of what I was about to step into. After encountering my peers in Sinjin's clubs and vanquishing my opponents in Death Valley, I thought I'd left real fear behind, but the thought of being trapped in an enclosed structure with a gang of potentially antagonistic vampires made me realize how stupid and insignificant as an individual I was. They could tear me apart in seconds if they wanted to. I tried to keep my cool, and slowed my breathing as I entered the building's entrance. I was stopped by a large doorman with a blacklight wand, which surprised me. He scanned my arms, neck, and head, and began to wave me in.

"Can't you smell if I'm vampire or not, from about a football field away?"

"Not that it's any of your business, but no, my sense of smell is gone. I got my face crushed in, and it's just now looking somewhat normal. But this light is not to tell if you're a vampire or not. That was understood just by you walking up. It's to see your blood and confirm if it's clean or corrupted."

"Corrupted? Isn't every vampire's blood corrupted."

"Not like that. This light can detect HIV, cancer, and several other things."

"Is HIV in vampires an actual thing? I mean, we're already basically dead, and even normal people live with HIV like it's nothing nowadays."

"HIV in vampires kills them. Drinking infected blood doesn't replenish a vampire. They keep hungering and decomposing, but now with a new virus inside them. The proximity to this place provides a lot of potentially infected blood on the menu. You must not be from here, or you'd know the process. What's with the accent, and the belt buckle? Are you from Texas, or something?" *Jesus, not again. Do I have a sign on my chest?*

"YES! Yes, I'm from Texas. Thank you for noticing." I entered with a smirk on my face and a chip on my shoulder.

Building 3 consisted of a large lobby, a clubhouse of sorts, and connected single-story apartments. This gathering was in the clubhouse, and was only attended by about two dozen vampires. I immediately felt a little more comfortable. In my mind, there would be over a hundred. Not that I could survive two dozen on one. They all looked different, but also very California at the same time. One was a drag queen, which I'd never seen in person before, and took a little getting used to. Some were dressed very fashionably, and some had different colored hair. They all stood in a circle, waiting for the leader to start the meeting. After a few minutes, that leader revealed himself, stepping into the center of the circle.

"Thank you for attending. You're here because someone has been stealing from the Black Moon. Someone's been skimming money from our various side businesses, the most lucrative of which, after overhead and other expenses are calculated, is this facility and its drug operation. This operation has been bleeding the most profit, no pun intended." Everyone laughed, and the mood lightened. The speaker had jet black, slick-backed hair and a pencil thin goatee you might not even detect if you were more than a hundred feet away. He wore cheap black sunglasses and a black leather motorcycle jacket. The comparison I kept returning to in my head was actually a vampire from the movie *Buffy the Vampire Slayer*. Having this image bouncing around in my head made me giggle out loud, and the place came to a silent halt. The speaker took off his glasses and did a double take, unable to recognize me. He regrouped, and resumed his lecture. "Does anyone here know who the culprit or culprits are?" He paused to allow for someone to speak up. Nothing but silence followed. "Is there no one who has any knowledge of the shit stain who is stealing from Alister and his cohorts? Remember, they're not just stealing from the Black Moon; they're stealing from you and me. They're making it difficult for night people to relish in some enjoyment, some normalcy. Even if our existence is limited; even if the freedom we strive for will forever be just out of reach, the Black Moon makes the transformation livable. They make happiness possible. And *this*?! This is how we repay them? Someone has to know something. SPEAK!"

Still, not one person parted their lips. Not even a whisper could be heard. I could tell things were about to nosedive. The speaker went from inspirational and captivating to angry and belligerent within seconds. His face, his voice, his eyes, now uncovered by the cheap shades, sparkled and cracked with shards of fire. He was about to erupt, and the smattering of collected "night people" started to move and jitter and look at each other with a queasy, nervous energy. I wondered when the proverbial other shoe would drop. I didn't have to wait long.

"Well, if no one will say, then I will have to find other sources of information!" One of this speaker's henchmen drug out young Ben from Building 2, and threw him in the center of the circle at the speaker's feet. The speaker grabbed Ben by the back of the neck, like a mother cat would do to its young, and lifted him a foot in the air, Ben's legs and feet kicking and twisting in an attempt to get away. "What do you have to say for yourself, Business?"

"I didn't do shit! And I don't know shit! Put me down you sick fuck!" Everyone burst out with laughter, but you had to hand it to the kid. He didn't seem willing to back down or show fear. And one major rule in his line of business, he wasn't going to snitch. Unfortunately, that bravado wasn't going to improve his situation.

"Now, I have it on good authority that you and your buddies Ethan, Lorenzo, and Sneakers have all been diverting funds into your own pockets, and that you planned on setting fires to the clubs and liquor stores in Huntington Beach and L.A. to atone for letting Jose get smoked without any assistance from any of you. Your need for vengeance, along with your own guilt sent you down a wrong path, to the land of bad decisions. Those decisions have consequences, little man. You know that. So, by the power vested in me by the House of the Black Moon, I sentence you to---"

"NO!," I shouted. I don't know how or why it slipped out, but vampire or not, I wasn't so morally devoid that I was alright with such a little kid getting executed in my presence. I at least had to speak on his behalf. Again, the crowd went silent, and the speaker eyed me curiously.

"WHO… are *you*?" he inquired hastily.

"I'm… My name's Davis. Davis McCarty. And what would your name be?" The mixed looks of shock and amusement on the attendees was humorous in hindsight, but I had clearly made a mistake by asking such a question. They took it as a sign of disrespect.

"What would *my* name be?" The man stood puzzled and pondering for a few seconds, still holding Ben in the air by the neck. "My name. Let me guess, you're not from around here."

"He's from Texas. Now let me go, bitch," Ben muttered through half-closed lips. I don't know if his plan was to provoke the speaker into letting hm go or killing him quickly. The man ignored Ben and returned his attention to me.

"My name is Raven Chastain, one of the longest surviving blood drinkers in the OC, and I run things around here for Alister Amaranth." I decided to conduct a test, and needed some mental and factual misdirection. The plan was to distract Raven long enough to figure out how to free Ben and escape.

"Oh, *you're* the one Daniel Sepulveda says is just a wannabe rock star bitch." The crowd gasped at the blatant disrespect, and then burst out laughing louder than they had all night to this point. "There's no way that's your real name. You must be one of those stereotypical, pretentious, bisexual vampires."

"Is that right, cowboy? Well, you must be the guy Daniel said he threw through a fucking building." *Oh shit.* "He said we might run into you. So, I think tonight is the last and only night we run into you. But first..." Raven lifted Ben higher and closer to him, and then sunk his teeth into the side of Ben's throat. Ben shook and writhed, trying to get away fruitlessly. I ran towards them, but was met with six vampires grabbing onto me, stretching my limbs, and keeping me still.

"Let him go!," I ordered. Raven turned Ben at an angle so they could both stare at me while Raven continued to feed. He then broke free of his bite, and wiped his mouth off dramatically.

"Anything you say, Davis." Raven spiked Ben to the ground like a football, and I could hear his skull make a thuddingly hollow crash onto the clubhouse's splintered, unraveling wood floor. Tears started to pour from my eyes, and an all-consuming rage I'd had yet to feel was burning through me from my toes upward. Raven had neither fed long enough, nor threw Ben hard enough to kill him, and he lay there moaning in agony. If he didn't die, soon, I knew his next sounds would be of utter misery, learning the brutal purgatory of vampire transformation. "Kill him," Raven ordered to the minions holding onto me. Neither he nor the others gathered around me could see the physical changes taking place under my clothing. My rage had unlocked some secret power like in a video game, and my muscles strained and grew tighter and larger. It was actually painful, almost unbearable, as my spine and hip bones detached to allow for me to increase in height. I could feel my hands and feet extend, and by my quick account, I must have gone from 5'9" to 5'11" in mere seconds, weighing at least thirty more pounds.

My reflexes improved, and before the first of the group reacted to Raven's command, I reversed his hold with my hand, breaking his right wrist in the process, and threw him into the three vampires on my left side. I then snapped the neck of one of the remaining two on my right, which didn't kill him – because he's a fucking vampire – and smashed in the skull of the third, which did kill him. I then stomped on the face of the broken necked vampire on the floor, turning it into gelatin. A random individual lunged toward me, and I kicked him like I was kicking off in the NFL, sending him flying some 25 feet backwards. The clubhouse welcome desk ended his journey, breaking his back. I killed four more vampires, all while making my way to the center of the room, and Raven. I noticed he wasn't moving at all. Just the opposite, he fell to his knees and sat there hands upward in his lap, staring wild-eyed at me. Chaos ensued around us, vampires running for the exits, some still running at me, when Raven yelled a loud, guttural roar.

"ENOUGH!" He stayed fixated on me. I slowed to a walk, and stopped before Ben.

"He has the Namtudari. He has the Luminastra Namtudari!" His words fell on deaf ears. "Don't any of you even know your history? Jesus, I weep for the next generation." He turned his words just to me directly. "You have it. I'm over a hundred years old, and thought it was just a myth. But, right before my eyes, you have it. Some hick from Texas."

"What the hell are you talking about?"

"The texts from the first vampire call it the Luminastra Namtudari. It's a sort of rebirth for a vampire, where they fully shed the original human body they're trapped in, and gain a new, more powerful one. Basically, the vampire version of a snake shedding its skin."

"Bullshit."

"You tell me, then. You're the one going through it. Do you think any random, newbie, *rookie* vampire can mow down even two or three veterans? By my count, you demolished, not defeated, but *demolished* eight vampires. You look like a bigger, stronger version of the idiot I saw when this meeting started. That's not a mirage, genius."

"How the hell would some generic movie vampire know any of this?"

"I'm not just some braindead biker, asshole. I took the time to learn and retain the information provided by my leader."

"Alister Amaranth?"

"The one and only."

I'm humble enough to admit that I'm not really the sharpest guy in the room. Therefore, it's taken me this entire time to realize that Alister Amaranth is the ultimate ringleader of this circus of damnation. I make an instant internal decision that before I kill, or attempt to kill, or even think of killing Alister, I must first sit down with him and gain some understanding, some knowledge of what I am. What we are. I must first decide what to do with Mr. Raven Chastain. My verdict is death, but as I advance toward him with a final blow in my thoughts, Ben kicks me inadvertently as he begins his metamorphosis. His display is one half epileptic seizure and one-half fish flopping on the dock, gills ablaze. I look at Raven, and he looks at me, and I have to forget him for a bit. I kneel down and grab hold of Ben, trying to console him and get his convulsions to stop. That won't do anything for the pain, though, and I feel helpless. I'm crying over him, and I don't know why the fact that he's a child makes me sympathize this deeply. Even with my new form, I'm just a newbie like Raven shared so eloquently. I have no solutions, save for two. I can either allow the transformation to continue, however violent and prolonged, or I can complete draining him. Feed on him like any other victim. Only one is merciful, so I hold him tighter and tighter, and unleash a set of teeth I'd never had before. These ones are new, and they include two fangs. I insert them into Ben's neck, and cover his mouth, to muffle the screams the best I can. I'm no longer a human or a normal vampire, but an all-powerful python constricting the life and afterlife out of a small child. In the procedure, I notice Ben stop struggling, and I look upon him, our eyes meeting. He raises his brows, and I can tell somehow that he's trying to say something. I stop momentarily, and let his limp head go.

"What is it, little man?" I ask. My eyes don't leave his, and I'm within a few inches of his face.

"Mayfield," he spirts out barely audibly.

"What, Ben?"

"Mayfield. My last name is Mayfield. In case you find out where my parents are... or if they're aliv---"

And then Ben Mayfield died in my arms. 11 years old, he looked more like nine. My head and heart were caught between two opposing reactions. On one end, I was still Davis, and good, and simple, and I was heartbroken for this little boy, regardless of his story or his choices. I wanted to avenge him, to mourn him. On the other end of the spectrum, my instinct was to discard his body, leave the scene, and begin the next phase of my mission. I tried to appease both voices on my shoulder. First order of business was to kill Raven, but when I looked up from Ben's lifeless body, I found only absence where Raven once stood. There was no point in obsessing about it; he was nowhere to be found. I had his scent though, so I would find him soon enough. I then ordered whoever was left in the room to make Ben disappear like they no doubt are able to do with other fatalities in the Horizon Vista, but that he needs to be buried. I felt that was important, respectful. These vampires didn't seem to know what Raven was going on about, but they believed what they saw with their eyes, which was a vampire dominant over them. They complied with my request with no resistance. For the third time in a few days, I prayed. No idea why, but the need compelled me, so before they moved Ben from the room, I placed my hand on his head and said a prayer to whatever God would hear me, asking that he travel safely to his next destination, if there was one.

Walking back to the filthy hovel I shared with Felix, outside was abuzz with humans and vampires alike moving about through the property, many leaving its confines for at least the night. It appears that the scene caused in the clubhouse had future repercussions no one wanted to be present for. This was the location I'd identified as optimal, though, and I wasn't going anywhere. This was in walking distance of the Black Moon, which meant I was in striking distance. The knowledge that Unholy Saint and whoever else was involved in a vast amount of illegal activity only added to my eagerness to put an end to them. A new feeling of righteousness came upon me, and there would be no joining this group of abominations. I opened the door to find Felix laying on his mattress waiting for me, a sarcastic smirk adorning his face.

"What the fuck did you do this t---" he stopped, puzzled. "Wait. What the holy fuck happened to your body? Did you go down to Muscle Beach and pump some iron, or pump a shitload of steroids?"

"So it's noticeable, then?"

"Well, not if no one's ever seen you before, or if you're fucking blind! Other than that, yeah, it's pretty noticeable."

"Something… happened in there tonight. To me."

"Yeah, no shit."

"I underwent a new level, a next level, of transformation, because of the situation I was in. There's a name for it, though. The lead vampire there called it something, but I can't remember exactly what right now. It wasn't English, that much I know."

"What exactly did happen, because about five minutes ago, everyone in here started getting all riled up, and I could hear a lot of activity."

Before I could get into it, blue and red lights that looked a hell of a lot like police lights became visible, and an uproar from the masses became audible as they scattered in various directions. I couldn't move Felix right now, so we sat tight, and if we came face to face with the police, I would decide then and there what to do. For now, we sat still and said nothing. We just looked at the window and the lights. Several minutes later, the lights faded away, and we were left in the room with silence.

"Do you think it's safe?" Felix questioned.

"I do."

"Good. Those chili dogs fucked up my insides and I've got to go, bad. Could you help a brother get to the toilet?"

I was thankful for the loud, abrupt laugh that shot out of my mouth. I didn't know if I would be capable of such a thing anymore. If there was a purpose, a reason for meeting someone and becoming part of their life, then the continued ability to laugh might have been mine for meeting Felix. I got him in the wheelchair, and we made the death march to the nastiest men's room on earth. Luckily, a half decent, half full roll of toilet paper was in our room, and Felix brought that with him. I got him in a somewhat suitable stall, and left him to his business. As I stepped outside the men's room and headed back to our allocated dwelling, my phone rang. It hadn't rung in what seemed like weeks. I looked at the screen, and it read 'Annie'. I couldn't believe it. I just stared at her name for a few seconds, and let the call die. It rang again immediately. Again, the screen read 'Annie'. I picked up the phone and gave a quiet, somber "Hello."

"Hi, Davis."

"You're alive!" I exclaimed, tears running down my face. I was so grateful.

"Yes."

"Why didn't you answer, when I called all those times?"

"I was upset with you, that you… that's not important. I called because I have some bad news. I'm so sorry. I debated so long… I'm so sorry."

"Annie. What is it?" In my heart, I knew before she said it.

"Davis. Your mom died." *Wait. Maybe not what I thought.*

"My mom? Valerie?"

"No, Davis. Your *real* mom. Mona."

My Adam's Apple sank to my stomach, and my heart to my knees. Instant grief juxtaposed by instant hollowness filled up in my insides, and a soft, weird murmur emitted from deep in my throat. I tried to speak, but nothing would come. Annie stayed silent on the other end, patient with my reaction. Finally, I was able to get out one word.

"How?"

"How did she go?"

"Yes."

"Peacefully, as far as I could tell. She was asleep in her chair in the living room. She had a heart attack, and may have not even been awake when it happened."

"*When* did it happen?"

"Five days ago."

"FIVE DAYS AGO?! And you're just calling me NOW?!"

"There was nothing you could do, Davis!" I could hear Annie trying to hold back sobs. "She went out of the blue, and you were here – I mean there - doing this, and you wouldn't have been able to attend her funeral. It was in the daytime." Annie paused and composed herself before resuming. "She had all her arrangements taken care of, and things went very quickly. I was able to help the pastor coordinate the funeral and it was lovely. Small and lovely, just like she directed it in her will. It was yesterday. Mabel Nadine said a few words, and she prayed for you."

"You helped?"

"Of course I did."

"Annie. Who found her?"

"Who found her at home in the chair?" She sounded coy.

"Yes."

"I did, Davis." I closed my eyes tight, attempting to dam up any more tears. I could hear Felix calling for me, and felt bad about keeping him waiting.

"You?"

"Yes… I had called her that day, and got no answer. After I tried a second time later in the evening, I got a weird feeling and thought I would check in on her. That's when I found her. She just looked asleep, but I knew she had passed. After the funeral, I talked it over with my parents, and then booked a flight to get out of town. I had to get away."

"Where did you go?"

"Newport Beach, California."

"*What*?"

"This morning, I flew to Newport Beach, California. Maybe you've heard of it."

"I'm in Newport Beach, right now, Annie."

"I know, Davis. I see you." I wondered, *what kind of existential, metaphysical shit had she gotten herself caught up in*?

"What do you mean, you *see* me? Like some sympathetic mind's eye type crap?"

"No, Davis. I SEE you. Look out your window." Felix's calls got louder and more frequent. I didn't believe that I was doing it, but I took a step to the window and pulled back the milk-white plastic painter's tarp used for a curtain. And there she was, staring at me, cellphone to her ear.

Annie Fucking Moore.

Chapter Twenty-Two: Did Your Eyes Have to Be So Blue?

"Where the FUCK ARE YOU?!," Felix roared through the still, silent retirement building. No one else was inside. Just me and him. I had to get him, so I put my finger to my lips in a "be quiet" gesture, and then pointed to the door I wanted Annie to go to, hung up, and went to rescue Felix from the noxious cesspool I'd left him imprisoned in for so long.

"I'm sorry, man. Really. I got caught up on a phone call."

"Phone call? You just chit chatting with your girlfriends while you each do your nails?"

"My grandmother died. Annie called to tell me."

"Oh, I'm sorry, man. I didn't know."

"I know you didn't. That's why I'm not pulling your trachea out with my teeth right now." He jerked his head around and up to look at me.

"What?!"

"I'm just fucking with you." A sad smile crossed my lips. "I've got to wheel you to the front door. I have to let Annie in." He jerked his head around identically.

"Let her in? You said she was on the phone."

"Correct. She was calling from outside the place."

"Well, how the fuck did---"

"That's what I'm going to ask her, Felix. All in good time."

"Well, you shouldn't bring her in here! This place is a hell hole." I agreed with Felix, but I had to get Annie out from in the open. It wouldn't be long before people, and others, would find their way back here after the drama died down. I also didn't know who might be watching. It wasn't safe for her. We got to the door, and I set Felix off to the side. I opened it and there she was.

"Hi," I offered, like a verbal olive branch. She just stood there, not sure of what to do.

"Hi. Have you been… working out or something? It didn't take you long to adopt the healthy Cali lifestyle."

"That's a complicated story… How did you find me?"

"I didn't find you… I tracked you."

"What do you mean?"

"I mean in Glendale, I put a tracking device in your truck, and another one in your backpack. I put a teeny tiny one in your wallet, but it either stopped working or fell out."

"I can't believe you. What possessed you to do something like that?"

"I love you, Davis." I moved closer to her, and she stepped back a little.

"Please. Don't worry. I'll protect you," I assured her.

"From what?"

"If I fail to protect you, you'll see."

"Whose blood is that on the sides of your mouth?"

"Another complicated story, and one for another time. I need to get you out of here, so we're all three going to relocate."

"All three? Who's the third?"

"Ah, yes." I shuffled back into the building and wheeled out Felix. "This is Felix. We met in Laughlin, and he's been my traveling companion ever since."

"And look where it got me," Felix interjected, now causing a sad smile on Annie's face. "Pleased to meet you, but this isn't a complete reunion until you two embrace." Annie and I looked at each other, and just slowly took one step at a time before standing two inches apart, our clothes touching. I held out my hand to shake hers, and she wrapped both arms around me. I did the same, and I squeezed hard, like I never wanted her to leave my clutch.

"You're hurting me, a little bit," she said, difficult to breathe in or out.

"Oh, I'm sorry. I'm so sorry." I grabbed both of her

cheeks and planted a soft kiss on her lips. I made sure to keep my lips sealed tight, as not to exhale my foul breath in her mouth a second time. "Thank you for being there for my Mona. I can't believe I'll really never see her again. I was holding out a modicum of hope. And I love you, too. I love you so much… Are we just throwing that around now?"

"Why not? You and I might not even live past tomorrow."

"You most certainly *are* living past tomorrow, unless we don't get the hell out of here, now. I've got another shirt in my backpack, and these pants are passable, so let's go."

"I need to eat, so can we go to In-N-Out Burger? My treat."

"Sure." I was surprised but relieved that she already had a place in mind. "But I don't eat food anymore, remember?"

"Felix does, and you can order something, so you don't stick out as a bloodthirsty demon of the night." I didn't detect the humor in her words, but she and Felix looked at each other, both with mischievous, shit-eating grins on their faces.

"Oh, got it. Yes, very funny. I'm a vampire, so…"

No one really said anything in the truck, save for Annie navigating us to the nearest In-N-Out. We went in and ordered, and sat down with our food, still not really speaking, until Felix finally broke the ice.

"These fries are shit, but damn if this isn't the best

fast-food burger I've ever had. Hands down."

"It's obvious you haven't had Whataburger," I countered. We both stared a hole through Annie.

"Well, Miss. You're the tiebreaker," Felix chuckled. Annie inhaled deep from her diaphragm, closed her eyes, and let out her judgement.

"Davis, we've established that I love you, and I'm just as much a Texan as you are, but this burger is better than Whatabur---"

"Blasphemy! Your Texas citizenship is revoked." We all laughed, but then I burst into tears. "She's gone, Annie. She's really gone?" I buried my head in her shoulder and cried. "It hurts. Why does it hurt this much?" She held me tight, caressing my hair with caring hands while Felix turned his head to either give me privacy and respect, or ignore my show of emotion.

"This is grief, Davis. She was your mom for all intents and purposes. Of course it's going to hurt. However long I'm with you here, I'll be here for you. And if we get out of this alive, I'll always be here for you." I lifted my head, wiped my eyes, and looked at her blankly. "Now can you tell me how the hell you gained so much muscle so quickly, and how your eye color changed?"

"Yeah, me, too," Felix joined in.

'Eye color? Did my eye color change?"

"Yes. Could you not tell?"

"Vampires don't... I don't... look in the mirror very

often… If I can help it. Plus, I'm going color blind." It wasn't until that moment that I realized I'd regained the ability to see the full spectrum.

"Your eyes are a hard cobalt blue, deep as the ocean."

Felix cocked his head. "Are you a writer, or sumthin?"

"I hope to be." This was a good time for me to bring up getting her the hell away from California.

"Then why aren't you back at Kansas? You can't ruin your future and your life over me."

"I have every intention of going back, but not until the fall. I couldn't sit through post-graduate writing and journalism with you fighting vampires and drinking human blood cross country like some undead Viking."

"Understood. But promise me. Promise me you'll go back to school when we get out of this. Or better yet, promise me you'll leave here tomorrow, no matter what happens between now and then."

"I most certainly will not." Felix tried to stand up on a broken leg and told us he was going to go have a cigarette. The mood was definitely now more personal than he was prepared for. He decided it best instead to wheel himself out. "I didn't fly out here after burying your mom just to sit by and prepare a place for you next to her. I plan on helping you."

"You can't help me! You can't stand up to them. You can't defeat them." She pursed her lips together and tried to bite her tongue, thinking hard about her next words and what she *wanted* to say.

"Back to your physical change. How did you go from a buck twenty to about 155, and how and why did your eye color change?"

"The truth? The short answer is I don't know. I was at a vampire "meeting" earlier, which ended up in me being held down while they fed on a human. A kid." Her face was gripped by astonishment and horror. "The need to rescue the child unlocked some… change in me. Kind of like the Incredible Hulk when he gets mad. My muscles grew, my height grew. I guess my eyes changed color. I don't know how or why."

"Did you rescue the boy?" I looked down at the table, ran my fingers through my hair, and thought back to Ben's face as he told me his last name. My body language gave Annie her answer, but I wanted to clarify anyway.

"He had been bitten, and partially fed on, which meant he would soon become a vampire. I couldn't let that happen, Annie. He's only 11. So I had to finish feeding, so he could pass peacefully, and honorably."

"Honorably?" She put her fist to her mouth, and bit down.

"As honorably as could be. It was intentional what the other vampire had done. It was a punishment for something Ben, the boy, had done or something they accused him of doing. Doing it in front of me was just a side bonus for them. They wanted me to watch, and then they were going to kill me, but they didn't factor the change that would occur in me. I killed more than a handful of them before tonight's lead vampire, a real douchebag looking guy named Raven, recognized what had happened. He had a word for it. Luminata something or other. Something like that. So I sacrificed the boy so he wouldn't become what I had. I never want to see someone go through that, unable to choose that reality. Unaware of what's going to happen to them."

"I know you would have never chosen a child to feed on for your own survival. I'm sorry you were put in that situation. Did you kill that Raven guy?"

"He escaped while I dealt with Ben. I don't know where he is now, but he can't be far. If his scent is within a half mile, I can hunt him down... Everything got a little hectic after that. The cops showed up, everyone scattered, I saw to Felix, and then you showed up. And now, here we are. You put a tracking device on me?"

"Three... tracking devices. And for the record, I was *pissed off* when I woke up in some rando's van and found out I had been drugged. What the actual fuck was that?"

"I apologize, but it was necessary. I had to keep you safe, and without making an agreement with Sinjin, neither of us would have walked out of there alive."

"How can you be so sure? How do you know you wouldn't have done that illuminati thing there?"

"I don't know, but I didn't do it up to that point, so... I couldn't take any chances... The way I feel about Mona right now, I couldn't live with myself if I lost you, too. If I was responsible for it..." More tears. Man. Feelings. They suck.

"So what now?"

"I mean it. Tomorrow, I need you to leave this place. You don't have to leave California, but it would be better if you... Yes, please leave California. My next move is to find somewhere to sleep throughout the day. Maybe that's the retirement home, maybe it's not. The next step is to visit the House of the Black Moon tomorrow night, as neither friend nor foe. It's to find and *speak* to Alister Amaranth. He runs this place and apparently every vampire around, and I need answers. He's got them. If anyone does, it's him. I guess step three is to take that knowledge and use it. Oh, and step four is to kill every last person inside the House of the Black Moon."

"DAVIS! That's the kind of stupid shit I'm here to prevent!"

"If I find out there's still a chance that killing Devin can bring me back my humanity, I have to take it. You'd want that, right? The chance to have a normal relationship now that we know how we both feel?"

"Of course. But it still sounds like a suicide mission."

"Maybe, but now that I've got this newfound power, the odds are far more even. I swear I could have ended every single vampire in that room tonight, without breaking a sweat. I'm not as afraid as I was, and I know that Raven went running to Alister and the band about what happened. This thing seems like a big deal. Raven said he thought it was just a myth."

"If the urge moves you, or the situation dictates it, you plan on killing them anyway."

"I don't think they deserve to live."

"Who are you to say? You're a vampire just like they are. You can't tell me that all of them came to be that way by choice."

"So maybe I don't kill all of them. Maybe I just kill the band. Cut off the head and the body will fall or something. This. All of this, and that place… needs to stop. Permanently."

Annie could tell we'd reached the point where nothing she could say would change my mind. So, she decided to stop talking. She grabbed ahold of my hand and stroked it gently, while she just looked into my eyes. For the first time, I felt what it was like to be loved romantically. There was a glassy gleam in her eyes, and I felt like her gaze penetrated me and kept going, through the west, and into the future. This is the love I'd always wished she felt for me, the love I needed. And now that it was here in my grasp, I knew that it might be the one and only time I'd ever see it. Finally, as we looked out the window to find Felix staring at us the same way he did at me in the Naked Huntress, she spoke.

"Goddamnit, Davis. Did your eyes have to be so blue?" I laughed, and I was instantly teleported back to junior high, a shy poor kid with a crush.

"Do we have an agreement?"

"Agreed, as long as you keep the tracking devices where I left them, and you keep your phone on you at all times. Call me as soon as either whatever happens is done or it looks like you're not going to make it."

"I'll try."

"Don't try. Promise. That's the only way I leave tomorrow."

"Ok, ok. I promise."

"Good. Since I'm leaving tomorrow, that means we can be together tonight. I'll get us two rooms at a nice hotel, instead of a homeless drug den, and Felix can sleep comfortably tonight while you and I spend some alone time together. You can both take hot showers and get clean, because you both need showers. Bad. Like really bad. Sound good?"

"Sure."

"Sure?" Annie made a face like she was about to become mentally unhinged. "Sure?"

"I mean, Thank you. That sounds nice."

"Damn right. Go get your handicapped friend, and let's do this."

Chapter Twenty-Three: Queen Size Bed

Bob Moore's bloated membership points with either of two different hotel chains secured us two rooms in town free of charge, and as Annie promised, they were *nice*. We checked in, Felix in his room, and us in ours, right next door. Annie set her things down and unpacked per some step-by-step ritual she was long familiar with. *She was only in town for one night*. I'd never stayed anywhere nicer than a cheap, bed-bug infested motel, and had no protocol to adhere to. I only had a backpack of wrinkled, stolen, or dirt cheap resell, clothes.

"I'm going to take a shower first, ok?" Annie stated like a question, but was really a declaration. I cut straight to something more serious.

"I'm going to have to feed again, tonight." My face must have looked grim, because she stepped back into the dresser.

"Oh. Okay. No worries. Don't leave the room. Don't kill someone. Not tonight. You can feed on me like we did in Glendale. How desperate is it? How much time do you have?"

"You can shower, and then I can shower. I have enough time to do that."

"Ok. I'll be quick."

As she hopped in the shower, I turned on the television, and, after figuring out how the remote worked, I put it on the news. Almost every story was negative, almost every outcome bad. I'd always known this about the news since I was little, and Mona would watch it religiously. The irony is that none of these stories even scratched the surface on just how evil the underworld was. What true evil was. As despicable as humans were, they were still a rung above vampires in the kindness department, while being a rung below them on the food chain. In what seemed like a flash, ten minutes had gone by, and Annie was out of the shower.

"Your turn, stinky." She gave me a kiss on the cheek as we switched spots in the bathroom. It seemed like we were a regular couple on vacation, but nothing could have been further from the truth. We hadn't really ever been a couple at all. The mixed signals put me on a roller coaster of joy and despair, and while in the shower, I stood with my head against the wall and wept quietly, thinking about all the banal details of regular life that would forever be out of reach to Annie and me. As a couple, we would never have the phone full of photos, or the memories on social media to look forward to. We wouldn't have a wedding, or kids, or family vacations. We didn't have a future, and part of me was relieved she agreed to fly away tomorrow. It prevented me from playing out an illogical fantasy or clinging on to hope that would never materialize. I must have taken too long, and she checked on me.

"Everything ok in there?"

"Yes, sorry. I have a lot of filth and grime built up on my body."

"Well, speed it up. I really want to cuddle now." *Cuddle*, I thought. *What else might she want to do*?

"I'm making sure to be cuddle approved."

"And make sure you brush your teeth. You've got what you need in there."

"Yes, Sargeant." There was just silence. *I thought it was funny.*

I got out of the shower to find a new pair of pajama pants and a t-shirt waiting for me, and they were the perfect size – for my *old body*. Annie had purchased them before even coming to find me. She had no idea I would be much more filled out. I tried them on, but there was no chance they'd fit. Luckily, she had a pair of her father's old boxers she wore as lounge around shorts, and I was able to fit in those. I fashioned a sleeveless muscle shirt out of the one she'd bought. It wasn't ideal but it did make my muscles look good in the mirror, the whole two seconds I could bring myself to look in it.

"Now come on out so we can spend some time together, and put the "do not disturb" sign on the door, so you can rest in total darkness tomorrow afternoon." She definitely had things planned out.

I came out and did a little turn for Annie, and she

laughed at my out-of-character performance. She looked tremendously sexy, wearing short, plaid pajama shorts and a thin, white tank top, no bra. She patted the bed next to her in a universal "come sit" directive. Instinctively, but nervously for some reason, I quickly complied. I didn't have any preconceived notions about what lay ahead for the night, because I didn't even know I'd be seeing Annie, but my heart and head were fighting each other in a metal death ball from some post-apocalyptic film, going round and round. There were words I wanted to say, but didn't know how or when to say them.

"Thank you," I started. "Thank you for always being my friend, and caring about me when literally nobody else did. Except for Nathan. I can't discredit his friendship. I know that you probably got some flak from your other rich friends about keeping me around. I'm not in the same stratosphere as them, in any way, shape, or form. I really never belonged in your world, so I don't know what I'm still doing here. But, again, thank you."

"Davis," Annie began but paused. Her eyes darted left and right while she manifested the correct words. "You had something about you that felt really comfortable and warm and genuine to me. In junior high, I thought you were cute, and our senior year, I thought you were really good looking. I was drawn to you. So, as far as my other friends go, I didn't care what they thought or what they might have said behind my back. Because I was happy with you in my world, and I maybe always thought you'd be in it. I was happy to make you my world, no matter how different our upbringings or circumstances were."

"Wow." I sat next to Annie, stunned, studying the pattern of the hotel carpet. That was a lot to take in, and in my brain, I just couldn't comprehend it. I don't think I'd be able to, if I had a thousand years to do so. "Why?"

"I can't explain why, any better than I just did. I think we were just meant to be."

"And now?"

"Well, I'm here, aren't I? I flew halfway across the country for you." I looked up from the carpet's hypnotic design and stared into Annie's eyes as she stared back into mine, and we edged up closer to one another and kissed a soft, delicate kiss. Then we shared a second one, a little more passionate than the first. And then… I started to sweat with hunger withdrawals.

"Uhhh, Annie? I need to feed soon. Like real soon." The mood dashed and the impending doom of "drink or kill" hanging over us, Annie shifted into high gear.

"Ohhh, shit! I'm sorry. I made you wait, and you DID! You were such a good sport. I'm so sorry. I feel like a dick."

"No, no, no. It's all good, I swear. I just can't wait anymore. My body kind of held out as long as it could."

"How do you want to do this? I didn't bring a knife, and you can't bite me, so…"

"What if I open you up with my nails?"

"Too risky. What if the toxin or whatever that's in a vampire's bite is also in their keratin?"

"In their what?"

"In their nails."

"Wait." I tried to think like a girl for a second. "Did you bring a travel kit?"

"Of course."

"Does it include a razor to shave your legs?"

"It does." A smile grazed her face.

"Bring it to me." Annie rose from the bed and grabbed her razor from her bag. "All I need is a small cut, but strategic enough that the blood will actually pour out with no trouble. You tell me where to make it."

"Where did the people at the Wet Beaver usually cut themselves?"

"Well, the people at the Naked Huntress usually cut their arms or bellies."

"You mean the titty bar? Don't think I didn't look up the place when your tracking device had you there for hours. I wonder how cutting their bellies helped the vampires feed." *Hours?* I thought. *Damn.*

"I'm running out of time." It was a good way to change the subject.

"My arm. It will heal, and I don't want any scars on my belly. It's too cute." When she uttered those words, her face looked extremely innocent.

"Ok, then. I'm going to cut the back of your forearm, and you're just going to bend your arm and hold it over my mouth. I'll take in what I can. I can't promise that I won't need to make another cut."

“Got it. Do you… Do you need to chain yourself to anything?”

“No. I’ll be on my best behavior, and there’s nothing in here I can’t break out of, now.”

“What do you mean?”

“You still don’t get it. Before this evening, I had the strength of maybe five really strong men. Now, I have the strength of maybe five really strong vampires.” Annie did math in her head, and then got very wide-eyed.

“So, like you’re roughly as strong as 25 men?”

“More or less. Yes.”

“Hot damn. My man is *strong*.”

“Am I? Your man?” Annie took the razor from my hand and put it to her right forearm.

“Do you want to be?” She made a short, quick slice to her skin, and then we waited to see its success rate. Sure enough, it reached the surface, and with a little double squeeze, it came pouring.

“I do,” I said as I sat on the hotel room floor and knelt below her dripping gift. She kept a consistent squeeze on her arm, and I drank. As I did, she chose to drop another bombshell on me, something she’s become quite adept at doing.

“I want to make love to you,” Annie conveyed, softly and sensually. I almost spit out a mouthful of plasma.

“Oh. Wow. Ok. I, uhhh. I…”

"So, even a badass vampire becomes a little boy when a girl offers sex?'.

"I… just wasn't expecting that. And I need to share something with you."

"That's what I'm hoping for."

"No. I need to… inform you of something."

"I'm all ears."

"Vampires can't… I can't… perform, without…" I looked up into her waiting eyes, she hanging off a cliff waiting for me to get out the words. "Without feeding."

"You need to be feeding on me to get it up?!"

"No. Not at the same time. Just within a short window. Like ten to 30 minutes after."

"OK. That's no problem. We're already in the room, you're already feeding, and who knows when and if we'll ever have this opportunity again… I'm just glad you didn't mean we would have to be a bloody mess while we did it."

"That would be a little much. I do have to get a substantial amount of blood in me to be able to… you know."

"My God. You're so sexy when you're shy. That must be what did it. In the beginning. I think your shyness is what attracted me to you. It's definitely a turn-on right now."

"Thank you. Glad I could oblige." It was a little difficult to speak while drinking blood from a slow faucet, so I intentionally got closer to her arm and fell silent.

"No, *I* need to oblige." Annie stood up, grabbed the razor from the end table and made a second cut in her arm. She also slipped off the pajama shorts to reveal a white satin and mesh thong. "How do you like it?" she asked.

"I... I... Like it. I like it... A lot."

"Good. Are you full yet?"

"Yes, I can be," I replied shakily. Annie smiled at me seductively, and started planting soft kisses on my arms. She took off my undersized shirt, tore it and wrapped her wounds, and continued her kisses along my neck and chest. My little friend was at attention almost instantly.

"Does that feel good?"

"Oh yes." I felt engulfed in a small heaven I never thought I'd ascend to.

"Will your saliva or whatever it is you inject in someone when you turn them infect me if we French kiss?" That was a damn good question.

"I don't know. No one's ever mentioned that, and you kissed me pretty hard once before, albeit for a few seconds."

"Well, until we know for sure; until you're able to receive a judge's ruling on that detail, I need us to hold off on such activity." She could tell I was disappointed. "Hey, I think it sucks, too. No worry. I'll make sure you're happy." She placed her hand on my crotch. "Oh,

Mr. McCarty. You're *already* happy." She began to take off her little tank top, when I grabbed her hand and held it in place.

"I don't want your first time to be with a vampire." You would have needed a bulldozer to pick her jaw up off the floor and a skilled optical surgeon to reimplant her eyes in their sockets.

"What?"

"I can't even kiss you. Not like I want to. I can't wake up with you in the morning and go down to breakfast and order French toast and bacon, and just smile and laugh over how awesome our first night together was. I love you, but I don't think I can do this."

"Uh, Davis---"

"No. Please. I've thought about it, and there's nothing you can say to change my mind. I love you too much to ruin such a milestone occasion."

"Davis!" Her snapped call of my name got my attention and buttoned me up quickly. "I'm... I'm not... a virgin." Now it was I who needed the bulldozer and eye surgeon.

"Um. You're... Umm. Come again?"

"I'm not a virgin." I placed my hand on the night table, grabbing the television remote and crushing it with the difficulty of crushing a potato chip over a ham and cheese sandwich.

"Oh. I see. I'm---"

"I'm sorry."

"No. No. I'm sorry. I didn't know. I just thought that---"

"Thought that what?"

"I mean, you never mentioned it, so I just thought it... I thought it never---"

"Never happened? Because I didn't tell you?"

"Yeah. I guess, kinda."

"That wasn't something that was just going to come out."

"Yeah, but we talked more and more ever since senior year, and we talked once we reunited, and... did it happen in that time before I saw you in the hardware store?" Her face scrunched up a little, and I couldn't tell if she was trying to remember, or if she was diplomatically trying to not pulverize my heart strings."

"Yesssss. And noooo?"

"Why did your answer sound like a question? And what does yes *and* no mean?"

"It means that I did have sex while you and I had been out of contact. But I also had sex once before we gradua-, before I, graduated from AHS."

"You had sex in *high school*?!"

"Well, yes, Davis. Just once. With Landon Walters, prom night."

"*Landon Walters*?!" I rolled my eyes so hard and melodramatically, I thought they might accidentally float away out of my head and onto the ceiling.

"What? Landon was sweet, and super cute."

"No! Don't, don't, don't, don't, don't, don't. I don't want to hear about Landon *Walters*... How did this happen?"

"Wait. You do or you don't want to hear about Landon Walters?"

"I don't want details, but how?"

"Well, it was senior prom, and everyone just planned on having sex that night. And, for some people," Annie took her two thumbs and pointed them at her own chest, "having sex at prom meant losing your virginity." I put my hands in my head, and just sat there. At first, Annie didn't know what to do, and was very hesitant to continue telling me anything, but then I could tell she was annoyed. I stopped her before she said something that escalated the frustrated interruption.

"I know. I know. We weren't together. You were a teenage girl, and practically everybody who was popular had lost their virginity by graduation. I'm not blaming you for anything, and I'm not judging you. I was just... I was just surprised, is all."

"OK. Understood. Thank you for saying that. I was about to get a little pissed off."

"Who were the other ones?"

"One. There was just another one. His name was Rob. Rob Oliveira. He was from Portugal. He had a Portuguese father, and a Minnesotan mom, and we met my first year at KU. That year, we went on a few dates, but nothing serious, and we didn't talk again until my second year, when we had two courses together. We tried dating again, and this time around was better. We were a couple, although a very take-it-slow couple, from October to February, until he dumped me right before Valentine's Day. I think maybe I took it too slow for such a global, mature guy." The sarcasm in her voice weighed a ton. "So, I've had sex a total of four times with two people. I'm sorry you weren't the first. I'm sorry you weren't the only. But you're here now. I don't want you to regret thissss... eeeeitherrrr... waaaay." Annie didn't look so good.

"You don't look so good. I think I drained you of too much blood."

"Nnnnooooo. I'mmmm FFF... Ffine... M-m-mmaaake. Lovvvvve to---." And Annie fell asleep. Damn.

I took off the torn portion of shirt she used as a tourniquet and replaced it with proper gauze and Band-Aids after cleansing it with Neosporin. I then put her pajama shorts back on her, maybe sneaking a short glance at the wonderful ass I may never touch. I made sure I'd cleaned up any and all traces of blood on my body and the room, and took inventory of myself in the mirror, a clear mistake. I couldn't see the man Annie supposedly loved. All I saw was the monster that killed those six people in the desert. I saw the man-made demon that enjoyed it. Transforming further and getting my color sight back only made my reflection more cruel. Now I could see every gray-green decaying hue in my damaged façade, as well as the pronounced, blackened veins under my flesh. All the while, this monster's visage was offset by the brand new, beautiful cobalt blue eyes now entrenched in my head. *What the hell am I? Does this Luminastra Namtudari mean anything? Why did it happen to me?* I didn't have any answers, but knew that I had to talk to Alister Amaranth. But first, I was going to turn out the lights, slink into bed next to Annie, and hold her, hopefully repurposing all the love that she infused in me with her blood back to her through the slimmest shade of warmth I could muster. Hopefully, that would be enough.

Unfortunately, two hours into her sleep and my loving, protecting night watch, I could hear her heart pumping strong and healthily. I could feel the pulse in her arms, and feet, and neck, and lips. Her *lips*, of all things. And I could smell the dried, crusting, scabbing blood from her arms, as her cuts used the wonder of life to heal them. And I was *hungry*. I tightened my eyes, forcing the tears to stay in them, and slowly uncoiled my serpent's arms from around her body. I lay her head gently on a pillow, and removed myself from the bed. I stood over her for a few moments, watching her peacefully at sleep, her eyes moving rapidly and disjointed. Her dreams would no doubt be adventures. Adventures based in truths that no good, God-fearing Texas girl should ever live through. *I had fed enough, hadn't I?* Nevertheless, I knew that I had to remove myself from the room completely. I grabbed the extra key card to Felix's room and went to check on him, to get some much-needed advice and perspective from my new comrade. Yet, when I opened the door and turned on the light, all I found was a very well-kept room with no one in it. It looked like no one had ever checked in at all. I did find a note on the desk. It read the following:

"Tell your girl thanks for the room. A shower and new clothes make me feel like a new man. I'm going to go check on an old friend while I'm here. Don't worry about my broken bones. I'll be fine. I'll be back after a while. See you then." I never saw Felix Hendry again.

Chapter Twenty-Four: A Funny Thing Happened on The Way...

After telling myself that Felix's apparent short interlude in the early hours of the morning was in fact a long-term absence, and subsequently weighing the pros and cons of said absence, I went back into mine and Annie's room, leaving a bottle of water and two Tylenol on the table next to her. I then went back to Felix's room so I could get some sleep before having to bid her farewell yet again. I couldn't be too close to her. Her blood felt, sounded, and *tasted* too good. Three hours later, which flew by like five minutes, Annie was waking me up by gently nudging my shoulder. I opened my eyes, and scratched my head, looking up at her beautiful face. She smelled of some really nice body lotion.

"You don't know how relieved I was to come in here and not find you and Felix in a naked lover's embrace." My gut laughed, but my throat was too dry to allow any sound to leave my mouth. It sounded more like the cackle of dice being thrown on a floor of bones. I grabbed the water bottle out of her hand and took a gulp.

“I didn’t know you were so funny.”

“Where is Felix, by the way?”

“He left me a note saying he was checking on an old friend, but I think he more or less flew the coup.”

“Why?”

“Why not, I suppose. I mean, the closer I get to the Black Moon, the more dangerous things become. The more vulnerable an already wounded soldier becomes.”

“I guess. Well, I hope he’s ok out there.”

“The guy’s been through more than I ever will be, and I can possibly live for a few hundred years. I think he’ll be just fine.”

“I have to head to John Wayne. My flight leaves in a little over an hour.”

“I’m really sorry last night didn’t turn out how we wanted it to.”

“Me, too. It’s ok. Had we not talked, and went right to it, I probably would have passed out from lack of blood even sooner than I did.”

“Why didn’t you ever mention that Rob guy?”

“You never asked.”

“I was afraid to.”

“And now we know why… Look, I’ve had boyfriends here and there ever since sixth grade, and I had genuine feelings for some of them… but for what it’s worth, I think I’ve only ever loved you.”

“Same here… Although, there’s this one stripper in Laughlin---”

“Davis McCarty, you are *NOT FUNNY*!’.

“I’m a little funny.” Annie smiled briefly but then swapped her face for a much more serious expression.

“Remember, you promised me you’ll call me if it doesn’t look like you’ll make it out of there, or after you have. Take the rest of the sunlight to sleep here in total darkness. I got the room for two days, so if you make it back here tonight, tomorrow before the sun comes up, all you have to do is leave. Just leave the keycard on the table by the bed. I love you, Davis, and I’m praying you come out of this.”

“I love you, too, Annie.”

She stooped down to give me a kiss on the cheek and rest her head against mine, and then walked to the door. Turning her head to face me once more, I could see the watery film of tears filling her eyes, and then she walked out and closed the door behind her. Tonight, I’ll head to the House of the Black Moon, and I’ll simply ask to speak with Alister Amaranth. Whatever happens, happens. But first, I’ll take full advantage of the chance at solitude and rejuvenation Annie reserved for me.

At 9:00pm, the alarm I set went off like bombs in WWII France, and I scrambled to get to its shutoff button. I got dressed in the new clothes Annie somehow had delivered to our room, these ones fitting my new physique perfectly. As I neared readiness, I knelt down, put my elbows on the bed, and once again prayed to some invisible God I’d never really believed in. I didn’t know if he was listening, or if he cared, but I had to say my peace, just in case. I prayed to come out of tonight a human being again. One that could pursue a relationship with Annie that might lead to marriage and kids, and a house with a wrap-around porch where we could enjoy a sweet tea and watch the sunset. Afterward, I got in the truck and drove the twenty minutes or so to the House of the Black Moon. I hadn't scouted it out ahead of time, and this was the first time putting my eyes on it. It was a lot larger than I had envisioned, and it, not surprisingly, was all black. A mediterranean style stucco estate with lots of columns and multiple balconies. A velvet rope lined the sidewalk, with a long line of people hoping to gain admittance. I thought to myself *Is this the American headquarters of the vampire community I'd been led to believe it is, is it a hot shot's personal mansion, or is it just a mega-sized club similar to the Wet Beaver, etc.?* I passed it up, detecting with my nose that the ratio of vampires to humans in line was twenty to one, and parked at Castaways Park, just like I had a few nights ago. I didn't need my vehicle trapped in the vicinity if I managed to get out of there. I also didn't have time to go stand in line with a bunch of wannabes and rejects. *If they have to stand there*, I reasoned, *they're not important enough to get in. Was I turning into the aristocratic vampire asshole I'd seen on television*? In any case, I was going to the front of the line, and I was going to get in sooner rather than later.

"The line forms to my left. Can I help you?" a larger doorman than I'd ever seen in person barked at me with a gruff expression and a disinterested voice.

"I'm here to see Alister Amaranth."

"You and everybody who's in the line - forming to my left."

"I'm Davis. Davis from Texas."

"And?" I'd expected that to be enough. I had no prepared response to his ambivalence.

"Umm. Can you use your walkie talkie thing to radio to someone who might know who I am and get that message to Alister? Tell them I *just* want to talk." He stared at me with fierce, commanding eyes, thinking that would be adequate to scare me off and have me get in the line. He was wrong, and I stared back just as fiercely. This was a virtual pissing contest. The doorman then smiled an arrogant smile, and broke the silence.

"OK, asshole. You asked for this… Hey, Cyrus. I've got a Davis from Texas here, asking to 'just talk' to Alister." We waited, looking at the walkie talkie for a few seconds.

"Send him up, now. Alister will meet him in the Lavender Room." The doorman's eyebrow raised, and he mouthed 'oh shit' to me before signing off with Cyrus.

"It looks like you're a VIP, Davis."

"I guess so. Where's the Lavender Room?"

"Go through these doors, take a left at the entry to the main floor, and follow the wall until you get to a guy guarding access to a stairwell. He'll know who you are, and he'll let you up the stairs. The Lavender Room will be the second door on the left, at the second floor. Try to stay alive."

I watched the doorman remove the ceremonial rope that prevented me from entering and stand aside to allow me in, and I held my head high, confidently striding through the ornate, imposing double doors. Once inside, I was greeted by the loudest, eardrum torturing techno music in the main room, with 90's hip hop faintly droning on elsewhere, and a complex array of eye-shattering lights pummeling the crowd as they danced and writhed and grinded upon each other. The middle of the main room looked large enough to house two of Mona's homes comfortably inside it, yards and all. I couldn't begin to estimate the population pounding and stomping on its marble floor. I imagined that this was what the most popular clubs in L.A., New York, and Miami must be like. Shaking my head to free myself of the mesmerizing effect of the display, I turned left and followed the wall like instructed, and soon got to the doorman at the stairs.

"Davis from Texas?" I thought it was funny how this was now a thing. Davis from Texas. *Would I forever be known as this*?

"The one and only."

"Up these steps to the second floor, second door on the left."

"Thank you."

"Don't mention it."

I ran my fingers against the walls as I ascended the stairs, catching muffled parts of various conversations behind closed doors, and bits and pieces of loud, rambunctious exchanges on the dance floor. I knocked on the door of the Lavender Room, and it opened automatically for me. No one behind it, I entered carefully, spotting Alister standing with his back to me, pouring a drink at a personal bar. A large, glossy-topped mahogany conference room table separated the two of us. A handful of comfy, black leather chairs around the room were the only other items in it. I closed the door, and all the noise and sound from outside the door was immediately canceled out by silence. I was impressed.

"Ahh, Davis," Alister addressed me with his back still turned. I took that as a sign that he either felt unthreatened or tried to project that perception. "Davis, Davis, Davis. You are unique in your stubbornness and persistence. I do want to give you credit for stifling your combative urges, and thank you for becoming more open to listening and learning. More importantly, Sinjin Pierce thanks you. You could have caused some serious tantrums in his respective establishments, but you played nice. I won't forget that. Now, as for the Horizon Vista, on the other hand. That scene wasn't so civil. Many of my brothers lost their lives under your boots, and much productivity was halted." Alister spun around to face me. "Neither will I forget that."

"That wasn't my fault. Your lapdog was going to slaughter a child."

"No, he was going to right an injustice and set an example by terminating an underperforming, insubordinate, disloyal employee." I was stunned.

"*Employee*? The kid was 11 years old, and moved into his "position" because Daniel had his predecessor killed – *in front of him*."

"Semantics."

"Semantics? What kind of heartless, soulless individual finds it acceptable to force a child into drug distribution, and to kill him in a gruesome, public execution?"

"A vampire."

"And how is that abandoned old folks home operation your highest revenue margin?"

"What would give you that idea?"

"Raven; he said so, plain as day."

"That idiot. Other than to make the others in attendance think the offense was more dire than it was, I have no idea why he would say that. It's unequivocally small potatoes in the grand scheme of things. Raven…" A hint of disgust danced across Alister's jaw. "I never would have given him such a high-ranking position, except for his status as an elder and his friendship with Daniel. I have to keep Daniel happy, because underneath that tall, lead singer swagger is a really insecure adolescent, starved for acceptance and affection. Really, though; Raven is such a poser. You would think he was a vamp tramp instead of an actual vampire."

"Vamp tramp?" I was intrigued.

"Yeah, vamp tramp. You've heard the term 'fag hag', right?"

"Yes."

"That's the vampire version. Just a faithful, devoted, blood drinker's fan. I mean how little self-esteem and common sense must someone have to fall into that category. It's like having daddy issues multiplied by fucking ever… We're going to have to agree to disagree on that whole Raven fracas. How can I help you, Davis? Wait, first tell me about the Luminastra Namtudari. Did that really happen?"

"That's one of the reasons I wanted to talk to you. What the *HELL* is the Luminastra Namtudari?!"

"Haha! God, you're a funny dude. Would you like a drink?"

"Water, please."

"Yes, sir. Right away, sir." Alister laughed at his own comment, and seemed to get all goofy on me for a second. "Sorry, sorry. I must have felt the need to add a little levity to the atmosphere. I can speak to the Namtudari for sure, but first, I believe a proper crash course in all things vampire is of the utmost importance. You need to know the past and present. You need to be able to separate the truth from fiction."

"Please, yes. I believe that will help."

"Okay, then. Have a seat. Where do we begin? Oh, yes! At the beginning. So, I don't know what you've researched, or discovered, or learned, but the first "vampire" was Aylash Revall, and he became so around 2,500 B.C. in Sumer, which you might know as Iraq. In some cultures, as a human, Aylash might be called an alchemist, or a sorcerer. He might even be called a witch or a wizard. What I know is that he was a mystical priest of sorts who went off on his own and attempted for most of his adult life to alter the natural and improve upon it.

He basically wanted the power of the divine to shine inside humanity. Not altogether a bad idea, but his methods for trying to attain it left something to be desired among his people. Like any insane but captivating figure, he did develop a small, fanatical following, but was shunned by the general public for the most part. He conducted experiments, and performed rituals, all for the ultimate purpose of overcoming or outlasting mortality. I know, it doesn't sound like all it's cracked up to be, immortality, but back then metaphorical fountains of youth stood like a pillar next to mythological ones. Aylash's experiments included living and dead subjects, all types of bodily fluids, and the best substances and solutions he could possess or create at the time.

"One day, after having previously tried so many different potions on himself and his most fervent disciples, he comes across a breakthrough: a liquid he ingests that makes him suffer in pain, boiling every system within his insides, turning his skin grayish white and jaundiced yellow green. His people think he's dying, and one half of them are trying to comfort him with water, food, and digestive medicines to hopefully expel the concoction, and the other half are trying to manhandle him onto a death bed to either prepare for his natural stoppage, or to sacrifice him to end his pain. He manages to push away and break free from all of them, and crawls outside where he falls into a large hole being dug to build a cistern. In the hole were two teenage girls hiding from their parents and chores. The two were startled and frightened by this horrific, suffering man, and started to climb out of the hole. Unfortunately for them, and unbeknownst to Aylash as to why, he feels the unquenchable urge to consume blood, and he grabs one of the teens and starts biting her all over her arms and neck. The second girl tries to rescue her friend and starts beating on him, but it's no use, and he shoves the first girl down to attack the second. In a moment of shear instinct shaking hands with ingenuity, his body directs him to her carotid artery, and he pops through that sucker with his teeth at full munch. He drinks her to death while his first victim just watches, paralyzed with terror. After he drops the one girl to the ground, he jumps on top of the other, and sinks his teeth into her. Her eyes turn a hazy, metallic gray, and her legs tremor and thrash violently. The frenzy gets Aylash's nether region all ablaze, and he rapes her while he feeds. Afterward, he sat there drunk on blood, his suffering subsided. He looks up to the sky to find his followers watching in stunned silence. Aylash lifted his hand to be pulled out of the hole, and as he's brought back up to the surface, the sun touches his skin and within seconds, he's burning and writhing in pain. Blisters and splotches form on his skin, and one of his men, Petras, throws a cloak over him and pushes him inside his domicile/laboratory."

Alister's tale is highly entertaining, and I'm on the edge of my seat, when we're interrupted by news of a confrontation down on the floor. As he instructs his assistant to not waste his time with trivial matters while he's occupied with me, I get a whiff of Devin Sikorsky in my nostrils. She's downstairs, and she's close. My eyes dilate, and my stomach churns. I want to fly down the stairs, find her, and crush her windpipe.

"Easy, tiger. You haven't heard anything yet. Devin

can wait." He knew everything I was feeling, without any communication at all. "May I continue?"

"Uh, yes. Please."

"For hours, Aylash's people are observing him and trying to feed him, but he'll only take water. Everything else seems trivial, and nauseating. The whole time, a crowd has been growing outside his house, with the parents of the two slain girls mourning in anguish, and demanding that the purveyor of their murders be brought out and dealt justice. The most physically imposing of Aylash's cult stand guard outside, preventing anyone from entering by force, while the rest of the group sit inside, concerned about their master. Then, about seven or so hours after he killed the girls, Revall goes through the same ravenous ordeal all over again, and just like before, his only priority is blood. The downside is, the only blood available belongs to his followers, so he rips into the nearest one, his loyal man Petras. Several people try at first to pull him off the poor disciple, but it's futile, and before you know it, Petras is no more. But now Aylash is satiated after just the one victim. His body returns to almost normal, and he calms his people down. In short order, they all realize that this is going to happen again, and they all surmise that if a live sacrifice is necessary, then it's better to bestow that fate upon someone else." I stop Alister right there, for a question.

"How do you know all this?" I threw out skeptically.

"The story was written down by Aylash, and separately by his follower, Tulonus. They both kept detailed journals of everything before and after the transformation, which the Sumerians call the Namtudari, loosely translated as birth/death/rebirth. Some fifteen years later, a third person started keeping his own accounts. To honor Petras, who died leaving behind a pregnant wife, Aylash suggested that his widow name their unborn son Sartep, which of course is Petras backward. Sartep ended up becoming Aylash's longest lasting follower. He also became the second ever vampire to walk the earth, and the person to continually update the writings so they never deteriorated. Copies were passed down to various vampires through history, and one of them is kept safely in the confines of this establishment."

"Did Aylash bite Sartep to turn him?"

"Yes. Whatever liquid poison Aylash concocted to send him to his fate, his followers destroyed it after seeing its terrifying result. Additionally, they set fire to the journal entries documenting the ingredients to the potion. At first, Aylash didn't blame them at all. It seemed as if he'd cursed himself to an abomination of an existence. Once he comprehended that he could continue living, however limited he might be, he tried to recreate the potion. Only, no one would drink it. They were all afraid. So, on they went, eventually worshipping Aylash as some sort of demonic angel. He's referenced several times in journals as the Lower God. Aylash must have felt lonely in his status, and having sought unsuccessfully to convince anyone to take his fateful drink, he tried a second option. A few days before Sartep's thirtieth birthday, Aylash crept into Sartep's room, wrapped himself around his follower, and asked if Sartep would trust him to conduct an experiment. Sartep agreed timidly, thinking he was going to be sodomized, and Aylash bit into his throat for just a fraction of time."

"Wait, wait. Go back. You mentioned Aylash's people realizing that they didn't want to become his dinner, so what did they do?"

"Well, that shouldn't be hard to deduce. They started grabbing other Sumerians. Nothing in the texts suggests that they even thought about using animals instead of humans, so they started with the homeless, then the criminals sentenced to die, then orphans, and random foreigners travelling through. Through trial and error, and Aylash's own developing palette, he could soon recognize quality blood from poor. A victim's diet, hydration level, and overall hygiene all factored into his experience. His findings, and maybe his downfall, all pointed to the hypothesis that the richest, most well-kept members of society had to have the healthiest, most sustaining blood. Thus, he and his followers expanded, or more accurately, selectively adjusted their menu to only provide a certain prey. This is when the public really took notice of disappearances and people found dead in and around Sumer."

"Wait… Go back *again*. What happened to the mob and the grieving parents of Aylash's first two victims?"

"Damn, dude! These are all *good* questions! Aside from the parents of the girl he raped while devouring, there's no further mention of the mob or the aftermath of the evening."

"And what of that girl's parents?"

"They kept asking for justice for their daughter, but

the ruling class either didn't take the story seriously, or someone within their ranks was protecting Aylash. Possibly both. The father decided to take matters into his own hands, and broke into Aylash's home in the middle of the night. Aylash hadn't yet fed, and drank of the man in short order. To avoid any questions or backlash from the wife, he travelled to their house and fed on her in her sleep. Both bodies were used as needed for Aylash's continued experimentation. His desire for purer and purer blood led to him lowering the age of his victims, and word started to spread about who was responsible for the kidnappings and murders. A large group of men under King Ur-Nanshe's rule marched through lower Sumer to Aylash's compound, and torched the home, with everything and everyone in it. Luckily, Aylash and half of his group were camped out in Tulonus' home, some fifty yards away. Whether or not someone had tipped off Aylash or his group, Tulonus had commandeered horses and a wagon, and he, Sartep, and a woman named Isa rode off inconspicuously, exiting Sumer for what is present day Pakistan. Aylash and the smallest four of his followers were covered underneath ragged stacks of straw and grain. By the time they got to their destination, the four hidden with Aylash had been reduced to one, a child named Muhabar. The other surviving members of his group would slowly trickle out of Sumer and convene with the fugitives in time. Isa and Muhabar would go on to become the third and fourth ever vampires on earth, respectively. This happened not long after Sartep's transformation."

"And not Tulonus?"

"No. For two reasons. One, he didn't want to

become what Aylash had, and two, they needed someone who could still move about in the daytime. A win-win as far as I'm concerned. Sartep's journal states that Tulonus died after an argument in an open-air market turned violent, and he was stabbed to death. The same night, Aylash and Isa hunted and killed Tulonus' slayer, skinning him alive and hanging him upside down in the market square."

"So, how long did Aylash live, and did he manifest any powers, or abilities similar to today's vampires?"

"After fleeing Sumer, Aylash was basically on the run for the rest of his existence. Rumor and truth both followed him, and he eventually succumbed, ending his struggle after 150 years. His final journal entry describes a man tired from running, hiding, and killing. No different than us. We don't do this very long, especially considering we can technically do it forever. During that time, though, he developed the same super speed, super strength, super hearing, wind-soaring, and everything else today's seasoned vampires can muster. He *even* underwent the *Luminastra Namtudari*." Alister did the spooky ghost hands at me.

"I've been waiting for this."

"What happened to you, when you got yours? What were the circumstances, and what was the physical change?"

"Raven had just finished dining on Ben, and dro---"

"Ben? You mean Business?" Anger filled my mouth, and I bit my lip at the possibility that Alister didn't even know Ben's real name. "Relax. I know his real name was

Ben."

"As soon as Raven had declared that Ben was going to die, I started to run at Raven, but was instantly stopped by about six of his loser buddies."

"Easy. Those are my brothers of the night. *Your* brothers of the night... Just kidding. Those guys are dipshits."

"Almost as soon as I was in their grip, I felt a change. I felt my muscles stretch and strain, and once Raven ordered his grunts to kill me, with Ben laying on the ground just seconds from transformation, my entire body went into hyperdrive. It was like I swallowed a smaller version of me, and now they were growing and pushing out of me. I'm taller and stronger than I ever would have been as a human."

"Oh, I'm aware. I remember the you I fought in Glendale. Your new and improved version might be able to survive a one-on-one contest with almost any vampire... Almost. Did your eye color change? I can't tell because I only see black and gray."

"It did. It's a really stark shade of blue."

"What the hell does "stark shade of blue" mean, Shakespeare?"

"Dark piercing blue."

"Fine."

"What caused Revall to go through his?"

"He spent his last 80 years on Earth shuttling back and forth between present day Hungary, Turkey, and

Serbia. Myths and legends have him spending a lot of time in Bulgaria and Romania, but neither his own journals, nor Sartep's, list anything more than a week or two in either of those territories. Aylash had apparently gotten too predictable in his route, and too trusting of his followers, and one night, the father of a slain Slavic boy and practically the entirety of his village lay in wait for Revall to travel through. They ambushed his caravan, killing almost all of his followers, and planned an especially gruesome justice for him. They tied his feet together and attached them to a horse facing one way. They then tied his hands together, and placed a noose around his neck and fastened both of those ropes to a horse facing the opposite direction. As the grieving father railed publicly against the evil that lay caught before them, and the village chieftains said prayers and sang hymns before obliterating Aylash's body, he undertook the Luminastra Namtudari. Same situation as you. Bigger, stronger, more uncontrollable, and more ravenous. He snapped the rope around his feet, and pulled the horse tied to his upper limbs toward him, causing it to fall to the ground. Once it did, he mounted its neck and bit a grapefruit sized hole in it. It took the villagers several seconds to get over the shock of what was unfolding before them, after which they attacked Revall with spears and hatchets. He blocked and dodged and swatted away every thrust and swing, and killed the entire mob. He placed the head of the slain boy, whom he killed two months prior, on a spear, and drove it into the ground, so that it would be the first thing passersby saw as they entered the village. He propped up the boy's father's head just behind it. Before you ask, I don't know why the Namtudari happened, to him or to you, and neither does anyone else, but it only seems to happen under complete and utter duress, and only to people who have been transformed by someone who's been transformed by Aylash Revall himself."

"So that means that..."

"It means that you and Devin Sikorsky, and whoever bit her, and yada-yada, are part of the same vampire family tree as the very first fucking vampire to ever exist."

"But wouldn't we all be---"

"Related? Like wouldn't we all be descendants of Adam and Eve or of Noah, because all but him and his family died in the flood?"

"Well, yeah."

"That I don't know, my man. I don't believe in any religion, so your guess is as good as mine." Just then, I felt my phone vibrate with a text message. "Go ahead and check it," Alister approved. His hearing or echolocation, what-have-you, was very good.

"I apologize. I'm just hoping that it's Annie or---"

"Felix. Yes, I know. How was the hotel?"

"How? How did you---"

"I could smell you, man. I could smell all of you." I looked down, and saw a Laughlin, Nevada number identified.

"I don't recognize the number. I'll just be a second." The message was typed out abruptly and choppy. It read

'SINJIN. CAN'T TALK. DON'T TRUST ALISTER. AFRAID OF YOU. ANNIE IN DANGER'. I didn't understand at first, but then it finally hit me. I had to play it cool. "It's just a scammer. Those bastards just don't quit." I hoped he bought it. I needed time to figure out if the message was true, or if this was just a trick. I never gave Sinjin my number, so I don't know how the hell he would have gotten it. I texted the number back, asking for clarification, and texted Annie as well, but had to stall while I waited. "How did you become a vampire, and how and why did you form a band?"

"Yes! I was hoping we'd get to that! I'll try to keep this as short as possible. I was born Harold Alister Wofford in Brockton, Massachusetts, in 1908. My father went into investment brokerage, and we moved to New York City in 1925. We weren't anything big; weren't even in the financial district. My father had a small office on the 11th floor of a building on 48th and 3rd. He did alright for himself, but put a lot of his own money in the market. On October 24th, 1929, the stock market crash hit. He worried, but didn't lose his shit until the 29th. He'd lost everything, not just for his clients, but his own investments as well. I was in my final year at City College and had already started working for him, and I walked into the office that Tuesday after class to see my father jumping out of the window. Instinctively, I leapt out the window after him, and was falling to my own death. About halfway down, my fall was intercepted by a mid-air tackle. I had no idea what was happening, but it was as if a hurricane had thrown me through a window back inside the building. Before I could even tend to the throbbing welp forming on my head, something was attacking me. It had bitten down on my throat, and blood was pouring from every direction. Just as quickly as it started, the creature was letting go of me, and standing up. That's when I realized it wasn't some winged beast, but a man." 'Do you really think dying is the best way to live your life', he asked me. I was puzzled by such an esoteric question. 'My name is Warren Winston, and I'm going to give you the chance at a second chance'. Every sentence, every phrase he uttered seemed more arcane and equivocal than the previous. Either way, he stood there and watched me go through the growing pains of vampire transformation, and when I thought I was finally going to die, suffocating on my own lack of oxygenated blood, he disappeared for a split second and returned with the eighth-floor cleaning lady. He threw her down on the floor next to me, and said 'feed'. I somehow knew what to do after that."

"Warren Winston. Where do I know that name?"

"If you've heard that name, it's because Sinjin Pierce said it. He probably told you the story of how his parents were killed and his siblings turned into vampires during a stop on a cross-country camping trip. I honestly think Sinjin is lonely as hell. He will talk your damn ear off."

"Yes! Yes, that's it. Jack and Milena."

"I was with Warren that night, one of the vile creatures that assisted in the carnage. I need to point out that the Warren in New York in 1929 and the Warren in Flagstaff in 1958 were two very different specimen. When he turned me, he was eloquent, debonair, and very charming. However, he got himself banished from the House of the Stone Sword, and all of New York, and somewhere along the way he'd gone off the deep end. We travelled west nomadically, where he envisioned creating an army of the night that would overthrow humankind and enslave them for our bidding and our nourishment. By the time we got to Sinjin's Winnebago, Warren was transforming as many able-bodied men and boys as he could, which is actually frowned upon by the overall community. No vampire has ever been known to impregnate a woman, but he tried merrily and voraciously, and even transformed a handful of females, ages 13 to 30, in hopes that a vampire could conceive with a vampire. That very experiment was referenced in Aylash Revall's journals from over 3,000 years ago. We relocated to California in 1980, some 250 vampires with Warren as their Julius Caesar. The House of the Black Moon was first established in 1916, and had been in permanent brick and mortar existence in some form since the late 40's. With his followers supporting him, Warren decapitated the House's captain and took it over. A failed attempt at the same act is what got him banned from New York. He thought everything was going to plan, but just two years later, Jack Pierce, Sinjin's older brother, committed suicide by laying out on the beach at sunrise. His flesh seared and burned, with no blood or oxygen in him. He washed out to sea, and was fished out by the coast guard. An autopsy revealed more questions than answers, an investigation stalled with Jack classified as a John Doe, and our kind had to really lay low for a long period. The other vampire strongholds around the country, and even across the ocean, started to question what the hell was going on in California.

"I referred to Warren as our Julius Caesar; well, you

know what happened to him, right?" I nodded and muttered 'et tu, Brute'. "It was during this time of fragile relations among the various networks of vampires and more hiding in the shadows than taking over the earth that Milena, Jack's sister, exacted revenge almost 25 years in the making. Under the guise of trying to arouse Warren sexually without the need to feed first, Milena stabbed Warren straight in the heart with two 12th century daggers, and as he stared frightfully into her eyes, she took an iron hammer, similar to Thor's, and caved the right side of his head and face in. I heard his gasp from several rooms away when the daggers went in, and tore off after him, but I was too late. He was dead. I avenged him instantly, driving my fist straight through Milena's chest and shoving her heart out the other side. Warren's army pledged their allegiance to me, and I became the custodian for the House of the Black Moon. Instead of overthrowing the human race, we now focus on constant partying, illicit drug use, and very loud music. Real contribution to the history."

"So, music. What's the deal behind forming a band and trying to attain popularity when you should probably be hiding yourselves from the general public?"

"The simplest answer? We just love music. It's the only thing that's probably kept the four of us, at least me and Devin for sure, from joining Jack Pierce on the beach at sunrise. I fell in love with "rock 'n' roll" as soon as I'd heard Little Richard, and then I spent decades listening to and learning every style of music I could get my hands on. Being here in California, I had nightly access to every kind of style in every kind of club imaginable. Rock one night, metal the next. Jazz on

Wednesday and punk on Thursday, you name it. In the 80's, the sunset strip was a haven for debaucherous behavior and flashy guitar acrobatics. It was the perfect setup for playing with my food, if you will. I eventually found like-minded vampires who could also play instruments, and we formed Unholy Saint. Or should I say, we formed Mortician, which became Cadaver, which became Black Orchid, which finally became Unholy Saint. The genres and songcraft evolved with each name change, until you have the band that exists today. Going as far as we can, in essence pretending to be something we're not, allows us to tour, which allows us to feed all over the country, keeping down the level of suspicion. And who would expect a group of vampires to be public figures. We give interviews, however seldom, during the day. They just happen to be indoors. We play festivals, but just ones that have all-night tents, so we can make the appearance without the hassle of declining to perform during the day. That our name is getting bigger and our popularity increasing, we'll just cross that bridge when we come to it. Because we all feel that the next album will make us Bonafide rock stars, headlining theaters and small arenas instead of just clubs and bars in places like Abilene, TX."

"Do you always seek to feed on your fans?" A tense bitterness arrived wholesale on my tongue, and deep inside my quivering intestines.

"That's a fair question. As honestly as I can put it, I don't care who I feed on. I don't care about humans and their everyday lives and struggles. I've pursued this existence – notice that I'll rarely use the word 'life' – long enough to know that survival of the fittest might be the greatest truth our planet has. I'm not saying the meek don't have a place here, but I'm saying their place, ultimately, is to satisfy the strong. Having said that, I don't condone Devin's method that night. We have protocols for multiple reasons, primarily to prevent being discovered, but I've noticed that Devin has met that inevitable existential melancholy that all vampires get, at one point or another. Comparable to a mid-life crisis, it typically occurs at the fifty-year mark, and she's been a night drinker for sixty now. How they deal with it determines if a vampire lasts a long time, or if they burn out and fade to dust. She's gotten careless, or carefree, and has taken to behaving in ways that could harm not only her, but the band. We have bodyguards on the road, but those bodyguards aren't there to protect us from our fans or the public; they're to protect us from *us*. Isaac was assigned to Devin on this tour, and in your town, he fucked up. She slipped away from him, and you got turned because of it. The punishment was that Isaac was fed to dogs in El Paso, his remaining carcass dumped in the Rio Grande."

"What I don't get is why Texas doesn't have a place like Sinjin's or why there was never a headquarters situated there. How did vampires decide where the 'Houses' would be?"

"Mostly the denseness of the population, but also the prominence and leadership of certain vampires. Your state's population would most assuredly demand a House. Trust me, there are a shit-ton of vampires in the Lone Star State. But there are no actual dynamic leaders in the whole bunch. Just a bunch of fucking cowboys all wanting to be desperados. We tend to call vampires with no community lone wolves, and I'll be damned if Texas isn't the Lone Wolf capital of the entire vampire world."

"You punished Isaac for my incident, but what are you to do with Devin?"

"What can I do? She's become like the most popular member of the band. And her songwriting is improving. I can't just kick her out."

"No. What do you do about her existential crisis? I'm sure that hasn't just up and vanished."

"True. True." Alister looked down at his right hand, running his thumb along the tips of his fingers. I could sense a deep contemplation in his head, and maybe the conflict of choosing his next words. "Getting off the road couldn't have come at a better time. It allows her to face her feelings and decide what's important. One major hurdle, which will either invigorate her or destroy her, is confronting you. She's got to distinguish you as friend or foe."

"I'll never be her friend. Let's get that clear."

"Oh, don't be so sure, Lone Wolf. I've seen the transformed, willing or not, grow to love their makers, and thrive within these walls. I've seen alliances form, and relationships crumble, but make no mistake, what you think you know doesn't mean about shit compared to the reality of things. The gravity of things. Hell, you might even end up being her lover, or her bass tech on tour. If she can convince you that here is the best place for you. If she can't, then we have a mutual dilemma. Because you somehow were gifted with the Luminastra

Namtudari, I doubt she can defeat you in combat. You're perfectly within your rights to get your revenge for what's been done to you, but I also can't just sit by and watch you kill my bass player. So I, we, may have to get involved."

Like this was playing out in a movie, Devin appeared in the doorway out of nowhere. This time, I didn't hear or smell her.

"Hi, Davis. Wanna talk?"

Chapter Twenty-Five: Crescendo

"I thought you'd *never* get here." Devin tended to look downward, a reticence in her I was just seeing for the first time. I didn't know if she was just playing the part to lure me in. We had left the confines of the Lavender Room and ambled along the catwalk strewn high above the dance floor, before exiting to a private balcony on the back end of the building.

"All of you ordered me at least once to not come here, accompanied by the threat of extreme torturous violence, and now you're surprised it took me so long to make it?" The look of frustrated confusion on my face could have been etched on stone tablets, with a latex mold made of it, to permanently commemorate my astonishment.

"Point taken. Things have changed, though."

"What things?"

"The Namtudari, for one."

"Really? Who cares? What's the big deal?" Her eyes bugged out a little, and her expression said, 'are you an idiot?', without her having to.

"The big deal is that no vampire here or anywhere that I know of has ever seen it happen. It was just words in an ancient book before you, not real. A myth."

"So, now I'm worthy of living? Or continuing, rather? I'm the vampire version of the guy you won't give the time of day until you see his $300,000 car?"

"It's not like that. And for the record, I doubt I'd ever be attracted to you. This does change things, though. It needs to be investigated. Analyzed."

"So I'd make a wonderful lab rat, you mean?"

"Well, yeah. Well said, Davis."

"Wrong answer." I lowered my shoulders, and hunched my back, and stalked toward Devin with aggression, and she backpedaled, caught off guard by my advance.

"Hold on. Hold on a minute! Are you going to kill me?"

"That was always my intention. And you are saying the exact opposite of the words someone who wants to live would say."

"Give me a second!" She was authentically afraid. I don't think Devin Sikorsky has been afraid of anything in quite a long time. Her teeth were chattering, and her hands trembled. Not detectable to the naked human eye, but obvious to me. "I'm failing to say what I want to, but my intent is not to hurt your feelings." Just then, my phone vibrated three times in four seconds. "Whoa. You're a popular guy, nowadays."

"If you'll excuse me for a second. Now would be the time to think of something intelligent and flattering to say."

One text from Annie and two from Laughlin. Annie's read 'I'm fine. Just sitting in my room worrying about you, after spending the evening with my mom. The whole ride home from the airport was a heated debate over whether or not I go back to KU. How are *you*?' Laughlin's read 'Trust me. Sent you a letter to the Huntress. Crystal's got a crush on you' and 'If they don't grab Annie, tonight, they'll do it tomorrow. Not a prank. Not a joke'. I had to think fast, but there was nothing I could do for Annie. If a gang of vampires burst into Bob Moore's home, they'd be done for.

'Everything alright?', Devin asked. Her voice sounded sincere.

"Yes. No problem. Where were we?"

"I was putting my foot in my mouth while trying to explain why you should join us and not kill me."

"No time like the right now."

"I can't take back anything I said in the past about you, or your town, or your fate, because it was the truth. You were no different than anyone else I'd fed on in the past. At least, that's what I thought. But now, I'm thinking maybe I got interrupted before killing you – *for a reason*. Maybe you were *meant* to become one of us.

Maybe, you were meant to attain the Luminastra Namtudari, and come here to California to become our king." I had to put my hand over my mouth to keep from laughing, and had to pause for a moment before responding.

"You can't be serious?"

"Oh, I'm dead serious. In one of Sartep's journal entries, he spoke of one of his final conversations with Aylash Revall. I know that Alister intended to give you a history lesson tonight, so I'm sure you know both those names now."

"Actually, I first discovered Revall's name on a website. It was-"

"Please not Carpathian Chalice."

"CarpathianChalice.com. Yes. That one."

"Jesus Christ. That website is full of such bullshit."

"They know who Aylash Revall is, and what time period he comes from."

"They also spout stupid shit, like how it's possible to become human again if you---"

"Kill the vampire who made you." I lowered my head and stared straight into Devin with one raised eyebrow. Her teeth and fingers started back up again.

"You don't honestly believe that, do you?" I didn't change my stare. "Come ON, Davis! That website is the vampire equivalent of a conspiracy theorist's wet dream."

"It was actually a real-life person who informed me about such a possibility. A second one told me of someone they knew who'd actually accomplished it."

"Who?"

"Who, what?"

"Who's the vampire that supposedly did this? Our community isn't that large, Davis. We're all interwoven or otherwise connected somehow. Except for maybe the homos in Texas."

"Ouch. You might want to cut down on the Texas bashing."

"Oh my God. You people do love your state, don't you?"

"They say New Yorkers are born tough. Well, Texans are born proud."

"I think I just threw up a little in my mouth. And I haven't eaten a meal in sixty years. So, who is it? Who's the magical former vampire?"

"Ruben Donovan." Three seconds after I said his name, the door to the balcony opened, and a sharp, whistling wind whirled past my ears. Just like that, Alister was leaning against its railing with a sour look on his face.

"Bullshit," he stated rather sternly.

"Did you hear me? Could you hear everything I was saying?"

"Pretty much. And the Ruben Donovan story is

bullshit."

"How do you know?"

"Because I've known Ruben Donovan ever since the day I ruined his burgeoning music career. He was never a vampire. He did have a really big mouth, though. So big that one day, I shut it for him, by ripping it from his skull."

"What are you talking about? Ruben Donovan died of throat cancer."

"*Throat cancer*?! That's a fucking laugh. My sense of smell can sniff out cancer, and his dumb ass didn't have cancer. Who told you that lame ass story?"

"My friend, Felix. They were friends."

"No they weren't! Felix Hendry never did anything in the Naked Huntress but sit and stare off into space. He'd order one damn drink and nurse it all goddamned night, until they had to kick him out of the place. Sinjin had a soft spot for the guy because he had Brittle Bone Disease or Multiple Sclerosis, or some shit. So, instead of banning him from the place when patrons and dancers alike started complaining about the creepy weird guy staring at them, he had management put him up in the VIP section in his own little corner, like a damn mascot or something… Felix Hendry? That's the whole reason you've been hunting us down?"

This question made a metaphorical light bulb turn on in Devin's head.

"No. The timeline doesn't add up. He came after us almost immediately after Abilene. We only played one or two shows before he showed up to kill me in Hobbs, New Mexico. Laughlin wasn't for a few more days, which is where he would have met Felix. He'd already had it in his head that he might be able to return to human if he killed me."

"Then what the hell, Davis?"

"Wait. Brittle Bone Disease and MS? Wasn't Felix's condition due to a war-time injury?" Alister laughed out for several seconds, doubled over holding his stomach like I was the best comedian he'd ever seen.

"Man, he completely pulled the wool over your eyes! Do you believe everything someone tells you? You need to send your vampire bullshit detector back for a refund. It's defective." I was starting to get pissed, and Alister knew it. His laughter ended abruptly, and he tried to affect a more serious expression.

"Go back to Ruben Donovan. You said you ripped his mouth off?"

"Indeed. I had always heard of his various tall tales when corresponding with Sinjin, or when we'd stop in. I'd been visiting the Naked Huntress, just like all of Sinjin's establishments, since he opened it, and I came through town every now and then. I had to comprehend the big picture when it came to what being in a successful, active band meant, so I started travelling with a few of them, first as a roadie, then a guitar tech, and eventually a road manager. When I couldn't help but feed on some of the crew… Sorry, I digress. That's a story for another day… So, Ruben had always been a musician trying to make it, and also always a big mouth.

I paid it no mind, until his stories starting involving vampires. Finally, it got to be too much. He started telling some story about becoming a vampire, killing other vampires, and returning to humanity. He did *not* tell it to Felix. I know that much. Word got back to me about the most extravagant and close to home of his stories, and I decided to make an example out of him." Devin leaned next to Alister and put her elbow on his shoulder, enthusiastic to hear the tale. "I wasn't too keen on how much predator/prey interaction Sinjin introduced with his clubs and their private lairs to begin with. However, this Ruben business had gone way too far. He shouldn't have even known about the existence of vampires, much less get so comfortable as to use them as fodder in his horseshit. I came in one night and summoned him to my table behind the shimmering door. I told him I was aware of his fabrications, and gave him a chance to come clean. Instead, he lied right to my face, burying himself deeper and deeper in a riverbed of deceit. I ripped his mandible from his face mid-sentence, and then reached into his throat and pulled out his cervical vertebrae. I was too disgusted with him to feed on his blood; I didn't want its corruption flowing through me."

"And the throat cancer diagnosis?"

"Who knows? Maybe Ruben started that lie himself to get sympathy or free drinks from people. Maybe Sinjin told the lie to cover up what happened. I can't say, and I don't really care. If Felix never told you that he went to the hospital to visit Ruben in treatment, or watched him die slowly of the disease, or attended a funeral where dozens of people broke down and wept over the incorrigible bastard that is cancer, then it didn't happen. No matter what, I know there wouldn't have been a body present, cuz it got ground up and added to dog food donations for the local animal shelter."

Devin was ready for Alister to leave us, so we could continue our conversation.

"Hey, do you think you could…"

"Give you some more time?"

"Yes."

"Okay, but clock's ticking." That piqued my interest, and I raised my eyebrows and gazed at Devin while Alister took his leave of the balcony.

"What does he mean by clock's ticking, and how is his hearing so good that he could catch every word we say from across the building and through walls? Does it even really matter that he left our presence?"

"You've got to remember that even though you're now equipped with some really powerful party tricks, Alister's been a vampire for almost one hundred years. With that comes a wealth of knowledge, experience, and skill. Skill that's ever evolving. You're still technically a baby in this world. Not a teenager, not even a toddler, but a full-fledged shitting your diaper baby. And confidence turned arrogance will get even a superior creature such as yourself hung upside down from this balcony if you proceed like a baby."

"Got it… So what is it that we really need to talk about?"

"Before we got interrupted, I was *trying* to tell you about one of Sartep's last conversations with Aylash. Aylash had confided in him that he saw a vision of the future. A future where one vampire would unite all the others and raise a kingdom."

"That sounds like Warren Winston."

"I know, but this came from Aylash Revall. The man who was able to transcend man's normal timeline and nature."

"For 150 years. Big whoop. And at what cost? His life's work and the destruction that it's caused over a millennia, was not worth its execution. All he's wrought upon the world is death."

"The point is that he was right. He was able, and his writings, and his vision should be looked to. At least heard, if not heeded."

"Do you actually think that I, Davis McCarty, born in fucking Merkel, Texas, am the chosen one, destined to lead a universal kingdom of vampires throughout the 21st century? Do you hear how insane that sounds?"

"It doesn't mean that it's not true. You started off on your journey thinking something was possible. Redemption. But it's not. You can't go back home, and you can't turn back time. Maybe your journey was all to bring you here, to this time, to this destiny?"

"Do you even want that to be true? Would you even care? Alister thinks the whole reason you fed on me so brazenly and ridiculously close to the venue that night is because subconsciously or otherwise, you might be done with existence."

"And you know what? He may be right, or may have been. But your whole transformation, and everything that's happened since – it's revitalized me. It's given me a reason to wake up at night. I can say that I might be an integral part of---"

"My story? Oh, I see. If I'm the chosen one, then you're the vampire that created the chosen one. Devin begat Davis, and Davis begat so on and so on. Wow. You vampires are self-centered as shit."

"You're one of us, Davis. Please stop trying to pretend you're not. You're no better, or no more moral than we are. You'll have to feed tonight, right? Sooner rather than later? Unless you're degrading yourself by drinking of an animal, you'll have to feed on a human being. A *living* human being. There's no integ---"

"But I don't have a choice. I wasn't given one. Remember?!"

"That's a moot point. We're over that, now."

"*I'M* NOT OVER IT!" Devin took two steps back, and I could feel her pulse racing, which was hard to hear in a vampire, as there almost wasn't one.

"What do you want to hear, Davis? That I'm sorry? That I apologize? Will that make you feel better?"

"I guess not. You won't mean it, so what's the point?"

"So then what's your play?" She swiped her hair to the side, stared deep into my eyes, and sighed as if she already knew the answer to her question. She didn't.

"I... I need some time. I need some time to think."

I walked back inside the club, looking down on its revelers from the rafters as they swayed and drank and partied the night away. Think is almost all I did this entire hellish, surreal road trip. *Why did I need more time? Was I getting cold feet? Did I believe her that killing her wouldn't turn me back? Did I even believe any more that it would? Was Alister right about Felix? Was Felix basically a liar?* My brain was a jumbled mess. The thoughts were crashing from every direction, like I was trapped in a raging storm at sea. I had to close my eyes, breathe deep, and focus on one thing, one image, at a time. I thought of Annie, and her beautiful, spotless, scarless (aside from the ones she endured for me) body. On one hand was the remote possibility that she and I could still be together. Furthermore, there was a real possibility that she was in danger. I didn't have any reason to doubt Sinjin. Supporting those two points would make the case for killing Devin and anyone else who came to her defense. As I looked at the vampires below me, and noticed their lack of worry, their lack of accountability, I thought to myself, *do they even deserve to live? How many innocent people will die tonight, just to satisfy this unholy, unnecessary group of heathens*? Another case for destroying not just her, but the whole lot. What if she was right about Aylash's vision, though? Could it be possible that a nobody from west Texas could be the most important vampire since the very first one, and maybe even more so? It didn't hurt my ego to envision it for a bit, fantasizing about what that might look like? When I was going to go back to the balcony to let Devin know that I couldn't make up my mind, and that I needed to feed before anything else was to take place, I noticed that she, Alister, Daniel Sepulveda, Robert M., and their bodyguard Cyrus were surrounding me from all sides. Alister was organizing a preemptive strike.

"I can't let you feed until we know what you're going to do. If we're friends, then we've got a beautiful, big-tittied sorority girl all lined up for you to rip into. If we're enemies, then I need you to be as weak as possible to... even the odds."

"You shouldn't corner a desperate animal, Alister."

"And you shouldn't assume that *you're* the desperate animal."

Daniel was starting to bounce around on the balls of his feet, antsy and frenetic. He couldn't hold his tongue any longer.

"How did you get to be so damn special? I don't find you to be particularly intimidating."

"Yes, you do. I'm not the same shy newbie that you met in Hobbs. And I'm fairly certain you're no longer the strongest guy on this floor. No shame in admitting that, or how scared you must be." This boiled Daniel to no end, and he began to run at me, when Alister stopped him.

"Daniel! Halt! Davis, we – I - would like us to get along. The four of us need to go on being a band. You need to be part of a vampire community. Taking on the long tradition of Texan lone wolf vampires will not get you anywhere but challenged at every stop. Others will see you as an alpha, and while that earns you some instant status or respect here, in other places it will just prompt contempt and/or opposition. Babies aren't supposed to hold such a high stature."

"I literally don't give two shits about anything you're saying. I don't care about your politics, or your traditions, or the absurd myths brought to light by an insane monster who's been dead longer than most nations have been alive. And the fact that you couldn't give me even a half hour longer to think things out before basically ambushing me is reason enough for me to just say fuck you and wipe you all off the face of the earth." All of a sudden, Robert M., who I've never seen show emotion, not even once, huffed like some caged bull, and ripped his shirt off to reveal a scar and laceration laced torso. "Oh, so now you have something to say? Go ahead, get it off your chest." Robert then stepped back, timidly, his mind snapped back from whatever rage gripped him. He was now a shy schoolboy.

"Go ahead, Robert," Alister directed. "Show him why the cat's got your tongue." Robert got within five feet of me, but didn't appear threatening. He opened his mouth wide and shined his cell phone's flashlight onto his face to reveal no tongue inside. He simply had no tongue. I tried not to have a visible reaction, but I'm not sure I was able to contain myself. "You see, Davis. Some vampires are not so kind to the ones they've created. Robert's maker controlled all he turned, and tortured them mercilessly. That was his way. He contributed to the vampires' bad reputation already forged by legend and fiction. Luckily, Robert was able to see the futility in remaining in such a faction, and managed to break free of his maker. And when that vampire came south looking for Robert, he found me. And a shit stain on our history was washed clean. I have taken in my brethren... Sorry, Devin; and sisters, too, and tried to enrich their existence. Or at the very least, enliven it. If you confront us, win or lose, we *all* lose."

I stood there solemnly for a few moments. The house music, which still filled the air with enough bass and treble to drown out one's thoughts, fell silent in my ears as I contemplated the next move. Then I made it.

"Nah. I think your road ends here. I am the one to end it."

"Before you go around killing us, you need to know that a contingent of my most blood-thirsty, inhumane associates are on the way to Abilene to kill Annie Moore's parents and abduct her. What they do or don't to her is all up to you. If you continue down the one path, her fate will be... Let's just say things will get messy."

"I texted with her tonight, and she's currently still safe in her bed, which tells me that your henchmen won't arrive until tomorrow, and we both know they have to wait until sundown before springing into action. By that time, I will have killed all five of you---." I looked disdainfully at Cyrus to let him know I wasn't excluding him from any confrontation. "And most likely killed many more of the vampires destroying their brain cells below. So playing the Annie card seems like a day late and a dollar short."

“Well-played, Davis. You’re correct; they won’t get there until tomorrow. However, don’t you want her to live? I can call them off if you just *cooperate*. No one’s going to force you to sign a contract or do anything you don’t want to. Just align with us. We don’t have to be enemies.”

“The fact that you would send vampires to kill the parents of the only woman I’ve ever loved, and kidnap and torture her, prove to me that we *are* enemies, and that your whole ‘I’m a humanitarian vampire, and kumbaya, let’s all be together’ schtick is total bullshit. You’re no different than the guy that made Robert or the fucktard villains in a horror movie. So why don’t we stop talki---”

Daniel Sepulveda flew at me, spearing me from the side, while Robert took a wildly curvy right at my head. The force I landed with was considerable, but I was not the same skinny weakling I had been. I held onto Daniel, and kneed him several times in the gut as I tried to get to a sitting position. While we lay entangled, Robert tried to stomp on my head, which may have been enough to kill me had he connected. But I caught his foot, turning his ankle 120 degrees, and whipped him over the railing of the catwalk. Daniel stayed face down, and punched me repeatedly in the ribs and abdomen while keeping me from standing. I grabbed him by each ear and pulled him up to my face so I could bite his nose. He screamed out in pain, and pushed away from me to prevent his nose from being torn off completely. All the while, Devin and Alister hadn’t moved. I got to my feet and noticed Cyrus walking casually toward me, in no real rush.

“My turn, faggot.” His choice of insult reminded me

of the kids back home at recess. He was not only very confident, but also apparently a little homophobic.

"Your turn it is. Where's your boss, Zander?"

"On his way to violate your girl's mom, and maybe her, too."

I threw an angry left hook, which he blocked easily, but at the expense of bruising his right forearm. He was unaware that this would happen. "Oh, you're not used to facing someone stronger than you. Get used to it." He then connected with a jab straight to my nose, which busted the rusty, decaying blood still left in me loose. My eyes watered, and I realized I would have to take this battle much more seriously. He faked a second jab, which caused me to bite, and then he connected with a right/left combination to my ribs and right cheek. I didn't go down, but I went backwards, which allowed Daniel to re-enter the fray, kicking me square in the back of the head. I sailed over the catwalk and fell to the dance floor below, causing everyone to scatter like medieval peasants running from leprosy.

"Had enough?" Alister called down from above.

"Are you dead, yet? Then no, not really."

I rose to my feet, a little sore from the fall, and brushed myself off. Daniel and Cyrus each jumped down to meet me, and as I watched their graceful descent, I noticed Robert out of the corner of my eye, galloping toward me. Before he could annihilate my chest with a clothesline, I ducked, watching him barrel forward. When he turned around, I hit him with a kick to the face that would deceive someone into thinking I'd been trained by a sensei. It snapped his neck so hard the back of his head smacked his shoulder blades, and he did a backflip, landing on his face and belly. He lay motionless, but I couldn't tell if he was dead. Cyrus moved in with a thick chain wrapped around his arm and hand.

"You made the wrong choice" he said. He may not have been wrong, but in my mind, it was the only choice.

"Then make me pay for it, tough guy."

Most of the crowd returned to the dance floor and gathered around us, now exhilarated by the site of a fight. For a split second, I wondered if they'd seen one so potentially epic. Some of them started to stir in a way that confirmed for me that they were considering assisting Cyrus.

"As you wish," Cyrus replied, and took a forceful, chained right cross, which insulted me with how telegraphed it was. He didn't respect my reflexes whatsoever. I dodged the punch, and we circled each other, neither wanting to make a mistake. When he crouched down to rise with an uppercut, I stuck a straight jab to his forehead, and then swept his legs out from under him, a move I was now considering my primary go-to. Daniel thought he could catch me from behind, but I was on to his strategy. I grabbed Cyrus by the ankle and demonstrated my strength, flinging him into Daniel, sending them both crashing against a row of barstools some thirty feet away. The crowd once again moved backward, confused and frightened by the display. Daniel and Cyrus stood up, both increasingly angry. They started their way back to me, when I thought I would test their loyalty. I walked over to Robert's prone, motionless body and stood over it.

"Take another step, and I'll rip off Robert's head." I grabbed a handful of his dark, sticky half-mullet, and yanked up. The two advancing opponents stopped where they stood.

"You wouldn't," Daniel debated, Alister and Devin still watching from above.

"Seriously? You know I would. Let's call Robert the first of many."

All the vampires witnessing this altercation were now uneasy and had decided in some hive-mind sort of telepathy that they would come to Robert M.'s rescue. They all stepped onto the dancefloor, and my enemies now numbered in the hundreds. The impending battle and my odds for surviving it now decreased, my Namtudari unveiled the Luminastra portion of its transformation. An energy started emitting from my hands, and I let Robert's hair go. It was a crackling, translucent white and blue, accompanied by a steaming mist. The pressure of the energy built up in my hands, and they shook with abandon while the veins in my arms pulsed and stretched, attempting to escape past the skin. When I couldn't take the pressure anymore, all I could do was hope to unleash it, and I aimed my hands palms up at the crowd. I felt like Iron Man as the blue and white energy shot from my palms in an uncontrollably violent spectacle, freezing, burning, and then crystallizing all caught in its trajectory. The members of the crowd remained stuck in their positions while steaming, smoky mist filled the room. The silhouettes of random vampires running for their lives darted out of the mist, while I squinted my eyes to try and locate Daniel and Cyrus.

As I stood there, I felt a faint grasping at my feet. It was Robert, who'd turned on his back, and was trying to grab me. I don't know if he was asking for mercy or trying weakly to fight back, but there was no power coming from his arms. He looked up at me, unable to speak of course, but pleading with me, with his wide-open mouth and swollen eyes. Without hesitation, I took my left hand, closed it into a tight, punishing fist, and punched through Robert's face, cracking the expensive tile floor beneath him. Devin finally chose to participate.

"NOOOO!," she howled in anguish. "ROBERT!" With tears streaming down her face, she leapt from the rafters high above me, and landed in a full sprint. I met her point of attack with a backhand that sent her sailing in a rainbow's shape, or an archer's arrow shot from long-range. She hit the ground hard, but appeared unfazed and undeterred by my blow, sprinting again in my direction. Kicking and punching for all her worth, Devin tried to avenge her bandmate all by herself. She managed to get her hand on my face, gouging a deep four-fingered wound down my cheek. My pain was matched by my rage, and I lifted her by the neck and tossed her through a glass wall into the manager's office behind the bar. I had no time to view the result of her voyage, as Daniel did manage to sneak up on me again, landing a pounding hammer of a fist down on the top of my skull. I could feel my bottom teeth collapse under the collision with my top ones, and a blinding headache followed. As I tried to shake my eye sockets from my jawbone, Daniel kicked me in the ribs, lifting me off the ground, while Cyrus simultaneously swung a baseball bat across my back. The bat broke on my spine, and I did a somersault, splashing onto the floor. Woozy and exhausted, I lay there, waiting to see which of them would attack next. It was Cyrus, who lazily put his foot on my throat.

"End of the line, Davis." His smirk was priceless.

"Agreed." I grabbed one half of the broken bat and forced it through his shin. Cyrus crumbled in agony next to me, and I grabbed him by the head, twisting his neck in a circle two and a half times. His face turned a purple/black/maroon, and I watched his eyes close forever.

"Motherfucker!," Daniel growled at me, frustrated by the inability of an estate full of vampires unable to kill a measly individual. "That's it, cabron. I'm going to end this right now." He jumped high into the air, intent on crashing down on me with both heavy-booted feet. I tried to move out of the way, but he caught me with one, landing square on my right arm. I felt my humerus bone fracture in multiple spots as it collided with my rib cage. Fortunately, the uneven landing caused Daniel to lose his balance, and he spun down awkwardly. He turned his back to me for a second, and that was my opportunity to regain my footing. I did so, clasping my hands around the back of his head, bringing my knee up to meet it. The sound my kneecap and his face combined to make was similar to hitting two iron hammers together in an echoey cavern, loud but hollow and haunting. I could see the intense look of pain on his face as Daniel flew backward, landing on the back of his head and neck some ten feet away. Holding my increasingly uncomfortable arm tight, I stumbled over to Daniel, stopping to grab the other half of the bat Cyrus broke on me. I knelt and straddled Daniel, trapping his arms between my thighs. His face looked broken; eyes, nose, and teeth destroyed. He struggled to breathe as I raised the bat above my head with both hands, prepared to drive it through his heart. Right before bringing it down, I could hear footsteps behind me, trampling slowly over broken glass and debris. They were dainty and measured.

"Not so fast." It was Alister. "It's unfortunate that you ended my drummer's affiliation with the band, and his life. It's quite possible you did the same with my bass player. I cannot, and will not, sit by and let you execute my lead singer. He's the fucking voice of Unholy Saint. Only a handful of bands in the history of rock music were able to continue successfully after replacing their lead singers. I'm not going to play the odds on us being one of them. So, please get your ass off Daniel and step away."

"You're now going to try an authoritarian approach? Where were you when I was killing Robert and the rest of your "brethren"? That is what you referred to them as, correct?"

"You smug son of a bitch. You're really on top of the world, aren't you? This is a far cry from the crybaby we encountered on the road. While you were struggling to stay alive, I was assessing your skills. Seeing how you fared against lesser competition. And if you must know, I'm not very impressed, aside from that cool thing you did with your hands."

Not knowing for sure, I volleyed back, "That was the Luminastra."

"Oh, no doubt. Don't you think you'll need to be whipping that back up right about now? I mean, you won't be defeating me without it. I venture to guess you won't even outlast Devin without---"

At that moment, Devin coasted into my chin with a stiff, flying right hook. She was shredded from the glass wall I threw her through, but still more than game for continued punishment. I rose to my feet, and we stood, facing each other. She used her knee to buckle mine, and then sent a succession of kicks to my face, before doing some acrobatic, ninja gymnastic move, ending with her bulldogging my face into the floor.

"I can't believe you destroyed Robert," she cried, with fierce, fiery tears and the expression of an insane asylum inmate. "He didn't deserve that. He was better than that."

"No sympathy for anything or anyone unless it's your friend? You're no different than any petty, hypocritical human, and Robert was no different than any of you. But I guess rhythm sections stick together, am I right?" *Hey, I knew them to be a rhythm section.*

Her rage seethed from deep inside her, and she tore at me with maniacal abandon. Punching, kicking, grabbing, etc. I finally identified her fighting style. It was rabid honey badger. She had no training. She probably hadn't had to fight like this since she became a vampire. Nothing like the paramilitary meatheads "protecting" the band, and nothing like Alister, I surmised. Something told me that when he finally entered the ring, he would be more formidable. Turns out 'finally' was now. He bolted at me like an Olympic champion, giving me just a second or two to dispatch Devin. I tried to grab her arm and hurl her out of our way, but Alister was too swift, and he caught her with one arm while elbowing me in the temple with his other.

"Playtime's over, Davis. You've ruined the night and damaged the framework of the band. This is unacceptable." He held me by the back of the neck and planted well-aimed knee strikes into the side of my head, eventually nailing me with his whole thigh. Each one penetrated my defenses a little more, and my head started to sway to and fro rather elastically. If I let him keep this up, I would soon be unconscious, so as he reared back for another blow to my cranium, I grasped his planted leg at the knee and squeezed it, crushing his assorted tendons. He crumpled to the floor and put a heel right to my nose as he scooted backward on his ass to get away. I regained my sight and crawled after him, but right into Devin and Daniel's waiting tandem field goal kicks to my face. I had to have lost consciousness for at least ten to thirty seconds. When I came to, the three of them were standing over me, debating over what to do next. I played asleep, listening as Daniel demanded they kill me instantly. Devin couldn't choose between a death sentence and a reconciliation, all due to the fact that I might be "the one." Alister, who all should know was the deciding and final vote, had a difficult time, weighing the grandiosity and prophecy of the Namtudari against the fact that he might soon lose his position as ruler over the vampires of California and the

House of the Black Moon.

"Why don't I make it easy for you?" I mumbled as I turned over on my back and again began to manifest the blue and white energy, with accompanying awesome steam mist. "Why don't I just kill the three of you, and end the deliberation?"

Daniel stepped on my left wrist and wanted one of them to stand on the other, thinking they might be able to stop me from freeze burning them. However, Alister simply hobbled away from the entire ordeal on his one good leg, and Devin just stared at me in amazement. I took that opportunity to hold Daniel's foot down while I aimed my right palm at his face. As much as he tried, he couldn't break my grip. He turned to look at Devin, bewildered by her lack of assistance, and then back down at me, uttering one last bit of wisdom.

"Fuck you, man!," he sneered so eloquently before I shot the full force of this newfound weapon directly into his face. His head and the upper most part of his torso exploded from his body and disintegrated in the air, while the rest of him stood frozen white and motionless. I still had no idea what the hell this was emanating from my body, but damn if it didn't pack a wallop and scare even the most seasoned of vampires shitless. Devin stood there dumbfounded, not saying a word, nor looking to defend herself. That was actually the best defense, because as a southern gentleman raised by a single mother, I couldn't attack a defenseless woman, vampire or not.

"I... What? How do we... What *are* you?" Devin questioned. I believe her questions came from a much more spiritual realm; her belief system shattered.

"What do you mean? I'm just a lonely loser from nowhere Texas that you messed up trying to kill, remember? That's basically what you've told me."

"I was wrong."

"Were you?"

"Did you ever read the Bible?"

"Only in church, or when I was forced to."

"I went to church, and read the bible, and I believed in God, but I never expected to see Jesus in person, on Earth… I've read the journals of all the previous vampires who kept any, and the transformation you've gone through is like seeing a prophecy come to life right in front of you."

"Pretty heavy stuff, I guess."

"Yup. Pretty heavy."

I looked around at the shambles that were left of the House of the Black Moon, and came to terms with how fleeting and temporary everything is. Less than six hours ago, this place was a swarming, pulsing mecca of a place. A dominion for people bound to my condition. Now it lay in a wreck, dozens of vampires dead forever, by my hands no less. Me, just a loser. A virgin. Who would have guessed that something that had been so vibrant, such a pillar, could be brought asunder so relatively quickly? So easily, by little ol' me? I determined that I don't want to be the savior of this place, or this community, or this race. I wanted to end it.

I wanted to get rid of Unholy Saint and their vice grip on my life. I wanted to see this building and everything in it burnt to the ground. I would have to take the lives of two more vampires if that were to happen. One stood in front of me, reverence and confusion swirling through her head. The other was making his way back from whatever hole he crawled into while his lead singer got his head blown off.

"It appears that we're all a little worse for wear, Davis."

"Yes, sir."

"Why don't we take a break, and get some blood in us? I know that I need it, and I can only assume that you do, too. You were trying to feed over an hour ago."

"I can only assume that you were feeding while I killed Daniel. I thought you couldn't let that happen."

"Oh, come on, Davis. You're able to project this nuclear death-ray shit from your body. How could I compete with that? How could I worry about writing songs and who's going to sing them, when some lighting bringer, Big Trouble in Little China fucker, is destroying my people left and right? Truth is, I kind of knew we were cooked in Glendale. Devin and I both tried to kill you, and we failed. That was before you even had this final boss transformation that enables you to vanquish multiple vampires in an instant. I should have abducted Annie far sooner. She seems to be the only bargaining chip you give a shit about. She must have like angelic pus---"

"Easy! You watch your mouth when you talk about

Annie Moore."

"Oooh. Touchy. A man defending his woman's honor. How sweet. What kind of life did you think you were going to have with her, Davis? You're a fucking vampire! You're like 70% not alive! Your high school reunion will be filled with questions from people asking about your skin, and your fangs. And what happens when the meathead jock that used to dunk your head in the toilet or the homecoming queen who used to laugh at you when she passed by go missing because you got hungry and felt the urge to eat them? Gonna teach your kids how to play soccer or take them to little league? WRONG!"

"Call off whatever order you gave, for her and her family."

"Why? Why would I do that? I think it's the only thing keeping me from perishing here."

"It's obviously not. Look around you. I did all this *after* knowing that you planned to kidnap her and kill her parents… Cancel the order."

"Oh my God. Did you just say that, Johnny Utah?" I was confused. I didn't know his vampire inside jokes. "And what if I don't? You're going to threaten me? You're going to kill me? You were going to do that anyway. So, let's get on with it, then." Alister pulled a sword out from behind his back. Not a European, knight-style sword like one of the several that adorn this place, but a Japanese Samurai looking sword, thinner and sharper. I thought back to the Ruben Donovan story that included a samurai sword, and wondered if it *was* true, and if this was the same sword. “This is hopefully just a little equalizer.”

Devin stepped backward and stood at the entrance to the dance floor, relegating herself to spectator. The fight, and the spark for that matter, had clearly gone out in her.

“Do you think that’s fair?” I asked Alister.

“Do you consider blowing some omnipotent goddamned lightning out of your hands fair, Davis?”

“I guess that’s a good point.”

I was going to have to be as fast as I possibly could to avoid his blade, and I was hoping that the blue and white energy stuff would reveal itself again, but since I had no idea how to summon it, I would just have to cross my fingers and wish for the best. We both looked like hobbled old boxers about to fall with one last swing, so I didn’t see this lasting much longer.

“Let’s do this,” Alister snickered, not terribly confident about his chances.

We inched closer, carefully, and finally got within striking distance when he raised his sword and brought it down diagonally. I managed to dodge it, and he was swinging again horizontally. I barely missed it cutting a deep gash in my belly. He was definitely skilled in wielding it.

“Okay. Okay, Davis. I see you.” Alister was a little pleasantly surprised at how much I still had left in the tank.

He tried sticking me directly with it three consecutive times, but I ducked each strike, devising a plan for how to go on the offensive. I waited for him to raise up and bring the sword down again, catching it in between my two hands. I then kicked him straight in the testicles, and kicked him again in the chest. The impact sent him flying backwards. He landed on his back with a loud crack, and sat back up slowly, running a diagnostic on his body before climbing back up to his feet. I ran and jumped at him, landing with a fist to his cheek, followed by another and another. He matched offense with offense, stabbing me in the arm and in the side. Each one only penetrated about an inch, as his strength was waning considerably. I swatted away a swing, knocked the sword out of his hands, and held them both together. I then punched him repeatedly in the side before pulling his shirt toward me and landing two missile-like headbutts to his eye socket. With Alister reeling and barely able to stand, I slid behind him and forced his sword to his own throat.

"Go ahead, Davis. End it. End me. Take your rightful place in Aylash's vision. Be the Black Moon."

"No. There will be no Black Moon. Your kind, our kind, is finished." I took a handful of his hair and pushed his head forward firmly. I then held his right wrist in my hand, and had him slice his own throat with the sharp steel. I let him go, and he turned facing me, his eyes wide, and his neck spewing the last blood he would ever drink from a gaping slit. In a last second decision to make sure he died, I swiped the sword from his hand and swung it with all my might, decapitating Alister Amaranth. His head rolled in the air while his body thudded, knees first to the floor. I could hear Devin crying as he lay on his belly, finally still after 113 years roaming this earth. His head, eyes opened, faced the high, intricate, gothic double doored entrance to the House of the Black Moon, and I found that fitting, the sun just now rising from the east.

"And now me?" Devin asked with a sour, defeated tinge to her voice.

"Yes... And now you," I replied solemnly.

"Please. Please don't destroy this. You're here for a reason, Davis. Even if you don't believe that, or can't grasp it right now. There's something more out there for our kind, and I'm sure it starts with you." I didn't respond at all. I just slowly took her hand and brought her close to a window, so she could see the early sunrise unveil its shroud from her Orange County.

"What is your real name?" I inquired.

"It's Annie. Actually, it's Elizabeth Ann Petrovsky. I was born in L.A. We moved to the O.C. when I was two."

"Annie. What a coincidence. What are the chan---"

"Please get it over with now."

"Sure."

"Are you going to cut off my head?"

"What?"

"Are you going to cut off my head? Or something of the sort? You punched through Robert's face. You blasted off Daniel's head. You sliced off Alister's. That seems to be the preferred modus operandi here. I was a little surprised when you didn't pull out the stake through the heart strategy, but it shows that you're listening. At least a little bit."

We didn't laugh, but her comments did cause a small smile to crack on our lips, cutting through the somber atmosphere of what was to come.

"No. I'm not going to cut off your head. I'm going to do what you did to me."

"What would that… Oh. You're going to bite my neck."

"Yes. The stories dictate that I have to drink the blood of my creator."

"Hmmm. Justice served… Well, alright then." I wrapped my arms around Devin's shoulders to secure her, and she provided no resistance whatsoever. Alister had been right about her vampire midlife crisis. Her face relaxed, almost relieved. Feeling that the fight was over, my grip became an embrace, and I hugged her, tighter and tighter. I hugged her like we were old friends saying goodbye for the last time. She got up on her tippy toes and stretched her head up to me, placing her forehead against mine. Then she gave me a soft kiss on the cheek followed by a firmer, longer kiss on the lips. I pulled back slightly, to not give her the impression I was kissing back, but also not severing our touch completely. I then gently pushed her head to one side, and placed my mouth on her neck, breathing in its scent. Her perfume and lotion did well to cover up the juxtaposition of semi-rotting flesh, but with my nose in her skin, I could smell the death on her before it came. I took my new fangs and clamped down on her neck, puncturing her vein, pouring into my mouth what blood remained in her. She moaned a haunting yet peaceful moan, and held onto my waist with both hands. Eventually that peace was disturbed by slight gasping and sputtering, the last water and oxygen syphoned from her body, then returned as she faded off into final sleep. I placed her on the floor, and looked out that window, exhausted and damaged from the night's confrontation. I took a look down at Devin, and studied her face. She authored my favorite song in the whole world. She tried to murder me, and in the process committed a much worse crime. Because of her, much more death cast its spell upon the world through me. I could never forgive her for that, and I didn't necessarily feel remorse for taking her life. Even still, seeing the harmless, childlike peace chiseled on her face did cause me to sympathize with her in some way, though. I just couldn't articulate how.

As I promised, I had to call Annie and tell her once it was done.

Except, my phone was missing. *Where the hell is my phone?*

Chapter Twenty-Six: Subside

I searched all over the battlefield for my phone. It must have fallen out in all the killing and getting the shit kicked out of me, etc. I found a phone behind the bar and called my number, listening for the vibration. I could hear the muffled sound as it rang, proving that it was still on the dance floor, but where? I called again and triangulated the vibration. My ears were improving their abilities in real time. As I narrowed down the location, I got closer and closer to Alister's headless corpse. I lifted him up slightly and looked under him, but nothing. I then reached into his pockets and found two cell phones, his and mine. He must have taken it from me after Devin and Daniel did that double team to my face. I had eight calls and twelve texts from Annie, and two more of each from Sinjin. I called her back, but got no answer. Her final text read "Boarding the plane now. Hopefully, you'll be alive when I get there," which she sent at 6:30am central time. I guess she was on her way. I called Sinjin.

"So, you won," he answered instead of the standard "Hello."

"Did I? It doesn't feel like it."

"Are they all dead?"

"All of Unholy Saint? Yes. Them, their bodyguard Cyrus, and about fifty other vampires."

"Wow. Look at the badass on you. Alister's plan for Annie. It actually went down last night. I had a feeling it would, so I took care of it." I didn't understand, and an anxiety filled level of concern washed over me. 'Don't worry. All is well."

"What are you saying? They went to grab her last night?"

"That's what I'm saying. I called in a few favors, rolling them up into one big return. The death squad, as I like to call it, that Alister sent to Texas; they were met by a few night drinkers of my own. They never made it Annie's house. Her and her parents are all fine." Just then, her name popped up on my screen for a brief moment.

"She just called, so I'm going to let you go, but I need to ask; why? Why did you help her? Why did you alert me? I thought you and Alister were friends, or allies, or whatever you were."

"The details aren't necessary, but I will give you a reason. Alister was a necessary evil to me, and vice versa. But he helped kill my parents and turn my siblings into perpetually 15- and 12-year-old monsters. Then, he killed my sister, a beautiful soul so selfless and loving that she was solely responsible for bartering to save my young life. What she became after joining Warren and

Alister was far and away different from my sensitive, talented big sister. But they couldn't eliminate all the humanity in her, and she got her revenge. Last night, in helping you, I got mine. And not for nothin', but from what I've heard about your recent physical changes, it sounds like there's a new sheriff in town. I just hope that you did the job thoroughly, and that you made Alister suffer."

"I'd say he suffered enough. Thank you. Thank you, a lot. I've got to call Annie."

"Until next time," Sinjin offered.

"There won't be a next time." This made him laugh.

"Oh, yes there will."

We hung up and I immediately called Annie back. She answered before I even heard a ringtone.

"Where are you?" she blurted out frantically.

"I'm... I'm at the House of the Black Moon. Or what's left of it."

"Are you okay?"

"Yes. I'm wounded. And beat up pretty badly, but I'm still here. They. They... aren't."

"Send me the address. I'm getting my rental car now... So are you back?"

"What?"

"Are you back? As in, back to normal?"

"OH!" I'd forgotten all about the entire reason I'd

made this insane, dangerous, bittersweet trip in the first place. To become HUMAN again!

"I don't feel any different, and---" I felt of the pointed fangs in my mouth. "---nothing's changed physically." The sun was now in the sky, even if the pollution and coastal clouds prevented it from shining brightly this early in the morning. "I'm going to take a step outside, and see if I'm affected by the morning."

"Please be careful."

With the phone at my ear, I walked past Alister's lonesome head and opened the heavy doors that separated me from possible freedom. I stepped out past the velvet roped sidewalk and onto the driveway, hoping for a positive sign. Through the overcast sky, miniscule bits of pain sprinkled all over my skin, and the surface of my flesh began to tickle and burn. I knew that I would have to go back in soon or risk further consequences.

"Nothing. No change. They were right. Returning to normal was a myth. I was lied to."

There was a stunned silence on the other end of the phone. After about seven seconds, Annie spoke again.

"I'm so sorry, Davis. I'm so, so sorry."

"Maybe you shouldn't come here."

'What? Why?"

"I haven't fed. This is by far the longest I've gone without drinking, and the adrenaline of warfare is fading quickly. I can't promise I won't hurt you."

"You can feed on me! We've already done that. It'll

be---”

“I can’t control myself right now!” I was about to lose my shit.

“Do you love me?”

“What?” My head was spinning, and the thought of living an eternity, or even a small piece of forever, still bound to this curse, without Annie, was fucking with me.

“DO YOU LOVE ME?!” She momentarily snapped me out of my mental downward spiral.

“Yes.”

“How long? How long have you loved me?’.

“A… A long time. Why?”

“Because we’re meant to be together, Davis. That’s why. That’s why you can feed on me for the rest of my days. As long as I’m alive.”

“Don’t say that. That will come faster than you think, even if you live a long life by human standards. We’ll grow apart, and I’ll become more detached from humanity, more grotesque.”

“You have no idea. You don’t know what’s to come. You didn’t know Unholy Saint were vampires, right?”

“Right.”

“Then you don’t know what you’ll devolve into, or *evolve* into. So far, your changes have been for the better, I think.”

The pangs of hunger reached into my stomach and

intestines and spread out among the network of arteries, veins, and blood vessels running through me. Every ounce of my body called out for relief, but I had none to give it. *Or did I?* I could almost taste the blood on Alister's mouth as he returned from abandoning Daniel to face me alone. And he spoke of a… buxom sorority girl they had lined up for me. There had to be humans chained up somewhere in the bowels of this estate.

"If you arrive, and I'm not at the door to greet you, do *not* come in. Please wait for me to text or call, or otherwise give you a signal. Please do that for me. I love you."

I couldn't wait to hear those sentiments returned, and hung up. I raced to the door Alister emerged from before our final clash, and smashed it in, me not having the proper clearance. Behind it lay a hallway of secret rooms not unlike something in the Naked Huntress, leading to another door at the end of the hall. I ripped that one off the hinges, and proceeded down a long, winding staircase into some dark unknown catacombs. At the bottom of the staircase rested three hallways, from one of which I could hear voices and screams. I followed it, and found a dungeon full of humans, most of them female, all of them adults. I found a large, primitive looking key and used it to open the iron-barred gate of these captives' cell. They cowered in the furthest corner, afraid I was there to feed or worse.

"Everybody, find the stairwell at the end of this hallway, and take it up to the first floor. You should be able to find the exit soon enough. It's morning, and there are no vampires alive in the building. Now go!"

They hesitated at first, unsure of my true intentions, so I instigated their movement.

"I said GO!" I pounded my fist against the black stone wall of the dungeon, causing the entire lower floor to vibrate and shuffle. This got everyone moving. They ran to the door, congesting the path, and had to integrate into small enough lines to go through it more orderly. Everyone escaped the cell save for the last one, coincidentally the aforementioned sorority girl. As she ran to leave, I grabbed her by the arm and covered her mouth. "Sorry. Please know I have no choice," I told her before feeding.

I sat in the cell alone and quiet for a minute or two, and then texted Annie, letting her know how to find me. I then went exploring the underground adventure land that lay beneath the Black Moon. Every hall, and every room in each hall, seemed to have a separate, designated purpose. All the feeding/torture rooms were grouped together, business offices and lounge rooms, the same. I came to the last door of the final subterranean hallway I walked through, and I noticed a scent from the other side of it. Something moving. Someone. Someone familiar. Raven Chastain.

I went to open the door carefully, only to find it locked. Instead of ripping it off toward me, I decided to kick it in. Much more difficult for a normal vampire, and impossible for a human, I thought it would shock the rat waiting on the other end. I was correct. I actually shoulder tackled the thing, conforming it to my body as I breezed into the room. Raven had been standing behind the door, prepared to ambush me when I opened it, and now he was stuck, crushed between it and a wall full of file cabinets.

"Oh, hello," I joked. "Fancy meeting you here. It's funny, but you were nowhere to be found last night, when all your friends were dying. Are you really that chicken shit?"

"I don't know *what* I am anymore, but I know I was going to wait out the fight, and I knew it was going to be you who won it. I've never seen anything like you, man. No one's ever seen anything like you. Now, could you please stop crushing me with this door?"

"Oh, yeah! Sorry. Let me get that for you." I made my voice as gentle and apologetic as possible, flung the door behind me, and then grabbed Raven by the throat. I raised him in the air as high as I could and was about to squish him into the floor, as satisfying a kill as I ever committed, when Annie's voice called out to me from behind.

"Davis, no!" I held him there, my nose snorting mucus and spit seeping through my clinched teeth. My entire being fought itself to listen to her words, and I almost ignored them, when she pleaded once more for me to stop. "Davis, please! Enough. For right now, let it be enough. Show me that there's some human still left in there."

I closed my eyes and counted to ten in my head, then let Raven's feet slowly touch the floor. He put both hands on my chest, fingers up in surrender.

"There isn't any human left, Annie." I planned to snap his neck and leave him there, when he spoke up.

"Wait, wait, wait, wait! Just wait! Please!"

"What is it?" I was uninterested, but still interested.

"You still have so much you don't know. You're in a room full of history, man. And you don't know about Aylash Revall."

"Of course, I do. Alister gave me an adequate history lesson. And if those journals are in these cabinets, I can learn the rest on my own."

"No, man. You don't know the truth. The Horizon Vista Retirement Community. It shut down because of the treatment and neglect of the residents."

"I know that. It's public knowledge. Time to say goodnight."

"NO! Man... You don't know the truth. It didn't shut down because of what the staff did, or didn't do. The killings and disappearances were committed by one of the *residents*. They were committed by Aylash Revall!"

"Sure, they were. He managed to live some 4,500 years, and ended up in an old folks' home in Orange County, California? Why couldn't you come up with something better, as long as you were hiding down here?" Annie had had enough of this conversation, and asked who this guy was. "Oh. Annie, meet Raven Chastain, the piece of shit who was going to execute a little boy, only to leave it for me to put him out of his misery."

"*This* is *that* guy?!" Annie stood there with her mouth wide open. Her eyes then squinted with contempt, and her lips melded together with scorn. "I was wrong. Go ahead and kill him."

"No, wait. Plea---"

"You heard the lady, Raven." I enveloped his skull with my now oversized hands and pressed them together until one hand's fingers interlocked with the other's. Annie turned away in horror and threw up, now experiencing the unrepentant extent of my brutality. Once the sounds of his death ceased, she relaxed her shoulders and returned upright. "Are you alright?"

"I'll be fine. With a few decades of therapy, sedatives, and wine, I'll be fine."

"I want to look in these cabinets before we go, but first..."

I grabbed Annie by the waist, and went in to plant a kiss on her burgundy lip sticked mouth, but she pushed me away, sending a jolt of pain down my broken arm. We locked eyes, and she made the weirdest face I'd ever seen her make.

"Gross! Look at you. You smell like a slaughterhouse, which from walking through the place to get down here, you turned it into." Somehow, coming from her, the comment caused me to feel some regret, and possibly a little shame. "And I love you, so don't take it personally; I just don't like that kissing you sometimes has come with being covered in various people's blood... I don't want to ever get used to that."

"Understood. We're going to need to get out of here soon. I'm surprised that neither non-vampire employees of this place nor the police have shown up. But I want to look through this stuff and take some of it with us. What kind of vehicle did you rent?"

"A Ford Explorer. Why?"

"Great. We can hold boxes in it, and keep me covered from the sun."

"So you're sure about not turning back? Not even a little?"

"A human couldn't have done to Raven what I just did. Not even Mr. Universe."

"OK. We'll worry about that later. I have a large, heavy blackout tarp in the rental to keep you protected. Let's look at what you want to look at, and load it up."

No one did appear, the property remained silent and empty, and we actually didn't rush at all. Over the next two hours, Annie and I dug through all kinds of boxes containing music files, business documentation, some of Aylash's original journals, and reprinted copies of his and multiple vampires' testimonies or memoirs. I painstakingly carried the ones I wanted to transport upstairs, and Annie backed both vehicles up as close to the front doors as possible, and we loaded up the boxes and a few artifacts. After I'd finished taking what I wanted, I set fire to the House of the Black Moon, and watched it burn from inside my truck until I could hear the familiar sounds of fire trucks and police cars speeding toward us. We parked the Explorer at Castaways Park, and took my truck to the same hotel we'd stayed at the night before. After taking a shower, and putting on some much-needed new clothes, we found a logistics company who could pack and ship the boxes in that vehicle back to Abilene. We did the same with everything in the Explorer, Annie driving it while I drove the truck covered almost 100% in dark black clothing, and under the relative protection of the sunset.

Once back at the hotel, I thought that Annie and I could finally try again at the delayed romantic evening we'd attempted previously. As we cuddled on the bed, though, I could feel her heartbeat, and the nervousness that permeated from her body outward was not of pre-sex jitters. It felt different. She was clearly troubled, and I could sense her biting her lip constantly. I'd actually been detecting this uncomfortableness for several hours.

"Annie, what's wrong?" I waited patiently for her answer, thinking it might have something to do with how she witnessed me killing Raven. I couldn't have been more wrong.

"Davis, when we were going through stuff in that file room, I came across something. I've been debating internally on whether or not to tell you. I figured you would just find it on your own anyway, so---"

"Annie. What is it?"

"That guy. Raven?"

"Yes."

"He said that Aylash Revall was still alive?"

"He did."

"Well... He... was... right."

"What do you mean, he was right?"

"Aylash Revall... Aylash Revall is alive."

The End

Epilogue

Whoever may be reading this, you're being allowed entrance into my story. My story so far. Not all the words are mine, though. I don't know big words. I would have never said or written something like *ominously*, *exasperation*, *assuredness*, *modicum*, *concoction*, or one of fifty other words found in this text. Also, I tend to speak with an accent, and if that accent was mimicked on paper, it would maybe make for some difficult reading. Luckily, I know a really gifted writer, my girlfriend Annie. She took everything I told her and typed it up into like a book. The only rules I gave her were to not add anything that didn't happen, and not to subtract anything that did. It's my cross to bear, and I'll take on the consequences for any wrong I've done. Incidentally, none of the crimes I committed in any of the cities I crossed through have caused the slightest commotion. An online article here or there, or two minutes on the local news, and then nothing. It's as if those people just faded from view, and everyone forgot about them.

I also asked Annie to keep Felix's accent as true to his speaking voice as she could. I couldn't hear any other *dialect* (Annie's choice of word) than Felix's in my head, and would want that to come across. I hope he gets to read this someday, wherever he is. If you run into him before I do, please tell him I don't have any hard feelings.

Sinjin Pierce divulged the full details of his intercepting of Alister's vampires in Abilene. Although very compelling, and one with some rather negative, far-reaching reverberations, it's a story for another time.

I took the music files I discovered and sent them anonymously to a recording studio in Austin. They in turn coordinated a deal with Unholy Saint's record label to complete the music, and the band's posthumous third full-length album will be released next fall. It's title, *Circus of Damnation*. The story of the band's "tragic and mysterious accident" at the House of the Black Moon captured the music world and pop culture's general attention, and they're now much more popular in death than they were... in... death.

After reading every single bit of the materials I took from the House of the Black Moon, I've now come to believe that Aylash Revall is indeed still alive. At least he was as of a year ago. Much older than the 150 years Alister Amaranth told me Revall walked the earth. I'm taking another trip, this one much farther, and much longer, in hopes of finding not only him, but a few more individuals tied to a much larger network of vampires. Two more Houses still exist, and I plan on visiting them. I may or may not let Annie come too, depending on who finally wins that argument. Since she managed to talk her father into releasing some $80,000 of her trust fund so she can "travel the world," I think she believes she's already won the argument.

One thing that *wasn't* mentioned in the above account, and which I wanted to come clean about, is that when going through the House of the Black Moon, we came across what looked like a million dollars in cash, and we took every bit of it. I kept $120K of it to fund my upcoming excursion, and sent the rest of the $775,458 equally and anonymously to the families of Lester Hansen, Aydin Morales, Oscar Jimenez, Helen Reid, Joan Ritter, Bob Walton, Jefferson Johnson, Robbie Whitaker, Sloan Salisbury, etc. etc. etc.

If we survive the journey, to France and the former Yugoslavia, I may have Annie write those details down as well. Until then…

Acknowledgements

I would like to thank my glorious wife and wonderful children for tolerating me while I persisted with this book, at times spending a little too much time and energy working on it than looking for a proper job. They are truly the most amazing gift a man can be given, and I hope that I make them proud.

I would also like to thank the family and friends who supported me during this difficult time, either financially or emotionally, or by helping directly with the completion of this book. Taking a gander at the untold number of rough drafts I provided, proofreading, formatting, making book cover suggestions, or getting hands on with the photoshopping, AI, etc. You are all most appreciated. Niki Simic, Jason Croft, and Stephanie Buduhan, you were particularly instrumental. Love you.

Finally, I would like to thank myself for finally completing an artistic project I'd started. Now maybe I can pull others out of "the Box" and finish them.

About the Author

William Xavier Chandler loves music, sports, food, bears, and virtually all other forms of art. Additionally, he loves speaking at length about these things. He thought he was going to be a rock star when he grew up, but maybe his calling is writing of a different sort. Maybe he'll know for sure if and when he grows up.

His family, especially his wife and two children, is the most important thing in his life.

He's lived his entire life in Texas, and probably always will. He hopes he's becoming a better person with each passing day. Already, the ratio of light to darkness within him has improved to 90/10.

Made in the USA
Coppell, TX
20 February 2026

71837625R00212